THE CROCODILE AND OTHER STORIES

THE CROCODILE AND OTHER STORIES

Fyodor Dostoevsky

Translated from the Russian by

Constance Garnett

Selected, with a Preface by

Michael Wood

riverrun

Constance Garnett's translations of Dostoevsky's works were first published in five volumes by Heinemann between 1917 and 1920

This edition published in 2019 by

riverrun

An imprint of

Quercus Editions Ltd
Carmelite House
50 Victoria Embankment
London EC4Y 0DZ

An Hachette UK company

A CIP catalogue record for this book is available from the British Library

PB ISBN 978 1 78747 824 4
EBOOK ISBN 978 1 78747 825 1

10 9 8 7

Typeset by CC Book Production
Printed and bound in Great Britain by Clays Ltd, Elcograf S.p.A.

Contents

Preface

FYODOR MIKHAILOVICH DOSTOEVSKY was a prolific author in many modes, but wrote relatively few short stories – wrote exactly as many stories as he wrote novels. Of course the count will vary to some degree if we regard the longer stories as novellas, but the overall picture remains the same, and rather surprising. The critic Georg Lukács famously said that Dostoevsky did not write novels – novels are irredeemably worldly and portray a universe without gods or without God. And in the same book, *The Theory of the Novel*, he suggested that great moments in the history of the novel were preceded and followed by major achievements in the short story form: Gogol before, let's say, and Hemingway after. What the proportional relation between the two forms in Dostoevsky's work suggests is something different but not unrelated: the short story looks at the same world as the novel, but it looks intermittently, looks when no one else is looking, so to speak.

There is nothing to be gained from worrying excessively about where we should place individual works by Dostoevsky – or anyone else, since classification will take us only so far – but it is always interesting to think about form as part of meaning.

As a short story writer Dostoevsky doesn't resemble Chekhov or Joyce – he doesn't work with economy and epiphanies. His short stories are different from each other in tone and style but all his narrators are voluble and not entirely in control of the plot line. The works all inhabit the same moral or philosophical dimension too. They rely on curiosity and exception. They resemble jokes and anecdotes, or what used to be called physiologies, the portraiture of strange characters, or perhaps more accurately the portraiture of character itself as strange. A supposed norm is always being violated, perhaps shown to be not a norm at all. Two of the pieces collected here are self-consciously called 'a story' in their subtitle, and each treats of 'a most unexpected adventure' or 'very unusual incident'. The sense of story here is not simply that of a narrative or a tale but of something that has to be told, like a hallucinated news item or a piece of gossip.

There is a real similarity to the novels here. In *The Idiot* and *The Brothers Karamazov*, for example, Dostoevsky argues that types and generalities either don't exist or are meaningless, that only the study of eccentric instances will yield true understanding. 'It happens sometimes that such a person [an eccentric] carries within himself the very heart of the universal, and the rest of the men of his epoch have for some reason been temporarily torn from it, as if by a gust of wind' (*The Brothers Karamazov*, 'From the Author'). The short stories share the climate of this claim, but there is something whispered and secretive about them. They don't come to grand conclusions ('No, gentlemen of the jury, they have their Hamlets, but we still have our Karamazovs'), they don't come to any conclusions, they scarcely end at all, it always seems possible to imagine their narrators still chattering after we have put the book down and gone away. This is a way of saying that in the stories the eccentric remains eccentric, even when you think you're ready for it, and part of Dostoevsky's amazing skill here is keeping suspense alive when there is every reason to think it should be dead.

A man goes mad because he is happy. No, because he can't bear the thought of being happy when so many others are not. No, because there is something about St Petersburg that explains such a pathology, although the story doesn't tell us what it is. A man is swallowed by a crocodile, but not seriously damaged. That is, not eaten and not impeded in his speech. He talks happily from inside the creature about his future fame and its attendant possibilities. The crocodile's owner is German, and no one in this story can think of anything but economic conditions and the significance of foreign imports for Russia's future. After his initial horror at the swallowing, and his fear that the crocodile might not survive the internal addition of a human, the owner himself eagerly looks forward to vastly increased revenues. One newspaper, making a slight mistake, reports the story as that of a man who swallowed a crocodile.

One could create similar pictures for all the stories gathered in this book, even when they concern a boy's first, almost unrecognised love, or the conversion of a modest, kindly young woman into a person who almost commits a murder – it's amazing what the nasty condescension of a husband can do. And I can't resist mentioning Dostoevsky's (to me improbable) gift for slapstick. When a senior civil servant decides to behave like a patronising, self-admiring monster at the wedding party of one of his subordinates, he steps into a plate of jelly as he enters the house, and by the time he is drunk enough to pass out, his face falls straight into a bowl of blancmange.

These stories have remarkable afterlives. The kindly young woman reappears as the heroine of Robert Bresson's film *Une femme douce* (1969), and Dostoevsky's 'White Nights' become the same director's *Quatre Nuits d'un rêveur* (1971). Luchino Visconti also made a film of 'White Nights' (1957). These works take Dostoevsky into different countries, of course, and not only geographically. With Bresson even the professional actors look like amateurs, and eccentricity turns into calm, almost normal desperation. Visconti's film, with its high-profile stars Maria Schell and Marcello Mastroianni and its low-key neorealist mood, makes us wonder how eccentricity could seem both ordinary and glamorous.

Once upon a time, let's say in 1959, when George Steiner wrote a book on the subject, it seemed as if English speakers had a cultural obligation to choose between Tolstoy and Dostoevsky – well, an obligation to choose Tolstoy, actually, after a decorous pause during which we pretended to be thinking. In 1951, Lionel Trilling had elegantly given us a reason for doing the right thing:

> We so happily give our assent to what Tolstoy shows us and so willingly call it reality because we have something to gain from its being reality. For it is the hope of every decent, reasonably honest person to be judged under the aspect of Tolstoy's representation of human nature.

What Trilling seems to me to have said (and said very well), although I am far from sure this is what he meant, is that Tolstoy shows us the world as it should be, while Dostoevsky shows us the world as it is. He often does this by means of what looks like fantasy; but then we do have a habit of calling fantastic all the aspects of reality we don't like.

Michael Wood

The Crocodile

and Other Stories

A Faint Heart

1848

UNDER THE SAME ROOF in the same flat on the same fourth storey lived two young men, colleagues in the service, Arkady Ivanovitch Nefedevitch and Vasya Shumkov . . . The author of course, feels the necessity of explaining to the reader why one is given his full title, while the other's name is abbreviated, if only that such a mode of expression may not be regarded as unseemly and rather familiar. But, to do so, it would first be necessary to explain and describe the rank and years and calling and duty in the service, and even, indeed, the characters of the persons concerned; and since there are so many writers who begin in that way the author of the proposed story, solely in order to be unlike them (that is, some people will perhaps say, entirely on account of his boundless vanity), decides to begin straightaway with action. Having completed this introduction, he begins.

Towards six o'clock on New Year's Eve Shumkov returned home. Arkady Ivanovitch, who was lying on the bed, woke up and looked at his friend with half-closed eyes. He saw that Vasya had on his very best trousers and a very clean shirt front. That, of course, struck him. 'Where had Vasya to go like that? And he had not dined at home either!' Meanwhile, Shumkov had lighted a candle, and Arkady Ivanovitch guessed immediately that his friend was intending to wake him accidentally. Vasya did, in fact, clear his throat twice, walked twice up and down the room, and at last, quite accidentally, let the pipe, which he had begun filling in the corner by the stove, slip out of his hands. Arkady Ivanovitch laughed to himself.

'Vasya, give over pretending!' he said.

'Arkasha, you are not asleep?'

'I really cannot say for certain; it seems to me I am not.'

'Oh, Arkasha! How are you, dear boy? Well, brother! Well, brother! . . . You don't know what I have to tell you!'

'I certainly don't know; come here.'

As though expecting this, Vasya went up to him at once, not at all anticipating, however, treachery from Arkady Ivanovitch. The other seized him very adroitly by the arms, turned him over, held him down, and began, as it is called, 'strangling' his victim, and apparently this proceeding afforded the light-hearted Arkady Ivanovitch great satisfaction.

'Caught!' he cried. 'Caught!'

'Arkasha, Arkasha, what are you about? Let me go. For goodness sake, let me go, I shall crumple my dress coat!'

'As though that mattered! What do you want with a dress coat? Why were you so confiding as to put yourself in my hands? Tell me, where have you been? Where have you dined?'

'Arkasha, for goodness sake, let me go!'

'Where have you dined?'

'Why, it's about that I want to tell you.'

'Tell away, then.'

'But first let me go.'

'Not a bit of it, I won't let you go till you tell me!'

'Arkasha! Arkasha! But do you understand, I can't – it is utterly impossible!' cried Vasya, helplessly wriggling out of his friend's powerful clutches, 'you know there are subjects!'

'How – subjects? . . .'

'Why, subjects that you can't talk about in such a position without losing your dignity; it's utterly impossible; it would make it ridiculous, and this is not a ridiculous matter, it is important.'

'Here, he's going in for being important! That's a new idea! You tell me so as to make me laugh, that's how you must tell me; I don't want anything important; or else you are no true friend of mine. Do you call yourself a friend? Eh?'

'Arkasha, I really can't!'

'Well, I don't want to hear . . .'

'Well, Arkasha!' began Vasya, lying across the bed and doing his utmost to put all the dignity possible into his words. 'Arkasha! If you like, I will tell you; only . . .'

'Well, what? . . .'

'Well, I am engaged to be married!'

Without uttering another word Arkady Ivanovitch took Vasya up in his arms like a baby, though the latter was by no means short, but rather long and thin, and began dexterously carrying him up and down the room, pretending that he was hushing him to sleep.

'I'll put you in your swaddling clothes, Master Bridegroom,' he kept saying. But seeing that Vasya lay in his arms, not stirring or uttering a word, he thought better of it at once, and reflecting that the joke had gone too far, set him down in the middle of the room and kissed him on the cheek in the most genuine and friendly way.

'Vasya, you are not angry?'

'Arkasha, listen . . .'

'Come, it's New Year's Eve.'

'Oh, I'm all right; but why are you such a madman, such a scatterbrain? How many times I have told you: Arkasha, it's really not funny, not funny at all!'

'Oh, well, you are not angry?'

'Oh, I'm all right; am I ever angry with anyone! But you have wounded me, do you understand?'

'But how have I wounded you? In what way?'

'I come to you as to a friend, with a full heart, to pour out my soul to you, to tell you of my happiness . . .'

'What happiness? Why don't you speak? . . .'

'Oh, well, I am going to get married!' Vasya answered with vexation, for he really was a little exasperated.

'You! You are going to get married! So you really mean it?' Arkasha cried at the top of his voice. 'No, no . . . but what's this? He talks like this and his tears are flowing . . . Vasya, my little Vasya, don't, my little son! Is it true, really?' And Arkady Ivanovitch flew to hug him again.

'Well, do you see, how it is now?' said Vasya. 'You are kind, of course, you are a friend, I know that. I come to you with such joy, such rapture, and all of a sudden I have to disclose all the joy of my heart, all my rapture struggling across the bed, in an undignified way . . . You understand, Arkasha,' Vasya went on, half laughing. 'You see, it made it seem comic: and in a sense I did not belong to myself at that minute. I could not let this be slighted . . . What's more, if you had asked me her name, I swear, I would sooner you killed me than have answered you.'

'But, Vasya, why did you not speak! You should have told me all about it sooner and I would not have played the fool!' cried Arkady Ivanovitch in genuine despair.

'Come, that's enough, that's enough! Of course, that's how it is . . . You know what it all comes from – from my having a good heart. What vexes me is, that I could not tell you as I wanted to, making you glad and happy, telling you nicely and initiating you into my secret properly . . . Really, Arkasha, I love you so much that I believe if it were not for you I shouldn't be getting married, and, in fact, I shouldn't be living in this world at all!'

Arkady Ivanovitch, who was excessively sentimental, cried and laughed at once as he listened to Vasya. Vasya did the same. Both flew to embrace one another again and forgot the past.

'How is it – how is it? Tell me all about it, Vasya! I am astonished, excuse me, brother, but I am utterly astonished; it's a perfect thunderbolt, by Jove! Nonsense, nonsense, brother, you have made it up, you've really made it up, you are telling fibs!' cried Arkady Ivanovitch, and he actually looked into Vasya's face with genuine uncertainty, but seeing in it the radiant confirmation of a positive intention of being married as soon as possible, threw himself on the bed and began rolling from side to side in ecstasy till the walls shook.

'Vasya, sit here,' he said at last, sitting down on the bed.

'I really don't know, brother, where to begin!'

They looked at one another in joyful excitement.

'Who is she, Vasya?'

'The Artemyevs! . . .' Vasya pronounced, in a voice weak with emotion.

'No?'

'Well, I did buzz into your ears about them at first, and then I shut up, and you noticed nothing. Ah, Arkasha, if you knew how hard it was to keep it from you; but I was afraid, afraid to speak! I thought it would all go wrong, and you know I was in love, Arkasha! My God! My God! You see this was the trouble,' he began, pausing continually from agitation, 'she had a suitor a year ago, but he was suddenly ordered somewhere; I knew him – he was a fellow, bless him! Well, he did not write at all, he simply vanished. They waited and waited, wondering what it meant . . . Four months ago he suddenly came back married, and has never set foot within their doors! It was coarse – shabby! And they had no one to stand up for them. She cried and cried, poor girl, and I fell in love with her . . . indeed, I had been in love with her long before, all the time! I began comforting her, and was always going there . . . Well, and I really don't know how it has all come about, only she came to love me; a week ago I could not restrain myself, I cried, I sobbed, and told her everything – well, that I love her – everything, in fact! . . . "I am ready to love you, too, Vassily Petrovitch, only I am a poor girl, don't make a mock of me; I don't dare to love anyone." Well, brother, you understand! You understand? . . . On that we got engaged on the spot. I kept thinking and thinking and thinking and thinking, I said to her, "How are we to tell your mother?" She said, "It will be hard, wait a little; she's afraid, and now maybe she would not let you have me; she keeps crying, too." Without telling her I blurted it out to her mother today. Lizanka fell on her knees before her, I did the same . . . well, she gave us her blessing. Arkasha, Arkasha! My dear fellow! We will live together. No, I won't part from you for anything.'

'Vasya, look at you as I may, I can't believe it. I don't believe it, I swear. I keep feeling as though . . . Listen, how can you be engaged to be married? . . . How is it I didn't know, eh? Do you know, Vasya, I will confess it to you now. I was thinking of getting married myself; but now since you are going to be married, it is just as good! Be happy, be happy! . . .'

'Brother, I feel so lighthearted now, there is such sweetness in my soul . . .' said Vasya, getting up and pacing about the room excitedly. 'Don't you feel the same? We shall be poor, of course, but we shall be happy; and you know it is not a wild fancy; our happiness is not a fairy tale; we shall be happy in reality! . . .'

'Vasya, Vasya, listen!'

'What?' said Vasya, standing before Arkady Ivanovitch.

'The idea occurs to me; I am really afraid to say it to you . . . Forgive me, and settle my doubts. What are you going to live on? You know I am delighted that you are going to be married, of course, I am delighted, and I don't know what to do with myself, but – what are you going to live on? Eh?'

'Oh, good heavens! What a fellow you are, Arkasha!' said Vasya, looking at Nefedevitch in profound astonishment. 'What do you mean? Even her old mother, even she did not think of that for two minutes when I put it all clearly before her. You had better ask what they are living on! They have five hundred roubles a year between the three of them: the pension, which is all they have, since the father died. She and her old mother and her little brother, whose schooling is paid for out of that income too – that is how they live! It's you and I are the capitalists! Some good years it works out to as much as seven hundred for me.'

'I say, Vasya, excuse me; I really . . . you know I . . . I am only thinking how to prevent things going wrong. How do you mean, seven hundred? It's only three hundred . . .'

'Three hundred! . . . And Yulian Mastakovitch? Have you forgotten him?'

'Yulian Mastakovitch? But you know that's uncertain, brother; that's not the same thing as three hundred roubles of secure salary, where every rouble is a friend you can trust. Yulian Mastakovitch, of course, he's a great man, in fact, I respect him, I understand him, though he is so far above us; and, by Jove, I love him, because he likes you and gives you something for your work, though he might not pay you, but simply order a clerk to work for him – but you will agree, Vasya . . . Let me tell you, too, I am not talking nonsense. I admit in all Petersburg you won't find a handwriting like your handwriting, I am ready to allow that to you,' Nefedevitch concluded, not without enthusiasm. 'But, God forbid! you may displease him all at once, you may not satisfy him, your work with him may stop, he may take another clerk – all sorts of things may happen, in fact! You know, Yulian Mastakovitch may be here today and gone tomorrow . . .'

'Well, Arkasha, the ceiling might fall on our heads this minute.'

'Oh, of course, of course, I mean nothing.'

'But listen, hear what I have got to say – you know, I don't see how he can part with me . . . No, hear what I have to say!

hear what I have to say! You see, I perform all my duties punctually; you know how kind he is, you know, Arkasha, he gave me fifty roubles in silver today!'

'Did he really, Vasya? A bonus for you?'

'Bonus, indeed, it was out of his own pocket. He said: "Why, you have had no money for five months, brother, take some if you want it; thank you, I am satisfied with you . . ." Yes, really! "Yes, you don't work for me for nothing," said he. He did, indeed, that's what he said. It brought tears into my eyes, Arkasha. Good heavens, yes!'

'I say, Vasya, have you finished copying those papers? . . .'

'No . . . I haven't finished them yet.'

'Vas . . . ya! My angel! What have you been doing?'

'Listen, Arkasha, it doesn't matter, they are not wanted for another two days, I have time enough . . .'

'How is it you have not done them?'

'That's all right, that's all right. You look so horror-stricken that you turn me inside out and make my heart ache! You are always going on at me like this! He's for ever crying out: Oh, oh, oh!!! Only consider, what does it matter? Why, I shall finish it, of course I shall finish it . . .'

'What if you don't finish it?' cried Arkady, jumping up, 'and he has made you a present today! And you going to be married . . . Tut, tut, tut! . . .'

'It's all right, it's all right,' cried Shumkov, 'I shall sit down directly, I shall sit down this minute.'

'How did you come to leave it, Vasya?'

'Oh, Arkasha! How could I sit down to work! Have I been in a fit state? Why, even at the office I could scarcely sit still, I could scarcely bear the beating of my heart . . . Oh! oh! Now I shall work all night, and I shall work all tomorrow night, and the night after, too – and I shall finish it.'

'Is there a great deal left?'

'Don't hinder me, for goodness sake, don't hinder me; hold your tongue.'

Arkady Ivanovitch went on tiptoe to the bed and sat down, then suddenly wanted to get up, but was obliged to sit down again, remembering that he might interrupt him, though he could not sit still for excitement: it was evident that the news had thoroughly upset him, and the first thrill of delight had not yet passed off. He glanced at Shumkov; the latter glanced at him, smiled, and shook his finger at him, then, frowning severely (as though all his energy and the success of his work depended upon it), fixed his eyes on the papers.

It seemed that he, too, could not yet master his emotion; he kept changing his pen, fidgeting in his chair, rearranging things, and setting to work again, but his hand trembled and refused to move.

'Arkasha, I've talked to them about you,' he cried suddenly, as though he had just remembered it.

'Yes,' cried Arkasha, 'I was just wanting to ask you that. Well?'

'Well, I'll tell you everything afterwards. Of course, it is my own fault, but it quite went out of my head that I didn't mean to say anything till I had written four pages, but I thought of you and of them. I really can't write, brother, I keep thinking about you . . .'

Vasya smiled.

A silence followed.

'Phew! What a horrid pen,' cried Shumkov, flinging it on the table in vexation. He took another.

'Vasya! listen! one word . . .'

'Well, make haste, and for the last time.'

'Have you a great deal left to do?'

'Ah, brother!' Vasya frowned, as though there could be nothing more terrible and murderous in the whole world than such a question. 'A lot, a fearful lot.'

'Do you know, I have an idea—'

'What?'

'Oh, never mind, never mind; go on writing.'

'Why, what? what?'

'It's past six, Vasya.'

Here Nefedevitch smiled and winked slyly at Vasya, though with a certain timidity, not knowing how Vasya would take it.

'Well, what is it?' said Vasya, throwing down his pen, looking him straight in the face and actually turning pale with excitement.

'Do you know what?'

'For goodness sake, what is it?'

'I tell you what, you are excited, you won't get much done . . . Stop, stop, stop! I have it, I have it – listen,' said Nefedevitch, jumping up from the bed in delight, preventing Vasya from speaking and doing his utmost to ward off all objections; 'first of all you must get calm, you must pull yourself together, mustn't you?'

'Arkasha, Arkasha!' cried Vasya, jumping up from his chair, 'I will work all night, I will, really.'

'Of course, of course, you won't go to bed till morning.'

'I won't go to bed, I won't go to bed at all.'

'No, that won't do, that won't do: you must sleep, go to bed at five. I will call you at eight. Tomorrow is a holiday; you can sit and scribble away all day long . . . Then the night and – but have you a great deal left to do?'

'Yes, look, look!'

Vasya, quivering with excitement and suspense, showed the manuscript: 'Look!'

'I say, brother, that's not much.'

'My dear fellow, there's some more of it,' said Vasya, looking very timidly at Nefedevitch, as though the decision whether he was to go or not depended upon the latter.

'How much?'

'Two signatures.'

'Well, what's that? Come, I tell you what. We shall have time to finish it, by Jove, we shall!'

'Arkasha!'

'Vasya, listen! Tonight, on New Year's Eve, everyone is at home with his family. You and I are the only ones without a home or relations . . . Oh, Vasya!'

Nefedevitch clutched Vasya and hugged him in his leonine arms.

'Arkasha, it's settled.'

'Vasya, boy, I only wanted to say this. You see, Vasya – listen, bandy-legs, listen! . . .'

Arkady stopped, with his mouth open, because he could not speak for delight. Vasya held him by the shoulders, gazed into his face and moved his lips, as though he wanted to speak for him.

'Well,' he brought out at last.

'Introduce me to them today.'

'Arkady, let us go to tea there. I tell you what, I tell you what. We won't even stay to see in the New Year, we'll come away earlier,' cried Vasya, with genuine inspiration.

'That is, we'll go for two hours, neither more nor less . . .'

'And then separation till I have finished . . .'

'Vasya, boy!'

'Arkady!'

Three minutes later Arkady was dressed in his best. Vasya did nothing but brush himself, because he had been in such haste to work that he had not changed his trousers.

They hurried out into the street, each more pleased than the other. Their way lay from the Petersburg Side to Kolomna. Arkady Ivanovitch stepped out boldly and vigorously, so that from his walk alone one could see how glad he was at the good fortune of his friend, who was more and more radiant with happiness. Vasya trotted along with shorter steps, though his deportment was none the less dignified. Arkady Ivanovitch, in fact, had never seen him before to such advantage. At that moment he actually felt more respect for him, and Vasya's physical defect, of which the reader is not yet aware (Vasya was slightly deformed), which always called forth a feeling of loving sympathy in Arkady Ivanovitch's kind heart, contributed to the deep tenderness the latter felt for him at this moment, a tenderness of which Vasya was in every way worthy. Arkady Ivanovitch felt ready to weep with happiness, but he restrained himself.

'Where are you going, where are you going, Vasya? It is nearer this way,' he cried, seeing that Vasya was making in the direction of Voznesenky.

'Hold your tongue, Arkasha.'

'It really is nearer, Vasya.'

'Do you know what, Arkasha?' Vasya began mysteriously, in a voice quivering with joy, 'I tell you what, I want to take Lizanka a little present.'

'What sort of present?'

'At the corner here, brother, is Madame Leroux's, a wonderful shop.'

'Well.'

'A cap, my dear, a cap; I saw such a charming little cap today. I inquired, I was told it was the *façon Manon Lescaut*

– a delightful thing. Cherry-coloured ribbons, and if it is not dear . . . Arkasha, even if it is dear . . .'

'I think you are superior to any of the poets, Vasya. Come along.'

They ran along, and two minutes later went into the shop. They were met by a black-eyed Frenchwoman with curls, who, from the first glance at her customers, became as joyous and happy as they, even happier, if one may say so. Vasya was ready to kiss Madame Leroux in his delight . . .

'Arkasha,' he said in an undertone, casting a casual glance at all the grand and beautiful things on little wooden stands on the huge table, 'lovely things! What's that? What's this? This one, for instance, this little sweet, do you see?' Vasya whispered, pointing to a charming cap further away, which was not the one he meant to buy, because he had already from afar descried and fixed his eyes upon the real, famous one, standing at the other end. He looked at it in such a way that one might have supposed someone was going to steal it, or as though the cap itself might take wings and fly into the air just to prevent Vasya from obtaining it.

'Look,' said Arkady Ivanovitch, pointing to one, 'I think that's better.'

'Well, Arkasha, that does you credit; I begin to respect you for your taste,' said Vasya, resorting to cunning with Arkasha in the tenderness of his heart, 'your cap is charming, but come this way.'

'Where is there a better one, brother?'

'Look; this way.'

'That,' said Arkady, doubtfully.

But when Vasya, incapable of restraining himself any longer, took it from the stand from which it seemed to fly spontaneously, as though delighted at falling at last into the hands of so good a customer, and they heard the rustle of its ribbons, ruches and lace, an unexpected cry of delight broke from the powerful chest of Arkady Ivanovitch. Even Madame Leroux, while maintaining her incontestable dignity and pre-eminence in matters of taste, and remaining mute from condescension, rewarded Vasya with a smile of complete approbation, everything in her glance, gesture and smile saying at once: 'Yes, you have chosen rightly, and are worthy of the happiness which awaits you.'

'It has been dangling its charms in coy seclusion,' cried Vasya, transferring his tender feelings to the charming cap. 'You have been hiding on purpose, you sly little pet!' And he kissed it, that is the air surrounding it, for he was afraid to touch his treasure.

'Retiring as true worth and virtue,' Arkady added enthusiastically, quoting humorously from a comic paper he had read that morning. 'Well, Vasya?'

'Hurrah, Arkasha! You are witty today. I predict you will make a sensation, as women say. Madame Leroux, Madame Leroux!'

'What is your pleasure?'

'Dear Madame Leroux.'

Madame Leroux looked at Arkady Ivanovitch and smiled condescendingly.

'You wouldn't believe how I adore you at this moment . . . Allow me to give you a kiss . . .' And Vasya kissed the shopkeeper.

She certainly at that moment needed all her dignity to maintain her position with such a madcap. But I contend that the innate, spontaneous courtesy and grace with which Madame Leroux received Vasya's enthusiasm, was equally befitting. She forgave him, and how tactfully, how graciously, she knew how to behave in the circumstances. How could she have been angry with Vasya?

'Madame Leroux, how much?'

'Five roubles in silver,' she answered, straightening herself with a new smile.

'And this one, Madame Leroux?' said Arkady Ivanovitch, pointing to his choice.

'That one is eight roubles.'

'There, you see – there, you see! Come, Madame Leroux, tell me which is nicer, more graceful, more charming, which of them suits you best?'

'The second is richer, but your choice *c'est plus coquet*.'

'Then we will take it.'

Madame Leroux took a sheet of very delicate paper, pinned it up, and the paper with the cap wrapped in it seemed even lighter than the paper alone. Vasya took it carefully, almost holding his breath, bowed to Madame Leroux, said something else very polite to her and left the shop.

'I am a lady's man, I was born to be a lady's man,' said Vasya, laughing a little noiseless, nervous laugh and dodging the passers-by, whom he suspected of designs for crushing his precious cap.

'Listen, Arkady, brother,' he began a minute later, and there was a note of triumph, of infinite affection in his voice. 'Arkady, I am so happy, I am so happy!'

'Vasya! how glad I am, dear boy!'

'No, Arkasha, no. I know that there is no limit to your affection for me; but you cannot be feeling one-hundreth part of what I am feeling at this moment. My heart is so full, so full! Arkasha, I am not worthy of such happiness. I feel that, I am conscious of it. Why has it come to me?' he said, his voice full of stifled sobs. 'What have I done to deserve it? Tell me. Look what lots of people, what lots of tears, what sorrow, what work-a-day life without a holiday, while I, I am loved by a girl like that, I . . . But you will see her yourself immediately, you will appreciate her noble heart. I was born in a humble station, now I have a grade in the service and an independent income – my salary. I was born with a physical defect, I am a little deformed. See, she loves me as I am. Yulian Mastakovitch was so kind, so attentive, so gracious today; he does not often talk to me; he came up to me: "Well, how goes it, Vasya" (yes, really, he called me Vasya), "are you going to have a good time for the holiday, eh?" he laughed.

'"Well, the fact is, your Excellency, I have work to do," but then I plucked up courage and said: "and maybe I shall have a good time, too, your Excellency." I really said it. He gave me the money, on the spot, then he said a couple of words more to me. Tears came into my eyes, brother, I actually cried, and he, too, seemed touched, he patted me on the shoulder, and said: "Feel always, Vasya, as you feel this now."'

Vasya paused for an instant. Arkady Ivanovitch turned away, and he, too, wiped away a tear with his fist.

'And, and . . .' Vasya went on, 'I have never spoken to you of this, Arkady. . . Arkady, you make me so happy with your affection, without you I could not live, – no, no, don't say anything, Arkady, let me squeeze your hand, let me . . . tha . . . ank . . . you . . .' Again Vasya could not finish.

Arkady Ivanovitch longed to throw himself on Vasya's neck, but as they were crossing the road and heard almost in their ears a shrill: 'Hi! there!' they ran frightened and excited to the pavement.

Arkady Ivanovitch was positively relieved. He set down Vasya's outburst of gratitude to the exceptional circumstances of the moment. He was vexed. He felt that he had done so little for Vasya hitherto. He felt actually ashamed of himself when Vasya began thanking him for so little. But they had all their lives before them, and Arkady Ivanovitch breathed more freely.

The Artemyevs had quite given up expecting them. The proof of it was that they had already sat down to tea! And the old, it seems, are sometimes more clear-sighted than the young, even when the young are so exceptional. Lizanka had very earnestly maintained, 'He isn't coming, he isn't coming, Mamma; I feel in my heart he is not coming'; while her mother on the contrary declared that she had a feeling that he would certainly come, that he would not stay away, that he would run round, that he could have no office work now, on New Year's Eve. Even as Lizanka opened the door she did not in the least expect to see them, and greeted them breathlessly, with her heart throbbing like a captured bird's, flushing and turning as red as a cherry, a fruit which she wonderfully resembled. Good heavens, what a surprise it was! What a joyful 'Oh!' broke from her lips. 'Deceiver! My darling!' she cried, throwing her arms round Vasya's neck. But imagine her amazement, her sudden confusion: just behind Vasya, as though trying to hide behind his back, stood Arkady Ivanovitch, a trifle out of countenance. It must be admitted that he was awkward in the company of women, very awkward indeed, in fact on one occasion something occurred . . . but of that later. You must put yourself in his place, however. There was nothing to laugh at; he was standing in the entry, in his goloshes and overcoat, and in a cap with flaps over the ears, which he would have hastened to pull off, but he had, all twisted round in a hideous way, a yellow knitted scarf, which, to make things worse, was knotted at the back. He had to disentangle all this, to take it off as quickly as possible, to show himself to more advantage, for there is no one who does not prefer to show himself to advantage. And then Vasya, vexatious insufferable Vasya, of course always the same dear kind Vasya, but now insufferable, ruthless Vasya. 'Here,' he shouted, 'Lizanka, I have brought you my Arkady? What do you think of him? He is my best friend, embrace him, kiss him, Lizanka, give him a kiss in advance; afterwards – you will know him better – you can take it back again.'

Well, what, I ask you, was Arkady Ivanovitch to do? And he had only untwisted half of the scarf so far. I really am sometimes ashamed of Vasya's excess of enthusiasm; it is, of course, the sign of a good heart, but . . . it's awkward, not nice!

At last both went in . . . The mother was unutterably delighted to make Arkady Ivanovitch's acquaintance, 'she had heard so much about him, she had . . .' But she did not finish. A joyful 'Oh!' ringing musically through the room interrupted her in the middle of a sentence. Good heavens! Lizanka was standing before the cap which had suddenly been unfolded before her gaze; she clasped her hands with the utmost simplicity, smiling such a smile . . . Oh, heavens! why had not Madame Leroux an even lovelier cap?

Oh, heavens! but where could you find a lovelier cap? It was quite first-rate. Where could you get a better one? I mean it seriously. This ingratitude on the part of lovers moves me, in fact, to indignation and even wounds me a little. Why, look at it for yourself, reader, look, what could be more beautiful than this little love of a cap? Come, look at it . . . But, no, no, my strictures are uncalled for; they had by now all agreed with me; it had been a momentary aberration; the blindness, the delirium of feeling; I am ready to forgive them . . . But then you must look . . . You must excuse me, kind reader, I am still talking about the cap: made of tulle, light as a feather, a broad cherry-coloured ribbon covered with lace passing between the tulle and the ruche, and at the back two wide long ribbons – they would fall down a little below the nape of the neck . . . All that the cap needed was to be tilted a little to the back of the head; come, look at it; I ask you, after that . . . but I see you are not looking . . . you think it does not matter. You are looking in a different direction . . . You are looking at two big tears, big as pearls, that rose in two jet-black eyes, quivered for one instant on the eyelashes, and then dropped on the ethereal tulle of which Madame Leroux's artistic masterpiece was composed . . . And again I feel vexed, those two tears were scarcely a tribute to the cap . . . No, to my mind, such a gift should be given in cool blood, as only then can its full worth be appreciated. I am, I confess, dear reader, entirely on the side of the cap.

They sat down – Vasya with Lizanka and the old mother with Arkady Ivanovitch; they began to talk, and Arkady Ivanovitch did himself credit, I am glad to say that for him. One would hardly, indeed, have expected it of him. After a couple of words about Vasya he most successfully turned the conversation to Yulian Mastakovitch, his patron. And he talked so cleverly, so cleverly that the subject was not exhausted for an hour. You ought to have seen with what dexterity, what tact, Arkady Ivanovitch touched upon certain peculiarities of Yulian Mastakovitch which directly or indirectly affected Vasya. The mother was fascinated, genuinely fascinated; she admitted it herself; she purposely called Vasya aside, and said to him that his friend was a most excellent and charming young man, and, what was of most account, such a serious, steady young man. Vasya almost laughed aloud with delight. He remembered how the serious Arkady had tumbled him on his bed for a quarter of an hour. Then the mother signed to Vasya to follow her quietly and cautiously into the next room. It must be admitted that she treated Lizanka rather unfairly: she behaved treacherously to her daughter, in the fullness of her heart, of course, and showed Vasya on the sly the present Lizanka was preparing to give him for the New Year. It was a paper-case, embroidered in beads and gold in a very choice design: on one side was depicted a stag, absolutely lifelike, running swiftly, and so well done! On the other side was the portrait of a celebrated General, also an excellent likeness. I cannot describe Vasya's raptures. Meanwhile, time was not being wasted in the parlour. Lizanka went straight up to Arkady Ivanovitch. She took his hand, she thanked him for something, and Arkady Ivanovitch gathered that she was referring to her precious Vasya. Lizanka was indeed deeply touched: she had heard that Arkady Ivanovitch was such a true friend of her betrothed, so loved him, so watched over him, guiding him at every step with helpful advice, that she, Lizanka, could hardly help thanking him, could not refrain from feeling grateful, and hoping that Arkady Ivanovitch might like her, if only half as well as Vasya. Then she began questioning him as to whether Vasya was careful of his health, expressed some apprehensions in regard to his marked impulsiveness of character, and his lack of knowledge of men and practical life; she said that she would in time watch over him religiously, that she would take care of and cherish his lot, and finally, she hoped that Arkady Ivanovitch would not leave them, but would live with them.

'We three shall live like one,' she cried, with extremely naïve enthusiasm.

But it was time to go. They tried, of course, to keep them, but Vasya answered point blank that it was impossible. Arkady Ivanovitch said the same. The reason was, of course, inquired into, and it came out at once that there was work to be done entrusted to Vasya by Yulian Mastakovitch, urgent, necessary, dreadful work, which must be handed in on the morning of the next day but one, and that it was not only unfinished, but had been completely laid aside. The mamma sighed when she heard of this, while Lizanka was positively scared, and hurried Vasya off in alarm. The last kiss lost nothing from this haste; though brief and hurried it was only the more warm and ardent. At last they parted and the two friends set off home.

Both began at once confiding to each other their impressions as soon as they found themselves in the street. And could they help it? Indeed, Arkady Ivanovitch was in love, desperately in love, with Lizanka. And to whom could he better confide his feelings than to Vasya, the happy man himself. And so he did; he was not bashful, but confessed everything at once to Vasya. Vasya laughed heartily and was immensely delighted, and even observed that this was all that was needed to make them greater friends than ever. 'You have guessed my feelings, Vasya,' said Arkady Ivanovitch. 'Yes, I love her as I love you; she will be my good angel as well as yours, for the radiance of your happiness will be shed on me, too, and I can bask in its warmth. She will keep house for me too, Vasya; my happiness will be in her hands. Let her keep house for me as she will for you. Yes, friendship for you is friendship for her; you are not separable for me now, only I shall have two beings like you instead of one . . .' Arkady paused in the fullness of his feelings, while Vasya was shaken to the depths of his being by his friend's words. The fact is, he had never expected anything of the sort from Arkady. Arkady Ivanovitch was not very great at talking as a rule, he was not fond of dreaming, either; now he gave way to the liveliest, freshest, rainbow-tinted day-dreams. 'How I will protect and cherish you both,' he began again. 'To begin with, Vasya, I will be godfather to all your children, every one of them; and secondly, Vasya, we must bestir ourselves about the future. We must buy furniture, and take a lodging so that you and she and I can each have a little room to ourselves. Do you know, Vasya, I'll run about tomorrow and look at the notices, on the gates! Three . . . no, two rooms, we should not need more. I really believe, Vasya, I talked nonsense this morning, there will be money enough; why, as soon as I glanced into her eyes I calculated at once that there would be enough to live on. It will all be for her. Oh, how we will work! Now, Vasya, we might venture up to twenty-five roubles for rent. A lodging is everything, brother. Nice rooms . . . and at once a man is cheerful, and his dreams are of the brightest hues. And, besides, Lizanka will keep the purse for both of us: not a farthing will be wasted. Do you suppose I would go to a restaurant? What do you take me for? Not on any account. And then we shall get a bonus and reward, for we shall be zealous in the service – oh! how we shall work, like oxen toiling in the fields . . . Only fancy,' and Arkady Ivanovitch's voice was faint with pleasure, 'all at once and quite unexpected, twenty-five or thirty roubles . . . Whenever there's an extra, there'll be a cap or a scarf or a pair of little stockings. She must knit me a scarf; look what a horrid one I've got, the nasty yellow thing, it did me a bad turn today! And you were a nice one, Vasya, to introduce me while I had my head in a halter . . . Though never mind that now. And look here, I undertake all the silver. I am bound to give you some little present – that will be an honour, that will flatter my vanity . . . My bonuses won't fail me, surely; you don't suppose they would give them to Skorohodov? No fear, they won't be landed in that person's pocket. I'll buy you silver spoons, brother, good knives – not silver knives, but thoroughly good ones; and a waistcoat, that is a waistcoat for myself. I shall be best man, of course. Only now, brother, you must keep at it, you must keep at it. I shall stand over you with a stick, brother, today and tomorrow and all night; I shall worry you to work. Finish, make haste and finish, brother. And then again to spend the evening, and then again both of us happy; we will go in for loto. We will spend the evening there – oh, it's jolly! Oh, the devil! How vexing it is I can't help you. I should like to take it and write it all for you . . . Why is it our handwriting is not alike?'

'Yes,' answered Vasya. 'Yes, I must make haste. I think it must be eleven o'clock; we must make haste . . . To work!' And saying this, Vasya, who had been all the time alternately smiling and trying to interrupt with some enthusiastic rejoinder the flow of his friend's feelings, and had, in short, been showing the most cordial response, suddenly subsided, sank into silence, and almost ran along the street. It seemed as though some burdensome idea had suddenly chilled his feverish head; he seemed all at once dispirited.

Arkady Ivanovitch felt quite uneasy; he scarcely got an answer to his hurried questions from Vasya, who confined himself to a word or two, sometimes an irrelevant exclamation.

'Why, what is the matter with you, Vasya?' he cried at last, hardly able to keep up with him. 'Can you really be so uneasy?'

'Oh, brother, that's enough chatter!' Vasya answered, with vexation.

'Don't be depressed, Vasya – come, come,' Arkady interposed. 'Why, I have known you write much more in a shorter time! What's the matter? You've simply a talent for it! You can write quickly in an emergency; they are not going to lithograph your copy. You've plenty of time! . . . The only thing is that you are excited now, and preoccupied and the work won't go so easily.'

Vasya made no reply, or muttered something to himself, and they both ran home in genuine anxiety.

Vasya sat down to the papers at once. Arkady Ivanovitch was quiet and silent; he noiselessly undressed and went to bed, keeping his eyes fixed on Vasya . . . A sort of panic came over him . . . 'What is the matter with him?' he thought to himself, looking at Vasya's face that grew whiter and whiter, at his feverish eyes, at the anxiety that was betrayed in every movement he made, 'why, his hand is shaking . . . what a stupid! Why did I not advise him to sleep for a couple of hours, till he had slept off his nervous excitement, anyway.' Vasya had just finished a page, he raised his eyes, glanced casually at Arkady and at once, looking down, took up his pen again.

'Listen, Vasya,' Arkady Ivanovitch began suddenly, 'wouldn't it be best to sleep a little now? Look, you are in a regular fever.'

Vasya glanced at Arkady with vexation, almost with anger, and made no answer.

'Listen, Vasya, you'll make yourself ill.'

Vasya at once changed his mind. 'How would it be to have tea, Arkady?' he said.

'How so? Why?'

'It will do me good. I am not sleepy, I'm not going to bed! I am going on writing. But now I should like to rest and have a cup of tea, and the worst moment will be over.'

'First-rate, brother Vasya, delightful! Just so. I was wanting to propose it myself. And I can't think why it did not occur to me to do so. But I say, Mavra won't get up, she won't wake for anything . . .'

'True.'

'That's no matter, though,' cried Arkady Ivanovitch, leaping out of bed. 'I will set the samovar myself. It won't be the first time . . .'

Arkady Ivanovitch ran to the kitchen and set to work to get the samovar; Vasya meanwhile went on writing. Arkady Ivanovitch, moreover, dressed and ran out to the baker's, so that Vasya might have something to sustain him for the night. A quarter of an hour later the samovar was on the table. They began drinking tea, but conversation flagged. Vasya still seemed preoccupied.

'Tomorrow,' he said at last, as though he had just thought of it, 'I shall have to take my congratulations for the New Year . . .'

'You need not go at all.'

'Oh yes, brother, I must,' said Vasya.

'Why, I will sign the visitors' book for you everywhere . . . How can you? You work tomorrow. You must work tonight, till five o'clock in the morning, as I said, and then get to bed. Or else you will be good for nothing tomorrow. I'll wake you at eight o'clock, punctually.'

'But will it be all right, your signing for me?' said Vasya, half assenting.

'Why, what could be better? Everyone does it.'

'I am really afraid.'

'Why, why?'

'It's all right, you know, with other people, but Yulian Mastakovitch . . . he has been so kind to me, you know, Arkasha, and when he notices it's not my own signature—'

'Notices! why, what a fellow you are, really, Vasya! How could he notice? . . . Come, you know I can imitate your signature awfully well, and make just the same flourish to it, upon my word I can. What nonsense! Who would notice?'

Vasya, made no reply, but emptied his glass hurriedly . . . Then he shook his head doubtfully.

'Vasya, dear boy! Ah, if only we succeed! Vasya, what's the matter with you, you quite frighten me! Do you know, Vasya, I am not going to bed now, I am not going to sleep! Show me, have you a great deal left?'

Vasya gave Arkady such a look that his heart sank, and his tongue failed him.

'Vasya, what is the matter? What are you thinking? Why do you look like that?'

'Arkady, I really must go tomorrow to wish Yulian Mastakovitch a happy New Year.'

'Well, go then!' said Arkady, gazing at him open-eyed, in uneasy expectation. 'I say, Vasya, do write faster; I am advising you for your good, I really am! How often Yulian Mastakovitch himself has said that what he likes particularly about your writing is its legibility. Why, it is all that Skoroplehin cares for, that writing should be good and distinct like a copy, so as afterwards to pocket the paper and take it home for his children to copy; he can't buy copybooks, the blockhead! Yulian Mastakovitch is always saying, always insisting: "Legible, legible, legible!" . . . What is the matter? Vasya, I really don't know how to talk to you . . . it quite frightens me . . . you crush me with your depression.'

'It's all right, it's all right,' said Vasya, and he fell back in his chair as though fainting. Arkady was alarmed.

'Will you have some water? Vasya! Vasya!'

'Don't, don't,' said Vasya, pressing his hand. 'I am all right, I only feel sad, I can't tell why. Better talk of something else; let me forget it.'

'Calm yourself, for goodness sake, calm yourself, Vasya. You will finish it all right, on my honour, you will. And even if you don't finish, what will it matter? You talk as though it were a crime!'

'Arkady,' said Vasya, looking at his friend with such meaning that Arkady was quite frightened, for Vasya had never been so agitated before. '. . . If I were alone, as I used to be . . . No! I don't mean that. I keep wanting to tell you as a friend, to confide in you . . . But why worry you, though? . . . You see, Arkady, to some much is given, others do a little thing as I do.

Well, if gratitude, appreciation, is expected of you . . . and you can't give it?'

'Vasya, I don't understand you in the least.'

'I have never been ungrateful,' Vasya went on softly, as though speaking to himself, 'but if I am incapable of expressing all I feel, it seems as though . . . it seems, Arkady, as though I am really ungrateful, and that's killing me.'

'What next, what next! As though gratitude meant nothing more than your finishing that copy in time? Just think what you are saying, Vasya? Is that the whole expression of gratitude?'

Vasya sank into silence at once, and looked open-eyed at Arkady, as though his unexpected argument had settled all his doubts. He even smiled, but the same melancholy expression came back to his face at once. Arkady, taking this smile as a sign that all his uneasiness was over, and the look that succeeded it as an indication that he was determined to do better, was greatly relieved.

'Well, brother Arkasha, you will wake up,' said Vasya, 'keep an eye on me; if I fall asleep it will be dreadful. I'll set to work now . . . Arkasha?'

'What?'

'Oh, it's nothing, I only . . . I meant . . .'

Vasya settled himself, and said no more, Arkady got into bed. Neither of them said one word about their friends, the Artemyevs. Perhaps both of them felt that they had been a little to blame, and that they ought not to have gone for their jaunt when they did. Arkady soon fell asleep, still worried about Vasya. To his own surprise he woke up exactly at eight o'clock in the morning. Vasya was asleep in his chair with the pen in his hand, pale and exhausted; the candle had burned out. Mavra was busy getting the samovar ready in the kitchen.

'Vasya, Vasya!' Arkady cried in alarm, 'when did you fall asleep?'

Vasya opened his eyes and jumped up from his chair.

'Oh!' he cried, 'I must have fallen asleep . . .'

He flew to the papers – everything was right; all were in order; there was not a blot of ink, nor spot of grease from the candle on them.

'I think I must have fallen asleep about six o'clock,' said Vasya. 'How cold it is in the night! Let us have tea, and I will go on again . . .'

'Do you feel better?'

'Yes, yes, I'm all right, I'm all right now.'

'A happy New Year to you, brother Vasya.'

'And to you too, brother, the same to you, dear boy.'

They embraced each other. Vasya's chin was quivering and his eyes were moist. Arkady Ivanovitch was silent, he felt sad. They drank their tea hastily.

'Arkady, I've made up my mind, I am going myself to Yulian Mastakovitch.'

'Why, he wouldn't notice—'

'But my conscience feels ill at ease, brother.'

'But you know it's for his sake you are sitting here; it's for his sake you are wearing yourself out.'

'Enough!'

'Do you know what, brother, I'll go round and see . . .'

'Whom?' asked Vasya.

'The Artemyevs. I'll take them your good wishes for the New Year as well as mine.'

'My dear fellow! Well, I'll stay here; and I see it's a good idea of yours; I shall be working here, I shan't waste my time. Wait one minute, I'll write a note.'

'Yes, do, brother, do, there's plenty of time. I've still to wash and shave and to brush my best coat. Well, Vasya, we are going to be contented and happy. Embrace me, Vasya.'

'Ah, if only we may, brother . . .'

'Does Mr Shumkov live here?' They heard a child's voice on the stairs.

'Yes, my dear, yes,' said Mavra, showing the visitor in.

'What's that? What is it?' cried Vasya, leaping up from the table and rushing to the entry, 'Petinka, you?'

'Good morning, I have the honour to wish you a happy New Year, Vassily Petrovitch,' said a pretty boy of ten years old with curly black hair. 'Sister sends you her love, and so does Mamma, and Sister told me to give you a kiss for her.'

Vasya caught the messenger up in the air and printed a long, enthusiastic kiss on his lips, which were very much like Lizanka's.

'Kiss him, Arkady,' he said, handing Petya to him, and

without touching the ground the boy was transferred to Arkady Ivanovitch's powerful and eager arms.

'Will you have some breakfast, dear?'

'Thank you, very much. We have had it already, we got up early today, the others have gone to church. Sister was two hours curling my hair, and pomading it, washing me and mending my trousers, for I tore them yesterday, playing with Sashka in the street, we were snowballing.'

'Well, well, well!'

'So she dressed me up to come and see you, and then pomaded my head and then gave me a regular kissing. She said: "Go to Vasya, wish him a happy New Year, and ask whether they are happy, whether they had a good night, and . . ." to ask something else – oh yes! whether you had finished the work you spoke of yesterday . . . when you were there. Oh, I've got it all written down,' said the boy, reading from a slip of paper which he took out of his pocket. 'Yes, they were uneasy.'

'It will be finished! It will be! Tell her that it will be. I shall finish it, on my word of honour!'

'And something else . . . Oh yes, I forgot. Sister sent a little note and a present, and I was forgetting it! . . .'

'My goodness! Oh, you little darling! Where is it? where is it? That's it, oh! Look, brother, see what she writes. The darling, the precious! You know I saw there yesterday a paper-case for me; it's not finished, so she says, "I am sending you a lock of my hair, and the other will come later." Look, brother, look!'

And overwhelmed with rapture he showed Arkady Ivanovitch a curl of luxuriant, jet-black hair; then he kissed it fervently and put it in his breast pocket, nearest his heart.

'Vasya, I shall get you a locket for that curl,' Arkady Ivanovitch said resolutely at last.

'And we are going to have hot veal, and tomorrow brains. Mamma wants to make cakes . . . but we are not going to have millet porridge,' said the boy, after a moment's thought, to wind up his budget of interesting items.

'Oh! what a pretty boy,' cried Arkady Ivanovitch. 'Vasya, you are the happiest of mortals.'

The boy finished his tea, took from Vasya a note, a thousand kisses, and went out happy and frolicsome as before.

'Well, brother,' began Arkady Ivanovitch, highly delighted, 'you see how splendid it all is; you see. Everything is going well, don't be downcast, don't be uneasy. Go ahead! Get it done, Vasya, get it done. I'll be home at two o'clock. I'll go round to them, and then to Yulian Mastakovitch.'

'Well, goodbye, brother; goodbye . . . Oh! if only . . . Very good, you go, very good,' said Vasya, 'then I really won't go to Yulian Mastakovitch.'

'Goodbye.'

'Stay, brother, stay, tell them . . . well, whatever you think fit. Kiss her . . . and give me a full account of everything afterwards.'

'Come, come – of course, I know all about it. This happiness has upset you. The suddenness of it all; you've not been yourself since yesterday. You have not got over the excitement of yesterday. Well, it's settled. Now try and get over it, Vasya. Goodbye, goodbye!'

At last the friends parted. All the morning Arkady Ivanovitch was preoccupied, and could think of nothing but Vasya. He knew his weak, highly nervous character. 'Yes, this happiness has upset him, I was right there,' he said to himself. 'Upon my word, he has made me quite depressed, too, that man will make a tragedy of anything! What a feverish creature! Oh, I must save him! I must save him!' said Arkady, not noticing that he himself was exaggerating into something serious a slight trouble, in reality quite trivial. Only at eleven o'clock he reached the porter's lodge of Yulian Mastakovitch's house, to add his modest name to the long list of illustrious persons who had written their names on a sheet of blotted and scribbled paper in the porter's lodge. What was his surprise when he saw just above his own the signature of Vasya Shumkov! It amazed him. 'What's the matter with him?' he thought. Arkady Ivanovitch, who had just been so buoyant with hope, came out feeling upset. There was certainly going to be trouble, but how? And in what form?

He reached the Artemyevs with gloomy forebodings; he seemed absent-minded from the first, and after talking a little with Lizanka went away with tears in his eyes; he was really anxious about Vasya. He went home running, and on the Neva came full tilt upon Vasya himself. The latter, too, was uneasy.

'Where are you going?' cried Arkady Ivanovitch.

Vasya stopped as though he had been caught in a crime.

'Oh, it's nothing, brother, I wanted to go for a walk.'

'You could not stand it, and have been to the Artemyevs? Oh, Vasya, Vasya! Why did you go to Yulian Mastakovitch?'

Vasya did not answer, but then with a wave of his hand, he said: 'Arkady, I don't know what is the matter with me. I . . .'

'Come, come, Vasya. I know what it is. Calm yourself. You've been excited, and overwrought ever since yesterday. Only think, it's not much to bear. Everybody's fond of you, everybody's ready to do anything for you; your work is getting on all right; you will get it done, you will certainly get it done. I know that you have been imagining something, you have had apprehensions about something . . .'

'No, it's all right, it's all right . . .'

'Do you remember, Vasya, do you remember it was the same with you once before; do you remember, when you got your promotion, in your joy and thankfulness you were so zealous that you spoilt all your work for a week? It is just the same with you now.'

'Yes, yes, Arkady; but now it is different, it is not that at all.'

'How is it different? And very likely the work is not urgent at all, while you are killing yourself . . .'

'It's nothing, it's nothing. I am all right, it's nothing. Well, come along!'

'Why, are you going home, and not to them?'

'Yes, brother, how could I have the face to turn up there? . . . I have changed my mind. It was only that I could not stay on alone without you; now you are coming back with me I'll sit down to write again. Let us go!'

They walked along and for some time were silent. Vasya was in haste.

'Why don't you ask me about them?' said Arkady Ivanovitch.

'Oh, yes! Well, Arkasha, what about them?'

'Vasya, you are not like yourself.'

'Oh, I am all right, I am all right. Tell me everything, Arkasha,' said Vasya, in an imploring voice, as though to avoid further explanations. Arkady Ivanovitch sighed. He felt utterly at a loss, looking at Vasya.

His account of their friends roused Vasya. He even grew talkative. They had dinner together. Lizanka's mother had filled Arkady Ivanovitch's pockets with little cakes, and eating them the friends grew more cheerful. After dinner Vasya promised to take a nap, so as to sit up all night. He did, in fact, lie down. In the morning, someone whom it was impossible to refuse had invited Arkady Ivanovitch to tea. The friends parted. Arkady promised to come back as soon as he could, by eight o'clock if possible. The three hours of separation seemed to him like three years. At last he got away and rushed back to Vasya. When he went into the room, he found it in darkness. Vasya was not at home. He asked Mavra. Mavra said that he had been writing all the time, and had not slept at all, then he had paced up and down the room, and after that, an hour before, he had run out, saying he would be back in half an hour; 'and when, says he, Arkady Ivanovitch comes in, tell him, old woman, says he,' Mavra told him in conclusion, 'that I have gone out for a walk,' and he repeated the order three or four times.

'He is at the Artemyevs,' thought Arkady Ivanovitch, and he shook his head.

A minute later he jumped up with renewed hope.

'He has simply finished,' he thought, 'that's all it is; he couldn't wait, but ran off there. But, no! he would have waited for me . . . Let's have a peep what he has there.'

He lighted a candle, and ran to Vasya's writing-table: the work had made progress and it looked as though there were not much left to do. Arkady Ivanovitch was about to investigate further, when Vasya himself walked in . . .

'Oh, you are here?' he cried, with a start of dismay.

Arkady Ivanovitch was silent. He was afraid to question Vasya. The latter dropped his eyes and remained silent too, as he began sorting the papers. At last their eyes met. The look in Vasya's was so beseeching, imploring, and broken, that Arkady shuddered when he saw it. His heart quivered and was full.

'Vasya, my dear boy, what is it? What's wrong?' he cried, rushing to him and squeezing him in his arms. 'Explain to me, I don't understand you, and your depression. What is the matter with you, my poor, tormented boy? What is it? Tell me all about it, without hiding anything. It can't be only this—'

Vasya held him tight and could say nothing. He could scarcely breathe.

'Don't, Vasya, don't! Well, if you don't finish it, what then? I don't understand you; tell me your trouble. You see it is for your sake I . . . Oh dear! oh dear!' he said, walking up and down the room and clutching at everything he came across, as though seeking at once some remedy for Vasya. 'I will go to Yulian Mastakovitch instead of you tomorrow. I will ask him – entreat him – to let you have another day. I will explain it all to him, anything, if it worries you so . . .'

'God forbid!' cried Vasya, and turned as white as the wall. He could scarcely stand on his feet.

'Vasya! Vasya!'

Vasya pulled himself together. His lips were quivering; he tried to say something, but could only convulsively squeeze Arkady's hand in silence. His hand was cold. Arkady stood facing him, full of anxious and miserable suspense. Vasya raised his eyes again.

'Vasya, God bless you, Vasya! You wring my heart, my dear boy, my friend.'

Tears gushed from Vasya's eyes; he flung himself on Arkady's bosom.

'I have deceived you, Arkady,' he said. 'I have deceived you. Forgive me, forgive me! I have been faithless to your friendship . . .'

'What is it, Vasya? What is the matter?' asked Arkady, in real alarm.

'Look!'

And with a gesture of despair Vasya tossed out of the drawer on to the table six thick manuscripts, similar to the one he had copied.

'What's this?'

'What I have to get through by the day after tomorrow. I haven't done a quarter! Don't ask me, don't ask me how it has happened,' Vasya went on, speaking at once of what was distressing him so terribly. 'Arkady, dear friend, I don't know myself what came over me. I feel as though I were coming out of a dream. I have wasted three weeks doing nothing. I kept . . . I . . . kept going to see her . . . My heart was aching, I was tormented by . . . the uncertainty . . . I could not write. I did not even think about it. Only now, when happiness is at hand for me, I have come to my senses.'

'Vasya,' began Arkady Ivanovitch resolutely, 'Vasya, I will save you. I understand it all. It's a serious matter; I will save you. Listen! listen to me: I will go to Yulian Mastakovitch tomorrow . . . Don't shake your head; no, listen! I will tell him exactly how it has all been; let me do that . . . I will explain to him . . . I will go into everything. I will tell him how crushed you are, how you are worrying yourself.'

'Do you know that you are killing me now?' Vasya brought out, turning cold with horror.

Arkady Ivanovitch turned pale, but at once controlling himself, laughed.

'Is that all? Is that all?' he said. 'Upon my word, Vasya, upon my word! Aren't you ashamed? Come, listen! I see that I am grieving you. You see I understand you; I know what is passing in your heart. Why, we have been living together for five years, thank God! You are such a kind, soft-hearted fellow, but weak, unpardonably weak. Why, even Lizaveta Mikalovna has noticed it. And you a dreamer, and that's a bad thing, too; you may go from bad to worse, brother. I tell you, I know what you want! You would like Yulian Mastakovitch, for instance, to be beside himself and, maybe, to give a ball, too, from joy, because you are going to get married . . . Stop, stop! you are frowning. You see that at one word from me you are offended on Yulian Mastakovitch's account. I'll let him alone. You know I respect him just as much as you do. But argue as you may, you can't prevent my thinking that you would like there to be no one unhappy in the whole world when you are getting married . . . Yes, brother, you must admit that you would like me, for instance, your best friend, to come in for a fortune of a hundred thousand all of a sudden, you would like all the enemies in the world to be suddenly, for no rhyme or reason, reconciled, so that in their joy they might all embrace one another in the middle of the street, and then, perhaps, come here to call on you. Vasya, my dear boy, I am not laughing; it is true; you've said as much to me long ago, in different ways. Because you are happy, you want everyone, absolutely everyone, to become happy at once. It hurts you and troubles you to be happy alone. And so you want at once to do your utmost to be worthy of that happiness, and maybe to do some great deed to satisfy your conscience. Oh! I understand how ready you are to distress yourself for having suddenly been remiss just where you ought to have shown your zeal, your capacity . . . well, maybe your gratitude, as you say. It is very bitter for you to think that Yulian Mastakovitch may frown and even be angry when he sees that you have not justified the expectations he had of you. It hurts you to think that you may hear reproaches from the man you look upon as your benefactor – and at such a moment! when your heart is full of joy and you don't know on whom to lavish your gratitude . . . Isn't that true? It is, isn't it?'

Arkady Ivanovitch, whose voice was trembling, paused, and drew a deep breath.

Vasya looked affectionately at his friend. A smile passed over his lips. His face even lighted up, as though with a gleam of hope.

'Well, listen, then,' Arkady Ivanovitch began again, growing more hopeful, 'there's no necessity that you should forfeit Yulian Mastakovitch's favour . . . Is there, dear boy? Is there any question of it? And since it is so,' said Arkady, jumping up, 'I shall sacrifice myself for you. I am going tomorrow to Yulian Mastakovitch, and don't oppose me. You magnify your failure to a crime, Vasya. Yulian Mastakovitch is magnanimous and merciful, and, what is more, he is not like you. He will listen to you and me, and get us out of our trouble, brother Vasya. Well, are you calmer?'

Vasya pressed his friend's hands with tears in his eyes.

'Hush, hush, Arkady,' he said, 'the thing is settled. I haven't finished, so very well; if I haven't finished, I haven't finished, and there's no need for you to go. I will tell him all about it, I will go myself. I am calmer now, I am perfectly calm; only you mustn't go . . . But listen . . .'

'Vasya, my dear boy,' Arkady Ivanovitch cried joyfully, 'I judged from what you said. I am glad that you have thought better of things and have recovered yourself. But whatever may befall you, whatever happens, I am with you, remember that. I see that it worries you to think of my speaking to Yulian Mastakovitch – and I won't say a word, not a word, you shall tell him yourself. You see, you shall go tomorrow . . . Oh no, you had better not go, you'll go on writing here, you see, and I'll find out about this work, whether it is very urgent or not, whether it must be done by the time or not, and if you don't finish it in time what will come of it. Then I will run back to you. Do you see, do you see! There is still hope; suppose the work is not urgent – it may be all right. Yulian Mastakovitch may not remember, then all is saved.'

Vasya shook his head doubtfully. But his grateful eyes never left his friend's face.

'Come, that's enough, I am so weak, so tired,' he said, sighing. 'I don't want to think about it. Let us talk of something else. I won't write either now; do you know, I'll only finish two short pages just to get to the end of a passage. Listen . . . I have long wanted to ask you, how is it you know me so well?'

Tears dropped from Vasya's eyes on Arkady's hand.

'If you knew, Vasya, how fond I am of you, you would not ask that – yes!'

'Yes, yes, Arkady, I don't know that, because I don't know why you are so fond of me. Yes, Arkady, do you know, even your love has been killing me? Do you know, ever so many times, particularly when I am thinking of you in bed (for I always think of you when I am falling asleep), I shed tears, and my heart throbs at the thought . . . at the thought . . . Well, at the thought that you are so fond of me, while I can do nothing to relieve my heart, can do nothing to repay you.'

'You see, Vasya, you see what a fellow you are! Why, how upset you are now,' said Arkady, whose heart ached at that moment and who remembered the scene in the street the day before.

'Nonsense, you want me to be calm, but I never have been so calm and happy! Do you know . . . Listen, I want to tell you all about it, but I am afraid of wounding you . . . You keep scolding me and being vexed; and I am afraid . . . See how I am trembling now, I don't know why. You see, this is what I want to say. I feel as though I had never known myself before – yes! Yes, I only began to understand other people too, yesterday. I did not feel or appreciate things fully, brother. My heart . . . was hard . . . Listen, how has it happened, that I have never done good to anyone, anyone in the world, because I couldn't – I am not even pleasant to look at . . . But everybody does me good! You, to begin with: do you suppose I don't see that? Only I said nothing; only I said nothing.'

'Hush, Vasya!'

'Oh, Arkasha! . . . it's all right,' Vasya interrupted, hardly able to articulate for tears. 'I talked to you yesterday about Yulian Mastakovitch. And you know yourself how stern and severe he is, even you have come in for a reprimand from him; yet he deigned to jest with me yesterday, to show his affection, and kind-heartedness, which he prudently conceals from everyone . . .'

'Come, Vasya, that only shows you deserve your good fortune.'

'Oh, Arkasha! How I longed to finish all this . . . No, I shall ruin my good luck! I feel that! Oh no, not through that,' Vasya added, seeing that Arkady glanced at the heap of urgent work lying on the table, 'that's nothing, that's only paper covered with writing . . . it's nonsense! That matter's settled . . . I went to see them today, Arkasha; I did not go in. I felt depressed and sad. I simply stood at the door. She was playing the piano, I listened. You see, Arkady,' he went on, dropping his voice, 'I did not dare to go in.

'I say, Vasya – what is the matter with you? You look at one so strangely.'

'Oh, it's nothing, I feel a little sick; my legs are trembling;

it's because I sat up last night. Yes! Everything looks green before my eyes. It's here, here—'

He pointed to his heart. He fainted. When he came to himself Arkady tried to take forcible measures. He tried to compel him to go to bed. Nothing would induce Vasya to consent. He shed tears, wrung his hands, wanted to write, was absolutely set on finishing his two pages. To avoid exciting him Arkady let him sit down to the work.

'Do you know,' said Vasya, as he settled himself in his place, 'an idea has occurred to me? There is hope.'

He smiled to Arkady, and his pale face lighted up with a gleam of hope.

'I will take him what is done the day after tomorrow. About the rest I will tell a lie. I will say it has been burned, that it has been sopped in water, that I have lost it . . . That, in fact, I have not finished it; I cannot lie. I will explain, do you know what? I'll explain to him all about it. I will tell him how it was that I could not. I'll tell him about my love; he has got married himself just lately, he'll understand me. I will do it all, of course, respectfully, quietly; he will see my tears and be touched by them . . .'

'Yes, of course, you must go, you must go and explain to him . . . But there's no need of tears! Tears for what? Really, Vasya, you quite scare me.'

'Yes, I'll go, I'll go. But now let me write, let me write, Arkasha. I am not interfering with anyone, let me write!'

Arkady flung himself on the bed. He had no confidence in

Vasya, no confidence at all. Vasya was capable of anything, but to ask for forgiveness for what? how? That was not the point. The point was, that Vasya had not carried out his obligations, that Vasya felt guilty *in his own eyes*, felt that he was ungrateful to destiny, that Vasya was crushed, overwhelmed by happiness and thought himself unworthy of it; that, in fact, he was simply trying to find an excuse to go off his head on that point, and that he had not recovered from the unexpectedness of what had happened the day before; 'that's what it is,' thought Arkady Ivanovitch. 'I must save him. I must reconcile him to himself. He will be his own ruin.' He thought and thought, and resolved to go at once next day to Yulian Mastakovitch, and to tell him all about it.

Vasya was sitting writing. Arkady Ivanovitch, worn out, lay down to think things over again, and only woke at daybreak.

'Damnation! Again!' he cried, looking at Vasya; the latter was still sitting writing.

Arkady rushed up to him, seized him and forcibly put him to bed. Vasya was smiling: his eyes were closing with sleep. He could hardly speak.

'I wanted to go to bed,' he said. 'Do you know, Arkady, I have an idea; I shall finish. I made my pen go faster! I could not have sat at it any longer; wake me at eight o'clock.'

Without finishing his sentence, he dropped asleep and slept like the dead.

'Mavra,' said Arkady Ivanovitch to Mavra, who came in

with the tea, 'he asked to be waked in an hour. Don't wake him on any account! Let him sleep ten hours, if he can. Do you understand?'

'I understand, sir.'

'Don't get the dinner, don't bring in the wood, don't make a noise or it will be the worse for you. If he asks for me, tell him I have gone to the office – do you understand?'

'I understand, bless you, sir; let him sleep and welcome! I am glad my gentlemen should sleep well, and I take good care of their things. And about that cup that was broken, and you blamed me, your Honour, it wasn't me, it was poor pussy broke it, I ought to have kept an eye on her. "S-sh, you confounded thing," I said.'

'Hush, be quiet, be quiet!'

Arkady Ivanovitch followed Mavra out into the kitchen, asked for the key and locked her up there. Then he went to the office. On the way he considered how he could present himself before Yulian Mastakovitch, and whether it would be appropriate and not impertinent. He went into the office timidly, and timidly inquired whether his Excellency were there; receiving the answer that he was not and would not be, Arkady Ivanovitch instantly thought of going to his flat, but reflected very prudently that if Yulian Mastakovitch had not come to the office he would certainly be busy at home. He remained. The hours seemed to him endless. Indirectly he inquired about the work entrusted to Shumkov, but no one knew anything about this.

All that was known was that Yulian Mastakovitch did employ him on special jobs, but what they were – no one could say. At last it struck three o'clock, and Arkady Ivanovitch rushed out, eager to get home. In the vestibule he was met by a clerk, who told him that Vassily Petrovitch Shumkov had come about one o'clock and asked, the clerk added, 'whether you were here, and whether Yulian Mastakovitch had been here.' Hearing this Arkady Ivanovitch took a sledge and hastened home, beside himself with alarm.

Shumkov was at home. He was walking about the room in violent excitement. Glancing at Arkady Ivanovitch, he immediately controlled himself, reflected, and hastened to conceal his emotion. He sat down to his papers without a word. He seemed to avoid his friend's questions, seemed to be bothered by them, to be pondering to himself on some plan, and deciding to conceal his decision, because he could not reckon further on his friend's affection. This struck Arkady, and his heart ached with a poignant and oppressive pain. He sat on the bed and began turning over the leaves of some book, the only one he had in his possession, keeping his eye on poor Vasya. But Vasya remained obstinately silent, writing, and not raising his head. So passed several hours, and Arkady's misery reached an extreme point. At last, at eleven o'clock, Vasya lifted his head and looked with a fixed, vacant stare at Arkady. Arkady waited. Two or three minutes passed; Vasya did not speak.

'Vasya!' cried Arkady.

Vasya made no answer.

'Vasya!' he repeated, jumping up from the bed, 'Vasya, what is the matter with you? What is it?' he cried, running up to him.

Vasya raised his eyes and again looked at him with the same vacant, fixed stare.

'He's in a trance!' thought Arkady, trembling all over with fear. He seized a bottle of water, raised Vasya, poured some water on his head, moistened his temples, rubbed his hands in his own – and Vasya came to himself. 'Vasya, Vasya!' cried Arkady, unable to restrain his tears. 'Vasya, save yourself, rouse yourself, rouse yourself! . . .' He could say no more, but held him tight in his arms. A look as of some oppressive sensation passed over Vasya's face; he rubbed his forehead and clutched at his head, as though he were afraid it would burst.

'I don't know what is the matter with me,' he added, at last. 'I feel torn to pieces. Come, it's all right, it's all right! Give over, Arkady; don't grieve,' he repeated, looking at him with sad, exhausted eyes. 'Why be so anxious? Come!'

'You, you comforting me!' cried Arkady, whose heart was torn. 'Vasya,' he said at last, 'lie down and have a little nap, won't you? Don't wear yourself out for nothing! You'll set to work better afterwards.'

'Yes, yes,' said Vasya, 'by all means, I'll lie down, very good. Yes! you see I meant to finish, but now I've changed my mind, yes . . .'

And Arkady led him to bed.

'Listen, Vasya,' he said firmly, 'we must settle this matter finally. Tell me what were you thinking about?'

'Oh!' said Vasya, with a flourish of his weak hand turning over on the other side.

'Come, Vasya, come, make up your mind. I don't want to hurt you. I can't be silent any longer. You won't sleep till you've made up your mind, I know.'

'As you like, as you like,' Vasya repeated enigmatically.

'He will give in,' thought Arkady Ivanovitch.

'Attend to me, Vasya,' he said, 'remember what I say, and I will save you tomorrow; tomorrow I will decide your fate! What am I saying, your fate? You have so frightened me, Vasya, that I am using your own words. Fate, indeed! It's simply nonsense, rubbish! You don't want to lose Yulian Mastakovitch's favour – affection, if you like. No! And you won't lose it, you will see. I—'

Arkady Ivanovitch would have said more, but Vasya interrupted him. He sat up in bed, put both arms around Arkady Ivanovitch's neck and kissed him.

'Enough,' he said in a weak voice, 'enough! Say no more about that!'

And again he turned his face to the wall.

'My goodness!' thought Arkady, 'my goodness! What is the matter with him? He is utterly lost. What has he in his mind! He will be his own undoing.'

Arkady looked at him in despair.

'If he were to fall ill,' thought Arkady, 'perhaps it would be better. His trouble would pass off with illness, and that might be the best way of settling the whole business. But what nonsense I am talking. Oh, my God!'

Meanwhile Vasya seemed to be asleep. Arkady Ivanovitch was relieved. 'A good sign,' he thought. He made up his mind to sit beside him all night. But Vasya was restless; he kept twitching and tossing about on the bed, and opening his eyes for an instant. At last exhaustion got the upper hand, he slept like the dead. It was about two o'clock in the morning, Arkady Ivanovitch began to doze in the chair with his elbow on the table.

He had a strange and agitated dream. He kept fancying that he was not asleep, and that Vasya was still lying on the bed. But strange to say, he fancied that Vasya was pretending, that he was deceiving him, that he was getting up, stealthily watching him out of the corner of his eye, and was stealing up to the writing-table. Arkady felt a scalding pain at his heart; he felt vexed and sad and oppressed to see Vasya not trusting him, hiding and concealing himself from him. He tried to catch hold of him, to call out, to carry him to the bed. Then Vasya kept shrieking in his arms, and he laid on the bed a lifeless corpse. He opened his eyes and woke up; Vasya was sitting before him at the table, writing.

Hardly able to believe his senses, Arkady glanced at the bed; Vasya was not there. Arkady jumped up in a panic, still under the influence of his dream. Vasya did not stir; he went on writing. All at once Arkady noticed with horror that Vasya was moving a dry pen over the paper, was turning over perfectly blank pages, and hurrying, hurrying to fill up the paper as though he were doing his work in a most thorough and efficient way. 'No, this is not a trance,' thought Arkady Ivanovitch, and he trembled all over.

'Vasya, Vasya, speak to me,' he cried, clutching him by the shoulder. But Vasya did not speak; he went on as before, scribbling with a dry pen over the paper.

'At last I have made the pen go faster,' he said, without looking up at Arkady.

Arkady seized his hand and snatched away the pen.

A moan broke from Vasya. He dropped his hand and raised his eyes to Arkady; then with an air of misery and exhaustion he passed his hand over his forehead as though he wanted to shake off some leaden weight that was pressing upon his whole being, and slowly, as though lost in thought, he let his head sink on his breast.

'Vasya, Vasya!' cried Arkady in despair. 'Vasya!'

A minute later Vasya looked at him, tears stood in his large blue eyes, and his pale, mild face wore a look of infinite suffering. He whispered something.

'What, what is it?' cried Arkady, bending down to him.

'What for, why are they doing it to me?' whispered Vasya. 'What for? What have I done?'

'Vasya, what is it? What are you afraid of? What is it?' cried Arkady, wringing his hands in despair.

'Why are they sending me for a soldier?' said Vasya, looking his friend straight in the face. 'Why is it? What have I done?'

Arkady's hair stood on end with horror; he refused to believe his ears. He stood over him, half dead.

A minute later he pulled himself together. 'It's nothing, it's only for the minute,' he said to himself, with pale face and blue, quivering lips, and he hastened to put on his outdoor things. He meant to run straight for a doctor. All at once Vasya called to him. Arkady rushed to him and clasped him in his arms like a mother whose child is being torn from her.

'Arkady, Arkady, don't tell anyone! Don't tell anyone, do you hear? It is my trouble, I must bear it alone.'

'What is it – what is it? Rouse yourself, Vasya, rouse yourself!'

Vasya sighed, and slow tears trickled down his cheeks.

'Why kill her? How is she to blame?' he muttered in an agonised, heart-rending voice. 'The sin is mine, the sin is mine!'

He was silent for a moment.

'Farewell, my love! Farewell, my love!' he whispered, shaking his luckless head. Arkady started, pulled himself together and would have rushed for the doctor. 'Let us go, it is time,' cried Vasya, carried away by Arkady's last movement. 'Let us go, brother, let us go; I am ready. You lead the way.' He paused and looked at Arkady with a downcast and mistrustful face.

'Vasya, for goodness sake, don't follow me! Wait for me here. I will come back to you directly, directly,' said Arkady

Ivanovitch, losing his head and snatching up his cap to run for a doctor. Vasya sat down at once; he was quiet and docile, but there was a gleam of some desperate resolution in his eyes. Arkady turned back, snatched up from the table an open pen-knife, looked at the poor fellow for the last time, and ran out of the flat.

It was eight o'clock. It had been broad daylight for some time in the room.

He found no one. He was running about for a full hour. All the doctors whose addresses he had got from the house porter when he inquired of the latter whether there were no doctor living in the building, had gone out, either to their work or on their private affairs. There was one who saw patients. This one questioned at length and in detail the servant who announced that Nefedevitch had called, asking him who it was, from whom he came, what was the matter, and concluded by saying that he could not go, that he had a great deal to do, and that patients of that kind ought to be taken to a hospital.

Then Arkady, exhausted, agitated, and utterly taken aback by this turn of affairs, cursed all the doctors on earth, and rushed home in the utmost alarm about Vasya. He ran into the flat. Mavra, as though there were nothing the matter, went on scrubbing the floor, breaking up wood and preparing to light the stove. He went into the room; there was no trace of Vasya, he had gone out.

'Which way? Where? Where will the poor fellow be off

to?' thought Arkady, frozen with terror. He began questioning Mavra. She knew nothing, had neither seen nor heard him go out, God bless him! Nefedevitch rushed off to the Artemyevs'.

It occurred to him for some reason that he must be there.

It was ten o'clock by the time he arrived. They did not expect him, knew nothing and had heard nothing. He stood before them frightened, distressed, and asked where was Vasya? The mother's legs gave way under her; she sank back on the sofa. Lizanka, trembling with alarm, began asking what had happened. What could he say? Arkady Ivanovitch got out of it as best he could, invented some tale which of course was not believed, and fled, leaving them distressed and anxious. He flew to his department that he might not be too late there, and he let them know that steps might be taken at once. On the way it occurred to him that Vasya would be at Yulian Mastakovitch's. That was more likely than anything: Arkady had thought of that first of all, even before the Artemyevs'. As he drove by his Excellency's door, he thought of stopping, but at once told the driver to go straight on. He made up his mind to try and find out whether anything had happened at the office, and if he were not there to go to his Excellency, ostensibly to report on Vasya. Someone must be informed of it.

As soon as he got into the waiting-room he was surrounded by fellow-clerks, for the most part young men of his own standing in the service. With one voice they began asking him what had happened to Vasya? At the same time they all told him that

Vasya had gone out of his mind, and thought that he was to be sent for a soldier as a punishment for having neglected his work. Arkady Ivanovitch, answering them in all directions, or rather avoiding giving a direct answer to anyone, rushed into the inner room. On the way he learned that Vasya was in Yulian Mastakovitch's private room, that everyone had been there and that Esper Ivanovitch had gone in there too. He was stopped on the way. One of the senior clerks asked him who he was and what he wanted? Without distinguishing the person he said something about Vasya and went straight into the room. He heard Yulian Mastakovitch's voice from within. 'Where are you going?' someone asked him at the very door. Arkady Ivanovitch was almost in despair; he was on the point of turning back, but through the open door he saw his poor Vasya. He pushed the door and squeezed his way into the room. Everyone seemed to be in confusion and perplexity, because Yulian Mastakovitch was apparently much chagrined. All the more important personages were standing about him talking, and coming to no decision. At a little distance stood Vasya. Arkady's heart sank when he looked at him. Vasya was standing, pale, with his head up, stiffly erect, like a recruit before a new officer, with his feet together and his hands held rigidly at his sides. He was looking Yulian Mastakovitch straight in the face. Arkady was noticed at once, and someone who knew that they lodged together mentioned the fact to his Excellency. Arkady was led up to him. He tried to make some answer to the questions put to him, glanced at

Yulian Mastakovitch and seeing on his face a look of genuine compassion, began trembling and sobbing like a child. He even did more, he snatched his Excellency's hand and held it to his eyes, wetting it with his tears, so that Yulian Mastakovitch was obliged to draw it hastily away, and waving it in the air, said, 'Come, my dear fellow, come! I see you have a good heart.' Arkady sobbed and turned an imploring look on everyone. It seemed to him that they were all brothers of his dear Vasya, that they were all worried and weeping about him. 'How, how has it happened? how has it happened?' asked Yulian Mastakovitch. 'What has sent him out of his mind?'

'Gra–gra–gratitude!' was all Arkady Ivanovitch could articulate.

Everyone heard his answer with amazement, and it seemed strange and incredible to everyone that a man could go out of his mind from gratitude. Arkady explained as best he could.

'Good heavens! what a pity!' said Yulian Mastakovitch at last. 'And the work entrusted to him was not important, and not urgent in the least. It was not worthwhile for a man to kill himself over it! Well, take him away! . . .' At this point Yulian Mastakovitch turned to Arkady Ivanovitch again, and began questioning him once more. 'He begs,' he said, pointing to Vasya, 'that some girl should not be told of this. Who is she – his betrothed, I suppose?'

Arkady began to explain. Meanwhile Vasya seemed to be thinking of something, as though he were straining his memory to the utmost to recall some important, necessary matter, which was particularly wanted at this moment. From time to time he looked round with a distressed face, as though hoping someone would remind him of what he had forgotten. He fastened his eyes on Arkady. All of a sudden there was a gleam of hope in his eyes; he moved with the left leg forward, took three steps as smartly as he could, clicking with his right boot as soldiers do when they move forward at the call from their officer. Everyone was waiting to see what would happen.

'I have a physical defect and am small and weak, and I am not fit for military service, your Excellency,' he said abruptly.

At that everyone in the room felt a pang at his heart, and firm as was Yulian Mastakovitch's character, tears trickled from his eyes.

'Take him away,' he said, with a wave of his hands.

'Present!' said Vasya in an undertone; he wheeled round to the left and marched out of the room. All who were interested in his fate followed him out. Arkady pushed his way out behind the others. They made Vasya sit down in the waiting-room till the carriage came which had been ordered to take him to the hospital. He sat down in silence and seemed in great anxiety. He nodded to any one he recognised as though saying goodbye. He looked round towards the door every minute, and prepared himself to set off when he should be told it was time. People crowded in a close circle round him; they were all shaking their heads and lamenting. Many of them were much impressed by his story, which had suddenly become known. Some discussed his illness, while others expressed their pity and high opinion of Vasya, saying that he was such a quiet, modest young man, that he had been so promising; people described what efforts he had made to learn, how eager he was for knowledge, how he had worked to educate himself. 'He had risen by his own efforts from a humble position,' someone observed. They spoke with emotion of his Excellency's affection for him. Some of them fell to explaining why Vasya was possessed by the idea that he was being sent for a soldier, because he had not finished his work. They said that the poor fellow had so lately belonged to the class liable for military service and had only received his first grade through the good offices of Yulian Mastakovitch, who had had the cleverness to discover his talent, his docility, and the rare mildness of his disposition. In fact, there was a great number of views and theories.

A very short fellow-clerk of Vasya's was conspicuous as being particularly distressed. He was not very young, probably about thirty. He was pale as a sheet, trembling all over and smiling queerly, perhaps because any scandalous affair or terrible scene both frightens, and at the same time somewhat rejoices the outside spectator. He kept running round the circle that surrounded Vasya, and as he was so short, stood on tiptoe and caught at the button of everyone – that is, of those with whom he felt entitled to take such a liberty – and kept saying that he knew how it had all happened, that it was not so simple, but a very important matter, that it couldn't be left without further inquiry; then stood on tiptoe again, whispered in someone's ear, nodded his head again two or three times, and ran round again. At last everything was over. The porter made his appearance, and an attendant from the hospital went up to Vasya and told him it was time to start. Vasya jumped up in a flutter and went with them, looking about him. He was looking about for someone.

'Vasya, Vasya!' cried Arkady Ivanovitch, sobbing. Vasya stopped, and Arkady squeezed his way up to him. They flung themselves into each other's arms in a last bitter embrace. It was sad to see them. What monstrous calamity was wringing the tears from their eyes! What were they weeping for? What was their trouble? Why did they not understand one another?

'Here, here, take it! Take care of it,' said Shumkov, thrusting a paper of some kind into Arkady's hand. 'They will take it away from me. Bring it me later on; bring it . . . take care of it . . .' Vasya could not finish, they called to him. He ran hurriedly downstairs, nodding to everyone, saying goodbye to everyone. There was despair in his face. At last he was put in the carriage and taken away. Arkady made haste to open the paper: it was Liza's curl of black hair, from which Vasya had never parted. Hot tears gushed from Arkady's eyes: oh, poor Liza!

When office hours were over, he went to the Artemyevs'. There is no need to describe what happened there! Even Petya, little Petya, though he could not quite understand what had happened to dear Vasya, went into a corner, hid his face in his little hands, and sobbed in the fullness of his childish heart. It was quite dusk when Arkady returned home. When he reached the Neva he stood still for a minute and turned a keen glance up the river into the smoky frozen thickness of the distance, which was suddenly flushed crimson with the last purple and blood-red glow of sunset, still smouldering on the misty horizon . . . Night lay over the city, and the wide plain of the Neva, swollen with frozen snow, was shining in the last gleams of the sun with myriads of sparks of gleaming hoar frost. There was a frost of twenty degrees. A cloud of frozen steam hung about the overdriven horses and the hurrying people. The condensed atmosphere quivered at the slightest sound, and from all the roofs on both sides of the river, columns of smoke rose up like giants and floated across the cold sky, intertwining and untwining as they went, so that it seemed new buildings were rising up above the old, a new town was taking shape in the air . . . It seemed as if all that world, with all its inhabitants, strong and weak, with all their habitations, the refuges of the poor, or the gilded palaces for the comfort of the powerful of this world was at that twilight hour like a fantastic vision of fairyland, like a dream which in its turn would vanish and pass away like vapour into the dark blue sky. A strange thought came to poor Vasya's forlorn friend. He started, and his heart seemed at that instant flooded with a hot rush of blood kindled by a powerful, overwhelming sensation he had never known before. He seemed only now to understand all the trouble, and to know why his poor Vasya had gone out of his mind, unable to bear his happiness. His lips twitched, his eyes lighted up, he turned pale, and as it were had a clear vision into something new.

He became gloomy and depressed, and lost all his gaiety. His old lodging grew hateful to him – he took a new room. He did not care to visit the Artemyevs, and indeed he could not. Two years later he met Lizanka in church. She was by then married; beside her walked a wet nurse with a tiny baby. They greeted each other, and for a long time avoided all mention of the past. Liza said that, thank God, she was happy, that she was not badly off, that her husband was a kind man and that she was fond of him . . . But suddenly in the middle of a sentence her eyes filled with tears, her voice failed, she turned away, and bowed down to the church pavement to hide her grief.

White Nights

A Sentimental Story from the Diary of a Dreamer

1848

First Night

IT WAS A WONDERFUL night, such a night as is only possible when we are young, dear reader. The sky was so starry, so bright that, looking at it, one could not help asking oneself whether ill-humoured and capricious people could live under such a sky. That is a youthful question too, dear reader, very youthful, but may the Lord put it more frequently into your heart! . . . Speaking of capricious and ill-humoured people, I cannot help recalling my moral condition all that day. From early morning I had been oppressed by a strange despondency. It suddenly seemed to me that I was lonely, that everyone was forsaking me and going away from me. Of course, anyone is entitled to ask who 'everyone' was. For though I had been living almost eight years in Petersburg I had hardly an acquaintance. But what did I want with acquaintances? I was acquainted with all Petersburg as it was; that was why I felt as though they were all deserting me when all Petersburg packed up and went to its summer villa. I felt afraid of being left alone, and for three whole days I wandered about the town in profound dejection, not knowing what to do with myself. Whether I walked in the Nevsky, went to the Gardens or sauntered on the embankment, there was not one face of those I had been accustomed to meet at the same time and place all the year. They, of course, do not know me, but I know them. I know them intimately, I have almost made a study of their faces, and am delighted when they are gay, and downcast when they are under a cloud. I have almost struck up a friendship with one old man whom I meet every blessed day, at the same hour in Fontanka. Such a grave, pensive countenance; he is always whispering to himself and brandishing his left arm, while in his right hand he holds a long gnarled stick with a gold knob. He even notices me and takes a warm interest in me. If I happen not to be at a certain time in the same spot in Fontanka, I am certain he feels disappointed. That is how it is that we almost bow to each other, especially when we are both in good humour. The other day, when we had not seen each other for two days and met on the third, we were actually touching our hats, but, realising in time, dropped our hands and passed each other with a look of interest.

I know the houses too. As I walk along they seem to run

forward in the streets to look out at me from every window, and almost to say: 'Good morning! How do you do? I am quite well, thank God, and I am to have a new storey in May,' or, 'How are you? I am being redecorated tomorrow'; or, 'I was almost burned down and had such a fright,' and so on. I have my favourites among them, some are dear friends; one of them intends to be treated by the architect this summer. I shall go every day on purpose to see that the operation is not a failure. God forbid! But I shall never forget an incident with a very pretty little house of a light pink colour. It was such a charming little brick house, it looked so hospitably at me, and so proudly at its ungainly neighbours, that my heart rejoiced whenever I happened to pass it. Suddenly last week I walked along the street, and when I looked at my friend I heard a plaintive, 'They are painting me yellow!' The villains! The barbarians! They had spared nothing, neither columns, nor cornices, and my poor little friend was as yellow as a canary. It almost made me bilious. And to this day I have not had the courage to visit my poor disfigured friend, painted the colour of the Celestial Empire.

So now you understand, reader, in what sense I am acquainted with all Petersburg.

I have mentioned already that I had felt worried for three whole days before I guessed the cause of my uneasiness. And I felt ill at ease in the street – this one had gone and that one had gone, and what had become of the other? – and at home I did not feel like myself either. For two evenings I was puzzling my brains to think what was amiss in my corner; why I felt so uncomfortable in it. And in perplexity I scanned my grimy green walls, my ceiling covered with a spider's web, the growth of which Matrona has so successfully encouraged. I looked over all my furniture, examined every chair, wondering whether the trouble lay there (for if one chair is not standing in the same position as it stood the day before, I am not myself). I looked at the window, but it was all in vain . . . I was not a bit the better for it! I even bethought me to send for Matrona, and was giving her some fatherly admonitions in regard to the spider's web and sluttishness in general; but she simply stared at me in amazement and went away without saying a word, so that the spider's web is comfortably hanging in its place to this day. I only at last this morning realised what was wrong. Aie! Why, they are giving me the slip and making off to their summer villas! Forgive the triviality of the expression, but I am in no mood for fine language . . . for everything that had been in Petersburg had gone or was going away for the holidays; for every respectable gentleman of dignified appearance who took a cab was at once transformed, in my eyes, into a respectable head of a household who after his daily duties were over, was making his way to the bosom of his family, to the summer villa; for all the passers-by had now quite a peculiar air which seemed to say to everyone they met: 'We are only here for the moment, gentlemen, and in another two hours we shall be going off to the summer villa.' If a window opened after delicate fingers, white as snow, had tapped upon the pane, and the head of a pretty girl was thrust out, calling to a street-seller with pots of flowers – at once on the spot I fancied that those flowers were being bought not simply in order to enjoy the flowers and the spring in stuffy town lodgings, but because they would all be very soon moving into the country and could take the flowers with them. What is more, I made such progress in my new peculiar sort of investigation that I could distinguish correctly from the mere air of each in what summer villa he was living. The inhabitants of Kamenny and Aptekarsky Islands or of the Peterhof Road were marked by the studied elegance of their manner, their fashionable summer suits, and the fine carriages in which they drove to town. Visitors to Pargolovo and places further away impressed one at first sight by their reasonable and dignified air; the tripper to Krestovsky Island could be recognised by his look of irrepressible gaiety. If I chanced to meet a long procession of waggoners walking lazily with the reins in their hands beside waggons loaded with regular mountains of furniture, tables, chairs, ottomans and sofas and domestic utensils of all sorts, frequently with a decrepit cook sitting on the top of it all, guarding her master's property as though it were the apple of her eye; or if I saw boats heavily loaded with household goods crawling along the Neva or Fontanka to the Black River or the Islands – the waggons and the boats were multiplied tenfold, a hundredfold, in my eyes. I fancied that everything was astir and moving, everything was going in regular caravans to the summer villas. It seemed as though Petersburg threatened to become a wilderness, so that at last I felt ashamed, mortified and sad that I had nowhere to go for the holidays and no reason to go away. I was ready to go away with every waggon, to drive off with every gentleman of respectable appearance who took a cab; but no one – absolutely no one – invited me; it seemed they had forgotten me, as though really I were a stranger to them!

I took long walks, succeeding, as I usually did, in quite forgetting where I was, when I suddenly found myself at the city gates. Instantly I felt light-hearted, and I passed the barrier and walked between cultivated fields and meadows, unconscious of fatigue, and feeling only all over as though a burden were falling off my soul. All the passers-by gave me such friendly looks that they seemed almost greeting me, they all seemed so pleased at something. They were all smoking cigars, every one of them. And I felt pleased as I never had before. It was as though I had suddenly found myself in Italy – so strong was the effect of nature upon a half-sick townsman like me, almost stifling between city walls.

There is something inexpressibly touching in nature round Petersburg, when at the approach of spring she puts forth all her might, all the powers bestowed on her by heaven, when she breaks into leaf, decks herself out and spangles herself with flowers . . . Somehow I cannot help being reminded of a frail, consumptive girl, at whom one sometimes looks with compassion, sometimes with sympathetic love, whom sometimes one simply does not notice; though suddenly in one instant she becomes, as though by chance, inexplicably lovely and exquisite, and, impressed and intoxicated, one cannot help asking oneself what power made those sad, pensive eyes flash with such fire? What summoned the blood to those pale, wan cheeks? What bathed with passion those soft features? What set that bosom heaving? What so suddenly called strength, life and beauty into the poor girl's face, making it gleam with such a smile, kindle with such bright, sparkling laughter? You look round, you seek for someone, you conjecture . . . But the moment passes, and next day you meet, maybe, the same pensive and preoccupied look as before, the same pale face, the same meek and timid movements, and even signs of remorse, traces of a mortal anguish and regret for the fleeting distraction . . . And you grieve that the momentary beauty has faded so soon never to return, that it flashed upon you so treacherously, so vainly, grieve because you had not even time to love her . . .

And yet my night was better than my day! This was how it happened.

I came back to the town very late, and it had struck ten as I was going towards my lodgings. My way lay along the canal embankment, where at that hour you never meet a soul. It is true that I live in a very remote part of the town. I walked along singing, for when I am happy I am always humming to myself like every happy man who has no friend or acquaintance with whom to share his joy. Suddenly I had a most unexpected adventure.

Leaning on the canal railing stood a woman with her elbows on the rail, she was apparently looking with great attention at the muddy water of the canal. She was wearing a very charming yellow hat and a jaunty little black mantle. 'She's a girl, and I am sure she is dark,' I thought. She did not seem to hear my footsteps, and did not even stir when I passed by with bated breath and loudly throbbing heart.

'Strange,' I thought; 'she must be deeply absorbed in something,' and all at once I stopped as though petrified. I heard a muffled sob. Yes! I was not mistaken, the girl was crying, and a minute later I heard sob after sob. Good heavens! My heart sank. And timid as I was with women, yet this was such a moment! . . . I turned, took a step towards her, and should certainly have pronounced the word 'Madam!' if I had not known that that exclamation has been uttered a thousand times in every Russian society novel. It was only that reflection stopped me. But while I was seeking for a word, the girl came to herself, looked round, started, cast down her eyes and slipped by me along the embankment. I at once followed her; but she, divining this, left the embankment, crossed the road and walked along the pavement. I dared not cross the street after her. My heart was fluttering like a captured bird. All at once a chance came to my aid.

Along the same side of the pavement there suddenly came

into sight, not far from the girl, a gentleman in evening dress, of dignified years, though by no means of dignified carriage; he was staggering and cautiously leaning against the wall. The girl flew straight as an arrow, with the timid haste one sees in all girls who do not want anyone to volunteer to accompany them home at night, and no doubt the staggering gentleman would not have pursued her, if my good luck had not prompted him.

Suddenly, without a word to anyone, the gentleman set off and flew full speed in pursuit of my unknown lady. She was racing like the wind, but the staggering gentleman was overtaking – overtook her. The girl uttered a shriek, and . . . I bless my luck for the excellent knotted stick, which happened on that occasion to be in my right hand. In a flash I was on the other side of the street; in a flash the obtrusive gentleman had taken in the position, and grasped the irresistible argument, fallen back without a word, and only when we were very far away protested against my action in rather vigorous language. But his words hardly reached us.

'Give me your arm,' I said to the girl. 'And he won't dare to annoy us further.'

She took my arm without a word, still trembling with excitement and terror. Oh, obtrusive gentleman! How I blessed you at that moment! I stole a glance at her, she was very charming and dark – I had guessed right.

On her black eyelashes there still glistened a tear – from her recent terror or her former grief – I don't know. But there was already a gleam of a smile on her lips. She too stole a glance at me, faintly blushed and looked down.

'There, you see; why did you drive me away? If I had been here, nothing would have happened . . .'

'But I did not know you; I thought that you too . . .'

'Why, do you know me now?'

'A little! Here, for instance, why are you trembling?'

'Oh, you are right at the first guess!' I answered, delighted that my girl had intelligence; that is never out of place in company with beauty. 'Yes, from the first glance you have guessed the sort of man you have to do with. Precisely; I am shy with women, I am agitated, I don't deny it, as much so as you were a minute ago when that gentleman alarmed you. I am in some alarm now. It's like a dream, and I never guessed even in my sleep that I should ever talk with any woman.'

'What? Really? . . .'

'Yes; if my arm trembles, it is because it has never been held by a pretty little hand like yours. I am a complete stranger to women; that is, I have never been used to them. You see, I am alone . . . I don't even know how to talk to them. Here, I don't know now whether I have not said something silly to you! Tell me frankly; I assured you beforehand that I am not quick to take offence? . . .'

'No, nothing, nothing, quite the contrary. And if you insist on my speaking frankly, I will tell you that women like such timidity; and if you want to know more, I like it too, and I won't drive you away till I get home.'

'You will make me,' I said, breathless with delight, 'lose my timidity, and then farewell to all my chances . . .'

'Chances! What chances – of what? That's not so nice.'

'I beg your pardon, I am sorry, it was a slip of the tongue; but how can you expect one at such a moment to have no desire . . .'

'To be liked, eh?'

'Well, yes; but do, for goodness sake, be kind. Think what I am! Here, I am twenty-six and I have never seen anyone. How can I speak well, tactfully, and to the point? It will seem better to you when I have told you everything openly . . . I don't know how to be silent when my heart is speaking. Well, never mind . . . Believe me, not one woman, never, never! No acquaintance of any sort! And I do nothing but dream every day that at last I shall meet some one. Oh, if only you knew how often I have been in love in that way . . .'

'How? With whom? . . .'

'Why, with no one, with an ideal, with the one I dream of in my sleep. I make up regular romances in my dreams. Ah, you don't know me! It's true, of course, I have met two or three women, but what sort of women were they? They were all landladies, that . . . But I shall make you laugh if I tell you that I have several times thought of speaking, just simply speaking, to some aristocratic lady in the street, when she is alone, I need hardly say; speaking to her, of course, timidly, respectfully, passionately; telling her that I am perishing in solitude, begging her not to send me away; saying that I have no chance of making the acquaintance of any woman; impressing upon her that it is a positive duty for a women not to repulse so timid a prayer from such a luckless man as me. That, in fact, all I ask is, that she should say two or three sisterly words with sympathy, should not repulse me at first sight; should take me on trust and listen to what I say; should laugh at me if she likes, encourage me, say two words to me, only two words, even though we never meet again afterwards! . . . But you are laughing; however, that is why I am telling you . . .'

'Don't be vexed; I am only laughing at your being your own enemy, and if you had tried you would have succeeded, perhaps, even though it had been in the street; the simpler the better . . . No kind-hearted woman, unless she were stupid or, still more, vexed about something at the moment, could bring herself to send you away without those two words which you ask for so timidly . . . But what am I saying? Of course she would take you for a madman. I was judging by myself; I know a good deal about other people's lives.'

'Oh, thank you,' I cried; 'you don't know what you have done for me now!'

'I am glad! I am glad! But tell me how did you find out that I was the sort of woman with whom . . . well, whom you think worthy . . . of attention and friendship . . . in fact, not a landlady as you say? What made you decide to come up to me?'

'What made me? . . . But you were alone; that gentleman was too insolent; it's night. You must admit that it was a duty . . .'

'No, no; I mean before, on the other side – you know you meant to come up to me.'

'On the other side? Really I don't know how to answer; I am afraid to . . . Do you know I have been happy today? I walked along singing; I went out into the country; I have never had such happy moments. You . . . perhaps it was my fancy . . . Forgive me for referring to it; I fancied you were crying, and I . . . could not bear to hear it . . . it made my heart ache . . . Oh, my goodness! Surely I might be troubled about you? Surely there was no harm in feeling brotherly compassion for you . . . I beg your pardon, I said compassion . . . Well, in short, surely you would not be offended at my involuntary impulse to go up to you? . . .'

'Stop, that's enough, don't talk of it,' said the girl, looking down, and pressing my hand. 'It's my fault for having spoken of it; but I am glad I was not mistaken in you . . . But here I am home; I must go down this turning, it's two steps from here . . . Goodbye, thank you! . . .'

'Surely . . . surely you don't mean . . . that we shall never see each other again? . . . Surely this is not to be the end?'

'You see,' said the girl, laughing, 'at first you only wanted two words, and now . . . However, I won't say anything . . . perhaps we shall meet . . .'

'I shall come here tomorrow,' I said. 'Oh, forgive me, I am already making demands . . .'

'Yes, you are not very patient . . . you are almost insisting.'

'Listen, listen!' I interrupted her. 'Forgive me if I tell you something else . . . I tell you what, I can't help coming here tomorrow, I am a dreamer; I have so little real life that I look upon such moments as this now, as so rare, that I cannot help going over such moments again in my dreams. I shall be dreaming of you all night, a whole week, a whole year. I shall certainly come here tomorrow, just here to this place, just at the same hour, and I shall be happy remembering today. This place is dear to me already. I have already two or three such places in Petersburg. I once shed tears over memories . . . like you . . . Who knows, perhaps you were weeping ten minutes ago over some memory . . . But, forgive me, I have forgotten myself again; perhaps you have once been particularly happy here . . .'

'Very good,' said the girl, 'perhaps I will come here tomorrow, too, at ten o'clock. I see that I can't forbid you . . . The fact is, I have to be here; don't imagine that I am making an appointment with you; I tell you beforehand that I have to be here on my own account. But . . . well, I tell you straight out, I don't mind if you do come. To begin with, something unpleasant might happen as it did today, but never mind that . . . In short, I should simply like to see you . . . to say two words to you. Only, mind, you must not think the worse of me now! Don't think I make appointments so lightly . . . I shouldn't make it except that . . . But let that be my secret! Only a compact beforehand . . .'

'A compact! Speak, tell me, tell me all beforehand; I agree to anything, I am ready for anything,' I cried delighted. 'I answer for myself, I will be obedient, respectful . . . you know me . . .'

'It's just because I do know you that I ask you to come tomorrow,' said the girl, laughing. 'I know you perfectly. But mind you will come on the condition, in the first place (only be good, do what I ask – you see, I speak frankly), you won't fall in love with me . . . That's impossible, I assure you. I am ready for friendship; here's my hand . . . But you mustn't fall in love with me, I beg you!'

'I swear,' I cried, gripping her hand . . .

'Hush, don't swear, I know you are ready to flare up like gunpowder. Don't think ill of me for saying so. If only you knew . . . I, too, have no one to whom I can say a word, whose advice I can ask. Of course, one does not look for an adviser in the street; but you are an exception. I know you as though we had been friends for twenty years . . . You won't deceive me, will you? . . .'

'You will see . . . the only thing is, I don't know how I am going to survive the next twenty-four hours.'

'Sleep soundly. Good night, and remember that I have trusted you already. But you exclaimed so nicely just now, "Surely one can't be held responsible for every feeling, even for brotherly sympathy!" Do you know, that was so nicely said, that the idea struck me at once, that I might confide in you?'

'For God's sake do; but about what? What is it?'

'Wait till tomorrow. Meanwhile, let that be a secret. So much the better for you; it will give it a faint flavour of romance. Perhaps I will tell you tomorrow, and perhaps not . . . I will talk to you a little more beforehand; we will get to know each other better . . .'

'Oh yes, I will tell you all about myself tomorrow! But what has happened? It is as though a miracle had befallen me . . . My God, where am I? Come, tell me aren't you glad that you were not angry and did not drive me away at the first moment, as any other woman would have done? In two minutes you have made me happy for ever. Yes, happy; who knows, perhaps, you have reconciled me with myself, solved my doubts! . . . Perhaps such moments come upon me . . . But there I will tell you all about it tomorrow, you shall know everything, everything . . .'

'Very well, I consent; you shall begin . . .'

'Agreed.'

'Goodbye till tomorrow!'

'Till tomorrow!'

And we parted. I walked about all night; I could not make up my mind to go home. I was so happy . . . Tomorrow!

Second Night

'WELL, so you have survived!' she said, pressing both my hands.

'I've been here for the last two hours; you don't know what a state I have been in all day.'

'I know, I know. But to business. Do you know why I have come? Not to talk nonsense, as I did yesterday. I tell you what, we must behave more sensibly in future. I thought a great deal about it last night.'

'In what way – in what must we be more sensible? I am ready for my part; but, really, nothing more sensible has happened to me in my life than this, now.'

'Really? In the first place, I beg you not to squeeze my hands so; secondly, I must tell you that I spent a long time thinking about you and feeling doubtful today.'

'And how did it end?'

'How did it end? The upshot of it is that we must begin all over again, because the conclusion I reached today was that I don't know you at all; that I behaved like a baby last night, like a little girl; and, of course, the fact of it is, that it's my soft heart that is to blame – that is, I sang my own praises, as one always does in the end when one analyses one's conduct. And therefore to correct my mistake, I've made up my mind to find out all about you minutely. But as I have no one from whom I can find out anything, you must tell me everything fully yourself. Well, what sort of man are you? Come, make haste – begin – tell me your whole history.'

'My history!' I cried in alarm. 'My history! But who has told you I have a history? I have no history . . .'

'Then how have you lived, if you have no history!' she interrupted, laughing.

'Absolutely without any history! I have lived, as they say, keeping myself to myself, that is, utterly alone – alone, entirely alone. Do you know what it means to be alone?'

'But how alone? Do you mean you never saw anyone?'

'Oh no, I see people, of course; but still I am alone.'

'Why, do you never talk to anyone?'

'Strictly speaking, with no one.'

'Who are you then? Explain yourself! Stay, I guess: most likely, like me you have a grandmother. She is blind and will never let me go anywhere, so that I have almost forgotten how to talk; and when I played some pranks two years ago, and she saw there was no holding me in, she called me up and pinned my dress to hers, and ever since we sit like that for days together; she knits a stocking, though she's blind, and I sit beside her, sew or read aloud to her – it's such a queer habit, here for two years I've been pinned to her . . .'

'Good heavens! what misery! But no, I haven't a grandmother like that.'

'Well, if you haven't why do you sit at home? . . .'

'Listen, do you want to know the sort of man I am?'

'Yes, yes!'

'In the strict sense of the word?'

'In the very strictest sense of the word.'

'Very well, I am a type!'

'Type, type! What sort of type?' cried the girl, laughing, as though she had not had a chance of laughing for a whole year. 'Yes, it's very amusing talking to you. Look, here's a seat, let us sit down. No one is passing here, no one will hear us, and – begin your history. For it's no good your telling me, I know you have a history; only you are concealing it. To begin with, what is a type?'

'A type? A type is an original, it's an absurd person!' I said, infected by her childish laughter. 'It's a character. Listen; do you know what is meant by a dreamer?'

'A dreamer! Indeed I should think I do know. I am a dreamer myself. Sometimes, as I sit by Grandmother, all sorts of things come into my head. Why, when one begins dreaming one lets one's fancy run away with one – why, I marry a Chinese Prince! . . . Though sometimes it is a good thing to dream! But, goodness knows! Especially when one has something to think of apart from dreams,' added the girl, this time rather seriously.

'Excellent! If you have been married to a Chinese Emperor, you will quite understand me. Come, listen . . . But one minute, I don't know your name yet.'

'At last! You have been in no hurry to think of it!'

'Oh, my goodness! It never entered my head, I felt quite happy as it was . . .'

'My name is Nastenka.'

'Nastenka! And nothing else?'

'Nothing else! Why, is not that enough for you, you insatiable person?'

'Not enough? On the contrary, it's a great deal, a very great deal, Nastenka; you kind girl, if you are Nastenka for me from the first.'

'Quite so! Well?'

'Well, listen, Nastenka, now for this absurd history.'

I sat down beside her, assumed a pedantically serious attitude, and began as though reading from a manuscript:

'There are, Nastenka, though you may not know it, strange nooks in Petersburg. It seems as though the same sun as shines for all Petersburg people does not peep into those spots, but some other different new one, bespoken expressly for those nooks, and it throws a different light on everything. In these corners, dear Nastenka, quite a different life is lived, quite unlike the life that is surging round us, but such as perhaps exists in some unknown realm, not among us in our serious, over-serious, time. Well, that life is a mixture of something purely fantastic, fervently ideal, with something (alas! Nastenka) dingily prosaic and ordinary, not to say incredibly vulgar.'

'Foo! Good heavens! What a preface! What do I hear?'

'Listen, Nastenka. (It seems to me I shall never be tired of calling you Nastenka.) Let me tell you that in these corners live strange people – dreamers. The dreamer – if you want an exact definition – is not a human being, but a creature of an intermediate sort. For the most part he settles in some inaccessible corner, as though hiding from the light of day; once he slips into his corner, he grows to it like a snail, or, anyway, he is in that respect very much like that remarkable creature, which is an animal and a house both at once, and is called a tortoise. Why do you suppose he is so fond of his four walls, which are invariably painted green, grimy, dismal and reeking unpardonably of tobacco smoke? Why is it that when this absurd gentleman is visited by one of his few acquaintances (and he ends by getting rid of all his friends), why does this absurd person meet him with such embarrassment, changing countenance and overcome with confusion, as though he had only just committed some crime within his four walls; as though he had been forging counterfeit notes, or as though he were writing verses to be sent to a journal with an anonymous letter, in which he states that the real poet is dead, and that his friend thinks it his sacred duty to publish his things? Why, tell me, Nastenka, why is it conversation is not easy between the two friends? Why is there no laughter? Why does no lively word fly from the tongue of the perplexed newcomer, who at other times may be very fond of laughter, lively words, conversation about the fair sex, and other cheerful subjects? And why does this friend, probably a new friend and on his first visit – for there will hardly be a second, and the friend will never come again – why is the friend himself so confused, so tongue-tied, in spite of his wit (if he has any), as he looks at the downcast face of his host, who in his turn becomes utterly helpless and at his wits' end after gigantic but fruitless efforts to smooth things over and enliven the conversation, to show his knowledge of polite society, to talk, too, of the fair sex, and by such humble endeavour, to please the poor man, who like a fish out of water has mistakenly come to visit him? Why does the gentleman, all at once remembering some very necessary business which never existed, suddenly seize his hat and hurriedly make off, snatching away his hand from the warm grip of his host, who was trying his utmost to show his regret and retrieve the lost position? Why does the friend chuckle as he goes out of the door, and swear never to come and see this queer creature again, though the queer creature is really a very good fellow, and at the same time he cannot refuse his imagination the little diversion of comparing the queer fellow's countenance during their conversation with the expression of an unhappy kitten treacherously captured, roughly handled, frightened and subjected to all sorts of indignities by children, till, utterly crestfallen, it hides away from them under a chair in the dark, and there must needs at its leisure bristle up, spit, and wash its insulted face with both paws, and long afterwards look angrily at life and nature, and even at the bits saved from the master's dinner for it by the sympathetic housekeeper?'

'Listen,' interrupted Nastenka, who had listened to me all

the time in amazement, opening her eyes and her little mouth. 'Listen; I don't know in the least why it happened and why you ask me such absurd questions; all I know is, that this adventure must have happened word for word to you.'

'Doubtless,' I answered, with the gravest face.

'Well, since there is no doubt about it, go on,' said Nastenka, 'because I want very much to know how it will end.'

'You want to know, Nastenka, what our hero, that is I – for the hero of the whole business was my humble self – did in his corner? You want to know why I lost my head and was upset for the whole day by the unexpected visit of a friend? You want to know why I was so startled, why I blushed when the door of my room was opened, why I was not able to entertain my visitor, and why I was crushed under the weight of my own hospitality?'

'Why, yes, yes,' answered Nastenka, 'that's the point. Listen. You describe it all splendidly, but couldn't you perhaps describe it a little less splendidly? You talk as though you were reading it out of a book.'

'Nastenka,' I answered in a stern and dignified voice, hardly able to keep from laughing, 'dear Nastenka, I know I describe splendidly, but, excuse me, I don't know how else to do it. At this moment, dear Nastenka, at this moment I am like the spirit of King Solomon when, after lying a thousand years under seven seals in his urn, those seven seals were at last taken off. At this moment, Nastenka, when we have met at last after such a long separation – for I have known you for ages, Nastenka, because

I have been looking for someone for ages, and that is a sign that it was you I was looking for, and it was ordained that we should meet now – at this moment a thousand valves have opened in my head, and I must let myself flow in a river of words, or I shall choke. And so I beg you not to interrupt me, Nastenka, but listen humbly and obediently, or I will be silent.'

'No, no, no! Not at all. Go on! I won't say a word!'

'I will continue. There is, my friend Nastenka, one hour in my day which I like extremely. That is the hour when almost all business, work and duties are over, and everyone is hurrying home to dinner, to lie down, to rest, and on the way all are cogitating on other more cheerful subjects relating to their evenings, their nights, and all the rest of their free time. At that hour our hero – for allow me, Nastenka, to tell my story in the third person, for one feels awfully ashamed to tell it in the first person – and so at that hour our hero, who had his work too, was pacing along after the others. But a strange feeling of pleasure set his pale, rather crumpled-looking face working. He looked not with indifference on the evening glow which was slowly fading on the cold Petersburg sky. When I say he looked, I am lying: he did not look at it, but saw it as it were without realising, as though tired or preoccupied with some other more interesting subject, so that he could scarcely spare a glance for anything about him. He was pleased because till next day he was released from business irksome to him, and happy as a schoolboy let out from the class-room to his games and mischief.

Take a look at him, Nastenka; you will see at once that joyful emotion has already had an effect on his weak nerves and morbidly excited fancy. You see he is thinking of something . . . Of dinner, do you imagine? Of the evening? What is he looking at like that? Is it at that gentleman of dignified appearance who is bowing so picturesquely to the lady who rolls by in a carriage drawn by prancing horses? No, Nastenka; what are all those trivialities to him now! He is rich now with his *own individual* life; he has suddenly become rich, and it is not for nothing that the fading sunset sheds its farewell gleams so gaily before him, and calls forth a swarm of impressions from his warmed heart. Now he hardly notices the road, on which the tiniest details at other times would strike him. Now "the Goddess of Fancy" (if you have read Zhukovsky, dear Nastenka) has already with fantastic hand spun her golden warp and begun weaving upon it patterns of marvellous magic life – and who knows, maybe, her fantastic hand has borne him to the seventh crystal heaven far from the excellent granite pavement on which he was walking his way? Try stopping him now, ask him suddenly where he is standing now, through what streets he is going – he will probably remember nothing, neither where he is going nor where he is standing now, and flushing with vexation he will certainly tell some lie to save appearances. That is why he starts, almost cries out, and looks round with horror when a respectable old lady stops him politely in the middle of the pavement and asks her way. Frowning with vexation he strides on, scarcely noticing that more than one passer-by smiles and turns round to look after him, and that a little girl, moving out of his way in alarm, laughs aloud, gazing open-eyed at his broad meditative smile and gesticulations. But fancy catches up in its playful flight the old woman, the curious passers-by, and the laughing child, and the peasants spending their nights in their barges on Fontanka (our hero, let us suppose, is walking along the canal-side at that moment), and capriciously weaves everyone and everything into the canvas like a fly in a spider's web. And it is only after the queer fellow has returned to his comfortable den with fresh stores for his mind to work on, has sat down and finished his dinner, that he comes to himself, when Matrona who waits upon him – always thoughtful and depressed – clears the table and gives him his pipe; he comes to himself then and recalls with surprise that he has dined, though he has absolutely no notion how it has happened. It has grown dark in the room; his soul is sad and empty; the whole kingdom of fancies drops to pieces about him, drops to pieces without a trace, without a sound, floats away like a dream, and he cannot himself remember what he was dreaming. But a vague sensation faintly stirs his heart and sets it aching, some new desire temptingly tickles and excites his fancy, and imperceptibly evokes a swarm of fresh phantoms. Stillness reigns in the little room; imagination is fostered by solitude and idleness; it is faintly smouldering, faintly simmering, like the water with which old Matrona is making her coffee as she moves quietly about in the kitchen close by. Now it breaks out spasmodically; and the book, picked up aimlessly and at random, drops from my dreamer's hand before he has reached the third page. His imagination is again stirred and at work, and again a new world, a new fascinating life opens vistas before him. A fresh dream – fresh happiness! A fresh rush of delicate, voluptuous poison! What is real life to him! To his corrupted eyes we live, you and I, Nastenka, so torpidly, slowly, insipidly; in his eyes we are all so dissatisfied with our fate, so exhausted by our life! And, truly, see how at first sight everything is cold, morose, as though ill-humoured among us . . . Poor things! thinks our dreamer. And it is no wonder that he thinks it! Look at these magic phantasms, which so enchantingly, so whimsically, so carelessly and freely group before him in such a magic, animated picture, in which the most prominent figure in the foreground is of course himself, our dreamer, in his precious person. See what varied adventures, what an endless swarm of ecstatic dreams. You ask, perhaps, what he is dreaming of. Why ask that? – why, of everything . . . of the lot of the poet, first unrecognised, then crowned with laurels; of friendship with Hoffmann, St Bartholomew's Night, of Diana Vernon, of playing the hero at the taking of Kazan by Ivan Vassilyevitch, of Clara Mowbray, of Effie Deans, of the council of the prelates and Huss before them, of the rising of the dead in *Robert the Devil* (do you remember the music, it smells of the churchyard!), of Minna and Brenda of the battle of Berezina, of the reading of a poem at Countess V. D.'s, of Danton, of Cleopatra *ei suoi amanti*, of a little house in Kolomna, of a little home of one's own and beside one a dear creature who listens to one on a winter's evening, opening her little mouth and eyes as you are listening to me now, my angel . . . No, Nastenka, what is there, what is there for him, voluptuous sluggard, in this life, for which you and I have such a longing? He thinks that this is a poor pitiful life, not foreseeing that for him too, maybe, sometime the mournful hour may strike, when for one day of that pitiful life he would give all his years of fantasy, and would give them not only for joy and for happiness, but without caring to make distinctions in that hour of sadness, remorse and unchecked grief. But so far that threatening time has not arrived – he desires nothing, because he is superior to all desire, because he has everything, because he is satiated, because he is the artist of his own life, and creates it for himself every hour to suit his latest whim. And you know this fantastic world of fairyland is so easily, so naturally created! As though it were not a delusion! Indeed, he is ready to believe at some moments that all his life is not suggested by feeling, is not mirage, not a delusion of the imagination, but that it is concrete, real, substantial! Why is it, Nastenka, why is it at such moments one holds one's breath? Why, by what sorcery, through what incomprehensible caprice, is the pulse quickened, does a tear start from the dreamer's eye, while his pale moist cheeks glow, while his whole being is suffused with an inexpressible sense of consolation? Why is it that whole sleepless nights pass like a flash in inexhaustible gladness and happiness, and when the dawn gleams rosy at the window and daybreak floods the gloomy room with uncertain, fantastic light, as in Petersburg, our dreamer, worn out and exhausted, flings himself on his bed and drops asleep with thrills of delight in his morbidly overwrought spirit, and with a weary sweet ache in his heart? Yes, Nastenka, one deceives oneself and unconsciously believes that real true passion is stirring one's soul; one unconsciously believes that there is something living, tangible in one's immaterial dreams! And is it delusion? Here love, for instance, is bound up with all its fathomless joy, all its torturing agonies in his bosom . . . Only look at him, and you will be convinced! Would you believe, looking at him, dear Nastenka, that he has never known her whom he loves in his ecstatic dreams? Can it be that he has only seen her in seductive visions, and that this passion has been nothing but a dream? Surely they must have spent years hand in hand together – alone the two of them, casting off all the world and each uniting his or her life with the other's? Surely when the hour of parting came she must have lain sobbing and grieving on his bosom, heedless of the tempest raging under the sullen sky, heedless of the wind which snatches and bears away the tears from her black eyelashes? Can all of that have been a dream – and that garden, dejected, forsaken, run wild with its little moss-grown paths, solitary, gloomy, where they used to walk so happily together, where they hoped, grieved, loved, loved each other so long, "so long and so fondly"? And that queer ancestral house where she spent so many years lonely and sad with her morose old husband, always silent and splenetic, who frightened them, while timid as children they hid their love from each other? What torments they suffered, what agonies of terror, how innocent, how pure was their love, and how (I need hardly say, Nastenka) malicious people were! And, good heavens! surely he met her afterwards, far from their native shores, under alien skies, in the hot south in the divinely eternal city, in the dazzling splendour of the ball to the crash of music, in a *palazzo* (it must be in a *palazzo*), drowned in a sea of lights, on the balcony, wreathed in myrtle and roses, where, recognising him, she hurriedly removes her mask and whispering, "I am free," flings herself trembling into his arms, and with a cry of rapture, clinging to one another, in one instant they forget their sorrow and their parting and all their agonies, and the gloomy house and the old man and the dismal garden in that distant land, and the seat on which with a last passionate kiss she tore herself away from his arms numb with anguish and despair . . . Oh, Nastenka, you must admit that one would start, betray confusion, and blush like a schoolboy who has just stuffed in his pocket an apple stolen from a neighbour's garden, when your uninvited visitor, some stalwart, lanky fellow, a festive soul fond of a joke, opens your door and shouts out as though nothing were happening; "My dear boy, I have this minute come from Pavlovsk." My goodness! the old count is dead, unutterable happiness is close at hand – and people arrive from Pavlovsk!'

Finishing my pathetic appeal, I paused pathetically. I

remembered that I had an intense desire to force myself to laugh, for I was already feeling that a malignant demon was stirring within me, that there was a lump in my throat, that my chin was beginning to twitch, and that my eyes were growing more and more moist.

I expected Nastenka, who listened to me opening her clever eyes, would break into her childish, irrepressible laugh; and I was already regretting that I had gone so far, that I had unnecessarily described what had long been simmering in my heart, about which I could speak as though from a written account of it, because I had long ago passed judgment on myself and now could not resist reading it, making my confession, without expecting to be understood; but to my surprise she was silent, waiting a little, then she faintly pressed my hand and with timid sympathy asked:

'Surely you haven't lived like that all your life?'

'All my life, Nastenka,' I answered; 'all my life, and it seems to me I shall go on so to the end.'

'No, that won't do,' she said uneasily, 'that must not be; and so, maybe, I shall spend all my life beside Grandmother. Do you know, it is not at all good to live like that?'

'I know, Nastenka, I know!' I cried, unable to restrain my feelings longer. 'And I realise now, more than ever, that I have lost all my best years! And now I know it and feel it more painfully from recognising that God has sent me you, my good angel, to tell me that and show it. Now that I sit beside you and talk to you it is strange for me to think of the future, for in the future – there is loneliness again, again this musty, useless life; and what shall I have to dream of when I have been so happy in reality beside you! Oh, may you be blessed, dear girl, for not having repulsed me at first, for enabling me to say that for two evenings, at least, I have lived.'

'Oh, no, no!' cried Nastenka and tears glistened in her eyes. 'No, it mustn't be so any more; we must not part like that! what are two evenings?'

'Oh, Nastenka, Nastenka! Do you know how far you have reconciled me to myself? Do you know now that I shall not think so ill of myself, as I have at some moments? Do you know that, maybe, I shall leave off grieving over the crime and sin of my life? for such a life is a crime and a sin. And do not imagine that I have been exaggerating anything – for goodness sake don't think that, Nastenka: for at times such misery comes over me, such misery . . . Because it begins to seem to me at such times that I am incapable of beginning a life in real life, because it has seemed to me that I have lost all touch, all instinct for the actual, the real; because at last I have cursed myself; because after my fantastic nights I have moments of returning sobriety, which are awful! Meanwhile, you hear the whirl and roar of the crowd in the vortex of life around you; you hear, you see, men living in reality; you see that life for them is not forbidden, that their life does not float away like a dream, like a vision; that their life is being eternally renewed, eternally youthful, and not one hour of it is the same as another; while fancy is so spiritless, monotonous to vulgarity and easily scared, the slave of shadows, of the idea, the slave of the first cloud that shrouds the sun, and overcasts with depression the true Petersburg heart so devoted to the sun – and what is fancy in depression! One feels that this *inexhaustible* fancy is weary at last and worn out with continual exercise, because one is growing into manhood, outgrowing one's old ideals: they are being shattered into fragments, into dust; if there is no other life, one must build one up from the fragments. And meanwhile the soul longs and craves for something else! And in vain the dreamer rakes over his old dreams, as though seeking a spark among the embers, to fan them into flame, to warm his chilled heart by the rekindled fire, and to rouse up in it again all that was so sweet, that touched his heart, that set his blood boiling, drew tears from his eyes, and so luxuriously deceived him! Do you know, Nastenka, the point I have reached? Do you know that I am forced now to celebrate the anniversary of my own sensations, the anniversary of that which was once so sweet, which never existed in reality – for this anniversary is kept in memory of those same foolish, shadowy dreams – and to do this because those foolish dreams are no more, because I have nothing to earn them with; you know even dreams do not come for nothing! Do you know that I love now to recall and visit at certain dates the places where I was once happy in my own way? I love to build up my present in harmony with the irrevocable past, and I often wander like a shadow, aimless, sad and dejected, about the streets and crooked lanes of Petersburg. What memories they are! To remember, for instance, that here just a year ago, just at this time, at this hour, on this pavement, I wandered just as lonely, just as dejected as today. And one remembers that then one's dreams were sad, and though the past was no better one feels as though it had somehow been better, and that life was more peaceful, that one was free from the black thoughts that haunt me now; that one was free from the gnawing of conscience – the gloomy, sullen gnawing which now gives me no rest by day or by night. And one asks oneself where are one's dreams. And one shakes one's head and says how rapidly the years fly by! And again one asks oneself what has one done with one's years. Where have you buried your best days? Have you lived or not? Look, one says to oneself, look how cold the world is growing. Some more years will pass, and after them will come gloomy solitude; then will come old age trembling on its crutch, and after it misery and desolation. Your fantastic world will grow pale, your dreams will fade and die and will fall like the yellow leaves from the trees . . . Oh, Nastenka! you know it will be sad to be left alone, utterly alone, and to have not even anything to regret – nothing, absolutely nothing . . . for all that you have lost, all that, all was nothing, stupid, simple nullity, there has been nothing but dreams!'

'Come, don't work on my feelings any more,' said Nastenka, wiping away a tear which was trickling down her cheek. 'Now it's over! Now we shall be two together. Now, whatever happens to me, we will never part. Listen; I am a simple girl, I have not had much education, though Grandmother did get a teacher for me, but truly I understand you, for all that you have described I have been through myself, when Grandmother pinned me to her dress. Of course, I should not have described it so well as you have; I am not educated,' she added timidly, for she was still feeling a sort of respect for my pathetic eloquence and lofty style; 'but I am very glad that you have been quite open with me. Now I know you thoroughly, all of you. And do you know what? I want to tell you my history too, all without concealment, and after that you must give me advice. You are a very clever man; will you promise to give me advice?'

'Ah, Nastenka,' I cried, 'though I have never given advice, still less sensible advice, yet I see now that if we always go on like this that it will be very sensible, and that each of us will give the other a great deal of sensible advice! Well, my pretty Nastenka, what sort of advice do you want? Tell me frankly; at this moment I am so gay and happy, so bold and sensible, that it won't be difficult for me to find words.'

'No, no!' Nastenka interrupted, laughing. 'I don't only want sensible advice, I want warm brotherly advice, as though you had been fond of me all your life!'

'Agreed, Nastenka, agreed!' I cried delighted; 'and if I had been fond of you for twenty years, I couldn't have been fonder of you than I am now.'

'Your hand,' said Nastenka.

'Here it is,' said I, giving her my hand.

'And so let us begin my history!'

Nastenka's History

'Half my story you know already – that is, you know that I have an old grandmother . . .'

'If the other half is as brief as that . . .' I interrupted, laughing.

'Be quiet and listen. First of all you must agree not to interrupt me, or else, perhaps I shall get in a muddle! Come, listen quietly.

'I have an old grandmother. I came into her hands when I was quite a little girl, for my father and mother are dead. It must be supposed that Grandmother was once richer, for now she recalls better days. She taught me French, and then got a teacher for me. When I was fifteen (and now I am seventeen) we gave up having lessons. It was at that time that I got into mischief; what I did I won't tell you; it's enough to say that it wasn't very important. But Grandmother called me to her one morning and said that as she was blind she could not look after me; she took a pin and pinned my dress to hers, and said that we should sit like that for the rest of our lives if, of course, I did not become a better girl. In fact, at first it was impossible to get away from her . . . I had to work, to read and to study all beside Grandmother. I tried to deceive her once, and persuaded Fekla to sit in my place. Fekla is our charwoman, she is deaf.

Fekla sat there instead of me; Grandmother was asleep in her arm-chair at the time, and I went off to see a friend close by. Well, it ended in trouble. Grandmother woke up while I was out, and asked some questions; she thought I was still sitting quietly in my place. Fekla saw that Grandmother was asking her something, but could not tell what it was; she wondered what to do, undid the pin and ran away . . .'

At this point Nastenka stopped and began laughing. I laughed with her. She left off at once.

'I tell you what, don't you laugh at Grandmother. I laugh because it's funny . . . What can I do, since Grandmother is like that; but yet I am fond of her in a way. Oh, well, I did catch it that time. I had to sit down in my place at once, and after that I was not allowed to stir.

'Oh, I forgot to tell you that our house belongs to us, that is to Grandmother; it is a little wooden house with three windows as old as Grandmother herself, with a little upper storey; well, there moved into our upper storey a new lodger.'

'Then you had an old lodger,' I observed casually.

'Yes, of course,' answered Nastenka, 'and one who knew how to hold his tongue better than you do. In fact, he hardly ever used his tongue at all. He was a dumb, blind, lame, dried-up little old man, so that at last he could not go on living, he died; so then we had to find a new lodger, for we could not live without a lodger – the rent, together with Grandmother's pension, is almost all we have. But the new lodger, as luck would have it, was a young man, a stranger not of these parts. As he did not haggle over the rent, Grandmother accepted him, and only afterwards she asked me: "Tell me, Nastenka, what is our lodger like – is he young or old?" I did not want to lie, so I told Grandmother that he wasn't exactly young and that he wasn't old.

'"And is he pleasant-looking?" asked Grandmother.

'Again I do not want to tell a lie: "Yes, he is pleasant looking, Grandmother," I said. And Grandmother said: "Oh, what a nuisance, what a nuisance! I tell you this, grandchild, that you may not be looking after him. What times these are! Why a paltry lodger like this, and he must be pleasant-looking too; it was very different in the old days!"'

'Grandmother was always regretting the old days – she was younger in old days, and the sun was warmer in old days, and cream did not turn so sour in old days – it was always the old days! I would sit still and hold my tongue and think to myself: why did Grandmother suggest it to me? Why did she ask whether the lodger was young and good-looking? But that was all, I just thought it, began counting my stitches again, went on knitting my stocking, and forgot all about it.

'Well, one morning the lodger came in to see us; he asked about a promise to paper his rooms. One thing led to another. Grandmother was talkative, and she said: "Go, Nastenka, into my bedroom and bring me my reckoner." I jumped up at once; I blushed all over, I don't know why, and forgot I was sitting pinned to grandmother; instead of quietly undoing the pin, so that the lodger should not see – I jumped so that Grandmother's chair moved. When I saw that the lodger knew all about me now, I blushed, stood still as though I had been shot, and suddenly began to cry – I felt so ashamed and miserable at that minute, that I didn't know where to look! Grandmother called out, "What are you waiting for?" and I went on worse than ever. When the lodger saw, saw that I was ashamed on his account, he bowed and went away at once!

'After that I felt ready to die at the least sound in the passage. "It's the lodger," I kept thinking; I stealthily undid the pin in case. But it always turned out not to be, he never came. A fortnight passed; the lodger sent word through Fekla that he had a great number of French books, and that they were all good books that I might read, so would not Grandmother like me to read them that I might not be dull? Grandmother agreed with gratitude, but kept asking if they were moral books, for if the books were immoral it would be out of the question, one would learn evil from them.'

'"And what should I learn, Grandmother? What is there written in them?"

'"Ah," she said, "what's described in them, is how young men seduce virtuous girls; how, on the excuse that they want to marry them, they carry them off from their parents' houses; how afterwards they leave these unhappy girls to their fate, and they perish in the most pitiful way. I read a great many books," said Grandmother, "and it is all so well described that one sits up all night and reads them on the sly. So mind you don't read them, Nastenka," said she. "What books has he sent?"

'"They are all Walter Scott's novels, Grandmother."

'"Walter Scott's novels! But stay, isn't there some trick about it? Look, hasn't he stuck a love-letter among them?"

'"No, Grandmother," I said, "there isn't a love-letter."

'"But look under the binding; they sometimes stuff it under the bindings, the rascals!"

'"No, Grandmother, there is nothing under the binding."

'"Well, that's all right."

'So we began reading Walter Scott, and in a month or so we had read almost half. Then he sent us more and more. He sent us Pushkin, too; so that at last I could not get on without a book, and left off dreaming of how fine it would be to marry a Chinese Prince.

'That's how things were when I chanced one day to meet our lodger on the stairs. Grandmother had sent me to fetch something. He stopped, I blushed and he blushed; he laughed, though, said good morning to me, asked after Grandmother, and said, "Well, have you read the books?" I answered that I had. "Which did you like best?" he asked. I said, "*Ivanhoe*, and Pushkin best of all," and so our talk ended for that time.

'A week later I met him again on the stairs. That time Grandmother had not sent me, I wanted to get something for myself. It was past two, and the lodger used to come home at that time. "Good afternoon," said he. I said good afternoon, too.

'"Aren't you dull," he said, "sitting all day with your grandmother?"

'When he asked that, I blushed, I don't know why; I felt ashamed, and again I felt offended – I suppose because other people had begun to ask me about that. I wanted to go away without answering, but I hadn't the strength.

'"Listen," he said, "you are a good girl. Excuse my speaking to you like that, but I assure you that I wish for your welfare quite as much as your grandmother. Have you no friends that you could go and visit?"

'I told him I hadn't any, that I had had no friends but Mashenka, and she had gone away to Pskov.

'"Listen," he said, "would you like to go to the theatre with me?"

'"To the theatre. What about Grandmother?"

'"But you must go without your Grandmother's knowing it," he said.

'"No," I said, "I don't want to deceive Grandmother. Goodbye."

'"Well, goodbye," he answered, and said nothing more.

'Only after dinner he came to see us; sat a long time talking to Grandmother; asked her whether she ever went out anywhere, whether she had acquaintances, and suddenly said: "I have taken a box at the opera for this evening; they are giving *The Barber of Seville*. My friends meant to go, but afterwards refused, so the ticket is left on my hands."

'"*The Barber of Seville*," cried Grandmother; "why, the same they used to act in old days?"

'"Yes, it's the same barber," he said, and glanced at me. I saw what it meant and turned crimson, and my heart began throbbing with suspense.

'"To be sure, I know it," said Grandmother; "why, I took the part of Rosina myself in old days, at a private performance!"

'"So wouldn't you like to go today?" said the lodger. "Or my ticket will be wasted."

'"By all means let us go," said Grandmother; "why shouldn't we? And my Nastenka here has never been to the theatre."

'My goodness, what joy! We got ready at once, put on our best clothes, and set off. Though Grandmother was blind, still she wanted to hear the music; besides, she is a kind old soul, what she cared most for was to amuse me, we should never have gone of ourselves.

'What my impressions of *The Barber of Seville* were I won't tell you; but all that evening our lodger looked at me so nicely, talked so nicely, that I saw at once that he had meant to test me in the morning when he proposed that I should go with him alone. Well, it was joy! I went to bed so proud, so gay, my heart beat so that I was a little feverish, and all night I was raving about *The Barber of Seville*.

'I expected that he would come and see us more and more often after that, but it wasn't so at all. He almost entirely gave up coming. He would just come in about once a month, and then only to invite us to the theatre. We went twice again. Only I wasn't at all pleased with that; I saw that he was simply sorry for me because I was so hardly treated by Grandmother, and that was all. As time went on, I grew more and more restless, I couldn't sit still, I couldn't read, I couldn't work; sometimes I laughed and did something to annoy Grandmother, at another time I would cry. At last I grew thin and was very nearly ill. The opera season was over, and our lodger had quite given up coming to see us; whenever we met – always on the same staircase, of course – he would bow so silently, so gravely, as though he did not want to speak, and go down to the front door, while I went on standing in the middle of the stairs, as red as a cherry, for all the blood rushed to my head at the sight of him.

'Now the end is near. Just a year ago, in May, the lodger came to us and said to Grandmother that he had finished his business here, and that he must go back to Moscow for a year. When I heard that, I sank into a chair half dead; Grandmother did not notice anything, and having informed us that he should be leaving us, he bowed and went away.

'What was I to do? I thought and thought and fretted and fretted, and at last I made up my mind. Next day he was to go away, and I made up my mind to end it all that evening when Grandmother went to bed. And so it happened. I made up all my clothes in a parcel – all the linen I needed – and with the parcel in my hand, more dead than alive, went upstairs to our lodger. I believe I must have stayed an hour on the staircase. When I opened his door he cried out as he looked at me. He thought I was a ghost, and rushed to give me some water, for I could hardly stand up. My heart beat so violently that my head ached, and I did not know what I was doing. When I recovered I began by laying my parcel on his bed, sat down beside it, hid my face in my hands and went into floods of tears. I think he understood it all at once, and looked at me so sadly that my heart was torn.

'"Listen," he began, "listen, Nastenka, I can't do anything; I am a poor man, for I have nothing, not even a decent berth. How could we live, if I were to marry you?"

'We talked a long time; but at last I got quite frantic, I said I could not go on living with Grandmother, that I should run away from her, that I did not want to be pinned to her, and that I would go to Moscow if he liked, because I could not live without him. Shame and pride and love were all clamouring in me at once, and I fell on the bed almost in convulsions, I was so afraid of a refusal.

'He sat for some minutes in silence, then got up, came up to me and took me by the hand.

'"Listen, my dear good Nastenka, listen; I swear to you that if I am ever in a position to marry, you shall make my happiness. I assure you that now you are the only one who could make me happy. Listen, I am going to Moscow and shall be there just a year; I hope to establish my position. When I come back, if you still love me, I swear that we will be happy. Now it is impossible, I am not able, I have not the right to promise anything. Well, I repeat, if it is not within a year it will certainly be some time;

that is, of course, if you do not prefer anyone else, for I cannot and dare not bind you by any sort of promise."

'That was what he said to me, and next day he went away. We agreed together not to say a word to Grandmother: that was his wish. Well, my history is nearly finished now. Just a year has past. He has arrived; he has been here three days, and, and—'

'And what?' I cried, impatient to hear the end.

'And up to now has not shown himself!' answered Nastenka, as though screwing up all her courage. 'There's no sign or sound of him.'

Here she stopped, paused for a minute, bent her head, and covering her face with her hands broke into such sobs that it sent a pang to my heart to hear them. I had not in the least expected such a *dénouement*.

'Nastenka,' I began timidly in an ingratiating voice, 'Nastenka! For goodness sake don't cry! How do you know? Perhaps he is not here yet . . .'

'He is, he is,' Nastenka repeated. 'He is here, and I know it. We *made an agreement* at the time, that evening, before he went away: when we said all that I have told you, and had come to an understanding, then we came out here for a walk on this embankment. It was ten o'clock; we sat on this seat. I was not crying then; it was sweet to me to hear what he said . . . And he said that he would come to us directly he arrived, and if I did not refuse him, then we would tell Grandmother about it all. Now he is here, I know it, and yet he does not come!'

And again she burst into tears.

'Good God, can I do nothing to help you in your sorrow?' I cried, jumping up from the seat in utter despair. 'Tell me, Nastenka, wouldn't it be possible for me to go to him?'

'Would that be possible?' she asked suddenly, raising her head.

'No, of course not,' I said pulling myself up; 'but I tell you what, write a letter.'

'No, that's impossible, I can't do that,' she answered with decision, bending her head and not looking at me.

'How impossible – why is it impossible?' I went on, clinging to my idea. 'But, Nastenka, it depends what sort of letter; there are letters and letters and . . . Ah, Nastenka, I am right; trust to me, trust to me, I will not give you bad advice. It can all be arranged! You took the first step – why not now?'

'I can't. I can't! It would seem as though I were forcing myself on him . . .'

'Ah, my good little Nastenka,' I said, hardly able to conceal a smile; 'no, no, you have a right to, in fact, because he made you a promise. Besides, I can see from everything that he is a man of delicate feeling; that he behaved very well,' I went on, more and more carried away by the logic of my own arguments and convictions. 'How did he behave? He bound himself by a promise: he said that if he married at all he would marry no one but you; he gave you full liberty to refuse him at once . . . Under such circumstances you may take the first step; you have the right, you are in the privileged position – if, for instance, you wanted to free him from his promise . . .'

'Listen; how would you write?'

'Write what?'

'This letter.'

'I tell you how I would write: "Dear Sir. . . ."'

'Must I really begin like that, "Dear Sir"?'

'You certainly must! Though, after all, I don't know, I imagine . . .'

'Well, well, what next?'

'"Dear Sir, – I must apologise for—' But, no, there's no need to apologise; the fact itself justifies everything. Write simply:

'"I am writing to you. Forgive me my impatience; but I have been happy for a whole year in hope; am I to blame for being unable to endure a day of doubt now? Now that you have come, perhaps you have changed your mind. If so, this letter is to tell you that I do not repine, nor blame you. I do not blame you because I have no power over your heart, such is my fate!

'"You are an honourable man. You will not smile or be vexed at these impatient lines. Remember they are written by a poor girl; that she is alone; that she has no one to direct her, no one to advise her, and that she herself could never control her heart. But forgive me that a doubt has stolen – if only for one instant – into my heart. You are not capable of insulting, even in thought, her who so loved and so loves you."'

'Yes, yes; that's exactly what I was thinking!' cried Nastenka, and her eyes beamed with delight. 'Oh, you have solved my difficulties: God has sent you to me! Thank you, thank you!'

'What for? What for? For God's sending me?' I answered, looking delighted at her joyful little face.

'Why, yes; for that too.'

'Ah, Nastenka! Why, one thanks some people for being alive at the same time with one; I thank you for having met me, for my being able to remember you all my life!'

'Well, enough, enough! But now I tell you what, listen: we made an agreement then that as soon as he arrived he would let me know, by leaving a letter with some good simple people of my acquaintance who know nothing about it; or, if it were impossible to write a letter to me, for a letter does not always tell everything, he would be here at ten o'clock on the day he arrived, where we had arranged to meet. I know he has arrived already; but now it's the third day, and there's no sign of him and no letter. It's impossible for me to get away from Grandmother in the morning. Give my letter tomorrow to those kind people I spoke to you about: they will send it on to him, and if there is an answer you bring it tomorrow at ten o'clock.'

'But the letter, the letter! You see, you must write the letter first! So perhaps it must all be the day after tomorrow.'

'The letter . . .' said Nastenka, a little confused, 'the letter . . . but . . .'

But she did not finish. At first she turned her little face away from me, flushed like a rose, and suddenly I felt in my hand a letter which had evidently been written long before, all ready and sealed up. A familiar sweet and charming reminiscence floated through my mind.

'R, o – Ro; s, i – si; n, a – na,' I began.

'Rosina!' we both hummed together; I almost embracing her with delight, while she blushed as only she could blush, and laughed through the tears which gleamed like pearls on her black eyelashes.

'Come, enough, enough! Goodbye now,' she said, speaking rapidly. 'Here is the letter, here is the address to which you are to take it. Goodbye, till we meet again! Till tomorrow!'

She pressed both my hands warmly, nodded her head, and flew like an arrow down her side street. I stood still for a long time following her with my eyes.

'Till tomorrow! till tomorrow!' was ringing in my ears as she vanished from my sight.

Third Night

TODAY was a gloomy, rainy day without a glimmer of sunlight, like the old age before me. I am oppressed by such strange thoughts, such gloomy sensations; questions still so obscure to me are crowding into my brain – and I seem to have neither power nor will to settle them. It's not for me to settle all this!

Today we shall not meet. Yesterday, when we said goodbye, the clouds began gathering over the sky and a mist rose. I said that tomorrow it would be a bad day; she made no answer, she did not want to speak against her wishes; for her that day was bright and clear, not one cloud should obscure her happiness.

'If it rains we shall not see each other,' she said, 'I shall not come.'

I thought that she would not notice today's rain, and yet she has not come.

Yesterday was our third interview, our third white night . . .

But how fine joy and happiness makes any one! How brimming over with love the heart is! One seems longing to pour out one's whole heart; one wants everything to be gay, everything to be laughing. And how infectious that joy is! There was such a softness in her words, such a kindly feeling in her heart towards me yesterday . . . How solicitous and friendly she was; how tenderly she tried to give me courage! Oh, the coquetry of happiness! While I . . . I took it all for the genuine thing, I thought that she . . .

But, my God, how could I have thought it? How could I have been so blind, when everything had been taken by another already, when nothing was mine; when, in fact, her very tenderness to me, her anxiety, her love . . . yes, love for me, was nothing else but joy at the thought of seeing another man so soon, desire to include me, too, in her happiness? . . . When he did not come, when we waited in vain, she frowned, she grew timid and discouraged. Her movements, her words, were no longer so light, so playful, so gay; and, strange to say, she redoubled her attentiveness to me, as though instinctively desiring to lavish on me what she desired for herself so anxiously, if her wishes were not accomplished. My Nastenka was so downcast, so dismayed, that I think she realised at last that I loved her, and was sorry for my poor love. So when we are unhappy we feel the unhappiness of others more; feeling is not destroyed but concentrated . . .

I went to meet her with a full heart, and was all impatience. I had no presentiment that I should feel as I do now, that it would not all end happily. She was beaming with pleasure; she was expecting an answer. The answer was himself. He was to come, to run at her call. She arrived a whole hour before I did. At first she giggled at everything, laughed at every word I said. I began talking, but relapsed into silence.

'Do you know why I am so glad,' she said, 'so glad to look at you? – why I like you so much today?'

'Well?' I asked, and my heart began throbbing.

'I like you because you have not fallen in love with me. You know that some men in your place would have been pestering and worrying me, would have been sighing and miserable, while you are so nice!'

Then she wrung my hand so hard that I almost cried out. She laughed.

'Goodness, what a friend you are!' she began gravely a minute later. 'God sent you to me. What would have happened to me if you had not been with me now? How disinterested you are! How truly you care for me! When I am married we will be great friends, more than brother and sister; I shall care almost as I do for him . . .'

I felt horribly sad at that moment, yet something like laughter was stirring in my soul.

'You are very much upset,' I said; 'you are frightened; you think he won't come.'

'Oh dear!' she answered; 'if I were less happy, I believe I should cry at your lack of faith, at your reproaches. However, you have made me think and have given me a lot to think about; but I shall think later, and now I will own that you are right. Yes, I am somehow not myself; I am all suspense, and feel everything as it were too lightly. But hush! that's enough about feelings . . .'

At that moment we heard footsteps, and in the darkness we saw a figure coming towards us. We both started; she almost cried out; I dropped her hand and made a movement as though to walk away. But we were mistaken, it was not he.

'What are you afraid of? Why did you let go of my hand?' she said, giving it to me again. 'Come, what is it? We will meet him together; I want him to see how fond we are of each other.'

'How fond we are of each other!' I cried. ('Oh, Nastenka, Nastenka,' I thought, 'how much you have told me in that saying! Such fondness at *certain* moments makes the heart cold and the soul heavy. Your hand is cold, mine burns like fire. How blind you are, Nastenka! . . . Oh, how unbearable a happy person is sometimes! But I could not be angry with you!')

At last my heart was too full.

'Listen, Nastenka!' I cried. 'Do you know how it has been with me all day?'

'Why, how, how? Tell me quickly! Why have you said nothing all this time?'

'To begin with, Nastenka, when I had carried out all your commissions, given the letter, gone to see your good friends, then . . . then I went home and went to bed.'

'Is that all?' she interrupted, laughing.

'Yes, almost all,' I answered restraining myself, for foolish tears were already starting into my eyes. 'I woke an hour before our appointment, and yet, as it were, I had not been asleep. I don't know what happened to me. I came to tell you all about it, feeling as though time were standing still, feeling as though one sensation, one feeling must remain with me from that time for ever; feeling as though one minute must go on for all eternity, and as though all life had come to a standstill for me . . . When I woke up it seemed as though some musical motif long familiar, heard somewhere in the past, forgotten and voluptuously sweet, had come back to me now. It seemed to me that it had been clamouring at my heart all my life, and only now . . .'

'Oh my goodness, my goodness,' Nastenka interrupted, 'what does all that mean? I don't understand a word.'

'Ah, Nastenka, I wanted somehow to convey to you that strange impression . . .' I began in a plaintive voice, in which there still lay hid a hope, though a very faint one.

'Leave off. Hush!' she said, and in one instant the sly puss had guessed.

Suddenly she became extraordinarily talkative, gay, mischievous; she took my arm, laughed, wanted me to laugh too, and every confused word I uttered evoked from her prolonged ringing laughter . . . I began to feel angry, she had suddenly begun flirting.

'Do you know,' she began, 'I feel a little vexed that you are not in love with me? There's no understanding human nature! But all the same, Mr Unapproachable, you cannot blame me for being so simple; I tell you everything, everything, whatever foolish thought comes into my head.'

'Listen! That's eleven, I believe,' I said as the slow chime of a bell rang out from a distant tower. She suddenly stopped, left off laughing and began to count.

'Yes, it's eleven,' she said at last in a timid, uncertain voice.

I regretted at once that I had frightened her, making her count the strokes, and I cursed myself for my spiteful impulse; I felt sorry for her, and did not know how to atone for what I had done.

I began comforting her, seeking for reasons for his not coming, advancing various arguments, proofs. No one could have been easier to deceive than she was at that moment; and, indeed, anyone at such a moment listens gladly to any consolation, whatever it may be, and is overjoyed if a shadow of excuse can be found.

'And indeed it's an absurd thing,' I began, warming to my task and admiring the extraordinary clearness of my argument, 'why, he could not have come; you have muddled and confused me, Nastenka, so that I too, have lost count of the time . . . Only think: he can scarcely have received the letter; suppose he is not able to come, suppose he is going to answer the letter, could not come before tomorrow. I will go for it as soon as it's light tomorrow and let you know at once. Consider, there are thousands of possibilities; perhaps he was not at home when the letter came, and may not have read it even now! Anything may happen, you know.'

'Yes, yes!' said Nastenka. 'I did not think of that. Of course anything may happen?' she went on in a tone that offered no opposition, though some other far-away thought could be heard like a vexatious discord in it. 'I tell you what you must do,' she said, 'you go as early as possible tomorrow morning, and if you get anything let me know at once. You know where I live, don't you?'

And she began repeating her address to me.

Then she suddenly became so tender, so solicitous with me. She seemed to listen attentively to what I told her; but when I asked her some question she was silent, was confused, and turned her head away. I looked into her eyes – yes, she was crying.

'How can you? How can you? Oh, what a baby you are! what childishness! . . . Come, come!'

She tried to smile, to calm herself, but her chin was quivering and her bosom was still heaving.

'I was thinking about you,' she said after a minute's silence. 'You are so kind that I should be a stone if I did not feel it. Do you know what has occurred to me now? I was comparing you two. Why isn't he you? Why isn't he like you? He is not as good as you, though I love him more than you.'

I made no answer. She seemed to expect me to say something.

'Of course, it may be that I don't understand him fully yet. You know I was always as it were afraid of him; he was always so grave, as it were so proud. Of course I know it's only that he seems like that, I know there is more tenderness in his heart than in mine . . . I remember how he looked at me when I went in to him – do you remember? – with my bundle; but yet I respect him too much, and doesn't that show that we are not equals?'

'No, Nastenka, no,' I answered, 'it shows that you love him more than anything in the world, and far more than yourself.'

'Yes, supposing that is so,' answered Nastenka naïvely. 'But do you know what strikes me now? Only I am not talking about him now, but speaking generally; all this came into my mind some time ago. Tell me, how is it that we can't all be like brothers together? Why is it that even the best of men always seem to hide something from other people and to keep something back? Why not say straight out what is in one's heart, when one knows that one is not speaking idly? As it is everyone seems harsher than he really is, as though all were afraid of doing injustice to their feelings, by being too quick to express them.'

'Oh, Nastenka, what you say is true; but there are many reasons for that,' I broke in, suppressing my own feelings at that moment more than ever.

'No, no!' she answered with deep feeling. 'Here you, for instance, are not like other people! I really don't know how to tell you what I feel; but it seems to me that you, for instance . . . at the present moment . . . it seems to me that you are sacrificing something for me,' she added timidly, with a fleeting glance at me. 'Forgive me for saying so, I am a simple girl, you know. I have seen very little of life, and I really sometimes don't know how to say things,' she added in a voice that quivered with some hidden feeling, while she tried to smile; 'but I only wanted to tell you that I am grateful, that I feel it all too . . . Oh, may God give you happiness for it! What you told me about your dreamer is quite untrue now – that is, I mean, it's not true of you. You are recovering, you are quite a different man from what you described. If you ever fall in love with someone, God give you happiness with her! I won't wish anything for her, for she will be happy with you. I know, I am a woman myself, so you must believe me when I tell you so.'

She ceased speaking, and pressed my hand warmly. I too could not speak without emotion. Some minutes passed.

'Yes, it's clear he won't come tonight,' she said at last raising her head. 'It's late.'

'He will come tomorrow,' I said in the most firm and convincing tone.

'Yes,' she added with no sign of her former depression. 'I see for myself now that he could not come till tomorrow. Well, goodbye, till tomorrow. If it rains perhaps I shall not come. But the day after tomorrow, I shall come. I shall come for certain, whatever happens; be sure to be here, I want to see you, I will tell you everything.'

And then when we parted she gave me her hand and said, looking at me candidly: 'We shall always be together, shan't we?'

Oh, Nastenka, Nastenka! If only you knew how lonely I am now!

As soon as it struck nine o'clock I could not stay indoors, but put on my things, and went out in spite of the weather. I was there, sitting on our seat. I went to her street, but I felt ashamed, and turned back without looking at their windows, when I was two steps from her door. I went home more depressed than I had ever been before. What a damp, dreary day! If it had been fine I should have walked about all night . . .

But tomorrow, tomorrow! Tomorrow she will tell me everything. The letter has not come today, however. But that was to be expected. They are together by now . . .

Fourth Night

MY God, how it has all ended! What it has all ended in! I arrived at nine o'clock. She was already there. I noticed her a good way off; she was standing as she had been that first time, with her elbows on the railing, and she did not hear me coming up to her.

'Nastenka!' I called to her, suppressing my agitation with an effort.

She turned to me quickly.

'Well?' she said. 'Well? Make haste!'

I looked at her in perplexity.

'Well, where is the letter? Have you brought the letter?' she repeated, clutching at the railing.

'No, there is no letter,' I said at last. 'Hasn't he been to you yet?' She turned fearfully pale and looked at me for a long time without moving. I had shattered her last hope.

'Well, God be with him,' she said at last in a breaking voice; 'God be with him if he leaves me like that.'

She dropped her eyes, then tried to look at me and could not. For several minutes she was struggling with her emotion. All at once she turned away, leaning her elbows against the railing and burst into tears.

'Oh don't, don't!' I began; but looking at her I had not the heart to go on, and what was I to say to her?

'Don't try and comfort me,' she said; 'don't talk about him; don't tell me that he will come, that he has not cast me off so cruelly and so inhumanly as he has. What for – what for? Can there have been something in my letter, that unlucky letter?'

At that point sobs stifled her voice; my heart was torn as I looked at her.

'Oh, how inhumanly cruel it is!' she began again. 'And not a line, not a line! He might at least have written that he does not want me, that he rejects me – but not a line for three days! How easy it is for him to wound, to insult a poor, defenceless girl, whose only fault is that she loves him! Oh, what I've suffered during these three days! Oh, dear! When I think that I was the first to go to him, that I humbled myself before him, cried, that I begged of him a little love! . . . and after that! Listen,' she said, turning to me, and her black eyes flashed, 'it isn't so! It can't be so; it isn't natural. Either you are mistaken or I; perhaps he has not received the letter? Perhaps he still knows nothing about it? How could anyone – judge for yourself, tell me, for goodness sake explain it to me, I can't understand it – how could any one behave with such barbarous coarseness as he has behaved to me? Not one word! Why, the lowest creature on earth is treated more compassionately. Perhaps he has heard something, perhaps someone has told him something about me,' she cried, turning to me inquiringly: 'What do you think?'

'Listen, Nastenka, I shall go to him tomorrow in your name.'

'Yes?'

'I will question him about everything; I will tell him everything.'

'Yes, yes?'

'You write a letter. Don't say no, Nastenka, don't say no! I will make him respect your action, he shall hear all about it, and if—'

'No, my friend, no,' she interrupted. 'Enough! Not another word, not another line from me – enough! I don't know him; I don't love him any more. I will . . . forget him.'

She could not go on.

'Calm yourself, calm yourself! Sit here, Nastenka,' I said, making her sit down on the seat.

'I am calm. Don't trouble. It's nothing. It's only tears, they will soon dry. Why, do you imagine I shall do away with myself, that I shall throw myself into the river?'

My heart was full: I tried to speak, but I could not.

'Listen,' she said, taking my hand. 'Tell me: you wouldn't have behaved like this, would you? You would not have abandoned a girl who had come to you of herself, you would not have thrown into her face a shameless taunt at her weak foolish heart? You would have taken care of her? You would have realised that she was alone, that she did not know how to look after herself, that she could not guard herself from loving you, that it was not her fault, not her fault – that she had done nothing . . . Oh dear, oh dear!'

'Nastenka!' I cried at last, unable to control my emotion. 'Nastenka, you torture me! You wound my heart, you are killing me, Nastenka! I cannot be silent! I must speak at last, give utterance to what is surging in my heart!'

As I said this I got up from the seat. She took my hand and looked at me in surprise.

'What is the matter with you?' she said at last.

'Listen,' I said resolutely. 'Listen to me, Nastenka! What I am going to say to you now is all nonsense, all impossible, all stupid! I know that this can never be, but I cannot be silent. For the sake of what you are suffering now, I beg you beforehand to forgive me!'

'What is it? What is it?' she said, drying her tears and looking at me intently, while a strange curiosity gleamed in her astonished eyes. 'What is the matter?'

'It's impossible, but I love you, Nastenka! There it is! Now everything is told,' I said with a wave of my hand. 'Now you will see whether you can go on talking to me as you did just now, whether you can listen to what I am going to say to you . . .'

'Well, what then?' Nastenka interrupted me. 'What of it? I knew you loved me long ago, only I always thought that you simply liked me very much . . . Oh dear, oh dear!'

'At first it was simply liking, Nastenka, but now, now! I am just in the same position as you were when you went to him with your bundle. In a worse position than you, Nastenka, because he cared for no one else as you do.'

'What are you saying to me! I don't understand you in the least. But tell me, what's this for; I don't mean what for, but why are you . . . so suddenly . . . Oh dear, I am talking nonsense! But you . . .'

And Nastenka broke off in confusion. Her cheeks flamed; she dropped her eyes.

'What's to be done, Nastenka, what am I to do? I am to blame. I have abused your . . . But no, no, I am not to blame, Nastenka; I feel that, I know that, because my heart tells me I am right, for I cannot hurt you in any way, I cannot wound you! I was your friend, but I am still your friend, I have betrayed no trust. Here my tears are falling, Nastenka. Let them flow, let them flow – they don't hurt anybody. They will dry, Nastenka.'

'Sit down, sit down,' she said, making me sit down on the seat. 'Oh, my God!'

'No, Nastenka, I won't sit down; I cannot stay here any longer, you cannot see me again; I will tell you everything and go away. I only want to say that you would never have found out that I loved you. I should have kept my secret. I would not have worried you at such a moment with my egoism. No! But I could not resist it now; you spoke of it yourself, it is your fault, your fault and not mine. You cannot drive me away from you . . .'

'No, no, I don't drive you away, no!' said Nastenka, concealing her confusion as best she could, poor child.

'You don't drive me away? No! But I meant to run from you myself. I will go away, but first I will tell you all, for when you were crying here I could not sit unmoved, when you wept, when you were in torture at being – at being – I will speak of it, Nastenka – at being forsaken, at your love being repulsed, I felt that in my heart there was so much love for you, Nastenka, so much love! And it seemed so bitter that I could not help you with my love, that my heart was breaking and I . . . I could not be silent, I had to speak, Nastenka, I had to speak!'

'Yes, yes! tell me, talk to me,' said Nastenka with an indescribable gesture. 'Perhaps you think it strange that I talk to you like this, but . . . speak! I will tell you afterwards! I will tell you everything.'

'You are sorry for me, Nastenka, you are simply sorry for me, my dear little friend! What's done can't be mended. What is said cannot be taken back. Isn't that so? Well, now you know. That's the starting-point. Very well. Now it's all right, only listen. When you were sitting crying I thought to myself (oh, let me tell you what I was thinking!), I thought, that (of course it cannot be, Nastenka), I thought that you . . . I thought that you somehow . . . quite apart from me, had ceased to love him. Then – I thought that yesterday and the day before yesterday, Nastenka – then I would – I certainly would – have succeeded in making you love me; you know, you said yourself, Nastenka, that you almost loved me. Well, what next? Well, that's nearly all I wanted to tell you; all that is left to say is how it would be if you loved me, only that, nothing more! Listen, my friend – for anyway you are my friend – I am, of course, a poor, humble man, of no great consequence; but that's not the point (I don't seem to be able to say what I mean, Nastenka, I am so confused), only I would love you, I would love you so, that even if you still loved him, even if you went on loving the man

I don't know, you would never feel that my love was a burden to you. You would only feel every minute that at your side was beating a grateful, grateful heart, a warm heart ready for your sake . . . Oh Nastenka, Nastenka! What have you done to me?'

'Don't cry; I don't want you to cry,' said Nastenka getting up quickly from the seat. 'Come along, get up, come with me, don't cry, don't cry,' she said, drying her tears with her handkerchief; 'let us go now; maybe I will tell you something . . . If he has forsaken me now, if he has forgotten me, though I still love him (I do not want to deceive you) . . . but listen, answer me. If I were to love you, for instance, that is, if I only . . . Oh my friend, my friend! To think, to think how I wounded you, when I laughed at your love, when I praised you for not falling in love with me. Oh dear! How was it I did not foresee this, how was it I did not foresee this, how could I have been so stupid? But . . . Well, I have made up my mind, I will tell you.'

'Look here, Nastenka, do you know what? I'll go away, that's what I'll do. I am simply tormenting you. Here you are remorseful for having laughed at me, and I won't have you . . . in addition to your sorrow . . . Of course it is my fault, Nastenka, but goodbye!'

'Stay, listen to me: can you wait?'

'What for? How?'

'I love him; but I shall get over it, I must get over it, I cannot fail to get over it; I am getting over it, I feel that . . . Who knows? Perhaps it will all end today, for I hate him, for he has been laughing at me, while you have been weeping here with me, for you have not repulsed me as he has, for you love me while he has never loved me, for in fact, I love you myself . . . Yes, I love you! I love you as you love me; I have told you so before, you heard it yourself – I love you because you are better than he is, because you are nobler than he is, because, because he—'

The poor girl's emotion was so violent that she could not say more; she laid her head upon my shoulder, then upon my bosom, and wept bitterly. I comforted her, I persuaded her, but she could not stop crying; she kept pressing my hand, and saying between her sobs: 'Wait, wait, it will be over in a minute! I want to tell you . . . you mustn't think that these tears – it's nothing, it's weakness, wait till it's over . . .' At last she left off crying, dried her eyes and we walked on again. I wanted to speak, but she still begged me to wait. We were silent . . . At last she plucked up courage and began to speak.

'It's like this,' she began in a weak and quivering voice, in which, however, there was a note that pierced my heart with a sweet pang; 'don't think that I am so light and inconstant, don't think that I can forget and change so quickly. I have loved him for a whole year, and I swear by God that I have never, never, even in thought, been unfaithful to him . . . He has despised me, he has been laughing at me – God forgive him! But he has insulted me and wounded my heart. I . . . I do not love him, for I can only love what is magnanimous, what understands me, what is generous; for I am like that myself and he is not worthy of me – well, that's enough of him. He has done better than if he had deceived my expectations later, and shown me later what he was . . . Well, it's over! But who knows, my dear friend,' she went on pressing my hand, 'who knows, perhaps my whole love was a mistaken feeling, a delusion – perhaps it began in mischief, in nonsense, because I was kept so strictly by Grandmother? Perhaps I ought to love another man, not him, a different man, who would have pity on me and . . . and . . . But don't let us say any more about that,' Nastenka broke off, breathless with emotion, 'I only wanted to tell you . . . I wanted to tell you that if, although I love him (no, did love him), if, in spite of this you still say . . . If you feel that your love is so great that it may at last drive from my heart my old feeling – if you will have pity on me – if you do not want to leave me alone to my fate, without hope, without consolation – if you are ready to love me always as you do now – I swear to you that gratitude . . . that my love will be at last worthy of your love . . . Will you take my hand?'

'Nastenka!' I cried, breathless with sobs. 'Nastenka, oh Nastenka!'

'Enough, enough! Well, now it's quite enough,' she said, hardly able to control herself. 'Well, now all has been said, hasn't it? Hasn't it? You are happy – I am happy too. Not another word about it, wait; spare me . . . talk of something else, for God's sake.'

'Yes, Nastenka, yes! Enough about that, now I am happy. I – Yes, Nastenka, yes, let us talk of other things, let us make haste and talk. Yes! I am ready.'

And we did not know what to say: we laughed, we wept, we said thousands of things meaningless and incoherent; at one moment we walked along the pavement, then suddenly turned back and crossed the road; then we stopped and went back again to the embankment; we were like children.

'I am living alone now, Nastenka,' I began, 'but tomorrow! Of course you know, Nastenka, I am poor, I have only got twelve hundred roubles, but that doesn't matter.'

'Of course not, and Granny has her pension, so she will be no burden. We must take Granny.'

'Of course we must take Granny. But there's Matrona.'

'Yes, and we've got Fekla too!'

'Matrona is a good women, but she has one fault: she has no imagination, Nastenka, absolutely none; but that doesn't matter.'

'That's all right – they can live together; only you must move to us tomorrow.'

'To you? How so? All right, I am ready.'

'Yes, hire a room from us. We have a top floor, it's empty. We had an old lady lodging there, but she has gone away; and I know Granny would like to have a young man. I said to her, "Why a young man?" And she said, "Oh, because I am old; only don't you fancy, Nastenka, that I want him as a husband for you." So I guessed it was with that idea.'

'Oh, Nastenka!'

And we both laughed.

'Come, that's enough, that's enough. But where do you live? I've forgotten.'

'Over that way, near X bridge, Barannikov's Buildings.'

'It's that big house?'

'Yes, that big house.'

'Oh, I know, a nice house; only you know you had better give it up and come to us as soon as possible.'

'Tomorrow, Nastenka, tomorrow; I owe a little for my rent there but that doesn't matter. I shall soon get my salary.'

'And do you know I will perhaps give lessons; I will learn something myself and then give lessons.'

'Capital! And I shall soon get a bonus.'

'So by tomorrow you will be my lodger.'

'And we will go to *The Barber of Seville*, for they are soon going to give it again.'

'Yes, we'll go,' said Nastenka, 'but better see something else and not *The Barber of Seville*.'

'Very well, something else. Of course that will be better, I did not think—'

As we talked like this we walked along in a sort of delirium, a sort of intoxication, as though we did not know what was happening to us. At one moment we stopped and talked for a long time at the same place; then we went on again, and goodness knows where we went; and again tears and again laughter. All of a sudden Nastenka would want to go home, and I would not dare to detain her but would want to see her to the house; we set off, and in a quarter of an hour found ourselves at the embankment by our seat. Then she would sigh, and tears would come into her eyes again; I would turn chill with dismay . . . But she would press my hand and force me to walk, to talk, to chatter as before.

'It's time I was home at last; I think it must be very late,' Nastenka said at last. 'We must give over being childish.'

'Yes, Nastenka, only I shan't sleep tonight; I am not going home.'

'I don't think I shall sleep either; only see me home.'

'I should think so!'

'Only this time we really must get to the house.'

'We must, we must.'

'Honour bright? For you know one must go home sometime!'

'Honour bright,' I answered laughing.

'Well, come along!'

'Come along! Look at the sky, Nastenka. Look! Tomorrow it will be a lovely day; what a blue sky, what a moon! Look; that yellow cloud is covering it now, look, look! No, it has passed by. Look, look!'

But Nastenka did not look at the cloud; she stood mute as though turned to stone; a minute later she huddled timidly close up to me. Her hand trembled in my hand: I looked at her. She pressed still more closely to me.

At that moment a young man passed by us. He suddenly stopped, looked at us intently, and then again took a few steps on. My heart began throbbing.

'Who is it, Nastenka?' I said in an undertone.

'It's he,' she answered in a whisper, huddling up to me, still more closely, still more tremulously . . . I could hardly stand on my feet.

'Nastenka, Nastenka! It's you!' I heard a voice behind us and at the same moment the young man took several steps towards us.

My God, how she cried out! How she started! How she tore herself out of my arms and rushed to meet him! I stood and looked at them, utterly crushed. But she had hardly given him her hand, had hardly flung herself into his arms, when she turned to me again, was beside me again in a flash, and before I knew where I was she threw both arms round my neck and gave me a warm, tender kiss. Then, without saying a word to me, she rushed back to him again, took his hand, and drew him after her.

I stood a long time looking after them. At last the two vanished from my sight.

Morning

MY night ended with the morning. It was a wet day. The rain was falling and beating disconsolately upon my windowpane; it was dark in the room and grey outside. My head ached and I was giddy; fever was stealing over my limbs.

'There's a letter for you, sir; the postman brought it,' Matrona said, stooping over me.

'A letter? From whom?' I cried, jumping up from my chair.

'I don't know, sir, better look – maybe it is written there whom it is from.'

I broke the seal. It was from her!

'Oh, forgive me, forgive me! I beg you on my knees to forgive me! I deceived you and myself. It was a dream, a mirage . . . My heart aches for you today; forgive me, forgive me!

'Don't blame me, for I have not changed to you in the least. I told you that I would love you, I love you now, I more than love you. Oh, my God! If only I could love you both at once! Oh, if only you were he!'

['Oh, if only he were you,' echoed in my mind. I remembered your words, Nastenka!]

'God knows what I would do for you now! I know that you are sad and dreary. I have wounded you, but you know when one loves a wrong is soon forgotten. And you love me.

'Thank you, yes, thank you for that love! For it will live in my memory like a sweet dream which lingers long after awakening; for I shall remember for ever that instant when you opened your heart to me like a brother and so generously accepted the gift of my shattered heart to care for it, nurse it, and heal it . . . If you forgive me, the memory of you will be exalted by a feeling of everlasting gratitude which will never be effaced from my soul . . . I will treasure that memory: I will be true to it, I will not betray it, I will not betray my heart: it is too constant. It returned so quickly yesterday to him to whom it has always belonged.

'We shall meet, you will come to us, you will not leave us, you will be for ever a friend, a brother to me. And when you see me you will give me your hand . . . yes? You will give it to me, you have forgiven me, haven't you? You love me *as before*?

'Oh, love me, do not forsake me, because I love you so at this moment, because I am worthy of your love, because I will deserve it . . . my dear! Next week I am to be married to him. He has come back in love, he has never forgotten me. You will not be angry at my writing about him. But I want to come and see you with him; you will like him, won't you?

'Forgive me, remember and love your

NASTENKA.'

I read that letter over and over again for a long time; tears gushed to my eyes. At last it fell from my hands and I hid my face.

'Dearie! I say, dearie—' Matrona began.

'What is it, Matrona?'

'I have taken all the cobwebs off the ceiling; you can have a wedding or give a party.'

I looked at Matrona. She was still a hearty, *youngish* old woman, but I don't know why all at once I suddenly pictured her with lustreless eyes, a wrinkled face, bent, decrepit . . . I don't know why I suddenly pictured my room grown old like Matrona. The walls and the floors looked discoloured, everything seemed dingy; the spiders' webs were thicker than ever. I don't know why, but when I looked out of the window it seemed to me that the house opposite had grown old and dingy too, that the stucco on the columns was peeling off and crumbling, that the cornices were cracked and blackened, and that the walls, of a vivid deep yellow, were patchy.

Either the sunbeams suddenly peeping out from the clouds for a moment were hidden again behind a veil of rain, and everything had grown dingy again before my eyes; or perhaps the whole vista of my future flashed before me so sad and forbidding, and I saw myself just as I was now, fifteen years hence, older, in the same room, just as solitary, with the same Matrona grown no cleverer for those fifteen years.

But to imagine that I should bear you a grudge, Nastenka! That I should cast a dark cloud over your serene, untroubled happiness; that by my bitter reproaches I should cause distress to your heart, should poison it with secret remorse and should force it to throb with anguish at the moment of bliss; that I should crush a single one of those tender blossoms which you have twined in your dark tresses when you go with him to the altar . . . Oh never, never! May your sky be clear, may your sweet smile be bright and untroubled, and may you be blessed for that moment of blissful happiness which you gave to another, lonely and grateful heart!

My God, a whole moment of happiness! Is that too little for the whole of a man's life?

A Little Hero

1857

AT THAT TIME I was nearly eleven, I had been sent in July to spent the holiday in a village near Moscow with a relation of mine called T., whose house was full of guests, fifty, or perhaps more . . . I don't remember, I didn't count. The house was full of noise and gaiety. It seemed as though it were a continual holiday, which would never end. It seemed as though our host had taken a vow to squander all his vast fortune as rapidly as possible, and he did indeed succeed, not long ago, in justifying this surmise, that is, in making a clean sweep of it all to the last stick.

Fresh visitors used to drive up every minute. Moscow was close by, in sight, so that those who drove away only made room for others, and the everlasting holiday went on its course. Festivities succeeded one another, and there was no end in sight to the entertainments. There were riding parties about the environs; excursions to the forest or the river; picnics, dinners in the open air; suppers on the great terrace of the house, bordered with three rows of gorgeous flowers that flooded with their fragrance the fresh night air, and illuminated the brilliant lights which made our ladies, who were almost every one of them pretty at all times, seem still more charming, with their faces excited by the impressions of the day, with their sparkling eyes, with their interchange of spritely conversation, their peals of ringing laughter; dancing, music, singing; if the sky were overcast tableaux vivants, charades, proverbs were arranged, private theatricals were got up. There were good talkers, story-tellers, wits.

Certain persons were prominent in the foreground. Of course backbiting and slander ran their course, as without them the world could not get on, and millions of persons would perish of boredom, like flies. But as I was at that time eleven I was absorbed by very different interests, and either failed to observe these people, or if I noticed anything, did not see it all. It was only afterwards that some things came back to my mind. My childish eyes could only see the brilliant side of the picture, and the general animation, splendour, and bustle – all that, seen and heard for the first time, made such an impression upon me that for the first few days, I was completely bewildered and my little head was in a whirl.

I keep speaking of my age, and of course I was a child, nothing more than a child. Many of these lovely ladies petted me without dreaming of considering my age. But strange to say, a sensation which I did not myself understand already had possession of me; something was already whispering in my heart, of which till then it had had no knowledge, no conception, and for some reason it began all at once to burn and throb, and often my face glowed with a sudden flush. At times I felt as it were abashed, and even resentful of the various privileges of my childish years. At other times a sort of wonder overwhelmed me, and I would go off into some corner where I could sit unseen, as though to take breath and remember something – something which it seemed to me I had remembered perfectly till then, and now had suddenly forgotten, something without which I could not show myself anywhere, and could not exist at all.

At last it seemed to me as though I were hiding something from everyone. But nothing would have induced me to speak of it to anyone, because, small boy that I was, I was ready to weep with shame. Soon in the midst of the vortex around me I was conscious of a certain loneliness. There were other children, but all were either much older or younger than I; besides, I was in no mood for them. Of course nothing would have happened to me if I had not been in an exceptional position. In the eyes of those charming ladies I was still the little unformed creature whom they at once liked to pet, and with whom they could play as though he were a little doll. One of them particularly, a fascinating, fair woman, with very thick luxuriant hair, such as I had never seen before and probably shall never see again, seemed to have taken a vow never to leave me in peace. I was confused, while she was amused by the laughter which she continually provoked from all around us by her wild, giddy pranks with me, and this apparently gave her immense enjoyment. At school among her schoolfellows she was probably nicknamed the Tease. She was wonderfully good-looking, and there was something in her beauty which drew one's eyes from the first moment. And certainly she had nothing in common with the ordinary modest little fair girls, white as down and soft as white mice, or pastors' daughters. She was not very tall, and was rather plump, but had soft, delicate, exquisitely cut features. There was something quick as lightning in her face, and indeed she was like fire all over, light, swift, alive. Her big open eyes seemed to flash sparks; they glittered like diamonds, and I would never exchange such blue sparkling eyes for any black ones, were they blacker than any Andalusian orb. And, indeed, my blonde was fully a match for the famous brunette whose praises were sung by a great and well-known poet, who, in a superb poem, vowed by all Castile that he was ready to break his bones to be permitted only to touch the mantle of his divinity with the tip of his finger. Add to that, that *my* charmer was the merriest in the world, the wildest giggler, playful as a child, although she had been married for the last five years. There was a continual laugh upon her lips, fresh as the morning rose that, with the first ray of sunshine, opens its fragrant crimson bud with the cool dewdrops still hanging heavy upon it.

I remember that the day after my arrival private theatricals were being got up. The drawing-room was, as they say, packed to overflowing; there was not a seat empty, and as I was somehow late I had to enjoy the performance standing. But the amusing play attracted me to move forwarder, and forwarder, and unconsciously I made my way to the first row where I stood at last leaning my elbows on the back of an arm-chair, in which a lady was sitting. It was my blonde divinity, but we had not yet made acquaintance. And I gazed as it happened, at her marvellous, fascinating shoulders, plump and white as milk, though it did not matter to me in the least whether I stared at a woman's exquisite shoulders or at the cap with flaming ribbons that covered the grey locks of a venerable lady in the front row. Near my blonde divinity sat a spinster lady not in her first youth, one of those who, as I chanced to observe later, always take refuge in the immediate neighbourhood of young and pretty women, selecting such as are not fond of cold-shouldering young men. But that is not the point, only this lady, noting my fixed gaze, bent down to her neighbour and with a simper whispered something in her ear. The blonde lady turned at once, and I remember that her glowing eyes so flashed upon me in the half-dark, that, not prepared to meet them, I started as though I were scalded. The beauty smiled.

'Do you like what they are acting?' she asked, looking into my face with a shy and mocking expression.

'Yes,' I answered, still gazing at her with a sort of wonder that evidently pleased her.

'But why are you standing? You'll get tired. Can't you find a seat?'

'That's just it, I can't,' I answered, more occupied with my grievance than with the beauty's sparkling eyes, and rejoicing in earnest at having found a kind heart to whom I could confide my troubles. 'I have looked everywhere, but all the chairs are taken,' I added, as though complaining to her that all the chairs were taken.

'Come here,' she said briskly, quick to act on every decision, and, indeed, on every mad idea that flashed on her giddy brain, 'come here, and sit on my knee.'

'On your knee,' I repeated, taken aback. I have mentioned already that I had begun to resent the privileges of childhood and to be ashamed of them in earnest. This lady, as though in derision, had gone ever so much further than the others. Moreover, I had always been a shy and bashful boy, and of late had begun to be particularly shy with women.

'Why yes, on my knee. Why don't you want to sit on my knee?' she persisted, beginning to laugh more and more, so that at last she was simply giggling, goodness knows at what, perhaps at her freak, or perhaps at my confusion. But that was just what she wanted.

I flushed, and in my confusion looked round trying to find where to escape; but seeing my intention she managed to catch hold of my hand to prevent me from going away, and pulling it towards her, suddenly, quite unexpectedly, to my intense astonishment, squeezed it in her mischievous warm fingers, and began to pinch my fingers until they hurt so much that I had to do my very utmost not to cry out, and in my effort to control myself made the most absurd grimaces. I was, besides, moved to the greatest amazement, perplexity, and even horror, at the discovery that there were ladies so absurd and spiteful as to talk nonsense to boys, and even pinch their fingers, for no earthly reason and before everybody. Probably my unhappy face reflected my bewilderment, for the mischievous creature laughed in my face, as though she were crazy, and meantime she was pinching my fingers more and more vigorously. She was highly delighted in playing such a mischievous prank and completely mystifying and embarrassing a poor boy. My position was desperate. In the first place I was hot with shame, because almost everyone near had turned round to look at us, some in wonder, others with laughter, grasping at once that the beauty was up to some mischief. I dreadfully wanted to scream, too, for she was wringing my fingers with positive fury just because I didn't scream; while I, like a Spartan, made up my mind to endure the agony, afraid by crying out of causing a general fuss, which was more than I could face. In utter despair I began at last struggling with her, trying with all my might to pull away my hand, but my persecutor was much stronger than I was. At last I could bear it no longer, and uttered a shriek – that was all she was waiting for! Instantly she let me go, and turned away as though nothing had happened, as though it was not she who had played the trick but someone else, exactly like some schoolboy who, as soon as the master's back is turned, plays some trick on someone near him, pinches some small weak boy, gives him a flip, a kick, or a nudge with his elbows, and instantly turns again, buries himself in his book and begins repeating his lessons, and so makes a fool of the infuriated teacher who flies down like a hawk at the noise.

But luckily for me the general attention was distracted at the moment by the masterly acting of our host, who was playing the chief part in the performance, some comedy of Scribe's. Everyone began to applaud; under cover of the noise I stole away and hurried to the furthest end of the room, from which, concealed behind a column, I looked with horror towards the place where the treacherous beauty was sitting. She was still laughing, holding her handkerchief to her lips. And for a long time she was continually turning round, looking for me in every direction, probably regretting that our silly tussle was so soon over, and hatching some other trick to play on me.

That was the beginning of our acquaintance, and from that evening she would never let me alone. She persecuted me without consideration or conscience, she became my tyrant and tormentor. The whole absurdity of her jokes with me lay in the fact that she pretended to be head over ears in love with me, and teased me before everyone. Of course for a wild creature as I was all this was so tiresome and vexatious that it almost reduced me to tears, and I was sometimes put in such a difficult position that I was on the point of fighting with my treacherous admirer. My naïve confusion, my desperate distress, seemed to egg her on to persecute me more; she knew no mercy, while I did not know how to get away from her. The laughter which always accompanied us, and which she knew so well how to excite, roused her to fresh pranks. But at last people began to think that she went a little too far in her jests. And, indeed, as I remember now, she did take outrageous liberties with a child such as I was.

But that was her character; she was a spoilt child in every respect. I heard afterwards that her husband, a very short, very fat, and very red-faced man, very rich and apparently very much occupied with business, spoilt her more than any one. Always busy and flying round, he could not stay two hours in one place. Every day he drove into Moscow, sometimes twice in the day, and always, as he declared himself, on business. It would be hard to find a livelier and more good-natured face than his facetious but always well-bred countenance. He not only loved his wife to the point of weakness, softness: he simply worshipped her like an idol.

He did not restrain her in anything. She had masses of friends, male and female. In the first place, almost everybody liked her; and secondly, the feather-headed creature was not herself over particular in the choice of her friends, though there was a much more serious foundation to her character than might be supposed from what I have just said about her. But of all her friends she liked best of all one young lady, a distant relation, who was also of our party now. There existed between them a tender and subtle affection, one of those attachments which sometimes spring up at the meeting of two dispositions often the very opposite of each other, of which one is deeper, purer and more austere, while the other, with lofty humility, and generous self-criticism, lovingly gives way to the other, conscious of the friend's superiority and cherishing the friendship as a happiness. Then begins that tender and noble subtlety in the relations of such characters, love and infinite indulgence on the one side, on the other love and respect – a respect approaching awe, approaching anxiety as to the impression made on the friend so highly prized, and an eager, jealous desire to get closer and closer to that friend's heart in every step in life.

These two friends were of the same age, but there was an immense difference between them in everything – in looks, to begin with. Mme M. was also very handsome, but there was something special in her beauty that strikingly distinguished her from the crowd of pretty women; there was something in her face that at once drew the affection of all to her, or rather, which aroused a generous and lofty feeling of kindliness in everyone who met her. There are such happy faces. At her side everyone grew as it were better, freer, more cordial; and yet her big mournful eyes, full of fire and vigour, had a timid and anxious look, as though every minute dreading something antagonistic and menacing, and this strange timidity at times cast so mournful a shade over her mild, gentle features which recalled the serene faces of Italian Madonnas, that looking at her one soon became oneself sad, as though for some trouble of one's own. The pale, thin face, in which, through the irreproachable beauty of the pure, regular lines and the mournful severity of some mute hidden grief, there often flitted the clear looks of early childhood, telling of trustful years and perhaps simple-hearted happiness in the recent past, the gentle but diffident, hesitating smile, all aroused such unaccountable sympathy for her that every heart was unconsciously stirred with a sweet and warm anxiety that powerfully interceded on her behalf even at a distance, and made even strangers feel akin to her. But the lovely creature seemed silent and reserved, though no one could have been more attentive and loving if anyone needed sympathy. There are women who are like sisters of mercy in life. Nothing can be hidden from them, nothing, at least, that is a sore or wound of the heart. Anyone who is suffering may go boldly and hopefully to them without fear of being a burden, for few men know the infinite patience of love, compassion and forgiveness that may be found in some women's hearts. Perfect treasures of sympathy, consolation and hope are laid up in these pure hearts, so often full of suffering of their own – for a heart which loves much grieves much – though their wounds are carefully hidden from the curious eye, for deep sadness is most often mute and concealed. They are not dismayed by the depth of the wound, nor by its foulness and its stench; anyone who comes to them is deserving of help; they are, as it were, born for heroism . . . Mme M. was tall, supple and graceful, but rather thin. All her movements seemed somehow irregular, at times slow, smooth, and even dignified, at times childishly hasty; and yet, at the same time, there was a sort of timid humility in her gestures, something tremulous and defenceless, though it neither desired nor asked for protection.

I have mentioned already that the outrageous teasing of the treacherous fair lady abashed me, flabbergasted me, and wounded me to the quick. But there was for that another secret, strange and foolish reason, which I concealed, at which I shuddered as at a skeleton. At the very thought of it, brooding, utterly alone and overwhelmed, in some dark mysterious corner to which the inquisitorial mocking eye of the blue-eyed rogue could not penetrate, I almost gasped with confusion, shame and fear – in short, I was in love; that perhaps is nonsense, that could hardly have been. But why was it, of all the faces surrounding me, only her face caught my attention? Why was it that it was only she whom I cared to follow with my eyes, though I certainly had no inclination in those days to watch ladies and seek their acquaintance? This happened most frequently on the evenings when we were all kept indoors by bad weather, and when, lonely, hiding in some corner of the big drawing-room, I stared about me aimlessly, unable to find anything to do, for except my teasing ladies, few people ever addressed me, and I was insufferably bored on such evenings. Then I stared at the people round me, listened to the conversation, of which I often did not understand one word, and at that time the mild eyes, the gentle smile and lovely face of Mme M. (for she was the object of my passion) for some reason caught my fascinated attention; and the strange, vague, but unutterably sweet impression remained with me. Often for hours together I could not tear myself away from her; I studied every gesture, every movement she made, listened to every vibration of her rich, silvery, but rather muffled voice; but strange to say, as the result of all my observations, I felt, mixed with a sweet and timid impression, a feeling of intense curiosity. It seemed as though I were on the verge of some mystery.

Nothing distressed me so much as being mocked at in the presence of Mme M. This mockery and humorous persecution, as I thought, humiliated me. And when there was a general burst of laughter at my expense, in which Mme M. sometimes could not help joining, in despair, beside myself with misery, I used to tear myself from my tormentor and run away upstairs, where I remained in solitude the rest of the day, not daring to show my face in the drawing-room. I did not yet, however, understand my shame nor my agitation; the whole process went on in me unconsciously. I had hardly said two words to Mme M., and indeed I should not have dared to. But one evening after an unbearable day I turned back from an expedition with the rest of the company. I was horribly tired and made my way home across the garden. On a seat in a secluded avenue I saw Mme M. She was sitting quite alone, as though she had purposely chosen this solitary spot, her head was drooping and she was mechanically twisting her handkerchief. She was so lost in thought that she did not hear me till I reached her.

Noticing me, she got up quickly from her seat, turned round, and I saw her hurriedly wipe her eyes with her handkerchief. She was crying. Drying her eyes, she smiled to me and walked back with me to the house. I don't remember what we talked about; but she frequently sent me off on one pretext or another, to pick a flower, or to see who was riding in the next avenue. And when I walked away from her, she at once put her handkerchief to her eyes again and wiped away rebellious tears, which would persist in rising again and again from her heart and dropping from her poor eyes. I realised that I was very much in her way when she sent me off so often, and, indeed, she saw herself that I noticed it all, but yet could not control herself, and that made my heart ache more and more for her. I raged at myself at that moment and was almost in despair; cursed myself for my awkwardness and lack of resource, and at the same time did not know how to leave her tactfully, without betraying that I had noticed her distress, but walked beside her in mournful bewilderment, almost in alarm, utterly at a loss and unable to find a single word to keep up our scanty conversation.

This meeting made such an impression on me that I stealthily watched Mme. M. the whole evening with eager curiosity, and never took my eyes off her. But it happened that she twice caught me unawares watching her, and on the second occasion, noticing me, she gave me a smile. It was the only time she smiled that evening. The look of sadness had not left her face, which was now very pale. She spent the whole evening talking to an ill-natured and quarrelsome old lady, whom nobody liked owing to her spying and backbiting habits, but of whom everyone was afraid, and consequently everyone felt obliged to be polite to her . . .

At ten o'clock Mme M.'s husband arrived. Till that moment I watched her very attentively, never taking my eyes off her mournful face; now at the unexpected entrance of her husband I saw her start, and her pale face turned suddenly as white as a handkerchief. It was so noticeable that other people observed it. I overheard a fragmentary conversation from which I guessed that Mme M. was not quite happy; they said her husband was as jealous as an Arab, not from love, but from vanity. He was before all things a European, a modern man, who sampled the newest ideas and prided himself upon them. In appearance he was a tall, dark-haired, particularly thick-set man, with European whiskers, with a self-satisfied, red face, with teeth white as sugar, and with an irreproachably gentlemanly deportment. He was called a *clever man*. Such is the name given in certain circles to a peculiar species of mankind which grows fat at other people's expense, which does absolutely nothing and has no desire to do anything, and whose heart has turned into a lump of fat from everlasting slothfulness and idleness. You continually hear from such men that there is nothing they can do owing to certain very complicated and hostile circumstances, which 'thwart their genius', and that it was 'sad to see the waste of their talents'. This is a fine phrase of theirs, their *mot d'ordre*, their watchword, a phrase which these well-fed, fat friends of ours bring out at every minute, so that it has long ago bored us as an arrant Tartuffism, an empty form of words. Some, however, of these amusing creatures, who cannot succeed in finding anything to do – though, indeed, they never seek it – try to make everyone believe that they have not a lump of fat for a heart, but on the contrary, something *very deep*, though what precisely the greatest surgeon would hardly venture to decide – from civility, of course. These gentlemen make their way in the world through the fact that all their instincts are bent in the direction of coarse sneering, short-sighted censure and immense conceit. Since they have nothing else to do but note and emphasise the mistakes and weaknesses of others, and as they have precisely as much good feeling as an oyster, it it not difficult for them with such powers of self-preservation to get on with people fairly successfully. They pride themselves extremely upon that. They are, for instance, as good as persuaded that almost the whole world owes them something; that it is theirs, like an oyster which they keep in reserve; that all are fools except themselves; that everyone is like an orange or a sponge, which they will squeeze as soon as they want the juice; that they are the masters everywhere, and that all this acceptable state of affairs is solely due to the fact that they are people of so much intellect and character. In their measureless conceit they do not admit any defects in themselves, they are like that species of practical rogues, innate Tartuffes and Falstaffs, who are such thorough rogues that at last they have come to believe that that is as it should be, that is, that they should spend their lives in knavishness; they have so often assured everyone that they are honest men, that they have come to believe that they are honest men, and that their roguery is honesty. They are never capable of inner judgment before their conscience, of generous self-criticism; for some things they are too fat. Their own priceless personality, their Baal and Moloch, their magnificent *ego* is always in their foreground everywhere. All nature, the whole world for them is no more than a splendid mirror created for the little god to admire himself continually in it, and to see no one and nothing behind himself; so it is not strange that he sees everything in the world in such a hideous light. He has a phrase in readiness for everything and – the acme of ingenuity on his part – the most fashionable phrase. It is just these people, indeed, who help to make the fashion, proclaiming at every crossroad an idea in which they scent success. A fine nose is just what they have for sniffing a fashionable phrase and making it their own before other people get hold of it, so that it seems to have originated with them. They have a particular store of phrases for proclaiming their profound sympathy for humanity, for defining what is the most correct and rational form of philanthropy, and continually attacking romanticism, in other words, everything fine and true, each atom of which is more precious than all their mollusc tribe. But they are too coarse to recognise the truth in an indirect, roundabout and unfinished form, and they reject everything that is immature, still fermenting and unstable. The well-nourished man has spent all his life in merry-making, with everything provided, has done nothing himself and does not know how hard every sort of work is, and so woe betide you if you jar upon his fat feelings by any sort of roughness; he'll never forgive you for that, he will always remember it and will gladly avenge it. The long and short of it is, that my hero is neither more nor less than a gigantic, incredibly swollen bag, full of sentences, fashionable phrases, and labels of all sorts and kinds.

M. M., however, had a speciality and was a very remarkable man; he was a wit, good talker and story-teller, and there was always a circle round him in every drawing-room. That evening he was particularly successful in making an impression. He took possession of the conversation; he was in his best form, gay, pleased at something, and he compelled the attention of all; but Mme. M. looked all the time as though she were ill; her face was so sad that I fancied every minute that tears would begin quivering on her long eyelashes. All this, as I have said, impressed me extremely and made me wonder. I went away with a feeling of strange curiosity, and dreamed all night of M. M., though till then I had rarely had dreams.

Next day, early in the morning, I was summoned to a rehearsal of some tableaux vivants in which I had to take part.

The tableaux vivants, theatricals, and afterwards a dance were all fixed for the same evening, five days later – the birthday of our host's younger daughter. To this entertainment, which was almost improvised, another hundred guests were invited from Moscow and from surrounding villas, so that there was a great deal of fuss, bustle and commotion. The rehearsal, or rather review of the costumes, was fixed so early in the morning because our manager, a well-known artist, a friend of our host's, who had consented through affection for him to undertake the arrangement of the tableaux and the training of us for them, was in haste now to get to Moscow to purchase properties and to make final preparations for the fête, as there was no time to lose. I took part in one tableau with Mme M. It was a scene from mediaeval life and was called 'The Lady of the Castle and Her Page'.

I felt unutterably confused on meeting Mme M. at the rehearsal. I kept feeling that she would at once read in my eyes all the reflections, the doubts, the surmises, that had arisen in my mind since the previous day. I fancied, too, that I was, as it were, to blame in regard to her, for having come upon her tears the day before and hindered her grieving, so that she could hardly help looking at me askance, as an unpleasant witness and unforgiven sharer of her secret. But, thank goodness, it went off without any great trouble; I was simply not noticed. I think she had no thoughts to spare for me or for the rehearsal; she was absent-minded, sad and gloomily thoughtful; it was evident that she was worried by some great anxiety. As soon as my part was over I ran away to change my clothes, and ten minutes later came out on the verandah into the garden. Almost at the same time Mme M. came out by another door, and immediately afterwards coming towards us appeared her self-satisfied husband, who was returning from the garden, after just escorting into it quite a crowd of ladies and there handing them over to a competent *cavalieré servente.* The meeting of the husband and wife was evidently unexpected. Mme M., I don't know why, grew suddenly confused, and a faint trace of vexation was betrayed in her impatient movement. The husband, who had been carelessly whistling an air and with an air of profundity stroking his whiskers, now, on meeting his wife, frowned and scrutinised her, as I remember now, with a markedly inquisitorial stare.

'You are going into the garden?' he asked, noticing the parasol and book in her hand.

'No, into the copse,' she said, with a slight flush.

'Alone?'

'With him,' said Mme M., pointing to me. 'I always go a walk alone in the morning,' she added, speaking in an uncertain, hesitating voice, as people do when they tell their first lie.

'H'm . . . and I have just taken the whole party there. They have all met there together in the flower arbour to see N. off. He is going away, you know . . . Something has gone wrong in Odessa. Your cousin' (he meant the fair beauty) 'is laughing and crying at the same time; there is no making her out. She says, though, that you are angry with N. about something and so wouldn't go and see him off. Nonsense, of course?'

'She's laughing,' said Mme M., coming down the verandah steps.

'So this is your daily *cavalieré servente*,' added M. M., with a wry smile, turning his lorgnette upon me.

'Page!' I cried, angered by the lorgnette and the jeer; and laughing straight in his face I jumped down the three steps of the verandah at one bound.

'A pleasant walk,' muttered M. M., and went on his way.

Of course, I immediately joined Mme M. as soon as she indicated me to her husband, and looked as though she had invited me to do so an hour before, and as though I had been accompanying her on her walks every morning for the last month. But I could not make out why she was so confused, so embarrassed, and what was in her mind when she brought herself to have recourse to her little lie? Why had she not simply said that she was going alone? I did not know how to look at her, but overwhelmed with wonder I began by degree very naïvely peeping into her face; but just as an hour before at the rehearsal she did not notice either my looks or any mute question. The same anxiety, only more intense and more distinct, was apparent in her face, in her agitation, in her walk. She was in haste, and walked more and more quickly and kept looking uneasily down every avenue, down every path in the wood that led in the direction of the garden. And I, too, was expecting something.

Suddenly there was the sound of horses' hoofs behind us. It was the whole party of ladies and gentlemen on horseback escorting N., the gentleman who was so suddenly deserting us.

Among the ladies was my fair tormentor, of whom M. M. had told us that she was in tears. But characteristically she was laughing like a child, and was galloping briskly on a splendid bay horse. On reaching us N. took off his hat, but did not stop, nor say one word to Mme M. Soon all the cavalcade disappeared from our sight. I glanced at Mme. M. and almost cried out in wonder; she was standing as white as a handkerchief and big tears were gushing from her eyes. By chance our eyes met: Mme M. suddenly flushed and turned away for an instant, and a distinct look of uneasiness and vexation flitted across her face. I was in the way, worse even than last time, that was clearer than day, but how was I to get away?

And, as though guessing my difficulty, Mme M. opened the book which she had in her hand, and colouring and evidently trying not to look at me she said, as though she had only suddenly realised it:

'Ah! It is the second part. I've made a mistake; please bring me the first.'

I could not but understand. My part was over, and I could not have been more directly dismissed.

I ran off with her book and did not come back. The first part lay undisturbed on the table that morning . . .

But I was not myself; in my heart there was a sort of haunting terror. I did my utmost not to meet Mme M. But I looked with wild curiosity at the self-satisfied person of M. M., as though there must be something special about him now. I don't understand what was the meaning of my absurd curiosity. I only remember that I was strangely perplexed by all that I had chanced to see that morning. But the day was only just beginning and it was fruitful in events for me.

Dinner was very early that day. An expedition to a neighbouring hamlet to see a village festival that was taking place there had been fixed for the evening, and so it was necessary to be in time to get ready. I had been dreaming for the last three days of this excursion, anticipating all sorts of delights. Almost all the company gathered together on the verandah for coffee. I cautiously followed the others and concealed myself behind the third row of chairs. I was attracted by curiosity, and yet I was very anxious not to be seen by Mme M. But as luck would have it I was not far from my fair tormentor. Something miraculous and incredible was happening to her that day; she looked twice as handsome. I don't know how and why this happens, but such miracles are by no means rare with women. There was with us at this moment a new guest, a tall, pale-faced young man, the official admirer of our fair beauty, who had just arrived from Moscow as though on purpose to replace N., of whom rumour said that he was desperately in love with the same lady. As for the newly arrived guest, he had for a long time past been on the same terms as Benedick with Beatrice, in Shakespeare's *Much*

Ado About Nothing. In short, the fair beauty was in her very best form that day. Her chatter and her jests were so full of grace, so trustfully naïve, so innocently careless, she was persuaded of the general enthusiasm with such graceful self-confidence that she really was all the time the centre of peculiar adoration. A throng of surprised and admiring listeners was continually round her, and she had never been so fascinating. Every word she uttered was marvellous and seductive, was caught up and handed round in the circle, and not one word, one jest, one sally was lost. I fancy no one had expected from her such taste, such brilliance, such wit. Her best qualities were, as a rule, buried under the most harum-scarum wilfulness, the most schoolboyish pranks, almost verging on buffoonery; they were rarely noticed, and, when they were, were hardly believed in, so that now her extraordinary brilliancy was accompanied by an eager whisper of amazement among all. There was, however, one peculiar and rather delicate circumstance, judging at least by the part in it played by Mme M.'s husband, which contributed to her success. The madcap ventured – and I must add to the satisfaction of almost everyone or, at any rate, to the satisfaction of all the young people – to make a furious attack upon him, owing to many causes, probably of great consequence in her eyes. She carried on with him a regular cross-fire of witticisms, of mocking and sarcastic sallies, of that most illusive and treacherous kind that, smoothly wrapped up on the surface, hit the mark without giving the victim anything to lay hold of, and exhaust him in fruitless efforts to repel the attack, reducing him to fury and comic despair.

I don't know for certain, but I fancy the whole proceeding was not improvised but premeditated. This desperate duel had begun earlier, at dinner. I call it desperate because M. M. was not quick to surrender. He had to call upon all his presence of mind, all his sharp wit and rare resourcefulness not to be completely covered with ignominy. The conflict was accompanied by the continual and irrepressible laughter of all who witnessed and took part in it. That day was for him very different from the day before. It was noticeable that Mme M. several times did her utmost to stop her indiscreet friend, who was certainly trying to depict the jealous husband in the most grotesque and absurd guise, in the guise of 'a bluebeard' it must be supposed, judging from all probabilities, from what has remained in my memory and finally from the part which I myself was destined to play in the affair.

I was drawn into it in a most absurd manner, quite unexpectedly. And as ill-luck would have it at that moment I was standing where I could be seen, suspecting no evil and actually forgetting the precautions I had so long practised. Suddenly I was brought into the foreground as a sworn foe and natural rival of M. M., as desperately in love with his wife, of which my persecutress vowed and swore that she had proofs, saying that only that morning she had seen in the copse . . .

But before she had time to finish I broke in at the most

desperate minute. That minute was so diabolically calculated, was so treacherously prepared to lead up to its finale, its ludicrous *dénouement*, and was brought out with such killing humour that a perfect outburst of irrepressible mirth saluted this last sally. And though even at the time I guessed that mine was not the most unpleasant part in the performance, yet I was so confused, so irritated and alarmed that, full of misery and despair, gasping with shame and tears, I dashed through two rows of chairs, stepped forward, and addressing my tormentor, cried, in a voice broken with tears and indignation:

'Aren't you ashamed . . . aloud . . . before all the ladies . . . to tell such a wicked . . . lie? . . . Like a small child . . . before all these men . . . What will they say? . . . A big girl like you . . . and married! . . .'

But I could not go on, there was a deafening roar of applause. My outburst created a perfect furore. My naïve gesture, my tears, and especially the fact that I seemed to be defending M. M., all this provoked such fiendish laughter, that even now I cannot help laughing at the mere recollection of it. I was overcome with confusion, senseless with horror and, burning with shame, hiding my face in my hands rushed away, knocked a tray out of the hands of a footman who was coming in at the door, and flew upstairs to my own room. I pulled out the key, which was on the outside of the door, and locked myself in. I did well, for there was a hue and cry after me. Before a minute had passed my door was besieged by a mob of the prettiest ladies. I heard their ringing laughter, their incessant chatter, their trilling voices; they were all twittering at once, like swallows. All of them, every one of them, begged and besought me to open the door, if only for a moment; swore that no harm should come to me, only that they wanted to smother me with kisses. But . . . what could be more horrible than this novel threat? I simply burned with shame the other side of the door, hiding my face in the pillows and did not open, did not even respond. The ladies kept up their knocking for a long time, but I was deaf and obdurate as only a boy of eleven could be.

But what could I do now? Everything was laid bare, everything had been exposed, everything I had so jealously guarded and concealed! . . . Everlasting disgrace and shame had fallen on me! But it is true that I could not myself have said why I was frightened and what I wanted to hide; yet I was frightened of something and had trembled like a leaf at the thought of *that something's* being discovered. Only till that minute I had not known what it was: whether it was good or bad, splendid or shameful, praiseworthy or reprehensible? Now in my distress, in the misery that had been forced upon me, I learned that it was *absurd* and *shameful.* Instinctively I felt at the same time that this verdict was false, inhuman, and coarse; but I was crushed, annihilated; consciousness seemed checked in me and thrown into confusion; I could not stand up against that verdict, nor criticise it properly. I was befogged; I only felt that my heart had been inhumanly and shamelessly wounded, and was brimming over with impotent tears. I was irritated; but I was boiling with indignation and hate such as I had never felt before, for it was the first time in my life that I had known real sorrow, insult, and injury – and it was truly that, without any exaggeration. The first untried, unformed feeling had been so coarsely handled in me, a child. The first fragrant, virginal modesty had been so soon exposed and insulted; and the first and perhaps very real and aesthetic impression had been so outraged. Of course there was much my persecutors did not know and did not divine in my sufferings. One circumstance, which I had not succeeded in analysing till then, of which I had been as it were afraid, partly entered into it. I went on lying on my bed in despair and misery, hiding my face in my pillow, and I was alternately feverish and shivery. I was tormented by two questions: first, what had the wretched fair beauty seen, and, in fact, what could she have seen that morning in the copse between Mme M. and me? And secondly, how could I now look Mme M. in the face without dying on the spot of shame and despair?

An extraordinary noise in the yard roused me at last from the state of semi-consciousness into which I had fallen. I got up and went to the window. The whole yard was packed with carriages, saddle-horses, and bustling servants. It seemed that they were all setting off; some of the gentlemen had already mounted their horses, others were taking their places in the carriages . . . Then I remembered the expedition to the village fête, and little by little an uneasiness came over me; I began anxiously looking for my pony in the yard; but there was no pony there, so they must have forgotten me. I could not restrain myself, and rushed headlong downstairs, thinking no more of unpleasant meetings or my recent ignominy . . .

Terrible news awaited me. There was neither a horse nor seat in any of the carriages to spare for me; everything had been arranged, all the seats were taken, and I was forced to give place to others. Overwhelmed by this fresh blow, I stood on the steps and looked mournfully at the long rows of coaches, carriages, and chaises, in which there was not the tiniest corner left for me, and at the smartly dressed ladies, whose horses were restlessly curveting.

One of the gentlemen was late. They were only waiting for his arrival to set off. His horse was standing at the door, champing the bit, pawing the earth with his hoofs, and at every moment starting and rearing. Two stable-boys were carefully holding him by the bridle, and everyone else apprehensively stood at a respectful distance from him.

A most vexatious circumstance had occurred, which prevented my going. In addition to the fact that new visitors had arrived, filling up all the seats, two of the horses had fallen ill, one of them being my pony. But I was not the only person to suffer: it appeared that there was no horse for our new visitor, the pale-faced young man of whom I have spoken already. To get over this difficulty our host had been obliged to have recourse to the extreme step of offering his fiery unbroken stallion, adding, to satisfy his conscience, that it was impossible to ride him, and that they had long intended to sell the beast for its vicious character, if only a purchaser could be found.

But, in spite of his warning, the visitor declared that he was a good horseman, and in any case ready to mount anything rather than not go. Our host said no more, but now I fancied that a sly and ambiguous smile was straying on his lips. He waited for the gentleman who had spoken so well of his own horsemanship, and stood, without mounting his horse, impatiently rubbing his hands and continually glancing towards the door; some similar feeling seemed shared by two stable-boys, who were holding the stallion, almost breathless with pride at seeing themselves before the whole company in charge of a horse which might any minute kill a man for no reason whatever. Something akin to their master's sly smile gleamed, too, in their eyes, which were round with expectation, and fixed upon the door from which the bold visitor was to appear. The horse himself, too, behaved as though he were in league with our host and the stable-boys. He bore himself proudly and haughtily, as though he felt that he was being watched by several dozen curious eyes and were glorying in his evil reputation exactly as some incorrigible rogue might glory in his criminal exploits. He seemed to be defying the bold man who would venture to curb his independence.

That bold man did at last make his appearance. Conscience-stricken at having kept everyone waiting, hurriedly drawing on his gloves, he came forward without looking at anything, ran down the steps, and only raised his eyes as he stretched out his hand to seize the mane of the waiting horse. But he was at once disconcerted by his frantic rearing and a warning scream from the frightened spectators. The young man stepped back and looked in perplexity at the vicious horse, which was quivering all over, snorting with anger, and rolling his bloodshot eyes ferociously, continually rearing on his hind legs and flinging up his forelegs as though he meant to bolt into the air and carry the two stable-boys with him. For a minute the young man stood completely nonplussed; then, flushing slightly with some embarrassment, he raised his eyes and looked at the frightened ladies.

'A very fine horse!' he said, as though to himself, 'and to my thinking it ought to be a great pleasure to ride him; but . . . but do you know, I think I won't go?' he concluded, turning to our host with the broad, good-natured smile which so suited his kind and clever face.

'Yet I consider you are an excellent horseman, I assure you,' answered the owner of the unapproachable horse, delighted, and he warmly and even gratefully pressed the young man's hand, 'just because from the first moment you saw the sort of brute you had to deal with,' he added with dignity. 'Would you believe me, though I have served twenty-three years in the hussars, yet I've had the pleasure of being laid on the ground three times, thanks to that beast, that is, as often as I mounted the useless animal. Tancred, my boy, there's no one here fit for you! Your rider, it seems, must be some Ilya Muromets, and he must be sitting quiet now in the village of Kapatcharovo, waiting for your teeth to fall out. Come, take him away, he has frightened people enough. It was waste of time to bring him out,' he cried, rubbing his hands complacently.

It must be observed that Tancred was no sort of use to his master and simply ate corn for nothing; moreover, the old hussar had lost his reputation for a knowledge of horseflesh by paying a fabulous sum for the worthless beast, which he had purchased only for his beauty . . . yet he was delighted now that Tancred had kept up his reputation, had disposed of another rider, and so had drawn closer on himself fresh senseless laurels.

'So you are not going?' cried the blonde beauty, who was particularly anxious that her *cavalieré servente* should be in attendance on this occasion. 'Surely you are not frightened?'

'Upon my word I am,' answered the young man.

'Are you in earnest?'

'Why, do you want me to break my neck?'

'Then make haste and get on my horse; don't be afraid, it is very quiet. We won't delay them, they can change the saddles in a minute! I'll try to take yours. Surely Tancred can't always be so unruly.'

No sooner said than done, the madcap leapt out of the saddle and was standing before us as she finished the last sentence.

'You don't know Tancred, if you think he will allow your

wretched side-saddle to be put on him! Besides, I would not let your break your neck, it would be a pity!' said our host, at that moment of inward gratification affecting, as his habit was, a studied brusqueness and even coarseness of speech which he thought in keeping with a jolly good fellow and an old soldier, and which he imagined to be particularly attractive to the ladies. This was one of his favourite fancies, his favourite whim, with which we were all familiar.

'Well, cry-baby, wouldn't you like to have a try? You wanted so much to go?' said the valiant horsewoman, noticing me and pointing tauntingly at Tancred, because I had been so imprudent as to catch her eye, and she would not let me go without a biting word, that she might not have dismounted from her horse absolutely for nothing.

'I expect you are not such a— We all know you are a hero and would be ashamed to be afraid; especially when you will be looked at, you fine page,' she added, with a fleeting glance at Mme M., whose carriage was the nearest to the entrance.

A rush of hatred and vengeance had flooded my heart, when the fair Amazon had approached us with the intention of mounting Tancred . . . But I cannot describe what I felt at this unexpected challenge from the madcap. Everything was dark before my eyes when I saw her glance at Mme M. For an instant an idea flashed through my mind . . . but it was only a moment, less than a moment, like a flash of gunpowder; perhaps it was the last straw, and I suddenly now was moved to rage as my spirit rose, so that I longed to put all my enemies to utter confusion, and to revenge myself on all of them and before everyone, by showing the sort of person I was. Or whether by some miracle, some prompting from mediaeval history, of which I had known nothing till then, sent whirling through my giddy brain, images of tournaments, paladins, heroes, lovely ladies, the clash of swords, shouts and the applause of the crowd, and amidst those shouts the timid cry of a frightened heart, which moves the proud soul more sweetly than victory and fame – I don't know whether all this romantic nonsense was in my head at the time, or whether, more likely, only the first dawning of the inevitable nonsense that was in store for me in the future, anyway, I felt that my hour had come. My heart leapt and shuddered, and I don't remember how, at one bound, I was down the steps and beside Tancred.

'You think I am afraid?' I cried, boldly and proudly, in such a fever that I could hardly see, breathless with excitement, and flushing till the tears scalded my cheeks. 'Well, you shall see!' And clutching at Tancred's mane I put my foot in the stirrup before they had time to make a movement to stop me; but at that instant Tancred reared, jerked his head, and with a mighty bound forward wrenched himself out of the hands of the petrified stable-boys, and dashed off like a hurricane, while everyone cried out in horror.

Goodness knows how I got my other leg over the horse while it was in full gallop; I can't imagine, either, how I did not lose hold of the reins. Tancred bore me beyond the trellis gate, turned sharply to the right and flew along beside the fence regardless of the road. Only at that moment I heard behind me a shout from fifty voices, and that shout was echoed in my swooning heart with such a feeling of pride and pleasure that I shall never forget that mad moment of my boyhood. All the blood rushed to my head, bewildering me and overpowering my fears. I was beside myself. There certainly was, as I remember it now, something of the knight-errant about the exploit.

My knightly exploits, however, were all over in an instant or it would have gone badly with the knight. And, indeed, I do not know how I escaped as it was. I did know how to ride, I had been taught. But my pony was more like a sheep than a riding horse. No doubt I should have been thrown off Tancred if he had had time to throw me, but after galloping fifty paces he suddenly took fright at a huge stone which lay across the road and bolted back. He turned sharply, galloping at full speed, so that it is a puzzle to me even now that I was not sent spinning out of the saddle and flying like a ball for twenty feet, that I was not dashed to pieces, and that Tancred did not dislocate his leg by such a sudden turn. He rushed back to the gate, tossing his head furiously, bounding from side to side as though drunk with rage, flinging his legs at random in the air, and at every leap trying to shake me off his back as though a tiger had leapt on him and were thrusting its teeth and claws into his back.

In another instant I should have flown off; I was falling; but several gentleman flew to my rescue. Two of them intercepted the way into the open country, two others galloped up, closing in upon Tancred so that their horses' sides almost crushed my legs, and both of them caught him by the bridle. A few seconds later we were back at the steps.

They lifted me down from the horse, pale and scarcely breathing. I was shaking like a blade of grass in the wind; it was the same with Tancred, who was standing, his hoofs as it were thrust into the earth and his whole body thrown back, puffing his fiery breath from red and streaming nostrils, twitching and quivering all over, seeming overwhelmed with wounded pride and anger at a child's being so bold with impunity. All around me I heard cries of bewilderment, surprise, and alarm.

At that moment my straying eyes caught those of Mme M., who looked pale and agitated, and – I can never forget that moment – in one instant my face was flooded with colour, glowed and burned like fire; I don't know what happened to me, but confused and frightened by my own feelings I timidly dropped my eyes to the ground. But my glance was noticed, it was caught, it was stolen from me. All eyes turned on Mme M., and finding herself unawares the centre of attention, she, too, flushed like a child from some naïve and involuntary feeling and made an unsuccessful effort to cover her confusion by laughing . . .

All this, of course, was very absurd-looking from outside, but at that moment an extremely naïve and unexpected circumstance saved me from being laughed at by everyone, and gave a special colour to the whole adventure. The lovely persecutor who was the instigator of the whole escapade, and who till then had been my irreconcileable foe, suddenly rushed up to embrace and kiss me. She had hardly been able to believe her eyes when she saw me dare to accept her challenge, and pick up the gauntlet she had flung at me by glancing at Mme M. She had almost died of terror and self-reproach when I had flown off on Tancred; now, when it was all over, and particularly when she caught the glance at Mme M., my confusion and my sudden flush of colour, when the romantic strain in her frivolous little head had given a new secret, unspoken significance to the moment – she was moved to such enthusiasm over my 'knightliness', that touched, joyful and proud of me, she rushed up and pressed me to her bosom. She lifted the most naïve, stern-looking little face, on which there quivered and gleamed two little crystal tears, and gazing at the crowd that thronged about her said in a grave, earnest voice, such as they had never heard her use before, pointing to me: *'Mais c'est très sérieux, messieurs, ne riez pas!'* She did not notice that all were standing, as though fascinated, admiring her bright enthusiasm. Her swift, unexpected action, her earnest little face, the simple-hearted naïveté, the unexpected feeling betrayed by the tears that welled in her invariably laughter-loving eyes, were such a surprise that everyone stood before her as though electrified by her expression, her rapid, fiery words and gestures. It seemed as though no one could take his eyes off her for fear of missing that rare moment in her enthusiastic face. Even our host flushed crimson as a tulip, and people declared that they heard him confess afterwards that 'to his shame' he had been in love for a whole minute with his charming guest. Well, of course, after this I was a knight, a hero.

'De Lorge! Toggenburg!' was heard in the crowd.

There was a sound of applause.

'Hurrah for the rising generation!' added the host.

'But he is coming with us, he certainly must come with us,' said the beauty; 'we will find him a place, we must find him a place. He shall sit beside me, on my knee . . . but no, no! That's a mistake! . . .' she corrected herself, laughing, unable to restrain her mirth at our first encounter. But as she laughed she stroked my hand tenderly, doing all she could to soften me, that I might not be offended.

'Of course, of course,' several voices chimed in; 'he must go, he has won his place.'

The matter was settled in a trice. The same old maid who had brought about my acquaintance with the blonde beauty was at once besieged with entreaties from all the younger people to remain at home and let me have her seat. She was forced to consent, to her intense vexation, with a smile and a stealthy hiss of anger. Her protectress, who was her usual refuge, my former foe and new friend, called to her as she galloped off on her spirited horse, laughing like a child, that she envied her and would have been glad to stay at home herself, for it was just going to rain and we should all get soaked.

And she was right in predicting rain. A regular downpour came on within an hour and the expedition was done for. We had to take shelter for some hours in the huts of the village, and had to return home between nine and ten in the evening in the damp mist that followed the rain. I began to be a little feverish. At the minute when I was starting, Mme M. came up to me and expressed surprise that my neck was uncovered and that I had nothing on over my jacket. I answered that I had not had time to get my coat. She took out a pin and pinned up the turned down collar of my shirt, took off her own neck a crimson gauze kerchief, and put it round my neck that I might not get a sore throat. She did this so hurriedly that I had not time even to thank her.

But when we got home I found her in the little drawing-room with the blonde beauty and the pale-faced young man who had gained glory for horsemanship that day by refusing to ride Tancred. I went up to thank her and give back the scarf. But now, after all my adventures, I felt somehow ashamed. I wanted to make haste and get upstairs, there at my leisure to reflect and consider. I was brimming over with impressions. As I gave back the kerchief I blushed up to my ears, as usual.

'I bet he would like to keep the kerchief,' said the young man laughing. 'One can see that he is sorry to part with your scarf.'

'That's it, that's it!' the fair lady put in. 'What a boy! Oh!' she said, shaking her head with obvious vexation, but she stopped in time at a grave glance from Mme M., who did not want to carry the jest too far.

I made haste to get away.

'Well, you are a boy,' said the madcap, overtaking me in the next room and affectionately taking me by both hands, 'why, you should have simply not returned the kerchief if you wanted so much to have it. You should have said you put it down somewhere, and that would have been the end of it. What a simpleton! Couldn't even do that! What a funny boy!'

And she tapped me on the chin with her finger, laughing at my having flushed as red as a poppy.

'I am your friend now, you know; am I not? Our enmity is over, isn't it? Yes or no?'

I laughed and pressed her fingers without a word.

'Oh, why are you so . . . why are you so pale and shivering? Have you caught a chill?'

'Yes, I don't feel well.'

'Ah, poor fellow? That's the result of over-excitement. Do you know what? You had better go to bed without sitting up for supper, and you will be all right in the morning. Come along.'

She took me upstairs, and there was no end to the care she lavished on me. Leaving me to undress she ran downstairs, got me some tea, and brought it up herself when I was in bed. She brought me up a warm quilt as well. I was much impressed and touched by all the care and attention lavished on me; or perhaps I was affected by the whole day, the expedition and feverishness. As I said good night to her I hugged her warmly, as though she were my dearest and nearest friend, and in my exhausted state all the emotions of the day came back to me in a rush; I almost shed tears as I nestled to her bosom. She noticed my overwrought condition, and I believe my madcap herself was a little touched.

'You are a very good boy,' she said, looking at me with gentle eyes, 'please don't be angry with me. You won't, will you?'

In fact, we became the warmest and truest of friends.

It was rather early when I woke up, but the sun was already flooding the whole room with brilliant light. I jumped out of bed feeling perfectly well and strong, as though I had had no fever the day before; indeed, I felt now unutterably joyful. I recalled the previous day and felt that I would have given any happiness if I could at that minute have embraced my new friend, the fair-haired beauty, again, as I had the night before; but it was very early and everyone was still asleep. Hurriedly dressing I went out into the garden and from there into the copse. I made my way where the leaves were thickest, where the fragrance of the trees was more resinous, and where the sun peeped in most gaily, rejoicing that it could penetrate the dense darkness of the foliage. It was a lovely morning.

Going on further and further, before I was aware of it I had reached the further end of the copse and came out on the river Moskva. It flowed at the bottom of the hill two hundred paces below. On the opposite bank of the river they were mowing. I watched whole rows of sharp scythes gleam all together in the sunlight at every swing of the mower and then vanish again like little fiery snakes going into hiding; I watched the cut grass flying on one side in dense rich swathes and being laid in long straight lines. I don't know how long I spent in contemplation. At last I was roused from my reverie by hearing a horse snorting and impatiently pawing the ground twenty paces from me, in the track which ran from the high road to the manor house. I don't know whether I heard this horse as soon as the rider rode up and stopped there, or whether the sound had long been in my ears without rousing me from my dreaming. Moved by curiosity I went into the copse, and before I had gone many steps I caught the sound of voices speaking rapidly, though in subdued tones. I went up closer, carefully parting the branches of the bushes that edged the path, and at once sprang back in amazement. I caught a glimpse of a familiar white dress and a soft feminine voice resounded like music in my heart. It was Mme M. She was standing beside a man on horseback who, stooping down from the saddle, was hurriedly talking to her, and to my amazement I recognised him as N., the young man who had gone away the morning before and over whose departure M. M. had been so busy. But people had said at the time that he was going far away to somewhere in the South of Russia, and so I was very much surprised at seeing him with us again so early, and alone with Mme M.

She was moved and agitated as I had never seen her before, and tears were glistening on her cheeks. The young man was holding her hand and stooping down to kiss it. I had come upon them at the moment of parting. They seemed to be in haste. At last he took out of his pocket a sealed envelope, gave it to Mme M., put one arm round her, still not dismounting, and gave her a long, fervent kiss. A minute later he lashed his horse and flew past me like an arrow. Mme M. looked after him for some moments, then pensively and disconsolately turned homewards. But after going a few steps along the track she seemed suddenly to recollect herself, hurriedly parted the bushes and walked on through the copse.

I followed her, surprised and perplexed by all that I had seen. My heart was beating violently, as though from terror. I was, as it were, benumbed and befogged; my ideas were shattered and turned upside down; but I remember I was for some reason, very sad. I got glimpses from time to time through the green foliage of her white dress before me: I followed her mechanically, never losing sight of her, though I trembled at the thought that she might notice me. At last she came out on the little path that led to the house. After waiting half a minute I, too, emerged from the bushes; but what was my amazement when I saw lying on the red sand of the path a sealed packet, which I recognised, from the first glance, as the one that had been given to Mme M. ten minutes before.

I picked it up. On both sides the paper was blank, there was no address on it. The envelope was not large, but it was fat and heavy, as though there were three or more sheets of notepaper in it.

What was the meaning of this envelope? No doubt it would explain the whole mystery. Perhaps in it there was said all that N. had scarcely hoped to express in their brief, hurried interview. He had not even dismounted . . . Whether he had been in haste or whether he had been afraid of being false to himself at the hour of parting – God only knows . . .

I stopped, without coming out on the path, threw the envelope in the most conspicuous place on it, and kept my eyes upon it, supposing that Mme M. would notice the loss and come back and look for it. But after waiting four minutes I could stand it no longer, I picked up my find again, put it in my pocket, and set off to overtake Mme M. I came upon her in the big avenue in the garden. She was walking straight towards the house with a swift and hurried step, though she was lost in thought, and her eyes were on the ground. I did not know what to do. Go up to her, give it her? That would be as good as saying that I knew everything, that I had seen it all. I should betray myself at the first word. And how should I look, at her? How would she look at me? I kept expecting that she would discover her loss and return on her tracks. Then I could, unnoticed, have flung the envelope on the path and she would have found it. But no! We were approaching the house; she had already been noticed . . .

As ill-luck would have it everyone had got up very early that day, because after the unsuccessful expedition of the evening before, they had arranged something new, of which I had heard nothing. All were preparing to set off, and were having breakfast in the verandah. I waited for ten minutes, that I might not be seen with Mme M., and making a circuit of the garden approached the house from the other side a long time after her. She was walking up and down the verandah with her arms folded, looking pale and agitated, and was obviously trying her utmost to suppress the agonising, despairing misery which could be plainly discerned in her eyes, her walk, her every movement. Sometimes she went down the verandah steps and walked a few paces among the flower-beds in the direction of the garden; her eyes were impatiently, greedily, even incautiously, seeking something on the sand of the path and on the floor of the verandah. There could be no doubt she had discovered her loss and imagined she had dropped the letter somewhere here, near the house – yes, that must be so, she was convinced of it.

Someone noticed that she was pale and agitated, and others made the same remark. She was besieged with questions about her health and condolences. She had to laugh, to jest, to appear lively. From time to time she looked at her husband, who was standing at the end of the terrace talking to two ladies, and the poor woman was overcome by the same shudder, the same embarrassment, as on the day of his first arrival. Thrusting my hand into my pocket and holding the letter tight in it, I stood at a little distance from them all, praying to fate that Mme M. should notice me. I longed to cheer her up, to relieve her anxiety if only by a glance; to say a word to her on the sly. But when she did chance to look at me I dropped my eyes.

I saw her distress and I was not mistaken. To this day I don't know her secret. I know nothing but what I saw and what I have just described. The intrigue was not such, perhaps, as one might suppose at the first glance. Perhaps that kiss was the kiss of farewell, perhaps it was the last slight reward for the sacrifice made to her peace and honour. N. was going away, he was leaving her, perhaps for ever. Even that letter I was holding in my hand – who can tell what it contained! How can one judge? and who can condemn? And yet there is no doubt that the sudden discovery of her secret would have been terrible – would have been a fatal blow for her. I still remember her face at that minute, it could not have shown more suffering. To feel, to know, to be convinced, to expect, as though it were one's execution, that in a quarter of an hour, in a minute perhaps, all might be discovered, the letter might be found by someone, picked up; there was no address on it, it might be opened, and then . . . What then? What torture could be worse than what was awaiting her? She moved about among those who would be her judges. In another minute their smiling, flattering faces would be menacing and merciless. She would read mockery, malice and icy contempt on those faces, and then her life would be plunged in everlasting darkness, with no dawn to follow. . . Yes, I did not understand it then as I understand it now. I could only have vague suspicions and misgivings, and a heartache at the thought of her danger, which I could not fully understand. But whatever lay hidden in her secret, much was expiated, if expiation were needed, by those moments of anguish of which I was witness and which I shall never forget.

But then came a cheerful summons to set off; immediately everyone was bustling about gaily; laughter and lively chatter were heard on all sides. Within two minutes the verandah was deserted. Mme M. declined to join the party, acknowledging at last that she was not well. But, thank God, all the others set off, everyone was in haste, and there was no time to worry her with commiseration, inquiries, and advice. A few remained at home. Her husband said a few words to her; she answered that she would be all right directly, that he need not be uneasy, that there was no occasion for her to lie down, that she would go into the garden, alone . . . with me . . . here she glanced at me. Nothing could be more fortunate! I flushed with pleasure, with delight; a minute later we were on the way.

She walked along the same avenues and paths by which she had returned from the copse, instinctively remembering the way she had come, gazing before her with her eyes fixed on the ground, looking about intently without answering me, possibly forgetting that I was walking beside her.

But when we had already reached the place where I had picked up the letter, and the path ended, Mme M. suddenly stopped, and in a voice faint and weak with misery said that she felt worse, and that she would go home. But when she reached the garden fence she stopped again and thought a minute; a smile of despair came on her lips, and utterly worn out and exhausted, resigned, and making up her mind to the worst, she turned without a word and retraced her steps, even forgetting to tell me of her intention.

My heart was torn with sympathy, and I did not know what to do.

We went, or rather I led her, to the place from which an hour before I had heard the tramp of a horse and their conversation. Here, close to a shady elm tree, was a seat hewn out of one huge stone, about which grew ivy, wild jasmine, and dog-rose; the whole wood was dotted with little bridges, arbours, grottoes, and similar surprises. Mme M. sat down on the bench and glanced unconsciously at the marvellous view that lay open before us. A minute later she opened her book, and fixed her eyes upon it without reading, without turning the pages, almost unconscious of what she was doing. It was about half-past nine. The sun was already high and was floating gloriously in the deep, dark blue sky, as though melting away in its own light. The mowers were by now far away; they were scarcely visible from our side of the river; endless ridges of mown grass crept after them in unbroken succession, and from time to time the faintly stirring breeze wafted their fragrance to us. The never ceasing concert of those who 'sow not, neither do they reap' and are free as the air they cleave with their sportive wings was all about us. It seemed as though at that moment every flower, every blade of grass was exhaling the aroma of sacrifice, was saying to its Creator, 'Father, I am blessed and happy.'

I glanced at the poor woman, who alone was like one dead amidst all this joyous life; two big tears hung motionless on her lashes, wrung from her heart by bitter grief. It was in my power to relieve and console this poor, fainting heart, only I did not know how to approach the subject, how to take the first step. I was in agonies. A hundred times I was on the point of going up to her, but every time my face glowed like fire.

Suddenly a bright idea dawned upon me. I had found a way of doing it; I revived.

'Would you like me to pick you a nosegay?' I said, in such a joyful voice that Mme M. immediately raised her head and looked at me intently.

'Yes, do,' she said at last in a weak voice, with a faint smile, at once dropping her eyes on the book again.

'Or soon they will be mowing the grass here and there will be no flowers,' I cried, eagerly setting to work.

I had soon picked my nosegay, a poor, simple one, I should have been ashamed to take it indoors; but how light my heart was as I picked the flowers and tied them up! The dog-rose and the wild jasmine I picked closer to the seat, I knew that not far off there was a field of rye, not yet ripe. I ran there for cornflowers; I mixed them with tall ears of rye, picking out the finest and most golden. Close by I came upon a perfect nest of forget-me-nots, and my nosegay was almost complete. Further away in the meadow there were dark-blue campanulas and wild pinks, and I ran down to the very edge of the river to get yellow water-lilies.

At last, making my way back, and going for an instant into the wood to get some bright green fan-shaped leaves of the maple to put round the nosegay, I happened to come across a whole family of pansies, close to which, luckily for me, the fragrant scent of violets betrayed the little flower hiding in the thick lush grass and still glistening with drops of dew. The nosegay was complete. I bound it round with fine long grass which twisted into a rope, and I carefully lay the letter in the centre, hiding it with the flowers, but in such a way that it could be very easily noticed if the slightest attention were bestowed upon my nosegay.

I carried it to Mme M.

On the way it seemed to me that the letter was lying too much in view: I hid it a little more. As I got nearer I thrust it still further in the flowers; and finally, when I was on the spot, I suddenly poked it so deeply into the centre of the nosegay that it could not be noticed at all from outside. My cheeks were positively flaming. I wanted to hide my face in my hands and run away at once, but she glanced at my flowers as though she had completely forgotten that I had gathered them. Mechanically, almost without looking, she held out her hand and took my present; but at once laid it on the seat as though I had handed it to her for that purpose and dropped her eyes to her book again, seeming lost in thought. I was ready to cry at this mischance. 'If only my nosegay were close to her,' I thought; 'if only she had not forgotten it!' I lay down on the grass not far off, put my right arm under my head, and closed my eyes as though I were overcome by drowsiness. But I waited, keeping my eyes fixed on her.

Ten minutes passed, it seemed to me that she was getting paler and paler . . . fortunately a blessed chance came to my aid.

This was a big, golden bee, brought by a kindly breeze, luckily for me. It first buzzed over my head, and then flew up to Mme M. She waved it off once or twice, but the bee grew more and more persistent. At last Mme M. snatched up my nosegay and waved it before my face. At that instant the letter dropped out from among the flowers and fell straight upon the open book. I started. For some time Mme M., mute with amazement, stared first at the letter and then at the flowers which she was holding in her hands, and she seemed unable to believe her eyes. All at once she flushed, started, and glanced at me. But I caught her movement and shut my eyes tight, pretending to be asleep. Nothing would have induced me to look her straight in the face at that moment. My heart was throbbing and leaping like a bird in the grasp of some village boy. I don't remember how long I lay with my eyes shut, two or three minutes. At last I ventured to open them. Mme M. was greedily reading the letter, and from her glowing cheeks, her sparkling, tearful eyes, her bright face, every feature of which was quivering with joyful emotion, I guessed that there was happiness in the letter and all her misery was dispersed like smoke. An agonising, sweet feeling gnawed at my heart, it was hard for me to go on pretending . . .

I shall never forget that minute!

Suddenly, a long way off, we heard voices:

'Mme M.! Natalie! Natalie!'

Mme M. did not answer, but she got up quickly from the seat, came up to me and bent over me. I felt that she was looking straight into my face. My eyelashes quivered, but I controlled myself and did not open my eyes. I tried to breathe more evenly and quietly, but my heart smothered me with its violent throbbing. Her burning breath scorched my cheeks; she bent close down to my face as though trying to make sure. At last a kiss and tears fell on my hand, the one which was lying on my breast.

'Natalie! Natalie! where are you,' we heard again, this time quite close.

'Coming,' said Mme M., in her mellow, silvery voice, which was so choked and quivering with tears and so subdued that no one but I could hear that, 'Coming!'

But at that instant my heart at last betrayed me and seemed to send all my blood rushing to my face. At that instant a swift, burning kiss scalded my lips. I uttered a faint cry. I opened my eyes, but at once the same gauze kerchief fell upon them, as though she meant to screen me from the sun. An instant later she was gone. I heard nothing but the sound of rapidly retreating steps. I was alone . . .

I pulled off her kerchief and kissed it, beside myself with rapture; for some moments I was almost frantic . . . Hardly able to breathe, leaning on my elbow on the grass, I stared unconsciously before me at the surrounding slopes, streaked with cornfields, at the river that flowed twisting and winding far away, as far as the eye could see, between fresh hills and villages that gleamed like dots all over the sunlit distance – at the dark-blue, hardly visible forests, which seemed as though smoking at the edge of the burning sky, and a sweet stillness inspired by the triumphant peacefulness of the picture gradually brought calm to my troubled heart. I felt more at ease and breathed more freely, but my whole soul was full of a dumb, sweet yearning, as though a veil had been drawn from my eyes as though at a foretaste of something. My frightened heart, faintly quivering with expectation, was groping timidly and joyfully towards some conjecture . . . and all at once my bosom heaved, began aching as though something had pierced it, and tears, sweet tears, gushed from my eyes. I hid my face in my hands, and quivering like a blade of grass, gave myself up to the first consciousness and revelation of my heart, the first vague glimpse of my nature. My childhood was over from that moment.

When two hours later I returned home I did not find Mme M. Through some sudden chance she had gone back to Moscow with her husband. I never saw her again.

An Unpleasant Predicament

1862

THIS UNPLEASANT BUSINESS occurred at the epoch when the regeneration of our beloved fatherland and the struggle of her valiant sons towards new hopes and destinies was beginning with irresistible force and with a touchingly naïve impetuosity. One winter evening in that period, between eleven and twelve o'clock, three highly respectable gentlemen were sitting in a comfortable and even luxuriously furnished room in a handsome house of two storeys on the Petersburg Side, and were engaged in a staid and edifying conversation on a very interesting subject. These three gentlemen were all of generals' rank. They were sitting round a little table, each in a soft and handsome arm-chair, and as they talked, they quietly and luxuriously sipped champagne. The bottle stood on the table on a silver stand with ice around it. The fact was that the host, a privy councillor called Stepan Nikiforovitch Nikiforov, an old bachelor of sixty-five, was celebrating his removal into a house he had just bought, and as it happened, also his birthday, which he had never kept before. The festivity, however, was not on a very grand scale; as we have seen already, there were only two guests, both of them former colleagues and former subordinates of Mr Nikiforov; that is, an actual civil councillor called Semyon Ivanovitch Shipulenko, and another actual civil councillor, Ivan Ilyitch Pralinsky. They had arrived to tea at nine o'clock, then had begun upon the wine, and knew that at exactly half-past eleven they would have to set off home. Their host had all his life been fond of regularity. A few words about him.

He had begun his career as a petty clerk with nothing to back him, had quietly plodded on for forty-five years, knew very well what to work towards, had no ambition to draw the stars down from heaven, though he had two stars already, and particularly disliked expressing his own opinion on any subject. He was honest, too, that is, it had not happened to him to do anything particularly dishonest; he was a bachelor because he was an egoist; he had plenty of brains, but he could not bear showing his intelligence; he particularly disliked slovenliness and enthusiasm, regarding it as moral slovenliness; and towards the end of his life had become completely absorbed in a voluptuous, indolent comfort and systematic solitude. Though he sometimes visited people of a rather higher rank than his own, yet from his youth up he could never endure entertaining visitors himself; and of late he had, if he did not play a game of patience, been satisfied with the society of his dining-room clock, and would spend the whole evening dozing in his arm-chair, listening placidly to its ticking under its glass case on the chimneypiece. In appearance he was closely shaven and extremely proper-looking, he was well-preserved, looking younger than his age; he promised to go on living many years longer, and closely followed the rules of the highest good breeding. His post was a fairly comfortable one: he had to preside somewhere and to sign something. In short, he was regarded as a first-rate man. He had only one passion, or more accurately, one keen desire: that was, to have his own house, and a house built like a gentleman's residence, not a commercial investment. His desire was at last realised: he looked out and bought a house on the Petersburg Side, a good way off, it is true, but it had a garden and was an elegant house. The new owner decided that it was better for being a good way off: he did not like entertaining at home, and for driving to see anyone or to the office he had a handsome carriage of a chocolate hue, a coachman, Mihey, and two little but strong and handsome horses. All this was honourably acquired by the careful frugality of forty years, so that his heart rejoiced over it.

This was how it was that Stepan Nikiforovitch felt such pleasure in his placid heart that he actually invited two friends to see him on his birthday, which he had hitherto carefully concealed from his most intimate acquaintances. He had special designs on one of these visitors. He lived in the upper storey of his new house, and he wanted a tenant for the lower half, which was built and arranged in exactly the same way. Stepan Nikiforovitch was reckoning upon Semyon Ivanovitch Shipulenko, and had twice that evening broached the subject in the course of conversation. But Semyon Ivanovitch made no response. The latter, too, was a man who had doggedly made a way for himself in the course of long years. He had black hair and whiskers, and a face that always had a shade of jaundice. He was a married man of morose disposition who liked to stay at home; he ruled his household with a rod of iron; in his official duties he had the greatest self-confidence. He, too, knew perfectly well what goal he was making for, and better still, what he never would reach. He was in a good position, and he was sitting tight there. Though he looked upon the new reforms with a certain distaste, he was not particularly agitated about them: he was extremely self-confident, and listened with a shade of ironical malice to Ivan Ilyitch Pralinsky expatiating on new themes. All of them had been drinking rather freely, however, so that Stepan Nikiforovitch himself condescended to take part in a slight discussion with Mr Pralinsky concerning the latest reforms. But we must say a few words about his Excellency, Mr Pralinsky, especially as he is the chief hero of the present story.

The actual civil councillor Ivan Ilyitch Pralinsky had only been 'his Excellency' for four months; in short, he was a young general. He was young in years, too – only forty-three, no more – and he looked and liked to look even younger. He was a tall, handsome man, he was smart in his dress, and prided himself on its solid, dignified character; with great aplomb he displayed an order of some consequence on his breast. From his earliest childhood he had known how to acquire the airs and graces of aristocratic society, and being a bachelor, dreamed of a wealthy and even aristocratic bride. He dreamed of many other things, though he was far from being stupid. At times he was a great talker, and even liked to assume a parliamentary pose. He came of a good family. He was the son of a general, and brought up in the lap of luxury; in his tender childhood he had been dressed in velvet and fine linen, had been educated at an aristocratic school, and though he acquired very little learning there he was successful in the service, and had worked his way up to being a general. The authorities looked upon him as a capable man, and even expected great things from him in the future. Stepan Nikiforovitch, under whom Ivan Ilyitch had begun his career in the service, and under whom he had remained until he was made a general, had never considered him a good businessman and had no expectations of him whatever. What he liked in him was that he belonged to a good family, had property – that is, a big block of buildings, let out in flats, in charge of an overseer – was connected with persons of consequence, and what was more, had a majestic bearing. Stepan Nikiforovitch blamed him inwardly for excess of imagination and instability. Ivan Ilyitch himself felt at times that he had too much *amour-propre* and even sensitiveness. Strange to say, he had attacks from time to time of morbid tenderness of conscience and even a kind of faint remorse. With bitterness and a secret soreness of heart he recognised now and again that he did not fly so high as he imagined. At such moments he sank into despondency, especially when he was suffering from haemorrhoids, called his life *une existence manquée*, and ceased – privately, of course – to believe even in his parliamentary capacities, calling himself a talker, a maker of phrases; and though all that, of course, did him great credit, it did not in the least prevent him from raising his head again half an hour later, and growing even more obstinately, even more conceitedly self-confident, and assuring himself that he would yet succeed in making his mark, and that he would be not only a great official, but a statesman whom Russia would long remember. He actually dreamed at times of monuments. From this it will be seen that Ivan Ilyitch aimed high, though he hid his vague hopes and dreams deep in his heart, even with a certain trepidation. In short, he was a good-natured man and a poet at heart. Of late years these morbid moments of disillusionment had begun to be more frequent. He had become peculiarly irritable, ready to take offence, and was apt to take any contradiction as an affront. But reformed Russia gave him great hopes. His promotion to general was the finishing touch. He was roused; he held his head up. He suddenly began talking freely and eloquently. He talked about the new ideas, which he very quickly and unexpectedly made his own and professed with vehemence. He sought opportunities for speaking, drove about the town, and in many places succeeded in gaining the reputation of a desperate Liberal, which flattered him greatly. That evening, after drinking four glasses, he was particularly exuberant. He wanted on every point to confute Stepan Nikiforovitch, whom he had not seen for some time past, and whom he had hitherto always respected and even obeyed. He considered him for some reason reactionary, and fell upon him with exceptional heat. Stepan Nikiforovitch hardly answered him, but only listened slyly, though the subject interested him. Ivan Ilyitch got hot, and in the heat of the discussion sipped his glass more often than he ought to have done. Then Stepan Nikiforovitch took the bottle and at once filled his glass again, which for some reason seemed to offend Ivan Ilyitch, especially as Semyon Ivanovitch Shipulenko, whom he particularly despised and indeed feared on account of his cynicism and ill-nature, preserved a treacherous silence and smiled more frequently than was necessary. 'They seem to take me for a schoolboy,' flashed across Ivan Ilyitch's mind.

'No, it was time, high time,' he went on hotly. 'We have put it off too long, and to my thinking humanity is the first consideration, humanity with our inferiors, remembering that they, too, are men. Humanity will save everything and bring out all that is . . .'

'He-he-he-he!' was heard from the direction of Semyon Ivanovitch.

'But why are you giving us such a talking-to?' Stepan

Nikiforovitch protested at last, with an affable smile. 'I must own, Ivan Ilyitch, I have not been able to make out, so far, what you are maintaining. You advocate humanity. That is love of your fellow-creatures, isn't it?'

'Yes, if you like. I . . .'

'Allow me! As far as I can see, that's not the only thing. Love of one's fellow-creatures has always been fitting. The reform movement is not confined to that. All sorts of questions have arisen relating to the peasantry, the law courts, economics, government contracts, morals and . . . and . . . and those questions are endless, and all together may give rise to great upheavals, so to say. That is what we have been anxious about, and not simply humanity . . .'

'Yes, the thing is a bit deeper than that,' observed Semyon Ivanovitch.

'I quite understand, and allow me to observe, Semyon Ivanovitch, that I can't agree to being inferior to you in depth of understanding,' Ivan Ilyitch observed sarcastically and with excessive sharpness. 'However, I will make so bold as to assert, Stepan Nikiforovitch, that you have not understood me either . . .'

'No, I haven't.'

'And yet I maintain and everywhere advance the idea that humanity and nothing else with one's subordinates, from the official in one's department down to the copying clerk, from the copying clerk down to the house serf, from the servant down to the peasant – humanity, I say, may serve, so to speak, as the corner-stone of the coming reforms and the reformation of things in general. Why? Because. Take a syllogism. I am human, consequently I am loved. I am loved, so confidence is felt in me. There is a feeling of confidence, and so there is trust. There is trust, and so there is love . . . that is, no, I mean to say that if they trust me they will believe in the reforms, they will understand, so to speak, the essential nature of them, will, so to speak, embrace each other in a moral sense, and will settle the whole business in a friendly way, fundamentally. What are you laughing at, Semyon Ivanovitch? Can't you understand?'

Stepan Nikiforovitch raised his eyebrows without speaking; he was surprised.

'I fancy I have drunk a little too much,' said Semyon Ivanovitch sarcastically, 'and so I am a little slow of comprehension. Not quite all my wits about me.'

Ivan Ilyitch winced.

'We should break down,' Stepan Nikiforovitch pronounced suddenly, after a slight pause of hesitation.

'How do you mean, we should break down?' asked Ivan Ilyitch, surprised at Stepan Nikiforovitch's abrupt remark.

'Why, we should break under the strain.' Stepan Nikiforovitch evidently did not care to explain further.

'I suppose you are thinking of new wine in old bottles?' Ivan Ilyitch replied, not without irony. 'Well, I can answer for myself, anyway.'

At that moment the clock struck half-past eleven.

'One sits on and on, but one must go at last,' said Semyon Ivanovitch, getting up. But Ivan Ilyitch was before him; he got up from the table and took his sable cap from the chimneypiece. He looked as though he had been insulted.

'So how is it to be, Semyon Ivanovitch? Will you think it over?' said Stepan Nikiforovitch, as he saw the visitors out.

'About the flat, you mean? I'll think it over, I'll think it over.'

'Well, when you have made up your mind, let me know as soon as possible.'

'Still on business?' Mr Pralinsky observed affably, in a slightly ingratiating tone, playing with his hat. It seemed to him as though they were forgetting him.

Stepan Nikiforovitch raised his eyebrows and remained mute, as a sign that he would not detain his visitors. Semyon Ivanovitch made haste to bow himself out.

'Well . . . after that what is one to expect . . . if you don't understand the simple rules of good manners . . .' Mr Pralinsky reflected to himself, and held out his hand to Stepan Nikiforovitch in a particularly offhand way.

In the hall Ivan Ilyitch wrapped himself up in his light, expensive fur coat; he tried for some reason not to notice Semyon Ivanovitch's shabby raccoon, and they both began descending the stairs.

'The old man seemed offended,' said Ivan Ilyitch to the silent Semyon Ivanovitch.

'No, why?' answered the latter with cool composure.

'Servile flunkey,' Ivan Ilyitch thought to himself.

They went out at the front door. Semyon Ivanovitch's sledge with a grey ugly horse drove up.

'What the devil! What has Trifon done with my carriage?' cried Ivan Ilyitch, not seeing his carriage.

The carriage was nowhere to be seen. Stepan Nikiforovitch's servant knew nothing about it. They appealed to Varlam, Semyon Ivanovitch's coachman, and received the answer that he had been standing there all the time and that the carriage had been there, but now there was no sign of it.

'An unpleasant predicament,' Mr Shipulenko pronounced. 'Shall I take you home?'

'Scoundrelly people!' Mr Pralinsky cried with fury. 'He asked me, the rascal, to let him go to a wedding close here in the Petersburg Side; some crony of his was getting married, deuce take her! I sternly forbade him to absent himself, and now I'll bet he has gone off there.'

'He certainly has gone there, sir,' observed Varlam; 'but he promised to be back in a minute, to be here in time, that is.'

'Well, there it is! I had a presentiment that this would happen! I'll give it to him!'

'You'd better give him a good flogging once or twice at the police station, then he will do what you tell him,' said Semyon Ivanovitch, as he wrapped the rug round him.

'Please don't you trouble, Semyon Ivanovitch!'

'Well, won't you let me take you along?'

'*Merci, bon voyage.*'

Semyon Ivanovitch drove off, while Ivan Ilyitch set off on foot along the wooden pavement, conscious of a rather acute irritation.

'Yes, indeed I'll give it to you now, you rogue! I am going on foot on purpose to make you feel it, to frighten you! He will come back and hear that his master has gone off on foot . . . the blackguard!'

Ivan Ilyitch had never abused anyone like this, but he was greatly angered, and besides, there was a buzzing in his head. He was not given to drink, so five or six glasses soon affected him. But the night was enchanting. There was a frost, but it was remarkably still and there was no wind. There was a clear, starry sky. The full moon was bathing the earth in soft silver light. It was so lovely that after walking some fifty paces Ivan Ilyitch almost forgot his troubles. He felt particularly pleased. People quickly change from one mood to another when they are a little drunk. He was even pleased with the ugly little wooden houses of the deserted street.

'It's really a capital thing that I am walking,' he thought; 'it's a lesson to Trifon and a pleasure to me. I really ought to walk oftener. And I shall soon pick up a sledge on the Great Prospect. It's a glorious night. What little houses they all are! I suppose small fry live here, clerks, tradesmen, perhaps . . . That Stepan Nikiforovitch! What reactionaries they all are, those old fogies! Fogies, yes, *c'est le mot*. He is a sensible man, though; he has that *bon sens*, sober, practical understanding of things. But they are old, old. There is a lack of . . . what is it? There is a lack of something . . . "We shall break down." What did he mean by that? He actually pondered when he said it. He didn't understand me a bit. And yet how could he help understanding? It was more difficult not to understand it than to understand it. The chief thing is that I am convinced, convinced in my soul. Humanity . . . the love of one's kind. Restore a man to himself, revive his personal dignity, and then . . . when the ground is prepared, get to work. I believe that's clear? Yes! Allow me, your Excellency; take a syllogism, for instance: we meet, for instance, a clerk, a poor, downtrodden clerk. "Well . . . who are you?" Answer: "A clerk." Very good, a clerk; further: "What sort of clerk are you?" Answer: "I am such and such a clerk," he says. "Are you in the service?" "I am." "Do you want to be happy?" "I do." "What do you need for happiness?" "This and that." "Why?" "Because . . ." and there the man understands me with a couple of words, the man's mine, the man is caught, so to speak, in a net, and I can do what I like with him, that is, for his good. Horrid man that Semyon Ivanovitch! And what a nasty phiz he has! . . . "Flog him in the police station," he said that on purpose. No, you are talking rubbish; you can flog, but I'm not going to; I shall punish Trifon with words, I shall punish him with reproaches, he will feel it. As for flogging, h'm! . . . It is an open question, h'm! . . . What about going to Emerance?

Oh, damnation take it, the cursed pavement!' he cried out, suddenly tripping up. 'And this is the capital. Enlightenment! One might break one's leg. H'm! I detest that Semyon Ivanovitch; a most revolting phiz. He was chuckling at me just now when I said they would embrace each other in a moral sense. Well, and they will embrace each other, and what's that to do with you? I am not going to embrace you; I'd rather embrace a peasant . . . If I meet a peasant, I shall talk to him. I was drunk, though, and perhaps did not express myself properly. Possibly I am not expressing myself rightly now . . . H'm! I shall never touch wine again. In the evening you babble, and next morning you are sorry for it. After all, I am walking quite steadily . . . But they are all scoundrels, anyhow!'

So Ivan Ilyitch meditated incoherently and by snatches, as he went on striding along the pavement. The fresh air began to affect him, set his mind working. Five minutes later he would have felt soothed and sleepy. But all at once, scarcely two paces from the Great Prospect, he heard music. He looked round. On the other side of the street, in a very tumble-down-looking long wooden house of one storey, there was a great fête, there was the scraping of violins, and the droning of a double bass, and the squeaky tooting of a flute playing a very gay quadrille tune. Under the windows stood an audience, mainly of women in a wadded pelisses with kerchiefs on their heads; they were straining every effort to see something through a crack in the shutters. Evidently there was a gay party within. The sound of the thud of dancing feet reached the other side of the street. Ivan Ilyitch saw a policeman standing not far off, and went up to him.

'Whose house is that, brother?' he asked, flinging his expensive fur coat open, just far enough to allow the policeman to see the imposing decoration on his breast.

'It belongs to the registration clerk Pseldonimov,' answered the policeman, drawing himself up instantly, discerning the decoration.

'Pseldonimov? Bah! Pseldonimov! What is he up to? Getting married?'

'Yes, your Honour, to a daughter of a titular councillor, Mlekopitaev, a titular councillor . . . used to serve in the municipal department. That house goes with the bride.'

'So that now the house is Pseldonimov's and not Mlekopitaev's?'

'Yes, Pseldonimov's, your Honour. It was Mlekopitaev's, but now it is Pseldonimov's.'

'H'm! I am asking you, my man, because I am his chief. I am a general in the same office in which Pseldonimov serves.'

'Just so, your Excellency.'

The policeman drew himself up more stiffly than ever, while Ivan Ilyitch seemed to ponder. He stood still and meditated . . .

Yes, Pseldonimov really was in his department and in his own office; he remembered that. He was a little clerk with a salary of ten roubles a month. As Mr Pralinsky had received his department very lately he might not have remembered precisely all his subordinates, but Pseldonimov he remembered just because of his surname. It had caught his eye from the very first, so that at the time he had had the curiosity to look with special attention at the possessor of such a surname. He remembered now a very young man with a long hooked nose, with tufts of flaxen hair, lean and ill-nourished, in an impossible uniform, and with unmentionables so impossible as to be actually unseemly; he remembered how the thought had flashed through his mind at the time: shouldn't he give the poor fellow ten roubles for Christmas, to spend on his wardrobe? But as the poor fellow's face was too austere, and his expression extremely unprepossessing, even exciting repulsion, the good-natured idea somehow faded away of itself, so Pseldonimov did not get his tip. He had been the more surprised when this same Pseldonimov had not more than a week before asked for leave to be married. Ivan Ilyitch remembered that he had somehow not had time to go into the matter, so that the matter of the marriage had been settled offhand, in haste. But yet he did remember exactly that Pseldonimov was receiving a wooden house and four hundred roubles in cash as dowry with his bride. The circumstance had surprised him at the time; he remembered that he had made a slight jest over the juxtaposition of the names Pseldonimov and Mlekopitaev. He remembered all that clearly.

He recalled it, and grew more and more pensive. It is well known that whole trains of thought sometimes pass through our brains instantaneously as though they were sensations without being translated into human speech, still less into literary language. But we will try to translate these sensations of our hero's, and present to the reader at least the kernel of them, so to say, what was most essential and nearest to reality in them. For many of our sensations when translated into ordinary language seem absolutely unreal. That is why they never find expression, though everyone has them. Of course Ivan Ilyitch's sensations and thoughts were a little incoherent. But you know the reason.

'Why,' flashed through his mind, 'here we all talk and talk, but when it comes to action – it all ends in nothing. Here, for instance, take this Pseldonimov: he has just come from his wedding full of hope and excitement, looking forward to his wedding feast . . . This is one of the most blissful days of his life . . . Now he is busy with his guests, is giving a banquet, a modest one, poor, but gay and full of genuine gladness . . . What if he knew that at this very moment I, I, his superior, his chief, am standing by his house listening to the music? Yes, really how would he feel? No, what would he feel if I suddenly walked in? H'm! . . . Of course at first he would be frightened, he would be dumb with embarrassment . . . I should be in his way, and perhaps should upset everything. Yes, that would be so if any other general went in, but not I . . . That's a fact, anyone else, but not I . . .

'Yes, Stepan Nikiforovitch! You did not understand me just now, but here is an example ready for you.

'Yes, we all make an outcry about acting humanely, but we are not capable of heroism, of fine actions.

'What sort of heroism? This sort. Consider: in the existing relations of the various members of society, for me, for me, after midnight to go in to the wedding of my subordinate, a registration clerk, at ten roubles the month – why, it would mean embarrassment, a revolution, the last days of Pompeii, a nonsensical folly. No one would understand it. Stepan Nikiforovitch would die before he understood it. Why, he said we should break down. Yes, but that's you old people, inert, paralytic people; but I shan't break down, I will transform the last day of Pompeii to a day of the utmost sweetness for my subordinate, and a wild action to an action normal, patriarchal, lofty and moral. How? Like this. Kindly listen . . .

'Here . . . I go in, suppose; they are amazed, leave off dancing, look wildly at me, draw back. Quite so, but at once I speak out: I go straight up to the frightened Pseldonimov, and with a most cordial, affable smile, in the simplest words, I say: "This is how it is, I have been at his Excellency Stepan Nikiforovitch's. I expect you know, close here in the neighbourhood . . ." Well, then, lightly, in a laughing way, I shall tell him of my adventure with Trifon. From Trifon I shall pass on to saying how I walked here on foot . . . "Well, I heard music, I inquired of a policeman, and learned, brother, that it was your wedding. Let me go in, I thought, to my subordinate's; let me see how my clerks enjoy themselves and . . . celebrate their wedding. I suppose you won't turn me out?" Turn me out! What a word for a subordinate! How the devil could he dream of turning me out! I fancy that he would be half crazy, that he would rush headlong to seat me in an arm-chair, would be trembling with delight, would hardly know what he was doing for the first minute!

'Why, what can be simpler, more elegant than such an action? Why did I go in? That's another question! That is, so to say, the moral aspect of the question. That's the pith.

'H'm, what was I thinking about, yes!

'Well, of course they will make me sit down with the most important guest, some titular councillor or a relation who's a retired captain with a red nose. Gogol describes these eccentrics so capitally. Well, I shall make acquaintance, of course, with the bride, I shall compliment her, I shall encourage the guests. I shall beg them not to stand on ceremony. To enjoy themselves, to go on dancing. I shall make jokes, I shall laugh; in fact, I shall be affable and charming. I am always affable and charming when I am pleased with myself . . . H'm . . . the point is that I believe I am still a little, well, not drunk exactly, but . . .

'Of course, as a gentleman I shall be quite on an equality with them, and shall not expect any especial marks of . . . But morally, morally, it is a different matter; they will understand and appreciate it . . . My actions will evoke their nobler feelings . . . Well, I shall stay for half an hour . . . even for an hour; I shall leave, of course, before supper; but they will be bustling about, baking and roasting, they will be making low bows, but

I will only drink a glass, congratulate them and refuse supper. I shall say – "business." And as soon as I pronounce the word "business", all of them will at once have sternly respectful faces. By that I shall delicately remind them that there is a difference between them and me. The earth and the sky. It is not that I want to impress that on them, but it must be done . . . it's even essential in a moral sense, when all is said and done. I shall smile at once, however, I shall even laugh, and then they will all pluck up courage again . . . I shall jest a little again with the bride; h'm! . . . I may even hint that I shall come again in just nine months and stand godfather, he-he! And she will be sure to be brought to bed by then. They multiply, you know, like rabbits. And they will all roar with laughter and the bride will blush; I shall kiss her feelingly on the forehead, even give her my blessing . . . and next day my exploit will be known at the office. Next day I shall be stern again, next day I shall be exacting again, even implacable, but they will all know what I am like. They will know my heart, they will know my essential nature: "He is stern as chief, but as a man he is an angel!" And I shall have conquered them; I shall have captured them by one little act which would never have entered your head; they would be mine; I should be their father, they would be my children . . . Come now, your Excellency Stepan Nikiforovitch, go and do likewise . . .

'But do you know, do you understand, that Pseldonimov will tell his children how the general himself feasted and even drank at his wedding! Why you know those children would tell their children, and those would tell their grandchildren as a most sacred story that a grand gentleman, a statesman (and I shall be all that by then), did them the honour, and so on, and so on. Why, I am morally elevating the humiliated, I restore him to himself . . . Why, he gets a salary of ten roubles a month! . . . If I repeat this five or ten times, or something of the sort, I shall gain popularity all over the place . . . My name will be printed on the hearts of all, and the devil only knows what will come of that popularity! . . .'

These, or something like these, were Ivan Ilyitch's reflections, (a man says all sorts of things sometimes to himself, gentlemen, especially when he is in rather an eccentric condition). All these meditations passed through his mind in something like half a minute, and of course he might have confined himself to these dreams and, after mentally putting Stepan Nikiforovitch to shame, have gone very peacefully home and to bed. And he would have done well. But the trouble of it was that the moment was an eccentric one.

As ill-luck would have it, at that very instant the self-satisfied faces of Stepan Nikiforovitch and Semyon Ivanovitch suddenly rose before his heated imagination.

'We shall break down!' repeated Stepan Nikiforovitch, smiling disdainfully.

'He-he-he,' Semyon Ivanovitch seconded him with his nastiest smile.

'Well, we'll see whether we do break down!' Ivan Ilyitch said resolutely, with a rush of heat to his face.

He stepped down from the pavement and with resolute steps went straight across the street towards the house of his registration clerk Pseldonimov.

His star carried him away. He walked confidently in at the open gate and contemptuously thrust aside with his foot the shaggy, husky little sheep-dog who flew at his legs with a hoarse bark, more as a matter of form than with any real intention. Along a wooden plank he went to the covered porch which led like a sentry box to the yard, and by three decaying wooden steps he went up to the tiny entry. Here, though a tallow candle or something in the way of a night-light was burning somewhere in a corner, it did not prevent Ivan Ilyitch from putting his left foot just as it was, in its golosh, into a galantine which had been stood out there to cool. Ivan Ilyitch bent down, and looking with curiosity, he saw that there were two other dishes of some sort of jelly and also two shapes apparently of blancmange. The squashed galantine embarrassed him, and for one brief instant the thought flashed through his mind, whether he should not slink away at once. But he considered this too low. Reflecting that no one would have seen him, and that they would never think he had done it, he hurriedly wiped his golosh to conceal all traces, fumbled for the felt-covered door, opened it and found himself in a very little anteroom. Half of it was literally piled up with greatcoats, wadded jackets, cloaks, capes, scarves and goloshes. In the other half the musicians had been installed; two violins, a flute, and a double bass, a band of four, picked up, of course, in the street. They were sitting at an unpainted wooden table, lighted by a single tallow candle, and with the utmost vigour were sawing out the last figure of the quadrille. From the open door into the drawing-room one could see the dancers in the midst of dust, tobacco smoke and fumes. There was a frenzy of gaiety. There were sounds of laughter, shouts and shrieks from the ladies. The gentlemen stamped like a squadron of horses. Above all the Bedlam there rang out words of command from the leader of the dance, probably an extremely free and easy, and even unbuttoned gentleman: 'Gentlemen advance, ladies' chain, set to partners!' and so on, and so on. Ivan Ilyitch in some excitement cast off his coat and goloshes, and with his cap in his hand went into the room. He was no longer reflecting, however.

For the first minute nobody noticed him; all were absorbed in dancing the quadrille to the end. Ivan Ilyitch stood as though entranced, and could make out nothing definite in the chaos. He caught glimpses of ladies' dresses, of gentlemen with cigarettes between their teeth. He caught a glimpse of a lady's pale blue scarf which flicked him on the nose. After the wearer a medical student, with his hair blown in all directions on his head, pranced by in wild delight and jostled violently against him on the way. He caught a glimpse, too, of an officer of some description, who looked half a mile high. Someone in an unnaturally shrill voice shouted, 'O-o-oh, Pseldonimov!' as the speaker flew by stamping. It was sticky under Ivan Ilyitch's feet; evidently the floor had been waxed. In the room, which was a very small one, there were about thirty people.

But a minute later the quadrille was over, and almost at once the very thing Ivan Ilyitch had pictured when he was dreaming on the pavement took place.

A stifled murmur, a strange whisper passed over the whole company, including the dancers, who had not yet had time to take breath and wipe their perspiring faces. All eyes, all faces began quickly turning towards the newly arrived guest. Then they all seemed to draw back a little and beat a retreat. Those who had not noticed him were pulled by their coats or dresses and informed. They looked round and at once beat a retreat with the others. Ivan Ilyitch was still standing at the door without moving a step forward, and between him and the company there stretched an ever widening empty space of floor strewn with countless sweet-meat wrappings, bits of paper and cigarette ends. All at once a young man in a uniform, with a shock of flaxen hair and a hooked nose, stepped timidly out into that empty space. He moved forward, hunched up, and looked at the unexpected visitor exactly with the expression with which a dog looks at its master when the latter has called him up and is going to kick him.

'Good evening, Pseldonimov, do you know me?' said Ivan Ilyitch, and felt at the same minute that he had said this very awkwardly; he felt, too, that he was perhaps doing something horribly stupid at that moment.

'You-our Ex-cel-len-cy!' muttered Pseldonimov.

'To be sure . . . I have called in to see you quite by chance, my friend, as you can probably imagine . . .'

But evidently Pseldonimov could imagine nothing. He stood with staring eyes in the utmost perplexity.

'You won't turn me out, I suppose . . . Pleased or not, you must make a visitor welcome . . .' Ivan Ilyitch went on, feeling that he was confused to a point of unseemly feebleness; that he was trying to smile and was utterly unable; that the humorous reference to Stepan Nikiforovitch and Trifon was becoming more and more impossible. But as ill-luck would have it, Pseldonimov did not recover from his stupefaction, and still gazed at him with a perfectly idiotic air. Ivan Ilyitch winced, he felt that in another minute something incredibly foolish would happen.

'I am not in the way, am I? . . . I'll go away,' he faintly articulated, and there was a tremor at the right corner of his mouth.

But Pseldonimov had recovered himself.

'Good heavens, your Excellency . . . the honour . . .' he muttered, bowing hurriedly. 'Graciously sit down, your Excellency . . .' And recovering himself still further, he motioned him with both hands to a sofa before which a table had been moved away to make room for the dancing.

Ivan Ilyitch felt relieved and sank on the sofa; at once someone flew to move the table up to him. He took a cursory look round and saw that he was the only person sitting down, all the others were standing, even the ladies. A bad sign. But it was not yet time to reassure and encourage them. The company still held back, while before him, bending double, stood Pseldonimov, utterly alone, still completely at a loss and very far from smiling. It was horrid; in short, our hero endured such misery at that moment that his Haroun al-Raschid-like descent upon his subordinates for the sake of principle might well have been reckoned an heroic action. But suddenly a little figure made its appearance beside Pseldonimov, and began bowing. To his inexpressible pleasure and even happiness, Ivan Ilyitch at once recognised him as the head clerk of his office, Akim Petrovitch Zubikov, and though, of course, he was not acquainted with him, he knew him to be a businesslike and exemplary clerk. He got up at once and held out his hand to Akim Petrovitch – his whole hand, not two fingers. The latter took it in both of his with the deepest respect. The general was triumphant, the situation was saved.

And now indeed Pseldonimov was no longer, so to say, the second person, but the third. It was impossible to address his remarks to the head clerk in his necessity, taking him for an acquaintance and even an intimate one, and Pseldonimov meanwhile could only be silent and be in a tremor of reverence. So that the proprieties were observed. And some explanation was essential, Ivan Ilyitch felt that; he saw that all the guests were expecting something, that the whole household was gathered together in the doorway, almost creeping, climbing over one another in their anxiety to see and hear him. What was horrid was that the head clerk in his foolishness remained standing.

'Why are you standing?' said Ivan Ilyitch, awkwardly motioning him to a seat on the sofa beside him.

'Oh, don't trouble . . . I'll sit here,' and Akim Petrovitch hurriedly sat down on a chair, almost as it was being put for him by Pseldonimov, who remained obstinately standing.

'Can you imagine what happened,' addressing himself exclusively to Akim Petrovitch in a rather quavering, though free and easy voice. He even drawled out his words, with special emphasis on some syllables, pronounced the vowel *ah* like *eh*; in short, felt and was conscious that he was being affected but could not control himself: some external force was at work. He was painfully conscious of many things at that moment.

'Can you imagine, I have only just come from Stepan Nikiforovitch Nikiforov's, you have heard of him perhaps, the privy councillor. You know . . . on that special committee . . .'

Akim Petrovitch bent his whole person forward respectfully: as much as to say, 'Of course we have heard of him.'

'He is your neighbour now,' Ivan Ilyitch went on, for one instant for the sake of ease and good manners addressing Pseldonimov, but he quickly turned away again, on seeing from the latter's eyes that it made absolutely no difference to him.

'The old fellow, as you know, has been dreaming all his life of buying himself a house . . . Well, and he has bought it. And a very pretty house too. Yes . . . And today was his birthday and he had never celebrated it before, he used even to keep it secret from us, he was too stingy to keep it, he-he. But now he is so delighted over his new house, that he invited Semyon Ivanovitch Shipulenko and me, you know.'

Akim Petrovitch bent forward again. He bent forward zealously. Ivan Ilyitch felt somewhat comforted. It had struck him, indeed, that the head clerk possibly was guessing that he was an indispensable *point d'appui* for his Excellency at that moment. That would have been more horrid than anything.

'So we sat together, the three of us, he gave us champagne, we talked about problems . . . even dis-pu-ted . . . He-he!'

Akim Petrovitch raised his eyebrows respectfully.

'Only that is not the point. When I take leave of him at last – he is a punctual old fellow, goes to bed early, you know, in his old age – I go out . . . My Trifon is nowhere to be seen! I am anxious, I make inquiries. "What has Trifon done with the carriage?" It comes out that hoping I should stay on, he had gone off to the wedding of some friends of his, or sister maybe . . . Goodness only knows. Somewhere here on the Petersburg Side. And took the carriage with him while he was about it.'

Again for the sake of good manners the general glanced in the direction of Pseldonimov. The latter promptly gave a wriggle, but not at all the sort of wriggle the general would have liked. 'He has no sympathy, no heart,' flashed through his brain.

'You don't say so!' said Akim Petrovitch, greatly impressed. A faint murmur of surprise ran through all the crowd.

'Can you fancy my position . . .' (Ivan Ilyitch glanced at them all.) 'There was nothing for it, I set off on foot, I thought I would trudge to the Great Prospect, and there find some cabby . . . he-he!'

'He-he-he!' Akim Petrovitch echoed. Again a murmur, but this time on a more cheerful note, passed through the crowd. At that moment the chimney of a lamp on the wall broke with a crash. Someone rushed zealously to see to it. Pseldonimov started and looked sternly at the lamp, but the general took no notice of it, and all was serene again.

'I walked . . . and the night was so lovely, so still. All at once I heard a band, stamping, dancing. I inquired of a policeman; it is Pseldonimov's wedding. Why, you are giving a ball to all Petersburg Side, my friend. Ha-ha.' He turned to Pseldonimov again.

'He-he-he! To be sure,' Akim Petrovitch responded. There was a stir among the guests again, but what was most foolish was that Pseldonimov, though he bowed, did not even now smile, but seemed as though he were made of wood. 'Is he a fool or what?' thought Ivan Ilyitch. 'He ought to have smiled at that point, the ass, and everything would have run easily.' There was a fury of impatience in his heart.

'I thought I would go in to see my clerk. He won't turn me out I expect . . . pleased or not, one must welcome a guest. You must please excuse me, my dear fellow. If I am in the way, I will go . . . I only came in to have a look . . .'

But little by little a general stir was beginning.

Akim Petrovitch looked at him with a mawkishly sweet expression as though to say, 'How could your Excellency be in the way?' all the guests stirred and began to display the first symptoms of being at their ease. Almost all the ladies sat down. A good sign and a reassuring one. The boldest spirits among them fanned themselves with their handkerchiefs. One of them in a shabby velvet dress said something with intentional loudness. The officer addressed by her would have liked to answer her as loudly, but seeing that they were the only ones speaking aloud, he subsided. The men, for the most part government clerks, with two or three students among them, looked at one another as though egging each other on to unbend, cleared their throats, and began to move a few steps in different directions. No one, however, was particularly timid, but they were all restive, and almost all of them looked with a hostile expression at the personage who had burst in upon them, to destroy their gaiety. The officer, ashamed of his cowardice, began to edge up to the table.

'But I say, my friend, allow me to ask you your name,' Ivan Ilyitch asked Pseldonimov.

'Porfiry Petrovitch, your Excellency,' answered the latter, with staring eyes as though on parade.

'Introduce me, Porfiry Petrovitch, to your bride . . . Take me to her . . . I . . .'

And he showed signs of a desire to get up. But Pseldonimov ran full speed to the drawing-room. The bride, however, was standing close by at the door, but as soon as she heard herself mentioned, she hid. A minute later Pseldonimov led her up by the hand. The guests all moved aside to make way for them. Ivan Ilyitch got up solemnly and addressed himself to her with a most affable smile.

'Very, very much pleased to make your acquaintance,' he pronounced with a most aristocratic half-bow, 'especially on such a day . . .'

He gave a meaning smile. There was an agreeable flutter among the ladies.

'*Charmée*,' the lady in the velvet dress pronounced, almost aloud.

The bride was a match for Pseldonimov. She was a thin little lady not more than seventeen, pale, with a very small face and a sharp little nose. Her quick, active little eyes were not at all embarrassed; on the contrary, they looked at him steadily and even with a shade of resentment. Evidently Pseldonimov was marrying her for her beauty. She was dressed in a white muslin dress over a pink slip. Her neck was thin, and she had a figure like a chicken's with the bones all sticking out. She was not equal to making any response to the general's affability.

'But she is very pretty,' he went on, in an undertone, as though addressing Pseldonimov only, though intentionally speaking so that the bride could hear.

But on this occasion, too, Pseldonimov again answered absolutely nothing, and did not even wriggle. Ivan Ilyitch fancied that there was something cold, suppressed in his eyes, as though he had something peculiarly malignant in his mind. And yet he had at all costs to wring some sensibility out of him. Why, that was the object of his coming.

'They are a couple, though!' he thought.

And he turned again to the bride, who had seated herself beside him on the sofa, but in answer to his two or three questions he got nothing but 'yes' or 'no' and hardly that.

'If only she had been overcome with confusion,' he thought to himself, 'then I should have begun to banter her. But as it is, my position is impossible.'

And as ill-luck would have it, Akim Petrovitch, too, was mute; though this was only due to his foolishness, it was still unpardonable.

'My friends! Haven't I perhaps interfered with your enjoyment?' he said, addressing the whole company.

He felt that the very palms of his hands were perspiring.

'No . . . don't trouble, your Excellency; we are beginning directly, but now . . . we are getting cool,' answered the officer.

The bride looked at him with pleasure; the officer was not old, and wore the uniform of some branch of the service. Pseldonimov was still standing in the same place, bending forward, and it seemed as though his hooked nose stood out further than ever. He looked and listened like a footman standing with the greatcoat on his arm, waiting for the end of his master's farewell conversation. Ivan Ilyitch made his comparison himself. He was losing his head; he felt that he was in an awkward position, that the ground was giving way under his feet, that he had got in somewhere and could not find his way out, as though he were in the dark.

Suddenly the guests all moved aside, and a short, thickset, middle-aged woman made her appearance, dressed plainly though she was in her best, with a big shawl on her shoulders, pinned at her throat, and on her head a cap to which she was evidently unaccustomed. In her hands she carried a small round tray on which stood a full but uncorked bottle of champagne and two glasses, neither more nor less. Evidently the bottle was intended for only two guests.

The middle-aged lady approached the general.

'Don't look down on us, your Excellency,' she said, bowing. 'Since you have deigned to do my son the honour of coming to his wedding, we beg you graciously to drink to the health of the young people. Do not disdain us; do us the honour.'

Ivan Ilyitch clutched at her as though she were his salvation. She was by no means an old woman – forty-five or forty-six, not more; but she had such a good-natured, rosy-cheeked, such a round and candid Russian face, she smiled so good-humouredly, bowed so simply, that Ivan Ilyitch was almost comforted and began to hope again.

'So you are the mo-other of your so-on?' he said, getting up from the sofa.

'Yes, my mother, your Excellency,' mumbled Pseldonimov, craning his long neck and thrusting forward his long nose again.

'Ah! I am delighted – de-ligh-ted to make your acquaintance.'

'Do not refuse us, your Excellency.'

'With the greatest pleasure.'

The tray was put down. Pseldonimov dashed forward to pour out the wine. Ivan Ilyitch, still standing, took the glass.

'I am particularly, particularly glad on this occasion, that I can . . .' he began, 'that I can . . . testify before all of you . . . In short, as your chief . . . I wish you, madam' (he turned to the bride), 'and you, friend Porfiry, I wish you the fullest, completest happiness for many long years.'

And he positively drained the glass with feeling, the seventh he had drunk that evening. Pseldonimov looked at him gravely and even sullenly. The general was beginning to feel an agonising hatred of him.

'And that scarecrow' (he looked at the officer) 'keeps obtruding himself. He might at least have shouted "hurrah!" and it would have gone off, it would have gone off . . .'

'And you too, Akim Petrovitch, drink a glass to their health,' added the mother, addressing the head clerk. 'You are his superior, he is under you. Look after my boy, I beg you as a mother. And don't forget us in the future, our good, kind friend, Akim Petrovitch.'

'How nice these old Russian women are,' thought Ivan Ilyitch. 'She has livened us all up. I have always loved the democracy . . .'

At that moment another tray was brought to the table; it was brought in by a maid wearing a crackling cotton dress that had never been washed, and a crinoline. She could hardly grasp the tray in both hands, it was so big. On it there were numbers of plates of apples, sweets, fruit meringues and fruit cheeses, walnuts and so on, and so on. The tray had been till then in the drawing-room for the delectation of all the guests, and especially the ladies. But now it was brought to the general alone.

'Do not disdain our humble fare, your Excellency. What we have we are pleased to offer,' the old lady repeated, bowing.

'Delighted!' said Ivan Ilyitch, and with real pleasure took a walnut and cracked it between his fingers. He had made up his mind to win popularity at all costs.

Meantime the bride suddenly giggled.

'What is it?' asked Ivan Ilyitch with a smile, encouraged by this sign of life.

'Ivan Kostenkinitch, here, makes me laugh,' she answered, looking down.

The general distinguished, indeed, a flaxen-headed young man, exceedingly good-looking, who was sitting on a chair at the other end of the sofa, whispering something to Madame Pseldonimov. The young man stood up. He was apparently very young and very shy.

'I was telling the lady about a "dream book", your Excellency,' he muttered as though apologising.

'About what sort of "dream book"?' asked Ivan Ilyitch condescendingly.

'There is a new "dream book", a literary one. I was telling the lady that to dream of Mr Panaev means spilling coffee on one's shirt front.'

'What innocence!' thought Ivan Ilyitch, with positive annoyance.

Though the young man flushed very red as he said it, he was incredibly delighted that he had said this about Mr Panaev.

'To be sure, I have heard of it . . .' responded his Excellency.

'No, there is something better than that,' said a voice quite close to Ivan Ilyitch. 'There is a new encyclopaedia being published, and they say Mr Kraevsky will write articles . . . and satirical literature.'

This was said by a young man who was by no means embarrassed, but rather free and easy. He was wearing gloves and a white waistcoat, and carried a hat in his hand. He did not dance, and looked condescending, for he was on the staff of a satirical paper called *The Firebrand*, and gave himself airs accordingly. He had come casually to the wedding, invited as an honoured guest of the Pseldonimovs', with whom he was on intimate terms and with whom only a year before he had lived in very poor lodgings, kept by a German woman. He drank vodka, however, and for that purpose had more than once withdrawn to a snug little back room to which all the guests knew their way. The general disliked him extremely.

'And the reason that's funny,' broke in joyfully the flaxen-headed young man, who had talked of the shirt front and at whom the young man on the comic paper looked with hatred in consequence, 'it's funny, your Excellency, because it is supposed by the writer that Mr Kraevsky does not know how to spell, and thinks that "satirical" ought to be written with a "y" instead of an "i".'

But the poor young man scarcely finished his sentence; he could see from his eyes that the general knew all this long ago, for the general himself looked embarrassed, and evidently because he knew it. The young man seemed inconceivably ashamed. He succeeded in effacing himself completely, and remained very melancholy all the rest of the evening.

But to make up for that, the young man on the staff of the *Firebrand* came up nearer, and seemed to be intending to sit down somewhere close by. Such free and easy manners struck Ivan Ilyitch as rather shocking.

'Tell me, please, Porfiry,' he began, in order to say something, 'why – I have always wanted to ask you about it in person – why you are called Pseldonimov instead of Pseudonimov? Your name surely must be Pseudonimov.'

'I cannot inform you exactly, your Excellency,' said Pseldonimov.

'It must have been that when his father went into the service they made a mistake in his papers, so that he has remained now Pseldonimov,' put in Akim Petrovitch. 'That does happen.'

'Un-doubted-ly,' the general said with warmth, 'un-doubt-ed-ly; for only think, Pseudonimov comes from the literary word "pseudonym", while Pseldonimov means nothing.'

'Due to foolishness,' added Akim Petrovitch.

'You mean what is due to foolishness?'

'The Russian common people in their foolishness often alter letters, and sometimes pronounce them in their own way. For instance, they say nevalid instead of invalid.'

'Oh, yes, nevalid, he-he-he . . .'

'Mumber, too, they say, your Excellency,' boomed out the tall officer, who had long been itching to distinguish himself in some way.

'What do you mean by mumber?'

'Mumber instead of number, your Excellency.'

'Oh, yes, mumber . . . instead of number . . . To be sure, to be sure . . . He-he-he!' Ivan Ilyitch had to do a chuckle for the benefit of the officer too.

The officer straightened his tie.

'Another thing they say is nigh by,' the young man on the comic paper put it. But his Excellency tried not to hear this. His chuckles were not at everybody's disposal.

'Nigh by, instead of near,' the young man on the comic paper persisted, in evident irritation.

Ivan Ilyitch looked at him sternly.

'Come, why persist?' Pseldonimov whispered to him.

'Why, I was talking. Mayn't one speak?' the latter protested in a whisper; but he said no more and with secret fury walked out of the room.

He made his way straight to the attractive little back room where, for the benefit of the dancing gentlemen, vodka of two sorts, salt fish, caviare into slices and a bottle of very strong sherry of Russian make had been set early in the evening on a little table, covered with a Yaroslav cloth. With anger in his heart he was pouring himself out a glass of vodka, when suddenly the medical student with the dishevelled locks, the foremost dancer and cutter of capers at Pseldonimov's ball, rushed in. He fell on the decanter with greedy haste.

'They are just going to begin!' he said rapidly, helping himself. 'Come and look, I am going to dance a solo on my head; after supper I shall risk the fish dance. It is just the thing for the wedding. So to speak, a friendly hint to Pseldonimov. She's a jolly creature, that Kleopatra Semyonovna, you can venture on anything you like with her.'

'He's a reactionary,' said the young man on the comic paper gloomily, as he tossed off his vodka.

'Who is a reactionary?'

'Why, the personage before whom they set those sweetmeats. He's a reactionary, I tell you.'

'What nonsense!' muttered the student, and he rushed out of the room, hearing the opening bars of the quadrille.

Left alone, the young man on the comic paper poured himself out another glass to give himself more assurance and independence; he drank and ate a snack of something, and never had the actual civil councillor Ivan Ilyitch made for himself a bitterer foe more implacably bent on revenge than was the young man on the staff of the *Firebrand* whom he had so slighted, especially after the latter had drunk two glasses of vodka. Alas! Ivan Ilyitch suspected nothing of the sort. He did not suspect another circumstance of prime importance either, which had an influence on the mutual relations of the guests and his Excellency. The fact was that though he had given a proper and even detailed explanation of his presence at his clerk's wedding, this explanation did not really satisfy anyone, and the visitors were still embarrassed. But suddenly everything was transformed as though by magic, all were reassured and ready to enjoy themselves, to laugh, to shriek, to dance, exactly as though the unexpected visitor were not in the room. The cause of it was a rumour, a whisper, a report which spread in some unknown way that the visitor was not quite . . . it seemed – was, in fact, 'a little top-heavy'. And though this seemed at first a horrible calumny, it began by degrees to appear to be justified; suddenly everything became clear. What was more, they felt all at once extraordinarily free. And it was just at this moment that the quadrille for which the medical student was in such haste, the last before supper, began.

And just as Ivan Ilyitch meant to address the bride again, intending to provoke her with some innuendo, the tall officer suddenly dashed up to her and with a flourish dropped on one knee before her. She immediately jumped up from the sofa, and whisked off with him to take her place in the quadrille. The officer did not even apologise, and she did not even glance at the general as she went away; she seemed, in fact, relieved to escape.

'After all, she has a right to be,' thought Ivan Ilyitch, 'and of course they don't know how to behave.' 'H'm! Don't you stand on ceremony, friend Porfiry,' he said, addressing Pseldonimov. 'Perhaps you have . . . arrangements to make . . . or something . . . please don't put yourself out.' 'Why does he keep guard over me?' he thought to himself.

Pseldonimov, with his long neck and his eyes fixed intently upon him, began to be insufferable. In fact, all this was not the thing, not the thing at all, but Ivan Ilyitch was still far from admitting this.

The quadrille began.

'Will you allow me, your Excellency?' asked Akim Petrovitch, holding the bottle respectfully in his hands and preparing to pour from it into his Excellency's glass.

'I . . . I really don't know, whether . . .'

But Akim Petrovitch, with reverent and radiant face, was already filling the glass. After filling the glass, he proceeded, writhing and wriggling, as it were stealthily, as it were furtively, to pour himself out some, with this difference, that he did not fill his own glass to within a finger length of the top, and this seemed somehow more respectful. He was like a woman in travail as he sat beside his chief. What could he talk about, indeed? Yet to entertain his Excellency was an absolute duty since he had the honour of keeping him company. The champagne served as a resource, and his Excellency, too, was pleased that he had filled his glass – not for the sake of the champagne, for it was warm and perfectly abominable, but just morally pleased.

'The old chap would like to have a drink himself,' thought Ivan Ilyitch, 'but he doesn't venture till I do. I mustn't prevent him. And indeed it would be absurd for the bottle to stand between us untouched.'

He took a sip, anyway it seemed better than sitting doing nothing.

'I am here,' he said, with pauses and emphasis, 'I am here, you know, so to speak, accidentally, and, of course, it may be . . . that some people would consider . . . it unseemly for me to be at such . . . a gathering.'

Akim Petrovitch said nothing, but listened with timid curiosity.

'But I hope you will understand, with what object I have come . . . I haven't really come simply to drink wine . . . he-he!'

Akim Petrovitch tried to chuckle, following the example of his Excellency, but again he could not get it out, and again he made absolutely no consolatory answer.

'I am here . . . in order, so to speak, to encourage . . . to show, so to speak, a moral aim,' Ivan Ilyitch continued, feeling vexed at Akim Petrovitch's stupidity, but he suddenly subsided into silence himself. He saw that poor Akim Petrovitch had dropped his eyes as though he were in fault. The general in some confusion made haste to take another sip from his glass, and Akim Petrovitch clutched at the bottle as though it were his only hope of salvation and filled the glass again.

'You haven't many resources,' thought Ivan Ilyitch, looking sternly at poor Akim Petrovitch. The latter, feeling that stern general-like eye upon him, made up his mind to remain silent for good and not to raise his eyes. So they sat beside each other for a couple of minutes – two sickly minutes for Akim Petrovitch.

A couple of words about Akim Petrovitch. He was a man of the old school, as meek as a hen, reared from infancy to obsequious servility, and at the same time a good-natured and even honourable man. He was a Petersburg Russian; that is, his father and his father's father were born, grew up and served in Petersburg and had never once left Petersburg. That is quite a special type of Russian. They have hardly any idea of Russia, though that does not trouble them at all. Their whole interest is confined to Petersburg and chiefly the place in which they serve. All their thoughts are concentrated on preference for farthing points, on the shop, and their month's salary. They don't know a single Russian custom, a single Russian song except 'Lutchinushka'. and that only because it is played on the barrel organs. However, there are two fundamental and invariable signs by which you can at once distinguish a Petersburg Russian from a real Russian. The first sign is the fact that Petersburg Russians, all without exception, speak of the newspaper as the *Academic News* and never call it the *Petersburg News*. The second and equally trustworthy sign is that Petersburg Russians never make use of the word 'breakfast', but always call it 'Frühstück' with especial emphasis on the first syllable. By these radical and distinguishing signs you can tell them apart; in short, this is a humble type which has been formed during the last thirty-five years. Akim Petrovitch, however, was by no means a fool. If the general had asked him a question about anything in his own province he would have answered and kept up a conversation; as it was, it was unseemly for a subordinate even to answer such questions as these, though Akim Petrovitch was dying from curiosity to know something more detailed about his Excellency's real intentions.

And meanwhile Ivan Ilyitch sank more and more into meditation and a sort of whirl of ideas; in his absorption he sipped his glass every half-minute. Akim Petrovitch at once zealously filled it up. Both were silent. Ivan Ilyitch began looking at the dances, and immediately something attracted his attention. One circumstance even surprised him . . .

The dances were certainly lively. Here people danced in the simplicity of their hearts to amuse themselves and even to romp wildly. Among the dancers few were really skilful, but the unskilled stamped so vigorously that they might have been taken for agile ones. The officer was among the foremost! he particularly liked the figures in which he was left alone, to perform a solo. Then he performed the most marvellous capers. For instance, standing upright as a post, he would suddenly bend over to one side, so that one expected him to fall over; but with the next step he would suddenly bend over in the opposite direction at the same acute angle to the floor. He kept the most serious face and danced in the full conviction that everyone was watching him. Another gentleman, who had had rather more than he could carry before the quadrille, dropped asleep beside his partner so that his partner had to dance alone. The young registration clerk, who had danced with the lady in the blue scarf through all the figures and through all the five quadrilles which they had danced that evening, played the same prank the whole time: that is, he dropped a little behind his partner, seized the end of her scarf, and as they crossed over succeeded in imprinting some twenty kisses on the scarf. His partner sailed along in front of him, as though she noticed nothing. The medical student really did dance on his head, and excited frantic enthusiasm, stamping, and shrieks of delight. In short, the absence of constraint was very marked. Ivan Ilyitch, whom the wine was beginning to affect, began by smiling, but by degrees a bitter doubt began to steal into his heart; of course he liked free and easy manners and unconventionality. He desired, he had even inwardly prayed for free and easy manners, when they had all held back, but now that unconventionality had gone beyond all limits. One lady, for instance, the one in the shabby dark blue velvet dress, bought fourth-hand, in the sixth figure pinned her dress so as to turn it into – something like trousers. This was the Kleopatra Semyonovna with whom one could venture to do anything, as her partner, the medical student, had expressed it. The medical student defied description: he was simply a Fokin. How was it? They had held back and now they were so quickly emancipated! One might think it nothing, but this transformation was somehow strange; it indicated something. It was as though they had forgotten Ivan Ilyitch's existence. Of course he was the first to laugh, and even ventured to applaud. Akim Petrovitch chuckled respectfully in unison, though, indeed, with evident pleasure and no suspicion that his Excellency was beginning to nourish in his heart a new gnawing anxiety.

'You dance capitally, young man,' Ivan Ilyitch was obliged to say to the medical student as he walked past him.

The student turned sharply towards him, made a grimace, and bringing his face close into unseemly proximity to the face of his Excellency, crowed like a cock at the top of his voice. This was too much. Ivan Ilyitch got up from the table. In spite of that, a roar of inexpressible laughter followed, for the crow was an extraordinarily good imitation, and the whole performance was utterly unexpected. Ivan Ilyitch was still standing in bewilderment, when suddenly Pseldonimov himself made his appearance, and with a bow, began begging him to come to supper. His mother followed him.

'Your Excellency,' she said, bowing, 'do us the honour, do not disdain our humble fare.'

'I . . . I really don't know,' Ivan Ilyitch was beginning. 'I did not come with that idea . . . I . . . meant to be going . . .'

He was, in fact, holding his hat in his hands. What is more, he had at that very moment taken an inward vow at all costs to depart at once and on no account whatever to consent to remain, and . . . he remained. A minute later he led the procession to the table. Pseldonimov and his mother walked in front, clearing the way for him. They made him sit down in the seat of honour, and again a bottle of champagne, opened but not begun, was set beside his plate. By way of *hors d'oeuvre* there were salt herrings and vodka. He put out his hand, poured out a large glass of vodka and drank it off. He had never drunk vodka before. He felt as though he were rolling down a hill, were flying, flying, flying, that he must stop himself, catch at something, but there was no possibility of it.

His position was certainly becoming more and more eccentric. What is more, it seemed as though fate were mocking at him. God knows what had happened to him in the course of an hour or so. When he went in he had, so to say, opened his arms to embrace all humanity, all his subordinates; and here not more than an hour had passed and in all his aching heart he felt and knew that he hated Pseldonimov and was cursing him, his wife and his wedding. What was more, he saw from his face, from his eyes alone, that Pseldonimov himself hated him, that he was looking at him with eyes that almost said: 'If only you would take yourself off, curse you! Foisting yourself on us!' All this he had read for some time in his eyes.

Of course as he sat down to table, Ivan Ilyitch would sooner have had his hand cut off than have owned, not only aloud, but even to himself, that this was really so. The moment had not fully arrived yet. There was still a moral vacillation. But his heart, his heart . . . it ached! It was clamouring for freedom, for air, for rest. Ivan Ilyitch was really too good-natured.

He knew, of course, that he ought long before to have gone away, not merely to have gone away but to have made his escape. That all this was not the same, but had turned out utterly different from what he had dreamed of on the pavement.

'Why did I come? Did I come here to eat and drink?' he asked himself as he tasted the salt herring. He even had attacks of scepticism. There was at moments a faint stir of irony in regard to his own fine action at the bottom of his heart. He actually wondered at times why he had come in.

But how could he go away? To go away like this without having finished the business properly was impossible. What would people say? They would say that he was frequenting low company. Indeed it really would amount to that if he did not end it properly. What would Stepan Nikiforovitch, Semyon Ivanovitch say (for of course it would be all over the place by tomorrow)? what would be said in the offices, at the Shembels', at the Shubins'? No, he must take his departure in such a way that all should understand why he had come, he must make clear his moral aim . . . And meantime the dramatic moment would not present itself. 'They don't even respect me,' he went on thinking. 'What are they laughing at? They are as free and easy as though they had no feeling . . . But I have long suspected that all the younger generation are without feeling! I must remain at all costs! They have just been dancing, but now at table they will all be gathered together . . . I will talk about questions, about reforms, about the greatness of Russia . . . I can still win their enthusiasm! Yes! Perhaps nothing is yet lost . . . Perhaps it is always like this in reality. What should I begin upon with them to attract them? What plan can I hit upon? I am lost, simply lost . . . And what is it they want, what is it they require? . . . I see they are laughing together there. Can it be at me, merciful heavens! But what is it I want . . . why is it I am here, why don't I go away, why do I go on persisting?' . . . He thought this, and a sort of shame, a deep unbearable shame, rent his heart more and more intensely.

But everything went on in the same way, one thing after another.

Just two minutes after he had sat down to the table one terrible thought overwhelmed him completely. He suddenly felt that he was horribly drunk; that is, not as he was before, but hopelessly drunk. The cause of this was the glass of vodka which he had drunk after the champagne, and which had immediately produced an effect. He was conscious, he felt in every fibre of his being that he was growing hopelessly feeble. Of course, his assurance was greatly increased, but consciousness had not deserted him, and it kept crying out: 'It is bad, very bad and, in fact, utterly unseemly!' Of course, his unstable drunken reflections could not rest long on one subject; there began to be apparent, and unmistakably so, even to himself, two opposite sides. On one side there was swaggering assurance, a desire to conquer, a disdain of obstacles and a desperate confidence that he would attain his object. The other side showed itself in the aching of his heart, and a sort of gnawing in his soul. 'What would they say? How would it all end? What would happen tomorrow, tomorrow, tomorrow? . . .'

He had felt vaguely before that he had enemies in the company. 'No doubt that was because I was drunk,' he thought with agonising doubt. What was his horror when he actually, by unmistakable signs, convinced himself now that he really had enemies at the table, and that it was impossible to doubt of it.

'And why – why?' he wondered.

At the table there were all the thirty guests, of whom several were quite tipsy. Others were behaving with a careless and sinister independence, shouting and talking at the top of their voices, bawling out the toasts before the time, and pelting the ladies with pellets of bread. One unprepossessing personage in a greasy coat had fallen off his chair as soon as he sat down, and remained so till the end of supper. Another one made desperate efforts to stand on the table, to propose a toast, and only the officer, who seized him by the tails of his coat, moderated his premature ardour. The supper was a pell-mell affair, although they had hired a cook who had been in the service of a general;

there was the galantine, there was tongue and potatoes, there were rissoles with green peas, there was, finally, a goose, and last of all blancmange. Among the drinks were beer, vodka and sherry. The only bottle of champagne was standing beside the general, which obliged him to pour it out for himself and also for Akim Petrovitch, who did not venture at supper to officiate on his own initiative. The other guests had to drink the toasts in Caucasian wine or anything else they could get. The table was made up of several tables put together, among them even a card-table. It was covered with many tablecloths, amongst them one coloured Yaroslav cloth; the gentlemen sat alternately with the ladies. Pseldonimov's mother would not sit down to the table; she bustled about and supervised. But another sinister female figure, who had not shown herself till then, appeared on the scene, wearing a reddish silk dress, with a very high cap on her head and a bandage round her face for toothache. It appeared that this was the bride's mother, who had at last consented to emerge from a back room for supper. She had refused to appear till then owing to her implacable hostility to Pseldonimov's mother, but to that we will refer later. This lady looked spitefully, even sarcastically, at the general, and evidently did not wish to be presented to him. To Ivan Ilyitch this figure appeared suspicious in the extreme. But apart from her, several other persons were suspicious and inspired involuntary apprehension and uneasiness. It even seemed that they were in some sort of plot together against Ivan Ilyitch. At any rate it seemed so to him, and throughout the whole supper he became more and more convinced of it. A gentleman with a beard, some sort of free artist, was particularly sinister; he even looked at Ivan Ilyitch several times, and then turning to his neighbour, whispered something. Another person present was unmistakably drunk, but yet, from certain signs, was to be regarded with suspicion. The medical student, too, gave rise to unpleasant expectations. Even the officer himself was not quite to be depended on. But the young man on the comic paper was blazing with hatred, he lolled in his chair, he looked so haughty and conceited, he snorted so aggressively! And though the rest of the guests took absolutely no notice of the young journalist, who had contributed only four wretched poems to the *Firebrand*, and had consequently become a Liberal and evidently, indeed, disliked him, yet when a pellet of bread aimed in his direction fell near Ivan Ilyitch, he was ready to stake his head that it had been thrown by no other than the young man in question.

All this, of course, had a pitiable effect on him.

Another observation was particularly unpleasant. Ivan Ilyitch became aware that he was beginning to articulate indistinctly and with difficulty, that he was longing to say a great deal, but that his tongue refused to obey him. And then he suddenly seemed to forget himself, and worst of all he would suddenly burst into a loud guffaw of laughter, *à propos* of nothing. This inclination quickly passed off after a glass of champagne which Ivan Ilyitch had not meant to drink, though he had poured it out and suddenly drunk it quite by accident. After that glass he felt at once almost inclined to cry. He felt that he was sinking into a most peculiar state of sentimentality; he began to be again filled with love, he loved everyone, even Pseldonimov, even the young man on the comic paper. He suddenly longed to embrace all of them, to forget everything and to be reconciled. What is more, to tell them everything openly, all, all; that is, to tell them what a good, nice man he was, with what wonderful talents. What services he would do for his country, how good he was at entertaining the fair sex, and above all, how progressive he was, how humanely ready he was to be indulgent to all, to the very lowest; and finally in conclusion to tell them frankly all the motives that had impelled him to turn up at Pseldonimov's uninvited, to drink two bottles of champagne and to make him happy with his presence.

'The truth, the holy truth and candour before all things! I will capture them by candour. They will believe me, I see it clearly; they actually look at me with hostility, but when I tell them all I shall conquer them completely. They will fill their glasses and drink my health with shouts. The officer will break his glass on his spur. Perhaps they will even shout hurrah! Even if they want to toss me after the Hussar fashion I will not oppose them, and indeed it would be very jolly! I will kiss the bride on her forehead; she is charming. Akim Petrovitch is a very nice man, too. Pseldonimov will improve, of course, later on. He will acquire, so to speak, a society polish . . . And although, of course, the younger generation has not that delicacy of feeling, yet . . . yet I will talk to them about the contemporary significance of Russia among the European States. I will refer to the peasant question, too; yes, and . . . and they will all like me and I shall leave with glory! . . .'

These dreams were, of course, extremely agreeable, but what was unpleasant was that in the midst of these roseate anticipations, Ivan Ilyitch suddenly discovered in himself another unexpected propensity, that was to spit. Anyway saliva began running from his mouth apart from any will of his own. He observed this on Akim Petrovitch, whose cheek he spluttered upon and who sat not daring to wipe it off from respectfulness. Ivan Ilyitch took his dinner napkin and wiped it himself, but this immediately struck him himself as so incongruous, so opposed to all common sense, that he sank into silence and began wondering. Though Akim Petrovitch emptied his glass, yet he sat as though he were scalded. Ivan Ilyitch reflected now that he had for almost a quarter of an hour been talking to him about some most interesting subject, but that Akim Petrovitch had not only seemed embarrassed as he listened, but positively frightened. Pseldonimov, who was sitting one chair away from him, also craned his neck towards him, and bending his head sideways, listened to him with the most unpleasant air. He actually seemed to be keeping a watch on him. Turning his eyes upon the rest of the company, he saw that many were looking straight at him and laughing. But what was strangest of all was, that he was not in the least embarrassed by it; on the contrary, he sipped his glass again and suddenly began speaking so that all could hear:

'I was saying just now,' he began as loudly as possible, 'I was saying just now, ladies and gentlemen, to Akim Petrovitch, that Russia . . . yes, Russia . . . in short, you understand, that I mean to s-s-say . . . Russia is living, it is my profound conviction, through a period of hu-hu-manity . . .'

'Hu-hu-manity . . .' was heard at the other end of the table.

'Hu-hu . . .'

'Tu-tu!'

Ivan Ilyitch stopped. Pseldonimov got up from his chair and began trying to see who had shouted. Akim Petrovitch stealthily shook his head, as though admonishing the guests. Ivan Ilyitch saw this distinctly, but in his confusion said nothing.

'Humanity!' he continued obstinately; 'and this evening . . . and only this evening I said to Stepan Niki-ki-forovitch . . . yes . . . that . . . that the regeneration, so to speak, of things . . .'

'Your Excellency!' was heard a loud exclamation at the other end of the table.

'What is your pleasure?' answered Ivan Ilyitch, pulled up short and trying to distinguish who had called to him.

'Nothing at all, your Excellency. I was carried away, continue! Con-ti-nue!' the voice was heard again.

Ivan Ilyitch felt upset.

'The regeneration, so to speak, of those same things.'

'Your Excellency!' the voice shouted again.

'What do you want?'

'How do you do!'

This time Ivan Ilyitch could not restrain himself. He broke off his speech and turned to the assailant who had disturbed the general harmony. He was a very young lad, still at school, who had taken more than a drop too much, and was an object of great suspicion to the general. He had been shouting for a long time past, and had even broken a glass and two plates, maintaining that this was the proper thing to do at a wedding. At the moment when Ivan Ilyitch turned towards him, the officer was beginning to pitch into the noisy youngster.

'What are you about? Why are you yelling? We shall turn you out, that's what we shall do.'

'I don't mean you, your Excellency, I don't mean you. Continue!' cried the hilarious schoolboy, lolling back in his chair. 'Continue, I am listening, and am very, ve-ry, ve-ry much pleased with you! Praisewor-thy, praisewor-thy!'

'The wretched boy is drunk,' said Pseldonimov in a whisper.

'I see that he is drunk, but . . .'

'I was just telling a very amusing ancedote, your Excellency!' began the officer, 'about a lieutenant in our company who was talking just like that to his superior officers; so this young man is imitating him now. To every word of his superior officers he said "praiseworthy, praiseworthy!" He was turned out of the army ten years ago on account of it.'

'Wha-at lieutenant was that?'

'In our company, your Excellency, he went out of his mind over the word "praiseworthy". At first they tried gentle methods, then they put him under arrest . . . His commanding officer admonished him in the most fatherly way, and he answered, "Praiseworthy, praiseworthy!" And strange to say, the officer was a fine-looking man, over six feet. They meant to court-martial him, but then they perceived that he was mad.'

'So . . . a schoolboy. A schoolboy's prank need not be taken seriously. For my part I am ready to overlook it . . .'

'They held a medical inquiry, your Excellency.'

'Upon my word, but he was alive, wasn't he?'

'What! Did they dissect him?'

A loud and almost universal roar of laughter resounded among the guests, who had till then behaved with decorum. Ivan Ilyitch was furious.

'Ladies and gentlemen!' he shouted, at first scarcely stammering, 'I am fully capable of apprehending that a man is not dissected alive. I imagined that in his derangement he had ceased to be alive . . . that is, that he had died . . . that is, I mean to say . . . that you don't like me . . . and yet I like you all . . . Yes, I like Por . . . Porfiry . . . I am lowering myself by speaking like this . . .'

At that moment Ivan Ilyitch spluttered so that a great dab of saliva flew on to the tablecloth in a most conspicuous place. Pseldonimov flew to wipe it off with a table-napkin. This last disaster crushed him completely.

'My friends, this is too much,' he cried in despair.

'The man is drunk, your Excellency,' Pseldonimov prompted him again.

'Porfiry, I see that you . . . all . . . yes! I say that I hope . . . yes, I call upon you all to tell me in what way have I lowered myself?'

Ivan Ilyitch was almost crying.

'Your Excellency, good heavens!'

'Porfiry, I appeal to you . . . Tell me, when I came . . . yes . . . yes, to your wedding, I had an object. I was aiming at moral elevation . . . I wanted it to be felt . . . I appeal to all: am I greatly lowered in your eyes or not?'

A deathlike silence. That was just it, a deathlike silence, and to such a downright question. 'They might at least shout at this minute!' flashed through his Excellency's head. But the guests only looked at one another. Akim Petrovitch sat more dead than alive, while Pseldonimov, numb with terror, was repeating to himself the awful question which had occurred to him more than once already.

'What shall I have to pay for all this tomorrow?'

At this point the young man on the comic paper, who was very drunk but who had hitherto sat in morose silence, addressed Ivan Ilyitch directly, and with flashing eyes began answering in the name of the whole company.

'Yes,' he said in a loud voice, 'yes, you have lowered yourself. Yes, you are a reactionary . . . re-ac-tion-ary!'

'Young man, you are forgetting yourself! To whom are you speaking, so to express it?' Ivan Ilyitch cried furiously, jumping up from his seat again.

'To you; and secondly, I am not a young man . . . You've come to give yourself airs and try to win popularity.'

'Pseldonimov, what does this mean?' cried Ivan Ilyitch.

But Pseldonimov was reduced to such horror that he stood still like a post and was utterly at a loss what to do. The guests, too, sat mute in their seats. All but the artist and the schoolboy, who applauded and shouted, 'Bravo, bravo!'

The young man on the comic paper went on shouting with unrestrained violence:

'Yes, you came to show off your humanity! You've hindered the enjoyment of everyone. You've been drinking champagne without thinking that it is beyond the means of a clerk at ten roubles a month. And I suspect that you are one of those high officials who are a little too fond of the young wives of their clerks! What is more, I am convinced that you support State monopolies . . . Yes, yes, yes!'

'Pseldonimov, Pseldonimov,' shouted Ivan Ilyitch, holding out his hands to him. He felt that every word uttered by the comic young man was a fresh dagger at his heart.

'Directly, your Excellency; please do not disturb yourself!' Pseldonimov cried energetically, rushing up to the comic young man, seizing him by the collar and dragging him away from the table. Such physical strength could indeed not have been expected from the weakly-looking Pseldonimov. But the comic young man was very drunk, while Pseldonimov was perfectly sober. Then he gave him two or three cuffs in the back, and thrust him out of the door.

'You are all scoundrels!' roared the young man of the comic paper. 'I will caricature you all tomorrow in the *Firebrand*.'

They all leapt up from their seats.

'Your Excellency, your Excellency!' cried Pseldonimov, his mother and several others, crowding round the general; 'your Excellency, do not be disturbed!'

'No, no,' cried the general, 'I am annihilated . . . I came . . . I meant to bless you, so to speak. And this is how I am paid, for everything, everything! . . .'

He sank on to a chair as though unconscious, laid both his arms on the table, and bowed his head over them, straight into a plate of blancmange. There is no need to describe the general horror. A minute later he got up, evidently meaning to go out, gave a lurch, stumbled against the leg of a chair, fell full length on the floor and snored . . .

This is what is apt to happen to men who don't drink when they accidentally take a glass too much. They preserve their consciousness to the last point, to the last minute, and then fall to the ground as though struck down. Ivan Ilyitch lay on the floor absolutely unconscious. Pseldonimov clutched at his hair and sat as though petrified in that position. The guests made haste to depart, commenting each in his own way on the incident. It was about three o'clock in the morning.

The worst of it was that Pseldonimov's circumstances were far worse than could have been imagined, in spite of the unattractiveness of his present surroundings. And while Ivan Ilyitch is lying on the floor and Pseldonimov is standing over him tearing his hair in despair, we will break off the thread of our story and say a few explanatory words about Porfiry Petrovitch Pseldonimov.

Not more than a month before his wedding he was in a state of hopeless destitution. He came from a province where his father had served in some department and where he had died while awaiting his trial on some charge. When five months before his wedding, Pseldonimov, who had been in hopeless misery in Petersburg for a whole year before, got his berth at ten roubles a month, he revived both physically and mentally, but he was soon crushed by circumstances again. There were only two Pseldonimovs left in the world, himself and his mother, who had left the province after her husband's death. The mother and son barely existed in the freezing cold, and sustained life on the most dubious substances. There were days when Pseldonimov himself went with a jug to the Fontanka for water to drink. When he got his place he succeeded in settling with his mother in a 'corner'. She took in washing, while for four months he scraped together every farthing to get himself boots and an overcoat. And what troubles he had to endure at his office; his superiors approached him with the question: 'How long was it since he had had a bath?' There was a rumour about him that under the collar of his uniform there were nests of bugs. But Pseldonimov was a man of strong character. On the surface he was mild and meek; he had the merest smattering of education, he was practically never heard to talk of anything. I do not know for certain whether he thought, made plans and theories, had dreams. But on the other hand there was being formed within him an instinctive, furtive, unconscious determination to fight his way out of his wretched circumstances. He had the persistence of an ant. Destroy an ants' nest, and they will begin at once re-erecting it; destroy it again, and they will begin again without wearying. He was a constructive house-building animal. One could see from his brow that he would make his way, would build his nest, and perhaps even save for a rainy day. His mother was the only creature in the world who loved him, and she loved him beyond everything. She was a woman of resolute character, hard-working and indefatigable, and at the same time good-natured. So perhaps they might have lived in their corner for five or six years till their circumstances changed, if they had not come across the retired titular councillor Mlekopitaev, who had been a clerk in the treasury and had served at one time in the provinces, but had latterly settled in Petersburg and had established himself there with his family. He knew Pseldonimov, and had at one time been under some obligation to his father. He had a little money, not a large sum, of course, but there it was; how much it was no one knew, not his wife, nor his elder daughter, nor his relations. He had two daughters, and as he was an awful bully, a drunkard, a domestic tyrant, and in addition to that an invalid, he took it into his head one day to marry one of his daughters to Pseldonimov: 'I knew his father,' he would say, 'he was a good fellow and his son will be a good fellow.' Mlekopitaev did exactly as he liked, his word was law. He was a very queer bully. For the most part he spent his time sitting in an arm-chair, having lost the use of his legs from some disease which did not, however, prevent him from drinking vodka. For days together he would be drinking and swearing. He was an ill-natured man. He always wanted to have someone whom he could be continually tormenting. And for that purpose he kept several distant relations: his sister, a sickly and peevish woman; two of his wife's sisters, also ill-natured and very free with their tongues, and his old aunt, who had through some accident a broken rib; he kept another dependant also, a Russianised German, for the sake of her talent for entertaining him with stories from the *Arabian Nights*. His sole gratification consisted in jeering at all these unfortunate women and abusing them every minute with all his energies; though the latter, not excepting his wife, who had been born with toothache, dared not utter a word in his presence. He set them at loggerheads at one another, inventing and fostering spiteful backbiting and dissensions among them, and then laughed and rejoiced seeing how they were ready to tear one another to pieces. He was very much delighted when his elder daughter, who had lived in great poverty for ten years with her husband, an officer of some sort, and was at last left a widow, came to live with him with three little sickly children. He could not endure her children, but as her arrival had increased the material upon which he could work his daily experiments, the old man was very much pleased. All these ill-natured women and sickly children, together with their tormentor, were crowded together in a wooden house on Petersburg Side, and did not get enough to eat because the old man was stingy and gave out to them money a farthing at a time, though he did not grudge himself vodka; they did not get enough sleep because the old man suffered from sleeplessness and insisted on being amused. In short, they all were in misery and cursed their fate. It was at that time that Mlekopitaev's eye fell upon Pseldonimov. He was struck by his long nose and submissive air. His weakly and unprepossessing younger daughter had just reached the age of seventeen. Though she had at one time attended a German school, she had acquired scarcely anything but the alphabet. Then she grew up rickety and anaemic in fear of her crippled drunken father's crutch, in a Bedlam of domestic backbiting, eavesdropping and scolding. She had never had any friends or any brains. She had for a long time been eager to be married. In company she sat mute, but at home with her mother and the women of the household she was spiteful and cantankerous. She was particularly fond of pinching and smacking her sister's children, telling tales of their pilfering bread and sugar, and this led to endless and implacable strife with her elder sister. Her old father himself offered her to Pseldonimov. Miserable as the latter's position was, he yet asked for a little time to consider. His mother and he hesitated for a long time. But with the young lady there was to come as dowry a house, and though it was a nasty little wooden house of one storey, yet it was property of a kind. Moreover, they would give with her four hundred roubles, and how long it would take him to save it up himself! 'What am I taking the man into my house for?' shouted the drunken bully. 'In the first place because you are all females, and I am sick of female society. I want Pseldonimov, too, to dance to my piping. For I am his benefactor. And in the second place I am doing it because you are all cross and don't want it, so I'll do it to spite you. What I have said, I have said! And you beat her, Porfiry, when she is your wife; she has been possessed of seven devils ever since she was born. You beat them out of her, and I'll get the stick ready.'

Pseldonimov made no answer, but he was already decided. Before the wedding his mother and he were taken into the house, washed, clothed, provided with boots and money for the wedding. The old man took them under his protection possibly just because the whole family was prejudiced against them. He positively liked Pseldonimov's mother, so that he actually restrained himself and did not jeer at her. On the other hand, he made Pseldonimov dance the Cossack dance a week before the wedding.

'Well, that's enough. I only wanted to see whether you

remembered your position before me or not,' he said at the end of the dance. He allowed just enough money for the wedding, with nothing to spare, and invited all his relations and acquaintances. On the Pseldonimovs' side there was no one but the young man who wrote for the *Firebrand*, and Akim Petrovitch, the guest of honour. Pseldonimov was perfectly aware that his bride cherished an aversion for him, and that she was set upon marrying the officer instead of him. But he put up with everything, he had made a compact with his mother to do so. The old father had been drunk and abusive and foul-tongued the whole of the wedding day and during the party in the evening. The whole family took refuge in the back rooms and were crowded there to suffocation. The front rooms were devoted to the dance and the supper. At last when the old man fell asleep dead drunk at eleven o'clock, the bride's mother, who had been particularly displeased with Pseldonimov's mother that day, made up her mind to lay aside her wrath, become gracious and join the company. Ivan Ilyitch's arrival had turned everything upside down. Madame Mlekopitaev was overcome with embarrassment, and began grumbling that she had not been told that the general had been invited. She was assured that he had come uninvited, but was so stupid as to refuse to believe it. Champagne had to be got. Pseldonimov's mother had only one rouble, while Pseldonimov himself had not one farthing. He had to grovel before his ill-natured mother-in-law, to beg for the money for one bottle and then for another. They pleaded for the sake of his future position in the service, for his career, they tried to persuade her. She did at last give from her own purse, but she forced Pseldonimov to swallow such a cupful of gall and bitterness that more than once he ran into the room where the nuptial couch had been prepared, and madly clutching at his hair and trembling all over with impotent rage, he buried his head in the bed destined for the joys of paradise. No, indeed, Ivan Ilyitch had no notion of the price paid for the two bottles of Jackson he had drunk that evening. What was the horror, the misery and even the despair of Pseldonimov when Ivan Ilyitch's visit ended in this unexpected way. He had a prospect again of no end of misery, and perhaps a night of tears and outcries from his peevish bride, and upbraidings from her unreasonable relations. Even apart from this his head ached already, and there was dizziness and mist before his eyes. And here Ivan Ilyitch needed looking after, at three o'clock at night he had to hunt for a doctor or a carriage to take him home, and a carriage it must be, for it would be impossible to let an ordinary cabby take him home in that condition. And where could he get the money even for a carriage? Madame Mlekopitaev, furious that the general had not addressed two words to her, and had not even looked at her at supper, declared that she had not a farthing. Possibly she really had not a farthing. Where could he get it? What was he to do? Yes, indeed, he had good cause to tear his hair.

*

Meanwhile Ivan Ilyitch was moved to a little leather sofa that stood in the dining-room. While they were clearing the tables and putting them away, Pseldonimov was rushing all over the place to borrow money, he even tried to get it from the servants, but it appeared that nobody had any. He even ventured to trouble Akim Petrovitch who had stayed after the other guests. But good-natured as he was, the latter was reduced to such bewilderment and even alarm at the mention of money that he uttered the most unexpected and foolish phrases:

'Another time, with pleasure,' he muttered, 'but now . . . you really must excuse me . . .'

And taking his cap, he ran as fast as he could out of the house. Only the good-natured youth who had talked about the dream book was any use at all; and even that came to nothing. He, too, stayed after the others, showing genuine sympathy with Pseldonimov's misfortunes. At last Pseldonimov, together with his mother and the young man, decided in consultation not to send for a doctor, but rather to fetch a carriage and take the invalid home, and meantime to try certain domestic remedies till the carriage arrived, such as moistening his temples and his head with cold water, putting ice on his head, and so on. Pseldonimov's mother undertook this task. The friendly youth flew off in search of a carriage. As there were not even ordinary cabs to be found on the Petersburg Side at that hour, he went off to some livery stables at a distance to wake up the coachmen. They began bargaining, and declared that five roubles would be little to ask for a carriage at that time of night. They agreed to come, however, for three. When at last, just before five o'clock, the young man arrived at Pseldonimov's with the carriage, they had changed their minds. It appeared that Ivan Ilyitch, who was still unconscious, had became so seriously unwell, was moaning and tossing so terribly, that to move him and take him home in such a condition was impossible and actually unsafe. 'What will it lead to next?' said Pseldonimov, utterly disheartened. What was to be done? A new problem arose: if the invalid remained in the house, where should he be moved and where could they put him? There were only two bedsteads in the house: one large double bed in which old Mlekopitaev and his wife slept, and another double bed of imitation walnut which had just been purchased and was destined for the newly married couple. All the other inhabitants of the house slept on the floor side by side on feather beds, for the most part in bad condition and stuffy, anything but presentable in fact, and even of these the supply was insufficient; there was not one to spare. Where could the invalid be put? A feather bed might perhaps have been found – it might in the last resort have been pulled from under someone, but where and on what could a bed have been made up? It seemed that the bed must be made up in the drawing-room, for that room was the furthest from the bosom of the family and had a door into the passage. But on what could the bed be made? Surely not upon chairs. We all know that beds can only be made up on chairs for schoolboys when they come home for the weekend, and it would be terribly lacking in respect to make up a bed in that way for a personage like Ivan Ilyitch. What would be said next morning when he found himself lying on chairs? Pseldonimov would not hear of that. The only alternative was to put him on the bridal couch. This bridal couch, as we have mentioned already, was in a little room that opened out of the dining-room, on the bedstead was a double mattress actually newly bought first-hand, clean sheets, four pillows in pink calico covered with frilled muslin cases. The quilt was of pink satin, and it was quilted in patterns. Muslin curtains hung down from a golden ring overhead, in fact it was all just as it should be, and the guests who had all visited the bridal chamber had admired the decoration of it; though the bride could not endure Pseldonimov, she had several times in the course of the evening run in to have a look at it on the sly. What was her indignation, her wrath, when she learned that they meant to move an invalid, suffering from something not unlike a mild attack of cholera, to her bridal couch! The bride's mother took her part, broke into abuse and vowed she would complain to her husband next day, but Pseldonimov asserted himself and insisted: Ivan Ilyitch was moved into the bridal chamber, and a bed was made up on chairs for the young people. The bride whimpered, would have liked to pinch him, but dared not disobey; her papa had a crutch with which she was very familiar, and she knew that her papa would call her to account next day. To console her they carried the pink satin quilt and the pillows in muslin cases into the drawing-room. At that moment the youth arrived with the carriage, and was horribly alarmed that the carriage was not wanted. He was left to pay for it himself, and he never had as much as a ten-kopeck piece. Pseldonimov explained that he was utterly bankrupt. They tried to parley with the driver. But he began to be noisy and even to batter on the shutters. How it ended I don't know exactly. I believe the youth was carried off to Peski by way of a hostage to Fourth Rozhdensky Street, where he hoped to rouse a student who was spending the night at a friend's, and to try whether he had any money. It was going on for six o'clock in the morning when the young people were left alone and shut up in the drawing-room. Pseldonimov's mother spent the whole night by the bedside of the sufferer. She installed herself on a rug on the floor and covered herself with an old coat, but could not sleep because she had to get up every minute: Ivan Ilyitch had a terrible attack of colic. Madame Pseldonimov, a woman of courage and greatness of soul, undressed him with her own hands, took off all his things, looked after him as if he were her own son, and spent the whole night carrying basins, etc., from the bedroom across the passage and bringing them back again empty. And yet the misfortunes of that night were not yet over.

Not more than ten minutes after the young people had been shut up alone in the drawing-room, a piercing shriek was suddenly heard, not a cry of joy, but a shriek of the most sinister kind.

The screams were followed by a noise, a crash, as though of the falling of chairs, and instantly there burst into the still dark room a perfect crowd of exclaiming and frightened women, attired in every kind of *déshabillé*. These women were the bride's mother, her elder sister, abandoning for the moment the sick children, and her three aunts, even the one with a broken rib dragged herself in. Even the cook was there, and the German lady who told stories, whose own feather bed, the best in the house, and her only property, had been forcibly dragged from under her for the young couple, trailed in together with the others. All these respectable and sharp-eyed ladies had, a quarter of an hour before, made their way on tiptoe from the kitchen across the passage, and were listening in the ante-room, devoured by unaccountable curiosity. Meanwhile someone lighted a candle, and a surprising spectacle met the eyes of all. The chairs supporting the broad feather bed only at the sides had parted under the weight, and the feather bed had fallen between them on the floor. The bride was sobbing with anger, this time she was mortally offended. Pseldonimov, morally shattered, stood like a criminal caught in a crime. He did not even attempt to defend himself. Shrieks and exclamations sounded on all sides. Pseldonimov's mother ran up at the noise, but the bride's mamma on this occasion got the upper hand. She began by showering strange and for the most part quite undeserved reproaches, such as: 'A nice husband you are, after this. What are you good for after such a disgrace?' and so on; and at last carried her daughter away from her husband, undertaking to bear the full responsibility for doing so with her ferocious husband, who would demand an explanation. All the others followed her out exclaiming and shaking their heads. No one remained with Pseldonimov except his mother, who tried to comfort him. But he sent her away at once.

He was beyond consolation. He made his way to the sofa and sat down in the most gloomy confusion of mind just as he was, barefooted and in nothing but his night attire. His thoughts whirled in a tangled criss-cross in his mind. At times he mechanically looked about the room where only a little while ago the dancers had been whirling madly, and in which the cigarette smoke still lingered. Cigarette ends and sweet-meat papers still littered the slopped and dirty floor. The wreck of the nuptial couch and the overturned chairs bore witness to the transitoriness to the fondest and surest earthly hopes and dreams. He sat like this almost an hour. The most oppressive thoughts kept coming into his mind, such as the doubt: What was in store for him in the office now? He recognised with painful clearness that he would have, at all costs, to exchange into another department; that he could not possibly remain where he was after all that had happened that evening. He thought, too, of Mlekopitaev, who would probably make him dance the Cossack dance next day to test his meekness. He reflected, too, that though Mlekopitaev had given fifty roubles for the wedding festivities, every farthing of which had been spent, he had not thought of giving him the four hundred roubles yet, no mention had been made of it, in fact. And, indeed, even the house had not been formally made over to him. He thought, too, of his wife, who had left him at the most critical moment of his life, of the tall officer who had dropped on one knee before her. He had noticed that already; he thought of the seven devils which according to the testimony of her own father were in possession of his wife, and of the crutch in readiness to drive them out . . . Of course he felt equal to bearing a great deal, but destiny had let loose such surprises upon him that he might well have doubts of his fortitude. So Pseldonimov mused dolefully. Meanwhile the candle end was going out, its fading light, falling straight upon Pseldonimov's profile, threw a colossal shadow of it on the wall, with a drawn-out neck, a hooked nose, and with two tufts of hair sticking out on his forehead and the back of his head. At last, when the air was growing cool with the chill of early morning, he got up, frozen and spiritually numb, crawled to the feather bed that was lying between the chairs, and without rearranging anything, without putting out the candle end, without even laying the pillow under his head, fell into a leaden, deathlike sleep, such as the sleep of men condemned to flogging on the tomorrow must be.

On the other hand, what could be compared with the agonising night spent by Ivan Ilyitch Pralinsky on the bridal couch of the unlucky Pseldonimov! For some time, headache, vomiting and other most unpleasant symptoms did not leave him for one second. He was in the torments of hell. The faint glimpses of consciousness that visited his brain, lighted up such an abyss of horrors, such gloomy and revolting pictures, that it would have been better for him not to have returned to consciousness. Everything was still in a turmoil in his mind, however. He recognised Pseldonimov's mother, for instance, heard her gentle admonitions, such as: 'Be patient, my dear; be patient, good sir, it won't be so bad presently.' He recognised her, but could give no logical explanation of her presence beside him. Revolting phantoms haunted him, most frequently of all he was haunted by Semyon Ivanovitch; but looking more intently, he saw that it was not Semyon Ivanovitch but Pseldonimov's nose. He had visions, too, of the free-and-easy artist, and the officer and the old lady with her face tied up. What interested him most of all was the gilt ring which hung over his head, through which the curtains hung. He could distinguish it distinctly in the dim light of the candle end which lighted up the room, and he kept wondering inwardly: What was the object of that ring, why was it there, what did it mean? He questioned the old lady several times about it, but apparently did not say what he meant; and she evidently did not understand it, however much he struggled to explain. At last by morning the symptoms had ceased and he fell into a sleep, a sound sleep without dreams. He slept about an hour, and when he woke he was almost completely conscious, with an insufferable headache, and a disgusting taste in his mouth and on his tongue, which seemed turned into a piece of cloth. He sat up in the bed, looked about him, and pondered. The pale light of morning peeping through the cracks of the shutters in a narrow streak, quivered on the wall. It was about seven o'clock in the morning. But when Ivan Ilyitch suddenly grasped the position and recalled all that had happened to him since the evening; when he remembered all his adventures at supper, the failure of his magnanimous action, his speech at table; when he realised all at once with horrifying clearness all that might come of this now, all that people would say and think of him; when he looked round and saw to what a mournful and hideous condition he had reduced the peaceful bridal couch of his clerk – oh, then such deadly shame, such agony overwhelmed him, that he uttered a shriek, hid his face in his hands and fell back on the pillow in despair. A minute later he jumped out of bed, saw his clothes carefully folded and brushed on a chair beside him, and seizing them, and as quickly as he could, in desperate haste began putting them on, looking round and seeming terribly frightened at something. On another chair close by lay his greatcoat and fur cap, and his yellow gloves were in his cap. He meant to steal away secretly. But suddenly the door opened and the elder Madame Pseldonimov walked in with an earthenware jug and basin. A towel was hanging over her shoulder. She set down the jug, and without further conversation told him that he must wash.

'Come, my good sir, wash; you can't go without washing . . .'

And at that instant Ivan Ilyitch recognised that if there was one being in the whole world whom he need not fear, and before whom he need not feel ashamed, it was that old lady. He washed. And long afterwards, at painful moments of his life, he recalled among other pangs of remorse all the circumstances of that waking, and that earthenware basin, and the china jug filled with cold water in which there were still floating icicles, and the oval cake of soap at fifteen kopecks, in pink paper with letters embossed on it, evidently bought for the bridal pair though it fell to Ivan Ilyitch to use it, and the old lady with the linen towel over her left shoulder. The cold water refreshed him, he dried his face, and without even thanking his sister of mercy, he snatched up his hat, flung over his shoulders the coat handed to him by Pseldonimov, and crossing the passage and the kitchen where the cat was already mewing, and the cook sitting up in her bed staring after him with greedy curiosity, ran out into the yard, into the street, and threw himself into the first sledge he came across. It was a frosty morning. A chilly yellow fog still hid the house and everything. Ivan Ilyitch turned up his collar. He thought that everyone was looking at him, that they were all recognising him, all . . .

For eight days he did not leave the house or show himself at the office. He was ill, wretchedly ill, but more morally than physically. He lived through a perfect hell in those days, and they must have been reckoned to his account in the other world. There were moments when he thought of becoming a monk and entering a monastery. There really were. His imagination, indeed, took special excursions during that period. He pictured subdued subterranean singing, an open coffin, living in a solitary cell, forests and caves; but when he came to himself he recognised almost at once that all this was dreadful nonsense and exaggeration, and was ashamed of this nonsense. Then began attacks of moral agony on the theme of his *existence manquée*. Then shame flamed up again in his soul, took complete possession of him at once, consumed him like fire and re-opened his wounds. He shuddered as pictures of all sorts rose before his mind. What would people say about him, what would they think when he walked into his office? what a whisper would dog his steps for a whole year, ten years, his whole life! His story would go down to posterity. He sometimes fell into such dejection that he was ready to go straight off to Semyon Ivanovitch and ask for his forgiveness and friendship. He did not even justify himself, there was no limit to his blame of himself. He could find no extenuating circumstances, and was ashamed of trying to.

He had thoughts, too, of resigning his post at once and devoting himself to human happiness as a simple citizen, in solitude. In any case he would have completely to change his whole circle of acquaintances, and so thoroughly as to eradicate all memory of himself. Then the thought occurred to him that this, too, was nonsense, and that if he adopted greater severity with his subordinates it might all be set right. Then he began to feel hope and courage again. At last, at the expiration of eight days of hesitation and agonies, he felt that he could not endure to be in uncertainty any longer, and *un beau matin* he made up his mind to go to the office.

He had pictured a thousand times over his return to the office as he sat at home in misery. With horror and conviction he told himself that he would certainly hear behind him an ambiguous whisper, would see ambiguous faces, would intercept ominous smiles. What was his surprise when nothing of the sort happened. He was greeted with respect; he was met with bows; everyone was grave; everyone was busy. His heart was filled with joy as he made his way to his own room.

He set to work at once with the utmost gravity, he listened to some reports and explanations, settled doubtful points. He felt as though he had never explained knotty points and given his decisions so intelligently, so judiciously as that morning. He saw that they were satisfied with him, that they respected him, that he was treated with respect. The most thin-skinned sensitiveness could not have discovered anything.

At last Akim Petrovitch made his appearance with some document. The sight of him sent a stab to Ivan Ilyitch's heart, but only for an instant. He went into the business with Akim Petrovitch, talked with dignity, explained things, and showed him what was to be done. The only thing he noticed was that he avoided looking at Akim Petrovitch for any length of time, or rather Akim Petrovitch seemed afraid of catching his eyes, but at last Akim Petrovitch had finished and began to collect his papers.

'And there is one other matter,' he began as drily as he could, 'the clerk Pseldonimov's petition to be transferred to another department. His Excellency Semyon Ivanovitch Shipulenko has promised him a post. He begs your gracious assent, your Excellency.'

'Oh, so he is being transferred,' said Ivan Ilyitch, and he felt as though a heavy weight had rolled off his heart. He glanced at Akim Petrovitch, and at that instant their eyes met. 'Certainly, I for my part . . . I will use,' answered Ivan Ilyitch; 'I am ready.'

Akim Petrovitch evidently wanted to slip away as quickly as he could. But in a rush of generous feeling Ivan Ilyitch determined to speak out. Apparently some inspiration had come to him again.

'Tell him,' he began, bending a candid glance full of profound meaning upon Akim Petrovitch, 'tell Pseldonimov that I feel no ill-will, no, I do not! . . . That on the contrary I am ready to forget all that is past, to forget it all . . .'

But all at once Ivan Ilyitch broke off, looking with wonder at the strange behaviour of Akim Petrovitch, who suddenly seemed transformed from a sensible person into a fearful fool. Instead of listening and hearing Ivan Ilyitch to the end, he suddenly flushed crimson in the silliest way, began with positively unseemly haste making strange little bows, and at the same time edging towards the door. His whole appearance betrayed a desire to sink through the floor, or more accurately, to get back to his table as quickly as possible. Ivan Ilyitch, left alone, got up from his chair in confusion; he looked in the looking-glass without noticing his face.

'No, severity, severity and nothing but severity,' he whispered almost unconsciously, and suddenly a vivid flush overspread his face. He felt suddenly more ashamed, more weighed down than he had been in the most insufferable moments of his eight days of tribulation. 'I did break down!' he said to himself, and sank helplessly into his chair.

The Crocodile

A true story of how a gentleman of a certain age and of respectable appearance was swallowed alive by the crocodile in the Arcade, and of the consequences that followed.

1865

Ohè Lambert! Où est Lambert?
As-tu vu Lambert?

I

ON THE THIRTEENTH of January of this present year, 1865, at half-past twelve in the day, Elena Ivanovna, the wife of my cultured friend Ivan Matveitch, who is a colleague in the same department, and may be said to be a distant relation of mine, too, expressed the desire to see the crocodile now on view at a fixed charge in the Arcade. As Ivan Matveitch had already in his pocket his ticket for a tour abroad (not so much for the sake of his health as for the improvement of his mind), and was consequently free from his official duties and had nothing whatever to do that morning, he offered no objection to his wife's irresistible fancy, but was positively aflame with curiosity himself.

'A capital idea!' he said, with the utmost satisfaction. 'We'll have a look at the crocodile! On the eve of visiting Europe it is as well to acquaint ourselves on the spot with its indigenous inhabitants.' And with these words, taking his wife's arm, he set off with her at once for the Arcade. I joined them, as I usually do, being an intimate friend of the family. I have never seen Ivan Matveitch in a more agreeable frame of mind than he was on that memorable morning – how true it is that we know not beforehand the fate that awaits us! On entering the Arcade he was at once full of admiration for the splendours of the building, and when we reached the shop in which the monster lately arrived in Petersburg was being exhibited, he volunteered to pay the quarter-rouble for me to the crocodile owner – a thing which had never happened before. Walking into a little room, we observed that besides the crocodile there were in it parrots of the species known as cockatoo, and also a group of monkeys in a special case in a recess. Near the entrance, along the left wall stood a big tin tank that looked like a bath covered with a thin iron grating, filled with water to the depth of two inches.

In this shallow pool was kept a huge crocodile, which lay like a log absolutely motionless and apparently deprived of all its faculties by our damp climate, so inhospitable to foreign visitors. This monster at first aroused no special interest in any one of us.

'So this is the crocodile!' said Elena Ivanovna, with a pathetic cadence of regret. 'Why, I thought it was . . . something different.'

Most probably she thought it was made of diamonds. The owner of the crocodile, a German, came out and looked at us with an air of extraordinary pride.

'He has a right to be,' Ivan Matveitch whispered to me, 'he knows he is the only man in Russia exhibiting a crocodile.'

This quite nonsensical observation I ascribe also to the extremely good-humoured mood which had overtaken Ivan Matveitch, who was on other occasions of rather envious disposition.

'I fancy your crocodile is not alive,' said Elena Ivanovna, piqued by the irresponsive stolidity of the proprietor, and addressing him with a charming smile in order to soften his churlishness – a manoeuvre so typically feminine.

'Oh, no, madam,' the latter replied in broken Russian; and instantly moving the grating half off the tank, he poked the monster's head with a stick.

Then the treacherous monster, to show that it was alive, faintly stirred its paws and tail, raised its snout and emitted something like a prolonged snuffle.

'Come, don't be cross, Karlchen,' said the German caressingly, gratified in his vanity.

'How horrid that crocodile is! I am really frightened,' Elena Ivanovna twittered, still more coquettishly. 'I know I shall dream of him now.'

'But he won't bite you if you do dream of him,' the German retorted gallantly, and was the first to laugh at his own jest, but none of us responded.

'Come, Semyon Semyonitch,' said Elena Ivanovna, addressing me exclusively, 'let us go and look at the monkeys. I am awfully fond of monkeys; they are such darlings . . . and the crocodile is horrid.'

'Oh, don't be afraid, my dear!' Ivan Matveitch called after us, gallantly displaying his manly courage to his wife. 'This drowsy denizen of the realms of the Pharaohs will do us no harm.' And he remained by the tank. What is more, he took his glove and began tickling the crocodile's nose with it, wishing, as he said afterwards, to induce him to snort. The proprietor showed his politeness to a lady by following Elena Ivanovna to the case of monkeys.

So everything was going well, and nothing could have been foreseen. Elena Ivanovna was quite skittish in her raptures over the monkeys, and seemed completely taken up with them. With shrieks of delight she was continually turning to me, as though determined not to notice the proprietor, and kept gushing with laughter at the resemblance she detected between these monkeys and her intimate friends and acquaintances. I, too, was amused, for the resemblance was unmistakable. The German did not know whether to laugh or not, and so at last was reduced to frowning. And it was at that moment that a terrible, I may say unnatural, scream set the room vibrating. Not knowing what to think, for the first moment I stood still, numb with horror, but noticing that Elena Ivanovna was screaming too, I quickly turned round – and what did I behold! I saw – oh heavens! – I saw the luckless Ivan Matveitch in the terrible jaws of the crocodile, held by them round the waist, lifted horizontally in the air and desperately kicking. Then – one moment, and no trace remained of him. But I must describe it in detail, for I stood all the while motionless, and had time to watch the whole process taking place before me with an attention and interest such as I never remember to have felt before. 'What,' I thought at that critical moment, 'what if all that had happened to me instead of to Ivan Matveitch – how unpleasant it would have been for me!'

But to return to my story. The crocodile began by turning the unhappy Ivan Matveitch in his terrible jaws so that he could swallow his legs first; then bringing up Ivan Matveitch, who kept trying to jump out and clutching at the sides of the tank, sucked him down again as far as his waist. Then bringing him up again, gulped him down, and so again and again. In this way Ivan Matveitch was visibly disappearing before our eyes. At last, with a final gulp, the crocodile swallowed my cultured friend entirely, this time leaving no trace of him. From the outside of the crocodile we could see the protuberances of Ivan Matveitch's figure as he passed down the inside of the monster. I was on the point of screaming again when destiny played another treacherous trick upon us. The crocodile made a tremendous effort, probably oppressed by the magnitude of the object he had swallowed, once more opened his terrible jaws, and with a final hiccup he suddenly let the head of Ivan Matveitch pop out for a second, with an expression of despair on his face. In that brief instant the spectacles dropped off his nose to the bottom of the tank. It seemed as though that despairing countenance had only popped out to cast one last look on the objects around it, to take its last farewell of all earthly pleasures. But it had not time to carry out its intention; the crocodile made another effort, gave a gulp and instantly it vanished again – this time for ever. This appearance and disappearance of a still living human head was so horrible, but at the same – either from its rapidity and unexpectedness or from the dropping of the spectacles – there was something so comic about it that I suddenly quite unexpectedly exploded with laughter. But pulling myself together and realising that to laugh at such a moment was not the thing for an old family friend, I turned at once to Elena Ivanovna and said with a sympathetic air:

'Now it's all over with our friend Ivan Matveitch!'

I cannot even attempt to describe how violent was the agitation of Elena Ivanovna during the whole process. After the first scream she seemed rooted to the spot, and stared at the catastrophe with apparent indifference, though her eyes looked as though they were starting out of her head; then she suddenly went off into a heart-rending wail, but I seized her hands. At this instant the proprietor, too, who had at first been also petrified by horror, suddenly clasped his hands and cried, gazing upwards:

'Oh my crocodile! *Oh mein allerliebster Karlchen! Mutter, Mutter, Mutter!*'

A door at the rear of the room opened at this cry, and the *Mutter*, a rosy-cheeked, elderly but dishevelled woman in a cap made her appearance, and rushed with a shriek to her German.

A perfect Bedlam followed. Elena Ivanovna kept shrieking out the same phrase, as though in a frenzy, 'Flay him! flay him!' apparently entreating them – probably in a moment of oblivion – to flay somebody for something. The proprietor and *Mutter* took no notice whatever of either of us; they were both bellowing like calves over the crocodile.

'He did for himself! He will burst himself at once, for he did swallow a *ganz* official!' cried the proprietor.

'Unser Karlchen, unser allerliebster Karlchen wird sterben,' howled his wife.

'We are bereaved and without bread!' chimed in the proprietor.

'Flay him! flay him! flay him!' clamoured Elena Ivanovna, clutching at the German's coat.

'He did tease the crocodile. For what did your man tease the crocodile?' cried the German, pulling away from her. 'You will if *Karlchen wird* burst, therefore pay, *das war mein Sohn, das war mein einziger Sohn.*'

I must own I was intently indignant at the sight of such egoism in the German and the cold-heartedness of his dishevelled *Mutter*; at the same time Elena Ivanovna's reiterated shriek of 'Flay him! flay him!' troubled me even more and absorbed at last my whole attention, positively alarming me. I may as well say straight off that I entirely misunderstood this strange exclamation: it seemed to me that Elena Ivanovna had for the moment taken leave of her senses, but nevertheless wishing to avenge the loss of her beloved Ivan Matveitch, was demanding by way of compensation that the crocodile should be severely thrashed, while she was meaning something quite different. Looking round at the door, not without embarrassment, I began to entreat Elena Ivanovna to calm herself, and above all not to use the shocking word 'flay'. For such a reactionary desire here, in the midst of the Arcade and of the most cultured society, not two paces from the hall where at this very minute Mr Lavrov was perhaps delivering a public lecture, was not only impossible but unthinkable, and might at any moment bring upon us the hisses of culture and the caricatures of Mr Stepanov. To my horror I was immediately proved to be correct in my alarmed suspicions: the curtain that divided the crocodile room from the little entry where the quarter-roubles were taken suddenly parted, and in the opening there appeared a figure with moustaches and beard, carrying a cap, with the upper part of its body bent a long way forward, though the feet were scrupulously held beyond the threshold of the crocodile room in order to avoid the necessity of paying the entrance money.

'Such a reactionary desire, madam,' said the stranger, trying to avoid falling over in our direction and to remain standing outside the room, 'does no credit to your development, and is conditioned by lack of phosphorus in your brain. You will be promptly held up to shame in the *Chronicle of Progress* and in our satirical prints . . .'

But he could not complete his remarks; the proprietor coming to himself, and seeing with horror that a man was talking in the crocodile room without having paid entrance money, rushed furiously at the progressive stranger and turned him out with a punch from each fist. For a moment both vanished from our sight behind a curtain, and only then I grasped that the whole uproar was about nothing. Elena Ivanovna turned out quite innocent; she had, as I have mentioned already, no idea whatever of subjecting the crocodile to a degrading corporal punishment, and had simply expressed the desire that he should be opened and her husband released from his interior.

'What! You wish that my crocodile be perished!' the proprietor yelled, running in again. 'No! let your husband be perished first, before my crocodile! . . . *Mein Vater* showed crocodile, *mein Grossvater* showed crocodile, *mein Sohn* will show crocodile, and I will show crocodile! All will show crocodile! I am known to *ganz Europa*, and you are not known to *ganz Europa*, and you must pay me a *Strafe*!'

'*Ja, ja*,' put in the vindictive German woman, 'we shall not let you go. *Strafe*, since Karlchen is burst!'

'And, indeed, it's useless to flay the creature,' I added calmly, anxious to get Elena Ivanovna away home as quickly as possible, 'as our dear Ivan Matveitch is by now probably soaring somewhere in the empyrean.'

'My dear –' we suddenly heard, to our intense amazement, the voice of Ivan Matveitch – 'my dear, my advice is to apply direct to the superintendent's office, as without the assistance of the police the German will never be made to see reason.'

These words, uttered with firmness and aplomb, and expressing an exceptional presence of mind, for the first minute so astounded us that we could not believe our ears. But, of course, we ran at once to the crocodile's tank, and with equal reverence and incredulity listened to the unhappy captive. His voice was muffled, thin and even squeaky, as though it came from a considerable distance. It reminded one of a jocose person who, covering his mouth with a pillow, shouts from an adjoining room, trying to mimic the sound of two peasants calling to one another in a deserted plain or across a wide ravine – a performance to which I once had the pleasure of listening in a friend's house at Christmas.

'Ivan Matveitch, my dear, and so you are alive!' faltered Elena Ivanovna.

'Alive and well,' answered Ivan Matveitch, 'and, thanks to the Almighty, swallowed without any damage whatever. I am only uneasy as to the view my superiors may take of the incident; for after getting a permit to go abroad I've got into a crocodile, which seems anything but clever.'

'But, my dear, don't trouble your head about being clever; first of all we must somehow excavate you from where you are,' Elena Ivanovna interrupted.

'Excavate!' cried the proprietor. 'I will not let my crocodile be excavated. Now the *Publikum* will come many more, and I will *fünfzig* kopecks ask and Karlchen will cease to burst.'

'Gott sei dank!' put in his wife.

'They are right,' Ivan Matveitch observed tranquilly; 'the principles of economics before everything.'

'My dear! I will fly at once to the authorities and lodge a complaint, for I feel that we cannot settle this mess by ourselves.'

'I think so too,' observed Ivan Matveitch; 'but in our age of industrial crisis it is not easy to rip open the belly of a crocodile without economic compensation, and meanwhile the inevitable question presents itself: What will the German take for his crocodile? And with it another: How will it be paid? For, as you know, I have no means . . .'

'Perhaps out of your salary . . .' I observed timidly, but the proprietor interrupted me at once.

'I will not the crocodile sell; I will for three thousand the crocodile sell! I will for four thousand the crocodile sell! Now the *Publikum* will come very many. I will for five thousand the crocodile sell!'

In fact he gave himself insufferable airs. Covetousness and a revolting greed gleamed joyfully in his eyes.

'I am going!' I cried indignantly.

'And I! I too! I shall go to Andrey Osipitch himself. I will soften him with my tears,' whined Elena Ivanovna.

'Don't do that, my dear,' Ivan Matveitch hastened to interpose. He had long been jealous of Andrey Osipitch on his wife's account, and he knew she would enjoy going to weep before a gentleman of refinement, for tears suited her.

'And I don't advise you to do so either, my friend,' he added, addressing me. 'It's no good plunging headlong in that slap-dash way; there's no knowing what it may lead to. You had much better go today to Timofey Semyonitch, as though to pay an ordinary visit; he is an old-fashioned and by no means brilliant man, but he is trustworthy, and what matters most of all, he is straightforward. Give him my greetings and describe the circumstances of the case. And since I owe him seven roubles over our last game of cards, take the opportunity to pay him the money; that will soften the stern old man. In any case his advice may serve as a guide for us. And meanwhile take Elena Ivanovna home . . . Calm yourself my dear,' he continued, addressing her. 'I am weary of these outcries and feminine squabblings, and should like a nap. It's soft and warm in here, though I have hardly had time to look round in this unexpected haven.'

‘Look round! Why, is it light in there?’ cried Elena Ivanovna in a tone of relief.

‘I am surrounded by impenetrable night,’ answered the poor captive; ‘but I can feel and, so to speak, have a look round with my hands . . . Goodbye; set your mind at rest and don’t deny yourself recreation and diversion. Till tomorrow! And you, Semyon Semyonitch, come to me in the evening, and as you are absent-minded and may forget it, tie a knot in your handkerchief.’

I confess I was glad to get away, for I was overtired and somewhat bored. Hastening to offer my arm to the disconsolate Elena Ivanovna, whose charms were only enhanced by her agitation, I hurriedly led her out of the crocodile room.

‘The charge will be another quarter-rouble in the evening,’ the proprietor called after us.

‘Oh, dear, how greedy they are!’ said Elena Ivanovna, looking at herself in every mirror on the walls of the Arcade, and evidently aware that she was looking prettier than usual.

‘The principles of economics,’ I answered with some emotion, proud that passers-by should see the lady on my arm.

‘The principles of economics,’ she drawled in a touching little voice. ‘I did not in the least understand what Ivan Matveitch said about those horrid economics just now.’

‘I will explain to you,’ I answered, and began at once telling her of the beneficial effects of the introduction of foreign capital into our country, upon which I had read an article in the *Petersburg News* and the *Voice* that morning.

'How strange it is,' she interrupted, after listening for some time. 'But do leave off, you horrid man. What nonsense you are talking . . . Tell me, do I look purple?'

'You look perfect, and not purple!' I observed, seizing the opportunity to pay her a compliment.

'Naughty man!' she said complacently. 'Poor Ivan Matveitch,' she added a minute later, putting her little head on one side coquettishly. 'I am really sorry for him. Oh, dear!' she cried suddenly, 'how is he going to have his dinner . . . and . . . and . . . what will he do . . . if he wants anything?'

'An unforeseen question,' I answered, perplexed in my turn. To tell the truth, it had not entered my head, so much more practical are women than we men in the solution of the problems of daily life!

'Poor dear! how could he have got into such a mess . . . nothing to amuse him, and in the dark . . . How vexing it is that I have no photograph of him . . . And so now I am a sort of widow,' she added, with a seductive smile, evidently interested in her new position. 'H'm! . . . I am sorry for him, though.'

It was, in short, the expression of the very natural and intelligible grief of a young and interesting wife for the loss of her husband. I took her home at last, soothed her, and after dining with her and drinking a cup of aromatic coffee, set off at six o'clock to Timofey Semyonitch, calculating that at that hour all married people of settled habits would be sitting or lying down at home.

Having written this first chapter in a style appropriate to the incident recorded, I intend to proceed in a language more natural though less elevated, and I beg to forewarn the reader of the fact.

II

THE venerable Timofey Semyonitch met me rather nervously, as though somewhat embarrassed. He led me to his tiny study and shut the door carefully, 'that the children may not hinder us,' he added with evident uneasiness. There he made me sit down on a chair by the writing-table, sat down himself in an easy chair, wrapped round him the skirts of his old wadded dressing-gown, and assumed an official and even severe air, in readiness for anything, though he was not my chief nor Ivan Matveitch's, and had hitherto been reckoned as a colleague and even a friend.

'First of all,' he said, 'take note that I am not a person in authority, but just such a subordinate official as you and Ivan Matveitch . . . I have nothing to do with it, and do not intend to mix myself up in the affair.'

I was surprised to find that he apparently knew all about it already. In spite of that I told him the whole story over in detail. I spoke with positive excitement, for I was at that moment fulfilling the obligations of a true friend. He listened without special surprise, but with evident signs of suspicion.

'Only fancy,' he said, 'I always believed that this would be sure to happen to him.'

'Why, Timofey Semyonitch? It is a very unusual incident in itself . . .'

'I admit it. But Ivan Matveitch's whole career in the service was leading up to this end. He was flighty – conceited indeed. It was always "progress" and ideas of all sorts, and this is what progress brings people to!'

'But this is a most unusual incident and cannot possibly serve as a general rule for all progressives.'

'Yes, indeed it can. You see, it's the effect of over-education, I assure you. For over-education leads people to poke their noses into all sorts of places, especially where they are not invited. Though perhaps you know best,' he added, as though offended. 'I am an old man and not of much education. I began as a soldier's son, and this year has been the jubilee of my service.'

'Oh, no, Timofey Semyonitch, not at all. On the contrary, Ivan Matveitch is eager for your advice; he is eager for your guidance. He implores it, so to say, with tears.'

'So to say, with tears! H'm! Those are crocodile's tears and one cannot quite believe in them. Tell me, what possessed him to want to go abroad? And how could he afford to go? Why, he has no private means!'

'He had saved the money from his last bonus,' I answered plaintively. 'He only wanted to go for three months – to Switzerland . . . to the land of William Tell.'

'William Tell? H'm!'

'He wanted to meet the spring at Naples, to see the museums, the customs, the animals . . .'

'H'm! The animals! I think it was simply from pride. What animals? Animals, indeed! Haven't we animals enough? We have museums, menageries, camels. There are bears quite close to Petersburg! And here he's got inside a crocodile himself . . .'

'Oh, come, Timofey Semyonitch! The man is in trouble, the man appeals to you as to a friend, as to an older relation, craves for advice – and you reproach him. Have pity at least on the unfortunate Elena Ivanovna!'

'You are speaking of his wife? A charming little lady,' said Timofey Semyonitch, visibly softening and taking a pinch of snuff with relish. 'Particularly prepossessing. And so plump, and always putting her pretty little head on one side . . . Very agreeable. Andrey Osipitch was speaking of her only the other day.'

'Speaking of her?'

'Yes, and in very flattering terms. Such a bust, he said, such eyes, such hair . . . A sugar-plum, he said, not a lady – and then he laughed. He is still a young man, of course.' Timofey Semyonitch blew his nose with a loud noise. 'And yet, young though he is, what a career he is making for himself.'

'That's quite a different thing, Timofey Semyonitch.'

'Of course, of course.'

'Well, what do you say then, Timofey Semyonitch?'

'Why, what can I do?'

'Give advice, guidance, as a man of experience, a relative! What are we to do? What steps are we to take? Go to the authorities and . . .'

'To the authorities? Certainly not,' Timofey Semyonitch replied hurriedly. 'If you ask my advice, you had better, above all, hush the matter up and act, so to speak, as a private person. It is a suspicious incident, quite unheard of. Unheard of, above all; there is no precedent for it, and it is far from creditable . . . And so discretion above all . . . Let him lie there a bit. We must wait and see . . .'

'But how can we wait and see, Timofey Semyonitch? What if he is stifled there?'

'Why should he be? I think you told me that he made himself fairly comfortable there?'

I told him the whole story over again. Timofey Semyonitch pondered.

'H'm!' he said, twisting his snuff-box in his hands. 'To my mind it's really a good thing he should lie there a bit, instead of going abroad. Let him reflect at his leisure. Of course he mustn't be stifled, and so he must take measures to preserve his health, avoiding a cough, for instance, and so on . . . And as for the German, it's my personal opinion he is within his rights, and even more so than the other side, because it was the other party who got into *his* crocodile without asking permission, and not *he* who got into Ivan Matveitch's crocodile without asking permission, though, so far as I recollect, the latter has no crocodile. And a crocodile is private property, and so it is impossible to slit him open without compensation.'

'For the saving of human life, Timofey Semyonitch.'

'Oh, well, that's a matter for the police. You must go to them.'

'But Ivan Matveitch may be needed in the department. He may be asked for.'

'Ivan Matveitch needed? Ha-ha! Besides, he is on leave, so that we may ignore him – let him inspect the countries of Europe! It will be a different matter if he doesn't turn up when his leave is over. Then we shall ask for him and make inquiries.'

'Three months! Timofey Semyonitch, for pity's sake!'

'It's his own fault. Nobody thrust him there. At this rate we should have to get a nurse to look after him at government expense, and that is not allowed for in the regulations. But the chief point is that the crocodile is private property, so that the principles of economics apply in this question. And the principles of economics are paramount. Only the other evening, at Luka Andreitch's, Ignaty Prokofyitch was saying so. Do you know Ignaty Prokofyitch? A capitalist, in a big way of business, and he speaks so fluently. "We need industrial development," he said; "there is very little development among us. We must create it. We must create capital, so we must create a middleclass, the so-called bourgeoisie. And as we haven't capital we must attract it from abroad. We must, in the first place, give facilities to foreign companies to buy up lands in Russia as is done now abroad. The communal holding of land is poison, is ruin." And, you know, he spoke with such heat; well, that's all right for him – a wealthy man, and not in the service. "With the communal system," he said, "there will be no improvement in industrial development or agriculture. Foreign companies," he said, "must as far as possible buy up the whole of our land in big lots, and then split it up, split it up, split it up, in the smallest parts possible –" and do you know he pronounced the words "split it up" with such determination – "and then sell it as private property. Or rather, not sell it, but simply let it. When," he said, "all the land is in the hands of foreign companies they can fix any rent they like. And so the peasant will work three times as much for his daily bread and he can be turned out at pleasure. So that he will feel it, will be submissive and industrious, and will work three times as much for the same wages. But as it is, with the commune, what does he care? He knows he won't die of hunger, so he is lazy and drunken. And meanwhile money will be attracted into Russia, capital will be created and the bourgeoisie will spring up. The English political and literary paper, *The Times*, in an article the other day on our finances stated that the reason our financial position was so unsatisfactory was that we had no middle class, no big fortunes, no accommodating proletariat." Ignaty Prokofyitch speaks well. He is an orator. He wants to lay a report on the subject before the authorities, and then to get it published in the *News*. That's something very different from verses like Ivan Matveitch's . . .'

'But how about Ivan Matveitch?' I put in, after letting the old man babble on.

Timofey Semyonitch was sometimes fond of talking and showing that he was not behind the times, but knew all about things.

'How about Ivan Matveitch? Why, I am coming to that. Here we are, anxious to bring foreign capital into the country – and only consider: as soon as the capital of a foreigner, who has been attracted to Petersburg, has been doubled through Ivan Matveitch, instead of protecting the foreign capitalist, we are proposing to rip open the belly of his original capital – the crocodile. Is it consistent? To my mind, Ivan Matveitch, as the true son of his fatherland, ought to rejoice and to be proud that through him the value of a foreign crocodile has been doubled and possibly even trebled. That's just what is wanted to attract capital. If one man succeeds, mind you, another will come with a crocodile, and a third will bring two or three of them at once, and capital will grow up about them – there you have a bourgeoisie. It must be encouraged.'

'Upon my word, Timofey Semyonitch!' I cried, 'you are demanding almost supernatural self-sacrifice from poor Ivan Matveitch.'

'I demand nothing, and I beg you, before everything – as I have said already – to remember that I am not a person in authority and so cannot demand anything of anyone. I am speaking as a son of the fatherland, that is, not as the *Son of the*

Fatherland, but as a son of the fatherland. Again, what possessed him to get into the crocodile? A respectable man, a man of good grade in the service, lawfully married – and then to behave like that! Is it consistent?'

'But it was an accident.'

'Who knows? And where is the money to compensate the owner to come from?'

'Perhaps out of his salary, Timofey Semyonitch?'

'Would that be enough?'

'No, it wouldn't, Timofey Semyonitch,' I answered sadly. 'The proprietor was at first alarmed that the crocodile would burst, but as soon as he was sure that it was all right, he began to bluster and was delighted to think that he could double the charge for entry.'

'Treble and quadruple perhaps! The public will simply stampede the place now, and crocodile owners are smart people. Besides, it's not Lent yet, and people are keen on diversions, and so I say again, the great thing is that Ivan Matveitch should preserve his incognito, don't let him be in a hurry. Let everybody know, perhaps, that he is in the crocodile, but don't let them be officially informed of it. Ivan Matveitch is in particularly favourable circumstances for that, for he is reckoned to be abroad. It will be said he is in the crocodile, and we will refuse to believe it. That is how it can be managed. The great thing is that he should wait; and why should he be in a hurry?'

'Well, but if . . .'

'Don't worry, he has a good constitution . . .'

'Well, and afterwards, when he has waited?'

'Well, I won't conceal from you that the case is exceptional in the highest degree. One doesn't know what to think of it, and the worst of it is there is no precedent. If we had a precedent we might have something to go by. But as it is, what is one to say? It will certainly take time to settle it.'

A happy thought flashed upon my mind.

'Cannot we arrange,' I said, 'that if he is destined to remain in the entrails of the monster and it is the will of Providence that he should remain alive, that he should send in a petition to be reckoned as still serving?'

'H'm! . . . Possibly as on leave and without salary . . .'

'But couldn't it be with salary?'

'On what grounds?'

'As sent on a special commission.'

'What commission and where?'

'Why, into the entrails, the entrails of the crocodile . . . So to speak, for exploration, for investigation of the facts on the spot. It would, of course, be a novelty, but that is progressive and would at the same time show zeal for enlightenment.'

Timofey Semyonitch thought a little.

'To send a special official,' he said at last, 'to the inside of a crocodile to conduct a special inquiry is, in my personal opinion, an absurdity. It is not in the regulations. And what sort of special inquiry could there be there?'

'The scientific study of nature on the spot, in the living subject. The natural sciences are all the fashion nowadays, botany . . . He could live there and report his observations . . . For instance, concerning digestion or simply habits. For the sake of accumulating facts.'

'You mean as statistics. Well, I am no great authority on that subject, indeed I am no philosopher at all. You say "facts" – we are overwhelmed with facts as it is, and don't know what to do with them. Besides, statistics are a danger.'

'In what way?'

'They are a danger. Moreover, you will admit he will report facts, so to speak, lying like a log. And, can one do one's official duties lying like a log? That would be another novelty and a dangerous one; and again, there is no precedent for it. If we had any sort of precedent for it, then, to my thinking, he might have been given the job.'

'But no live crocodiles have been brought over hitherto, Timofey Semyonitch.'

'H'm . . . yes,' he reflected again. 'Your objection is a just one, if you like, and might indeed serve as a ground for carrying the matter further; but consider again, that if with the arrival of living crocodiles government clerks begin to disappear, and then on the ground that they are warm and comfortable there, expect to receive the official sanction for their position, and then take their ease there . . . you must admit it would be a bad example.

We should have everyone trying to go the same way to get a salary for nothing.'

'Do your best for him, Timofey Semyonitch. By the way, Ivan Matveitch asked me to give you seven roubles he had lost to you at cards.'

'Ah, he lost that the other day at Nikifor Nikiforitch's. I remember. And how gay and amusing he was – and now!'

The old man was genuinely touched.

'Intercede for him, Timofey Semyonitch!'

'I will do my best. I will speak in my own name, as a private person, as though I were asking for information. And meanwhile, you find out indirectly, unofficially, how much would the proprietor consent to take for his crocodile?'

Timofey Semyonitch was visibly more friendly.

'Certainly,' I answered. 'And I will come back to you at once to report.'

'And his wife . . . is she alone now? Is she depressed?'

'You should call on her, Timofey Semyonitch.'

'I will. I thought of doing so before; it's a good opportunity . . . And what on earth possessed him to go and look at the crocodile. Though, indeed, I should like to see it myself.'

'Go and see the poor fellow, Timofey Semyonitch.'

'I will. Of course, I don't want to raise his hopes by doing so. I shall go as a private person . . . Well, goodbye, I am going to Nikifor Nikiforitch's again; shall you be there?'

'No, I am going to see the poor prisoner.'

'Yes, now he is a prisoner! . . . Ah, that's what comes of thoughtlessness!'

I said goodbye to the old man. Ideas of all kinds were straying through my mind. A good-natured and most honest man, Timofey Semyonitch, yet, as I left him, I felt pleased at the thought that he had celebrated his fiftieth year of service, and that Timofey Semyonitchs are now a rarity among us. I flew at once, of course, to the Arcade to tell poor Ivan Matveitch all the news. And, indeed, I was moved by curiosity to know how he was getting on in the crocodile and how it was possible to live in a crocodile. And, indeed, was it possible to live in a crocodile at all? At times it really seemed to me as though it were all an outlandish, monstrous dream, especially as an outlandish monster was the chief figure in it.

III

AND yet it was not a dream, but actual, indubitable fact. Should I be telling the story if it were not? But to continue.

It was late, about nine o'clock, before I reached the Arcade, and I had to go into the crocodile room by the back entrance, for the German had closed the shop earlier than usual that evening. Now in the seclusion of domesticity he was walking about in a greasy old frock-coat, but he seemed three times as pleased as he had been in the morning. It was evidently that he had no apprehensions now, and that the public had been coming 'many more'. The *Mutter* came out later, evidently to keep an eye on me. The German and the *Mutter* frequently whispered together. Although the shop was closed he charged me a quarter-rouble. What unnecessary exactitude!

'You will every time pay; the public will one rouble, and you one quarter pay; for you are the good friend of your good friend; and I a friend respect . . .'

'Are you alive, are you alive, my cultured friend?' I cried, as I approached the crocodile, expecting my words to reach Ivan Matveitch from a distance and to flatter his vanity.

'Alive and well,' he answered, as though from a long way off or from under the bed, though I was standing close beside him. 'Alive and well; but of that later . . . How are things going?'

As though purposely not hearing the question, I was just beginning with sympathetic haste to question him how he was, what it was like in the crocodile, and what, in fact, there was inside a crocodile. Both friendship and common civility demanded this. But with capricious annoyance he interrupted me.

'How are things going?' he shouted, in a shrill and on this occasion particularly revolting voice, addressing me peremptorily as usual.

I described to him my whole conversation with Timofey Semyonitch down to the smallest detail. As I told my story I tried to show my resentment in my voice.

'The old man is right,' Ivan Matveitch pronounced as

abruptly as usual in his conversation with me. 'I like practical people, and can't endure sentimental milk-sops. I am ready to admit, however, that your idea about a special commission is not altogether absurd. I certainly have a great deal to report, both from a scientific and from an ethical point of view. But now all this has taken a new and unexpected aspect, and it is not worthwhile to trouble about mere salary. Listen attentively. Are you sitting down?'

'No, I am standing up.'

'Sit down on the floor if there is nothing else, and listen attentively.'

Resentfully I took a chair and put it down on the floor with a bang, in my anger.

'Listen,' he began dictatorially. 'The public came today in masses. There was no room left in the evening, and the police came in to keep order. At eight o'clock, that is, earlier than usual, the proprietor thought it necessary to close the shop and end the exhibition to count the money he had taken and prepare for tomorrow more conveniently. So I know there will be a regular fair tomorrow. So we may assume that all the most cultivated people in the capital, the ladies and the best society, the foreign ambassadors, the leading lawyers and so on, will all be present. What's more, people will be flowing here from the remotest provinces of our vast and interesting empire. The upshot of it is that I am the cynosure of all eyes, and though hidden to sight, I am eminent. I shall teach the idle crowd. Taught by experience,

I shall be an example of greatness and resignation to fate! I shall be, so to say, a pulpit from which to instruct mankind. The mere biological details I can furnish about the monster I am inhabiting are of priceless value. And so, far from repining at what has happened, I confidently hope for the most brilliant of careers.'

'You won't find it wearisome?' I asked sarcastically.

What irritated me more than anything was the extreme pomposity of his language. Nevertheless, it all rather disconcerted me. 'What on earth, what, can this frivolous blockhead find to be so cocky about?' I muttered to myself. 'He ought to be crying instead of being cocky.'

'No!' he answered my observation sharply, 'for I am full of great ideas, only now can I at leisure ponder over the amelioration of the lot of humanity. Truth and light will come forth now from the crocodile. I shall certainly develop a new economic theory of my own and I shall be proud of it – which I have hitherto been prevented from doing by my official duties and by trivial distractions. I shall refute everything and be a new Fourier. By the way, did you give Timofey Semyonitch the seven roubles?'

'Yes, out of my own pocket,' I answered, trying to emphasise that fact in my voice.

'We will settle it,' he answered superciliously. 'I confidently expect my salary to be raised, for who should get a raise if not I? I am of the utmost service now. But to business. My wife?'

'You are, I suppose, inquiring after Elena Ivanovna?'

'My wife?' he shouted, this time in a positive squeal.

There was no help for it! Meekly, though gnashing my teeth, I told him how I had left Elena Ivanovna. He did not even hear me out.

'I have special plans in regard to her,' he began impatiently. 'If I am celebrated *here*, I wish her to be celebrated *there*. Savants, poets, philosophers, foreign mineralogists, statesmen, after conversing in the morning with me, will visit her *salon* in the evening. From next week onwards she must have an "At Home" every evening. With my salary doubled, we shall have the means for entertaining, and as the entertainment must not go beyond tea and hired footmen – that's settled. Both here and there they will talk of me. I have long thirsted for an opportunity for being talked about, but could not attain it, fettered by my humble position and low grade in the service. And now all this has been attained by a simple gulp on the part of the crocodile. Every word of mine will be listened to, every utterance will be thought over, repeated, printed. And I'll teach them what I am worth! They shall understand at last what abilities they have allowed to vanish in the entrails of a monster. "This man might have been Foreign Minister or might have ruled a kingdom," some will say. "And that man did not rule a kingdom," others will say. In what way am I inferior to a Garnier-Pagesishky or whatever they are called? My wife must be a worthy second – I have brains, she has beauty and charm. "She is beautiful, and that is why she is his wife," some will say. "She is beautiful *because* she is his wife," others will amend. To be ready for anything let Elena Ivanovna buy tomorrow the Encyclopaedia edited by Andrey Kraevsky, that she may be able to converse on any topic. Above all, let her be sure to read the political leader in the *Petersburg News*, comparing it every day with the *Voice*. I imagine that the proprietor will consent to take me sometimes with the crocodile to my wife's brilliant *salon*. I will be in a tank in the middle of the magnificent drawing-room, and I will scintillate with witticisms which I will prepare in the morning. To the statesmen I will impart my projects; to the poet I will speak in rhyme; with the ladies I can be amusing and charming without impropriety, since I shall be no danger to their husbands' peace of mind. To all the rest I shall serve as a pattern of resignation to fate and the will of Providence. I shall make my wife a brilliant literary lady; I shall bring her forward and explain her to the public; as my wife she must be full of the most striking virtues; and if they are right in calling Andrey Alexandrovitch our Russian Alfred de Musset, they will be still more right in calling her our Russian Yevgenia Tour.'

I must confess that although this wild nonsense was rather in Ivan Matveitch's habitual style, it did occur to me that he was in a fever and delirious. It was the same, everyday Ivan Matveitch, but magnified twenty times.

'My friend,' I asked him, 'are you hoping for a long life? Tell me, in fact, are you well? How do you eat, how do you sleep, how do you breathe? I am your friend, and you must admit that the incident is most unnatural, and consequently my curiosity is most natural.'

'Idle curiosity and nothing else,' he pronounced sententiously, 'but you shall be satisfied. You ask how I am managing in the entrails of the monster? To begin with, the crocodile, to my amusement, turns out to be perfectly empty. His inside consists of a sort of huge empty sack made of gutta-percha, like the elastic goods sold in the Gorohovy Street, in the Morskaya, and, if I am not mistaken, in the Voznesensky Prospect. Otherwise, if you think of it, how could I find room?'

'Is it possible?' I cried, in a surprise that may well be understood. 'Can the crocodile be perfectly empty?'

'Perfectly,' Ivan Matveitch maintained sternly and impressively. 'And in all probability, it is so constructed by the laws of Nature. The crocodile possesses nothing but jaws furnished with sharp teeth, and besides the jaws, a tail of considerable length – that is all, properly speaking. The middle part between these two extremities is an empty space enclosed by something of the nature of gutta-percha, probably really gutta-percha.'

'But the ribs, the stomach, the intestines, the liver, the heart?' I interrupted quite angrily.

'There is nothing, absolutely nothing of all that, and probably there never has been. All that is the idle fancy of frivolous travellers. As one inflates an air-cushion, I am now with my person inflating the crocodile. He is incredibly elastic. Indeed, you might, as the friend of the family, get in with me if you were generous and self-sacrificing enough – and even with you here there would be room to spare. I even think that in the last resort I might send for Elena Ivanovna. However, this void, hollow formation of the crocodile is quite in keeping with the teachings of natural science. If, for instance, one had to construct a new crocodile, the question would naturally present itself. What is the fundamental characteristic of the crocodile? The answer is clear: to swallow human beings. How is one, in constructing the crocodile, to secure that he should swallow people? The answer is clearer still: construct him hollow. It was settled by physics long ago that Nature abhors a vacuum. Hence the inside of the crocodile must be hollow so that it may abhor the vacuum, and consequently swallow and so fill itself with anything it can come across. And that is the sole rational cause why every crocodile swallows men. It is not the same in the constitution of man: the emptier a man's head is, for instance, the less he feels the thirst to fill it, and that is the one exception to the general rule. It is all as clear as day to me now. I have deduced it by my own observation and experience, being, so to say, in the very bowels of Nature, in its retort, listening to the throbbing of its pulse. Even etymology supports me, for the very word "crocodile" means voracity. Crocodile – *crocodillo* – is evidently an Italian word, dating perhaps from the Egyptian Pharaohs, and evidently derived from the French verb *croquer*, which means to eat, to devour, in general to absorb nourishment. All these remarks I intend to deliver as my first lecture in Elena Ivanovna's *salon* when they take me there in the tank.'

'My friend, oughtn't you at least to take some purgative?' I cried involuntarily.

'He is in a fever, a fever, he is feverish!' I repeated to myself in alarm.

'Nonsense!' he answered contemptuously. 'Besides, in my present position it would be most inconvenient. I knew, though, you would be sure to talk of taking medicine.'

'But, my friend, how . . . how do you take food now? Have you dined today?'

'No, but I am not hungry, and most likely I shall never take food again. And that, too, is quite natural; filling the whole interior of the crocodile I make him feel always full. Now he need not be fed for some years. On the other hand, nourished by me, he will naturally impart to me all the vital juices of his body; it is the same as with some accomplished coquettes who embed themselves and their whole persons for the night in raw steak, and then, after their morning bath, are fresh, supple, buxom and fascinating. In that way nourishing the crocodile, I myself obtain nourishment from him, consequently we mutually nourish one another. But as it is difficult even for a crocodile to digest a man like me, he must, no doubt, be conscious of a certain weight in his stomach – an organ which he does not, however, possess – and that is why, to avoid causing the creature suffering, I do not often turn over, and although I could turn over I do not do so from humanitarian motives. This is the one drawback of my present position, and in an allegorical sense Timofey Semyonitch was right in saying I was lying like a log. But I will prove that even lying like a log – nay, that only lying like a log – one can revolutionise the lot of mankind. All the great ideas and movements of our newspapers and magazines have evidently been the work of men who were lying like logs; that is why they call them divorced from the realities of life – but what does it matter, their saying that! I am constructing now a complete system of my own, and you wouldn't believe how easy it is! You have only to creep into a secluded corner or into a crocodile, to shut your eyes, and you immediately devise a perfect millennium for mankind. When you went away this afternoon I set to work at once and have already invented three systems, now I am preparing the fourth. It is true that at first one must refute everything that has gone before, but from the crocodile it is so easy to refute it; besides, it all becomes clearer, seen from the inside of the crocodile . . . There are some drawbacks, though small ones, in my position, however; it is somewhat damp here and covered with a sort of slime; moreover, there is a smell of india-rubber like the smell of my old goloshes. That is all, there are no other drawbacks.'

'Ivan Matveitch,' I interrupted, 'all this is a miracle in which I can scarcely believe. And can you, can you intend never to dine again?'

'What trivial nonsense you are troubling about, you

thoughtless, frivolous creature! I talk to you about great ideas, and you . . . Understand that I am sufficiently nourished by the great ideas which light up the darkness in which I am enveloped. The good-natured proprietor has, however, after consulting the kindly *Mutter*, decided with her that they will every morning insert into the monster's jaws a bent metal tube, something like a whistle pipe, by means of which I can absorb coffee or broth with bread soaked in it. The pipe has already been bespoken in the neighbourhood, but I think this is superfluous luxury. I hope to live at least a thousand years, if it is true that crocodiles live so long, which, by the way – good thing I thought of it – you had better look up in some natural history tomorrow and tell me, for I may have been mistaken and have mixed it up with some excavated monster. There is only one reflection rather troubles me: as I am dressed in cloth and have boots on, the crocodile can obviously not digest me. Besides, I am alive, and so am opposing the process of digestion with my whole will power; for you can understand that I do not wish to be turned into what all nourishment turns into, for that would be too humiliating for me. But there is one thing I am afraid of: in a thousand years the cloth of my coat, unfortunately of Russian make, may decay, and then, left without clothing, I might perhaps, in spite of my indignation, begin to be digested; and though by day nothing would induce me to allow it, at night, in my sleep, when a man's will deserts him, I may be overtaken by the humiliating destiny of a potato, a pancake, or veal. Such an idea reduces me to fury. This alone is an argument for the revision of the tariff and the encouragement of the importation of English cloth, which is stronger and so will withstand Nature longer when one is swallowed by a crocodile. At the first opportunity I will impart this idea to some statesman and at the same time to the political writers on our Petersburg dailies. Let them publish it abroad. I trust this will not be the only idea they will borrow from me. I foresee that every morning a regular crowd of them, provided with quarter-roubles from the editorial office, will be flocking round me to seize my ideas on the telegrams of the previous day. In brief, the future presents itself to me in the rosiest light.'

'Fever, fever!' I whispered to myself.

'My friend, and freedom?' I asked, wishing to learn his views thoroughly. 'You are, so to speak, in prison, while every man has a right to the enjoyment of freedom.'

'You are a fool,' he answered. 'Savages love independence, wise men love order; and if there is no order . . .'

'Ivan Matveich, spare me, please!'

'Hold your tongue and listen!' he squealed, vexed at my interrupting him. 'Never has my spirit soared as now. In my narrow refuge there is only one thing that I dread – the literary criticisms of the monthlies and the hiss of our satirical papers. I am afraid that thoughtless visitors, stupid and envious people and nihilists in general, may turn me into ridicule. But I will take measures. I am impatiently awaiting the response of the public tomorrow, and especially the opinion of the newspapers. You must tell me about the papers tomorrow.'

'Very good; tomorrow I will bring a perfect pile of papers with me.'

'Tomorrow it is too soon to expect reports in the newspapers, for it will take four days for it to be advertised. But from today come to me every evening by the back way through the yard. I am intending to employ you as my secretary. You shall read the newspapers and magazines to me, and I will dictate to you my ideas and give you commissions. Be particularly careful not to forget the foreign telegrams. Let all the European telegrams be here every day. But enough; most likely you are sleepy by now. Go home, and do not think of what I said just now about criticisms: I am not afraid of it, for the critics themselves are in critical position. One has only to be wise and virtuous and one will certainly get on to a pedestal. If not Socrates, then Diogenes, or perhaps both of them together – that is my future rôle among mankind.'

So frivolously and boastfully did Ivan Matveitch hasten to express himself before me, like feverish weak-willed women who, as we are told by the proverb, cannot keep a secret. All that he told me about the crocodile struck me as most suspicious. How was it possible that the crocodile was absolutely hollow? I don't mind betting that he was bragging from vanity and partly to humiliate me. It is true that he was an invalid and one must make allowances for invalids; but I must frankly confess, I never could endure Ivan Matveitch. I have been trying all my life, from a child up, to escape from his tutelage and have not been able to; A thousand times over I have been tempted to break with him altogether, and every time I have been drawn to him again, as though I were still hoping to prove something to him or to revenge myself on him. A strange thing, this friendship! I can positively assert that nine-tenths of my friendship for him was made up of malice. On this occasion, however, we parted with genuine feeling.

'Your friend a very clever man!' the German said to me in an undertone as he moved to see me out; he had been listening all the time attentively to our conversation.

'*À propos*,' I said, 'while I think of it: how much would you ask for your crocodile in case anyone wanted to buy it?'

Ivan Matveitch, who heard the question, was waiting with curiosity for the answer; it was evident that he did not want the German to ask too little; anyway, he cleared his throat in a peculiar way on hearing my question.

At first the German would not listen – was positively angry.

'No one will dare my own crocodile to buy!' he cried furiously, and turned as red as a boiled lobster. 'Me not want to sell the crocodile! I would not for the crocodile a million thalers take. I took a hundred and thirty thalers from the public today, and I shall tomorrow ten thousand take, and then a hundred thousand every day I shall take. I will not him sell.'

Ivan Matveitch positively chuckled with satisfaction.

Controlling myself – for I felt it was a duty to my friend – I hinted coolly and reasonably to the crazy German that his calculations were not quite correct, that if he makes a hundred thousand every day, all Petersburg will have visited him in four days, and then there will be no one left to bring him roubles, that life and death are in God's hands, that the crocodile may burst or Ivan Matveitch may fall ill and die, and so on and so on.

The German grew pensive.

'I will him drops from the chemist's get,' he said, after pondering, 'and will save your friend that he die not.'

'Drops are all very well,' I answered, 'but consider, too, that the thing may get into the law courts. Ivan Matveitch's wife may demand the restitution of her lawful spouse. You are intending to get rich, but do you intend to give Elena Ivanovna a pension?'

'No, me not intend,' said the German in stern decision.

'No, we not intend,' said the *Mutter*, with positive malignancy.

'And so would it not be better for you to accept something now, at once, a secure and solid though moderate sum, than to leave things to chance? I ought to tell you that I am inquiring simply from curiosity.'

The German drew the *Mutter* aside to consult with her in a corner where there stood a case with the largest and ugliest monkey of his collection.

'Well, you will see!' said Ivan Matveitch.

As for me, I was at that moment burning with the desire, first, to give the German a thrashing, next, to give the *Mutter* an even sounder one, and, thirdly, to give Ivan Matveitch the soundest thrashing of all for his boundless vanity. But all this paled beside the answer of the rapacious German.

After consultation with the *Mutter* he demanded for his crocodile fifty thousand roubles in bonds of the last Russian loan with lottery voucher attached, a brick house in Gorohovy Street with a chemist's shop attached, and in addition the rank of Russian colonel.

'You see!' Ivan Matveitch cried triumphantly. 'I told you so! Apart from this last senseless desire for the rank of a colonel, he is perfectly right, for he fully understands the present value of the monster he is exhibiting. The economic principle before everything!'

'Upon my word!' I cried furiously to the German. 'But what should you be made a colonel for? What exploit have you performed? What service have you done? In what way have you gained military glory? You are really crazy!'

'Crazy!' cried the German, offended. 'No, a person very sensible, but you very stupid! I have a colonel deserved for that I have a crocodile shown and in him a live *Hofrath* sitting! And a Russian can a crocodile not show and a live *Hofrath* in him sitting! Me extremely clever man and much wish colonel to be!'

'Well, goodbye, then, Ivan Matveitch!' I cried, shaking with fury, and I went out of the crocodile room almost at a run.

I felt that in another minute I could not have answered for myself. The unnatural expectations of these two blockheads were insupportable. The cold air refreshed me and somewhat moderated my indignation. At last, after spitting vigorously fifteen times on each side, I took a cab, got home, undressed and flung myself into bed. What vexed me more than anything was my having become his secretary. Now I was to die of boredom there every evening, doing the duty of a true friend! I was ready to beat myself for it, and I did, in fact, after putting out the candle and pulling up the bedclothes, punch myself several times on the head and various parts of my body. That somewhat relieved me, and at last I fell asleep fairly soundly, in fact, for I was very tired. All night long I could dream of nothing but monkeys, but towards morning I dreamed of Elena Ivanovna.

IV

THE monkeys I dreamed about, I surmise, because they were shut up in the case at the German's; but Elena Ivanovna was a different story.

I may as well say at once, I loved the lady, but I make haste – post-haste – to make a qualification. I loved her as a father, neither more nor less. I judge that because I often felt an irresistible desire to kiss her little head or her rosy cheek. And although I never carried out this inclination, I would not have refused even to kiss her lips. And not merely her lips, but her teeth, which always gleamed so charmingly like two rows of pretty, well-matched pearls when she laughed. She laughed extraordinarily often. Ivan Matveitch in demonstrative moments used to call her his 'darling absurdity' – a name extremely happy and appropriate. She was a perfect sugar-plum, and that was all one could say of her. Therefore I am utterly at a loss to understand what possessed Ivan Matveitch to imagine his wife as a Russian Yevgenia Tour? Anyway, my dream, with the exception of the monkeys, left a most pleasant impression upon me, and going over all the incidents of the previous day as I drank my morning cup of tea, I resolved to go and see Elena Ivanovna at once on my way to the office – which, indeed, I was bound to do as the friend of the family.

In a tiny little room out of the bedroom – the so-called little drawing-room, though their big drawing-room was little too – Elena Ivanovna was sitting, in some half-transparent morning wrapper, on a smart little sofa before a little tea-table, drinking coffee out of a little cup in which she was dipping a minute biscuit. She was ravishingly pretty, but struck me as being at the same time rather pensive.

'Ah, that's you, naughty man!' she said, greeting me with an absent-minded smile. 'Sit down, feather-head, have some coffee. Well, what were you doing yesterday? Were you at the masquerade?'

'Why, were you? I don't go, you know. Besides, yesterday I was visiting our captive . . .' I sighed and assumed a pious expression as I took the coffee.

'Whom? . . . What captive? . . . Oh, yes! Poor fellow! Well, how is he – bored? Do you know . . . I wanted to ask you . . . I suppose I can ask for a divorce now?'

'A divorce!' I cried in indignation and almost spilled the coffee. 'It's that swarthy fellow,' I thought to myself bitterly.

There was a certain swarthy gentleman with little moustaches who was something in the architectural line, and who came far too often to see them, and was extremely skilful in amusing Elena Ivanovna. I must confess I hated him and there was no doubt that he had succeeded in seeing Elena Ivanovna yesterday either at the masquerade or even here, and putting all sorts of nonsense into her head.

'Why,' Elena Ivanovna rattled off hurriedly, as though it were a lesson she had learned, 'if he is going to stay on in the crocodile, perhaps not come back all his life, while I sit waiting for him here. A husband ought to live at home, and not in a crocodile . . .'

'But this was an unforeseen occurrence,' I was beginning, in very comprehensible agitation.

'Oh, no, don't talk to me, I won't listen, I won't listen,' she cried, suddenly getting quite cross. 'You are always against me, you wretch! There's no doing anything with you, you will never give me any advice! Other people tell me that I can get a divorce because Ivan Matveitch will not get his salary now.'

'Elena Ivanovna! is it you I hear!' I exclaimed pathetically. 'What villain could have put such an idea into your head? And divorce on such a trivial ground as a salary is quite impossible. And poor Ivan Matveitch, poor Ivan Matveitch is, so to speak, burning with love for you even in the bowels of the monster. What's more, he is melting away with love like a lump of sugar. Yesterday while you were enjoying yourself at the masquerade, he was saying that he might in the last resort send for you as his lawful spouse to join him in the entrails of the monster, especially as it appears the crocodile is exceedingly roomy, not only able to accommodate two but even three persons . . .'

And then I told her all that interesting part of my conversation the night before with Ivan Matveitch.

'What, what!' she cried, in surprise. 'You want me to get into the monster too, to be with Ivan Matveitch? What an idea! And how am I to get in there, in my hat and crinoline? Heavens, what foolishness! And what should I look like while I was getting into it, and very likely there would be someone there to see me! It's absurd! And what should I have to eat there? And . . . and . . . and what should I do there when . . . Oh, my goodness, what will they think of next? . . . And what should I have to amuse me there? . . . You say there's a smell of gutta-percha? And what should I do if we quarrelled – should we have to go on staying there side by side? Foo, how horrid!'

'I agree, I agree with all those arguments, my sweet Elena Ivanovna,' I interrupted, striving to express myself with that natural enthusiasm which always overtakes a man when he feels the truth is on his side. 'But one thing you have not appreciated in all this, you have not realised that he cannot live without you if he is inviting you there; that is a proof of love, passionate, faithful, ardent love . . . You have thought too little of his love, dear Elena Ivanovna !'

'I won't, I won't, I won't hear anything about it!' waving me off with her pretty little hand with glistening pink nails that had just been washed and polished. 'Horrid man! You will reduce me to tears! Get into it yourself, if you like the prospect. You are his friend, get in and keep him company, and spend your life discussing some tedious science . . .'

'You are wrong to laugh at this suggestion –' I checked the frivolous woman with dignity – 'Ivan Matveitch has invited me as it is. You, of course, are summoned there by duty; for me, it would be an act of generosity. But when Ivan Matveitch described to me last night the elasticity of the crocodile, he hinted very plainly that there would be room not only for you two, but for me also as a friend of the family, especially if I wished to join you, and therefore . . .'

'How so, the three of us?' cried Elena Ivanovna, looking at me in surprise. 'Why, how should we . . . are we going to be all three there together? Ha-ha-ha! How silly you both are! Ha-ha-ha! I shall certainly pinch you all the time, you wretch! Ha-ha-ha! Ha-ha-ha!'

And falling back on the sofa, she laughed till she cried. All this – the tears and the laughter – were so fascinating that I could not resist rushing eagerly to kiss her hand, which she did not oppose, though she did pinch my ears lightly as a sign of reconciliation.

Then we both grew very cheerful, and I described to her in detail all Ivan Matveitch's plans. The thought of her evening receptions and her *salon* pleased her very much.

'Only I should need a great many new dresses,' she observed, 'and so Ivan Matveitch must send me as much of his salary as possible and as soon as possible. Only . . . only I don't know about that,' she added thoughtfully. 'How can he be brought here in the tank? That's very absurd. I don't want my husband to be carried about in a tank. I should feel quite ashamed for my visitors to see it . . . I don't want that, no, I don't.'

'By the way, while I think of it, was Timofey Semyonitch here yesterday?'

'Oh, yes, he was; he came to comfort me, and do you know, we played cards all the time. He played for sweet-meats, and if I lost he was to kiss my hands. What a wretch he is! And only fancy, he almost came to the masquerade with me, really!'

'He was carried away by his feelings!' I observed. 'And who would not be with you, you charmer?'

'Oh, get along with your compliments! Stay, I'll give you a pinch as a parting present. I've learned to pinch awfully well lately. Well, what do you say to that? By the way, you say Ivan Matveitch spoke several times of me yesterday?'

'N-no, not exactly . . . I must say he is thinking more now of the fate of humanity, and wants . . .'

'Oh, let him! You needn't go on! I am sure it's fearfully boring. I'll go and see him some time. I shall certainly go tomorrow. Only not today; I've got a headache, and besides, there will such a lot of people there today . . . They'll say, "That's his wife," and I shall feel ashamed . . . Goodbye. You will be . . . there this evening, won't you?'

'To see him, yes. He asked me to go and take him the papers.'

'That's capital. Go and read to him. But don't come and see me today. I am not well, and perhaps I may go and see someone. Goodbye, you naughty man.'

'It's that swarthy fellow is going to see her this evening,' I thought.

At the office, of course, I gave no sign of being consumed by these cares and anxieties. But soon I noticed some of the most progressive papers seemed to be passing particularly rapidly from hand to hand among my colleagues, and were being read with an extremely serious expression of face. The first one that reached me was the *News-sheet*, a paper of no particular party but humanitarian in general, for which it was regarded with contempt among us, though it was read. Not without surprise I read in it the following paragraph:

'Yesterday strange rumours were circulating among the spacious ways and sumptuous buildings of our vast metropolis. A certain well-known *bon-vivant* of the highest society, probably weary of the *cuisine* at Borel's and at the X. Club, went into the Arcade, into the place where an immense crocodile recently brought to the metropolis is being exhibited, and insisted on its being prepared for his dinner. After bargaining with the proprietor he at once set to work to devour him (that is, not the proprietor, a very meek and punctilious German, but his crocodile), cutting juicy morsels with his penknife from the living animal, and swallowing them with extraordinary rapidity. By degrees the whole crocodile disappeared into the vast recesses of his stomach, so that he was even on the point of attacking an ichneumon, a constant companion of the crocodile, probably imagining that the latter would be as savoury. We are by no means opposed to that new article of diet with which foreign *gourmands* have long been familiar. We have, indeed, predicted that it would come. English lords and travellers make up regular parties for catching crocodiles in Egypt, and consume the back of the monster cooked like beefsteak, with mustard, onions and potatoes. The French who followed in the train of Lesseps prefer the paws baked in hot ashes, which they do, however, in opposition to the English, who laugh at them. Probably both ways would be appreciated among us. For our part, we are delighted at a new branch of industry, of which our great and varied fatherland stands pre-eminently in need. Probably before a year is out crocodiles will be brought in hundreds to replace this first one, lost in the stomach of a Petersburg *gourmand*. And why should not the crocodile be acclimatised among us in Russia? If the water of the Neva is too cold for these interesting strangers, there are ponds in the capital and rivers and lakes outside it. Why not breed crocodiles at Pargolovo, for instance, or at Pavlovsk, in the Presensky Ponds and in Samoteka in Moscow? While providing agreeable, wholesome nourishment for our fastidious *gourmands*, they might at the same time entertain the ladies who walk about these ponds and instruct the children in natural history. The crocodile skin might be used for making jewel-cases, boxes, cigar-cases, pocket-books, and possibly more than one thousand saved up in the greasy notes that are peculiarly beloved of merchants might be laid by in crocodile skin. We hope to return more than once to this interesting topic.'

Though I had foreseen something of the sort, yet the reckless inaccuracy of the paragraph overwhelmed me. Finding no one with whom to share my impression, I turned to Prohor Savvitch who was sitting opposite to me, and noticed that the latter had been watching me for some time, while in his hand he held the *Voice* as though he were on the point of passing it to me. Without a word he took the *News-sheet* from me, and as he handed me the *Voice* he drew a line with his nail against an article to which he probably wished to call my attention. This Prohor Savvitch was a very queer man; a taciturn old bachelor, he was not on intimate terms with any of us, scarcely spoke to anyone in the office, always had an opinion of his own about everything, but could not bear to impart it to anyone. He lived alone. Hardly anyone among us had ever been in his lodging.

This was what I read in the *Voice*:

'Everyone knows that we are progressive and humanitarian and want to be on a level with Europe in this respect. But in spite of all our exertions and the efforts of our paper we are still far from maturity, as may be judged from the shocking incident which took place yesterday in the Arcade and which we predicted long ago. A foreigner arrives in the capital bringing with him a crocodile which he begins exhibiting in the Arcade. We immediately hasten to welcome a new branch of useful industry such as our powerful and varied fatherland stands in great need of. Suddenly yesterday at four o'clock in the afternoon a gentleman of exceptional stoutness enters the foreigner's shop in an intoxicated condition, pays his entrance money, and immediately without any warning leaps into the jaws of the crocodile, who was forced, of course, to swallow him, if only from an instinct of self-preservation, to avoid being crushed. Tumbling into the inside of the crocodile, the stranger at once dropped asleep. Neither the shouts of the foreign proprietor, nor the lamentations of his terrified family, nor threats to send for the police made the slightest impression. Within the crocodile was heard nothing but laughter and a promise to flay him (*sic*), though the poor mammal, compelled to swallow such a mass, was vainly shedding tears. An uninvited guest is worse than a Tartar. But in spite of the proverb the insolent visitor would not leave. We do not know how to explain such barbarous incidents which prove our lack of culture and disgrace us in the eyes of foreigners. The recklessness of the Russian temperament has found a fresh outlet. It may be asked what was the object of the uninvited visitor? A warm and comfortable abode? But there are many excellent houses in the capital with very cheap and comfortable lodgings, with the Neva water laid on, and a staircase lighted by gas, frequently with a hall-porter maintained by the proprietor. We would call our readers' attention to the barbarous treatment of domestic animals: it is difficult, of course, for the crocodile to digest such a mass all at once, and now he lies swollen out to the size of a mountain, awaiting death in insufferable agonies. In Europe persons guilty of inhumanity towards domestic animals have long been punished by law. But in spite of our European enlightenment, in spite of our European pavements, in spite of the European architecture of our houses, we are still far from shaking off our time-honoured traditions:

> "Though the houses are new, the conventions are old."

'And, indeed, the houses are not new, at least the staircases in them are not. We have more than once in our paper alluded to the fact that in the Petersburg Side in the house of the merchant Lukyanov the steps of the wooden staircase have decayed, fallen away, and have long been a danger for Afimya Skapidarov, a soldier's wife who works in the house, and is often obliged to go up the stairs with water or armfuls of wood. At last our predictions have come true: yesterday evening at half-past eight Afimya Skapidarov fell down with a basin of soup and broke her leg. We do not know whether Lukyanov will mend his staircase now, Russians are often wise after the event, but the victim of Russian carelessness has by now been taken to the hospital. In the same way we shall never cease to maintain that the house-porters who clear away the mud from the wooden pavement in the Viborgsky Side ought not to spatter the legs of passers-by, but should throw the mud up into heaps as is done in Europe,' and so, and so on.

'What's this?' I asked in some perplexity, looking at Prohor Savvitch. 'What's the meaning of it?'

'How do you mean?'

'Why, upon my word! Instead of pitying Ivan Matveitch, they pity the crocodile!'

'What of it? They have pity even for a beast, a *mammal*. We must be up to Europe, mustn't we? They have a very warm feeling for crocodiles there too. He-he-he!'

Saying this, queer old Prohor Savvitch dived into his papers and would not utter another word.

I stuffed the *Voice* and the *News-sheet* into my pocket and collected as many old copies of the newspapers as I could find for Ivan Matveitch's diversion in the evening, and though the evening was far off, yet on this occasion I slipped away from the office early to go to the Arcade and look, if only from a distance, at what was going on there, and to listen to the various remarks and currents of opinion. I foresaw that there would be a regular crush there, and turned up the collar of my coat to meet it. I somehow felt rather shy – so unaccustomed are we to publicity. But I feel that I have no right to report my own prosaic feelings when faced with this remarkable and original incident.

Bobok

From Somebody's Diary

1873

SEMYON ARDALYONOVITCH said to me all of a sudden the day before yesterday: 'Why, will you ever be sober, Ivan Ivanovitch? Tell me that, pray.'

A strange requirement. I did not resent it, I am a timid man; but here they have actually made me out mad. An artist painted my portrait as it happened: 'After all, you are a literary man,' he said. I submitted, he exhibited it. I read: 'Go and look at that morbid face suggesting insanity.'

It may be so, but think of putting it so bluntly into print. In print everything ought to be decorous; there ought to be ideals, while instead of that . . .

Say it indirectly, at least; that's what you have style for. But no, he doesn't care to do it indirectly. Nowadays humour and a fine style have disappeared, and abuse is accepted as wit. I do not resent it: but God knows I am not enough of a literary man to go out of my mind. I have written a novel, it has not been published. I have written articles – they have been refused. Those articles I took about from one editor to another; everywhere they refused them: you have no salt they told me. 'What sort of salt do you want?' I asked with a jeer. 'Attic salt?'

They did not even understand. For the most part I translate from the French for the booksellers. I write advertisements for shopkeepers too: 'Unique opportunity! Fine tea, from our own plantations . . .' I made a nice little sum over a panegyric on his deceased Excellency Pyotr Matveyitch. I compiled the 'Art of Pleasing the Ladies', a commission from a bookseller. I have brought out some six little works of this kind in the course of my life. I am thinking of making a collection of the *bon mots* of Voltaire, but am afraid it may seem a little flat to our people. Voltaire's no good now; nowadays we want a cudgel, not Voltaire. We knock each other's last teeth out nowadays. Well, so that's the whole extent of my literary activity. Though indeed I do send round letters to the editors gratis and fully signed. I give them all sorts of counsels and admonitions, criticise and point out the true path. The letter I sent last week to an editor's office was the fortieth I had sent in the last two years. I have wasted four roubles over stamps alone for them. My temper is at the bottom of it all.

I believe that the artist who painted me did so not for the

sake of literature, but for the sake of two symmetrical warts on my forehead, a natural phenomenon, he would say. They have no ideas, so now they are out for phenomena. And didn't he succeed in getting my warts in his portrait – to the life. That is what they call realism.

And as to madness, a great many people were put down as mad among us last year. And in such language! 'With such original talent' . . . 'and yet, after all, it appears' . . . 'however, one ought to have foreseen it long ago.' That is rather artful; so that from the point of view of pure art one may really commend it. Well, but after all, these so-called madmen have turned out cleverer than ever. So it seems the critics can call them mad, but they cannot produce anyone better.

The wisest of all, in my opinion, is he who can, if only once a month, call himself a fool – a faculty unheard of nowadays. In old days, once a year at any rate a fool would recognise that he was a fool, but nowadays not a bit of it. And they have so muddled things up that there is no telling a fool from a wise man. They have done that on purpose.

I remember a witty Spaniard saying when, two hundred and fifty years ago, the French built their first madhouses: 'They have shut up all their fools in a house apart, to make sure that they are wise men themselves.' Just so: you don't show your own wisdom by shutting someone else in a madhouse. 'K. has gone out of his mind, means that we are sane now.' No, it doesn't mean that yet.

Hang it though, why am I maundering on? I go on grumbling and grumbling. Even my maidservant is sick of me. Yesterday a friend came to see me. 'Your style is changing,' he said; 'it is choppy: you chop and chop – and then a parenthesis, then a parenthesis in the parenthesis, then you stick in something else in brackets, then you begin chopping and chopping again.'

The friend is right. Something strange is happening to me. My character is changing and my head aches. I am beginning to see and hear strange things, not voices exactly, but as though some one beside me were muttering, '*Bobok, bobok, bobok!*'

What's the meaning of this *bobok*? I must divert my mind.

I went out in search of diversion, I hit upon a funeral. A distant relation – a collegiate counsellor, however. A widow and five daughters, all marriageable young ladies. What must it come to even to keep them in slippers. Their father managed it, but now there is only a little pension. They will have to eat humble pie. They have always received me ungraciously. And indeed I should not have gone to the funeral now had it not been for a peculiar circumstance. I followed the procession to the cemetery with the rest; they were stuck-up and held aloof from me. My uniform was certainly rather shabby. It's five-and-twenty years, I believe, since I was at the cemetery; what a wretched place!

To begin with the smell. There were fifteen hearses, with palls varying in expensiveness; there were actually two catafalques. One was a general's and one some lady's. There were many mourners, a great deal of feigned mourning and a great deal of open gaiety. The clergy have nothing to complain of; it brings them a good income. But the smell, the smell. I should not like to be one of the clergy here.

I kept glancing at the faces of the dead cautiously, distrusting my impressionability. Some had a mild expression, some looked unpleasant. As a rule the smiles were disagreeable, and in some cases very much so. I don't like them; they haunt one's dreams.

During the service I went out of the church into the air: it was a grey day, but dry. It was cold too, but then it was October. I walked about among the tombs. They are of different grades. The third grade cost thirty roubles; it's decent and not so very dear. The first two grades are tombs in the church and under the porch; they cost a pretty penny. On this occasion they were burying in tombs of the third grade six persons, among them the general and the lady.

I looked into the graves – and it was horrible: water and such water! Absolutely green, and . . . but there, why talk of it! The gravedigger was bailing it out every minute. I went out while the service was going on and strolled outside the gates. Close by was an almshouse, and a little further off there was a restaurant. It was not a bad little restaurant: there was lunch and everything. There were lots of the mourners here. I noticed a great deal of gaiety and genuine heartiness. I had something to eat and drink.

Then I took part in the bearing of the coffin from the church to the grave. Why is it that corpses in their coffins are so heavy?

They say it is due to some sort of inertia, that the body is no longer directed by its owner . . . or some nonsense of that sort, in opposition to the laws of mechanics and common sense. I don't like to hear people who have nothing but a general education venture to solve the problems that require special knowledge; and with us that's done continually. Civilians love to pass opinions about subjects that are the province of the soldier and even of the field-marshal; while men who have been educated as engineers prefer discussing philosophy and political economy.

I did not go to the requiem service. I have some pride, and if I am only received owing to some special necessity, why force myself on their dinners, even if it be a funeral dinner. The only thing I don't understand is why I stayed at the cemetery; I sat on a tombstone and sank into appropriate reflections.

I began with the Moscow exhibition and ended with reflecting upon astonishment in the abstract. My deductions about astonishment were these:

'To be surprised at everything is stupid of course, and to be astonished at nothing is a great deal more becoming and for some reason accepted as good form. But that is not really true. To my mind to be astonished at nothing is much more stupid than to be astonished at everything. And, moreover, to be astonished at nothing is almost the same as feeling respect for nothing. And indeed a stupid man is incapable of feeling respect.'

'But what I desire most of all is to feel respect. I *thirst* to feel respect,' one of my acquaintances said to me the other day.

He thirsts to feel respect! Goodness, I thought, what would happen to you if you dared to print that nowadays?

At that point I sank into forgetfulness. I don't like reading the epitaphs of tombstones: they are everlastingly the same. An unfinished sandwich was lying on the tombstone near me; stupid and inappropriate. I threw it on the ground, as it was not bread but only a sandwich. Though I believe it is not a sin to throw bread on the earth, but only on the floor. I must look it up in Suvorin's calendar.

I suppose I sat there a long time – too long a time, in fact; I must have lain down on a long stone which was of the shape of a marble coffin. And how it happened I don't know, but I began to hear things of all sorts being said. At first I did not pay attention to it, but treated it with contempt. But the conversation went on. I heard muffled sounds as though the speakers' mouths were covered with a pillow, and at the same time they were distinct and very near. I came to myself, sat up and began listening attentively.

'Your Excellency, it's utterly impossible. You lead hearts, I return your lead, and here you play the seven of diamonds. You ought to have given me a hint about diamonds.'

'What, play by hard and fast rules? Where is the charm of that?'

'You must, your Excellency. One can't do anything without something to go upon. We must play with dummy, let one hand not be turned up.'

'Well, you won't find a dummy here.'

What conceited words! And it was queer and unexpected. One was such a ponderous, dignified voice, the other softly suave; I should not have believed it if I had not heard it myself. I had not been to the requiem dinner, I believe. And yet how could they be playing preference here and what general was this? That the sounds came from under the tombstones of that there could be no doubt. I bent down and read on the tomb:

'Here lies the body of Major-General Pervoyedov . . . a cavalier of such and such orders.' H'm! 'Passed away in August of this year . . . fifty-seven . . . Rest, beloved ashes, till the joyful dawn!'

H'm, dash it, it really is a general! There was no monument on the grave from which the obsequious voice came, there was only a tombstone. He must have been a fresh arrival. From his voice he was a lower court councillor.

'Oh-ho-ho-ho!' I heard in a new voice a dozen yards from the general's resting-place, coming from quite a fresh grave. The voice belonged to a man and a plebeian, mawkish with its affectation of religious fervour. 'Oh-ho-ho-ho!'

'Oh, here he is hicupping again!' cried the haughty and disdainful voice of an irritated lady, apparently of the highest society. 'It is an affliction to be by this shopkeeper!'

'I didn't hiccup; why, I've had nothing to eat. It's simply my nature. Really, madam, you don't seem able to get rid of your caprices here.'

'Then why did you come and lie down here?'

'They put me here, my wife and little children put me here, I did not lie down here of myself. The mystery of death! And I would not have lain down beside you not for any money; I lie here as befitting my fortune, judging by the price. For we can always do that – pay for a tomb of the third grade.'

'You made money, I suppose? You fleeced people?'

'Fleece you, indeed! We haven't seen the colour of your money since January. There's a little bill against you at the shop.'

'Well, that's really stupid; to try and recover debts here is too stupid, to my thinking! Go to the surface. Ask my niece – she is my heiress.'

'There's no asking anyone now, and no going anywhere. We have both reached our limit and, before the judgment-seat of God, are equal in our sins.'

'In our sins,' the lady mimicked him contemptuously. 'Don't dare to speak to me.'

'Oh-ho-ho-ho!'

'You see, the shopkeeper obeys the lady, your Excellency.'

'Why shouldn't he?'

'Why, your Excellency, because, as we all know, things are different here.'

'Different? How?'

'We are dead, so to speak, your Excellency.'

'Oh, yes! But still . . .'

Well, this is an entertainment, it is a fine show, I must say! If it has come to this down here, what can one expect on the surface? But what a queer business! I went on listening, however, though with extreme indignation.

'Yes, I should like a taste of life! Yes, you know . . . I should like a taste of life.' I heard a new voice suddenly somewhere in the space between the general and the irritable lady.

'Do you hear, your Excellency, our friend is at the same game again. For three days at a time he says nothing, and then he bursts out with "I should like a taste of life, yes, a taste of life!" And with such appetite, he-he!'

'And such frivolity.'

'It gets hold of him, your Excellency, and do you know, he is growing sleepy, quite sleepy – he has been here since April; and then all of a sudden "I should like a taste of life!"'

'It is rather dull, though,' observed his Excellency.

'It is, your Excellency. Shall we tease Avdotya Ignatyevna again, he-he?'

'No, spare me, please. I can't endure that quarrelsome virago.'

'And I can't endure either of you,' cried the virago disdainfully. 'You are both of you bores and can't tell me anything ideal. I know one little story about you, your Excellency – don't turn up your nose, please – how a manservant swept you out from under a married couple's bed one morning.'

'Nasty woman,' the general muttered through his teeth.

'Avdotya Ignatyevna, ma'am,' the shopkeeper wailed suddenly again, 'my dear lady, don't be angry, but tell me, am I going through the ordeal by torment now, or is it something else?'

'Ah, he is at it again, as I expected! For there's a smell from him which means he is turning round!'

'I am not turning round, ma'am, and there's no particular smell from me, for I've kept my body whole as it should be, while you're regularly high. For the smell is really horrible even for a place like this. I don't speak of it, merely from politeness.'

'Ah, you horrid, insulting wretch! He positively stinks and talks about me.'

'Oh-ho-ho-ho! If only the time for my requiem would come quickly: I should hear their tearful voices over my head, my wife's lament and my children's soft weeping! . . .'

'Well, that's a thing to fret for! They'll stuff themselves with funeral rice and go home . . . Oh, I wish somebody would wake up!'

'Avdotya Ignatyevna,' said the insinuating government clerk, 'wait a bit, the new arrivals will speak.'

'And are there any young people among them?'

'Yes, there are, Avdotya Ignatyevna. There are some not more than lads.'

'Oh, how welcome that would be!'

'Haven't they begun yet?' inquired his Excellency.

'Even those who came the day before yesterday haven't awakened yet, your Excellency. As you know, they sometimes don't speak for a week. It's a good job that today and yesterday and the day before they brought a whole lot. As it is, they are all last year's for seventy feet round.'

'Yes, it will be interesting.'

'Yes, your Excellency, they buried Tarasevitch, the privy councillor, today. I knew it from the voices. I know his nephew, he helped to lower the coffin just now.'

'H'm, where is he, then?'

'Five steps from you, your Excellency, on the left . . . Almost at your feet. You should make his acquaintance, your Excellency.'

'H'm, no – it's not for me to make advances.'

'Oh, he will begin of himself, your Excellency. He will be flattered. Leave it to me, your Excellency, and I . . .'

'Oh, oh! . . . What is happening to me?' croaked the frightened voice of a new arrival.

'A new arrival, your Excellency, a new arrival, thank God! And how quick he's been! Sometimes they don't say a word for a week.'

'Oh, I believe it's a young man!' Avdotya Ignatyevna cried shrilly.

'I . . . I . . . it was a complication, and so sudden!' faltered the young man again. 'Only the evening before, Schultz said to me, "There's a complication," and I died suddenly before morning. Oh! oh!'

'Well, there's no help for it, young man,' the general observed graciously, evidently pleased at a new arrival. 'You must be comforted. You are kindly welcome to our Vale of Jehoshaphat, so to call it. We are kind-hearted people, you will come to know us and appreciate us. Major-General Vassili Vassilitch Pervoyedov, at your service.'

'Oh, no, no! Certainly not! I was at Schultz's; I had a complication, you know, at first it was my chest and a cough, and then I caught a cold: my lungs and influenza . . . and all of a sudden, quite unexpectedly . . . the worst of all was its being so unexpected.'

'You say it began with the chest,' the government clerk put in suavely, as though he wished to reassure the new arrival.

'Yes, my chest and catarrh and then no catarrh, but still the chest, and I couldn't breathe . . . and you know . . .'

'I know, I know. But if it was the chest you ought to have gone to Ecke and not to Schultz.'

'You know, I kept meaning to go to Botkin's, and all at once . . .'

'Botkin is quite prohibitive,' observed the general.

'Oh, no, he is not forbidding at all; I've heard he is so attentive and foretells everything beforehand.'

'His Excellency was referring to his fees,' the government clerk corrected him.

'Oh, not at all, he only asks three roubles, and he makes such an examination, and gives you a prescription . . . and I was very anxious to see him, for I have been told . . . Well, gentlemen, had I better go to Ecke or to Botkin?'

'What? To whom?' The general's corpse shook with agreeable laughter. The government clerk echoed it in falsetto.

'Dear boy, dear, delightful boy, how I love you!' Avdotya Ignatyevna squealed ecstatically. 'I wish they had put someone like you next to me.'

No, that was too much! And these were the dead of our times! Still, I ought to listen to more and not be in too great a hurry to draw conclusions. That snivelling new arrival – I remember him just now in his coffin – had the expression of a frightened chicken, the most revolting expression in the world! However, let us wait and see.

But what happened next was such a Bedlam that I could not keep it all in my memory. For a great many woke up at once; an official – a civil councillor – woke up, and began discussing at once the project of a new sub-committee in a government department and of the probable transfer of various functionaries in connection with the sub-committee – which very greatly interested the general. I must confess I learned a great deal that was new myself, so much so that I marvelled at the channels by which one may sometimes in the metropolis learn government news. Then an engineer half woke up, but for a long time muttered absolute nonsense, so that our friends left off worrying him and let him lie till he was ready. At last the distinguished lady who had been buried in the morning under the catafalque showed symptoms of the deanimation of the tomb. Lebeziatnikov (for the obsequious lower court councillor whom I detested and who lay beside General Pervoyedov was called, it appears, Lebeziatnikov) became much excited, and surprised that they were all waking up so soon this time. I must own I was surprised too; though some of those who woke had been buried for three days, as, for instance, a very young girl of sixteen who kept giggling . . . giggling in a horrible and predatory way.

'Your Excellency, privy councillor Tarasevitch is waking!' Lebeziatnikov announced with extreme fussiness.

'Eh? What?' the privy councillor, waking up suddenly, mumbled, with a lisp of disgust. There was a note of ill-humoured peremptoriness in the sound of his voice.

I listened with curiosity – for during the last few days I had heard something about Tarasevitch – shocking and upsetting in the extreme.

'It's I, your Excellency, so far only I.'

'What is your petition? What do you want?'

'Merely to inquire after your Excellency's health; in these unaccustomed surroundings everyone feels at first, as it were, oppressed . . . General Pervoyedov wishes to have the honour of making your Excellency's acquaintance, and hopes . . .'

'I've never heard of him.'

'Surely, your Excellency! General Pervoyedov, Vassili Vassilitch . . .'

'Are you General Pervoyedov?'

'No, your Excellency, I am only the lower court councillor Lebeziatnikov, at your service, but General Pervoyedov . . .'

'Nonsense! And I beg you to leave me alone.'

'Let him be.' General Pervoyedov at last himself checked with dignity the disgusting officiousness of his sycophant in the grave.

'He is not fully awake, your Excellency, you must consider that; it's the novelty of it all. When he is fully awake he will take it differently.'

'Let him be,' repeated the general.

'Vassili Vassilitch! Hey, your Excellency!' a perfectly new voice shouted loudly and aggressively from close beside Avdotya Ignatyevna. It was a voice of gentlemanly insolence, with the languid pronunciation now fashionable and an arrogant drawl. 'I've been watching you all for the last two hours. Do you remember me, Vassili Vassilitch? My name is Klinevitch, we met at the Volokonskys' where you, too, were received as a guest, I am sure I don't know why.'

'What, Count Pyotr Petrovitch? . . . Can it be really you . . . and at such an early age? How sorry I am to hear it.'

'Oh, I am sorry myself, though I really don't mind, and I want to amuse myself as far as I can everywhere. And I am not a count but a baron, only a baron. We are only a set of scurvy barons, risen from being flunkeys, but why I don't know and I don't care. I am only a scoundrel of the pseudo-aristocratic society, and I am regarded as "a charming *polisson*". My father is a wretched little general, and my mother was at one time received *en haut lieu.* With the help of the Jew Zifel I forged fifty thousand rouble notes last year and then I informed against him, while Julie Charpentier de Lusignan carried off the money to Bordeaux. And only fancy, I was engaged to be married – to a girl still at school, three months under sixteen, with a dowry of ninety thousand. Avdotya Ignatyevna, do you remember how you seduced me fifteen years ago when I was a boy of fourteen in the Corps des Pages?'

'Ah, that's you, you rascal! Well, you are a godsend, anyway, for here . . .'

'You were mistaken in suspecting your neighbour, the business gentleman, of unpleasant fragrance . . . I said nothing, but I laughed. The stench came from me: they had to bury me in a nailed-up coffin.'

'Ugh, you horrid creature! Still, I am glad you are here; you can't imagine the lack of life and wit here.'

'Quite so, quite so, and I intend to start here something original. Your Excellency – I don't mean you, Pervoyedov – your Excellency the other one, Tarasevitch, the privy councillor! Answer! I am Klinevitch, who took you to Mlle Furie in Lent, do you hear?'

'I do, Klinevitch, and I am delighted, and trust me . . .'

'I wouldn't trust you with a halfpenny, and I don't care. I simply want to kiss you, dear old man, but luckily I can't. Do you know, gentlemen, what this *grand-père*'s little game was?

He died three or four days ago, and would you believe it, he left a deficit of four hundred thousand government money from the fund for widows and orphans. He was the sole person in control of it for some reason, so that his accounts were not audited for the last eight years. I can fancy what long faces they all have now, and what they call him. It's a delectable thought, isn't it? I have been wondering for the last year how a wretched old man of seventy, gouty and rheumatic, succeeded in preserving the physical energy for his debaucheries – and now the riddle is solved! Those widows and orphans – the very thought of them must have egged him on! I knew about it long ago, I was the only one who did know; it was Julie told me, and as soon as I discovered it, I attacked him in a friendly way at once in Easter week: "Give me twenty-five thousand, if you don't they'll look into your accounts tomorrow." And just fancy, he had only thirteen thousand left then, so it seems it was very apropos his dying now. *Grand-père, grand-père*, do you hear?'

'*Cher* Klinevitch, I quite agree with you, and there was no need for you . . . to go into such details. Life is so full of suffering and torment and so little to make up for it . . . that I wanted at last to be at rest, and so far as I can see I hope to get all I can from here too.'

'I bet that he already sniffed Katiche Berestov!'

'Who? What Katiche?' There was a rapacious quiver in the old man's voice.

'A-ah, what Katiche? Why, here on the left, five paces from me and ten from you. She has been here for five days, and if only you knew, *grand-père*, what a little wretch she is! Of good family and breeding and a monster, a regular monster! I did not introduce her to anyone there, I was the only one who knew her . . . Katiche, answer!'

'He-he-he!' the girl responded with a jangling laugh, in which there was a note of something as sharp as the prick of a needle. 'He-he-he!'

'And a little blonde?' the *grand-père* faltered, drawling out the syllables.

'He-he-he!'

'I . . . have long . . . I have long,' the old man faltered breathlessly, 'cherished the dream of a little fair thing of fifteen and just in such surroundings.'

'Ach, the monster!' cried Avdotya Ignatyevna.

'Enough!' Klinevitch decided. 'I see there is excellent material. We shall soon arrange things better. The great thing is to spend the rest of our time cheerfully; but what time? Hey, you, government clerk, Lebeziatnikov or whatever it is, I hear that's your name!'

'Semyon Yesveitch Lebeziatnikov, lower court councillor, at your service, very, very, very much delighted to meet you.'

'I don't care whether you are delighted or not, but you seem to know everything here. Tell me first of all how it is we can talk? I've been wondering ever since yesterday. We are dead and yet we are talking and seem to be moving – and yet we are not talking and not moving. What jugglery is this?'

'If you want an explanation, Baron, Platon Nikolaevitch could give you one better than I.'

'What Platon Nikolaevitch is that? To the point. Don't beat about the bush.'

'Platon Nikolaevitch is our home-grown philosopher, scientist and Master of Arts. He has brought out several philosophical works, but for the last three months he has been getting quite drowsy, and there is no stirring him up now. Once a week he mutters something utterly irrelevant.'

'To the point, to the point!'

'He explains all this by the simplest fact, namely, that when we were living on the surface we mistakenly thought that death there was death. The body revives, as it were, here, the remains of life are concentrated, but only in consciousness. I don't know how to express it, but life goes on, as it were, by inertia. In his opinion everything is concentrated somewhere in consciousness and goes on for two or three months . . . sometimes even for half a year . . . There is one here, for instance, who is almost completely decomposed, but once every six weeks he suddenly utters one word, quite senseless of course, about some *bobok*,* "Bobok bobok," but you see that an imperceptible speck of life is still warm within him.'

---

* *i.e.* small bean.

'It's rather stupid. Well, and how is it I have no sense of smell and yet I feel there's a stench?'

'That . . . he-he . . . Well, on that point our philosopher is a bit foggy. It's apropos of smell, he said, that the stench one perceives here is, so to speak, moral – he-he! It's the stench of the soul, he says, that in these two or three months it may have time to recover itself . . . and this is, so to speak, the last mercy . . . Only, I think, Baron, that these are mystic ravings very excusable in his position . . .'

'Enough; all the rest of it, I am sure, is nonsense. The great thing is that we have two or three months more of life and then – bobok! I propose to spend these two months as agreeably as possible, and so to arrange everything on a new basis. Gentlemen! I propose to cast aside all shame.'

'Ah, let us cast aside all shame, let us!' many voices could be heard saying; and strange to say, several new voices were audible, which must have belonged to others newly awakened. The engineer, now fully awake, boomed out his agreement with peculiar delight. The girl Katiche giggled gleefully.

'Oh, how I long to cast off all shame!' Avdotya Ignatyevna exclaimed rapturously.

'I say, if Avdotya Ignatyevna wants to cast off all shame . . .'

'No, no, no, Klinevitch, I was ashamed up there all the same, but here I should like to cast off shame, I should like it awfully.'

'I understand, Klinevitch,' boomed the engineer, 'that you want to rearrange life here on new and rational principles.'

'Oh, I don't care a hang about that! For that we'll wait for Kudeyarov who was brought here yesterday. When he wakes he'll tell you all about it. He is such a personality, such a titanic personality! Tomorrow they'll bring along another natural scientist, I believe, an officer for certain, and three or four days later a journalist, and, I believe, his editor with him. But deuce take them all, there will be a little group of us anyway, and things will arrange themselves. Though meanwhile I don't want us to be telling lies. That's all I care about, for that is one thing that matters. One cannot exist on the surface without lying, for life and lying are synonymous, but here we will amuse ourselves by not lying. Hang it all, the grave has some value after all! We'll all tell our stories aloud, and we won't be ashamed of anything. First of all I'll tell you about myself. I am one of the predatory kind, you know. All that was bound and held in check by rotten cords up there on the surface. Away with cords and let us spend these two months in shameless truthfulness! Let us strip and be naked!'

'Let us be naked, let us be naked!' cried all the voices.

'I long to be naked, I long to be,' Avdotya Ignatyevna shrilled.

'Ah . . . ah, I see we shall have fun here; I don't want Ecke after all.'

'No, I tell you. Give me a taste of life!'

'He-he-he!' giggled Katiche.

'The great thing is that no one can interfere with us, and

though I see Pervoyedov is in a temper, he can't reach me with his hand. *Grand-père*, do you agree?'

'I fully agree, fully, and with the utmost satisfaction, but on condition that Katiche is the first to give us her biography.'

'I protest! I protest with all my heart!' General Pervoyedov brought out firmly.

'Your Excellency!' the scoundrel Lebeziatnikov persuaded him in a murmur of fussy excitement, 'your Excellency, it will be to our advantage to agree. Here, you see, there's this girl's . . . and all their little affairs.'

'There's the girl, it's true, but . . .'

'It's to our advantage, your Excellency, upon my word it is! If only as an experiment, let us try it . . .'

'Even in the grave they won't let us rest in peace.'

'In the first place, General, you were playing preference in the grave, and in the second we don't care a hang about you,' drawled Klinevitch.

'Sir, I beg you not to forget yourself.'

'What? Why, you can't get at me, and I can tease you from here as though you were Julie's lapdog. And another thing, gentlemen, how is he a general here? He was a general there, but here is mere refuse.'

'No, not mere refuse . . . Even here . . .'

'Here you will rot in the grave and six brass buttons will be all that will be left of you.'

'Bravo, Klinevitch, ha-ha-ha!' roared voices.

'I have served my sovereign . . . I have the sword . . .'

'You sword is only fit to prick mice, and you never drew it even for that.'

'That makes no difference; I formed a part of the whole.'

'There are all sorts of parts in a whole.'

'Bravo, Klinevitch, bravo! Ha-ha-ha!'

'I don't understand what the sword stands for,' boomed the engineer.

'We shall run away from the Prussians like mice, they'll crush us to powder!' cried a voice in the distance that was unfamiliar to me, that was positively spluttering with glee.

'The sword, sir, is an honour,' the general cried, but only I heard him. There arose a prolonged and furious roar, clamour, and hubbub, and only the hysterically impatient squeals of Avdotya Ignatyevna were audible.

'But do let us make haste! Ah, when are we going to begin to cast off all shame!'

'Oh-ho-ho! . . . The soul does in truth pass through torments!' exclaimed the voice of the plebeian, 'and . . .'

And here I suddenly sneezed. It happened suddenly and unintentionally, but the effect was striking: all became as silent as one expects it to be in a churchyard, it all vanished like a dream. A real silence of the tomb set in. I don't believe they were ashamed on account of my presence: they had made up their minds to cast off all shame! I waited five minutes – not a word, not a sound. It cannot be supposed that they were afraid of my informing the police; for what could the police do to them? I must conclude that they had *some secret* unknown to the living, which they carefully concealed from every mortal.

'Well, my dears,' I thought, 'I shall visit you again.' And with those words, I left the cemetery.

No, that I cannot admit; no, I really cannot! The *bobok* case does not trouble me (so that is what that bobok signified!).

Depravity in such a place, depravity of the last aspirations, depravity of sodden and rotten corpses – and not even sparing the last moments of consciousness! Those moments have been granted, vouchsafed to them, and . . . and, worst of all, in such a place! No, that I cannot admit.

I shall go to other tombs, I shall listen everywhere. Certainly one ought to listen everywhere and not merely at one spot in order to form an idea. Perhaps one may come across something reassuring.

But I shall certainly go back to those. They promised their biographies and anecdotes of all sorts. Tfoo! But I shall go, I shall certainly go; it is a question of conscience!

I shall take it to the *Citizen*; the editor there has had his portrait exhibited too. Maybe he will print it.

A Gentle Spirit

1876

Part I

WHO I WAS AND WHO SHE WAS

OH, WHILE SHE is still here, it is still all right; I go up and look at her every minute; but tomorrow they will take her away – and how shall I be left alone? Now she is on the table in the drawing-room, they put two card tables together, the coffin will be here tomorrow – white, pure white 'gros de Naples' – but that's not it . . .

I keep walking about, trying to explain it to myself. I have been trying for the last six hours to get it clear, but still I can't think of it all as a whole.

The fact is, I walk to and fro, and to and fro.

This is how it was. I will simply tell it in order. (Order!)

Gentlemen, I am far from being a literary man and you will see that; but no matter, I'll tell it as I understand it myself. The horror of it for me is that I understand it all!

It was, if you care to know, that is to take it from the beginning, that she used to come to me simply to pawn things, to pay for advertising in the *Voice* to the effect that a governess was quite willing to travel, to give lessons at home, and so on, and so on. That was at the very beginning, and I, of course, made no difference between her and the others: 'She comes,' I thought, 'like anyone else,' and so on.

But afterwards I began to see a difference. She was such a slender, fair little thing, rather tall, always a little awkward with me, as though embarrassed (I fancy she was the same with all strangers, and in her eyes, of course, I was exactly like anybody else – that is, not as a pawnbroker but as a man).

As soon as she received the money she would turn round at once and go away. And always in silence. Other women argue so, entreat, haggle for me to give them more; this one did not ask for more . . .

I believe I am muddling it up.

Yes; I was struck first of all by the things she brought: poor little silver gilt earrings, a trashy little locket, things not worth sixpence. She knew herself that they were worth next to nothing, but I could see from her face that they were treasures to her, and I found out afterwards as a fact that they were all that was left her belonging to her father and mother.

Only once I allowed myself to scoff at her things. You see I never allow myself to behave like that. I keep up a gentlemanly tone with my clients: few words, politeness and severity. 'Severity, severity!'

But once she ventured to bring her last rag, that is, literally the remains of an old hareskin jacket, and I could not resist saying something by way of a joke. My goodness! how she flared up! Her eyes were large, blue and dreamy but – how they blazed. But she did not drop one word; picking up her 'rags' she walked out.

It was then for the first time I noticed her *particularly*, and thought something of the kind about her – that is, something of a particular kind. Yes, I remember another impression – that is, if you will have it, perhaps the chief impression, that summed up everything. It was that she was terribly young, so young that she looked just fourteen. And yet she was within three months of sixteen. I didn't mean that, though, that wasn't what summed it all up. Next day she came again. I found out later that she had been to Dobronravov's and to Mozer's with that jacket, but they take nothing but gold and would have nothing to say to it. I once took some stones from her (rubbishy little ones) and, thinking it over afterwards, I wondered: I, too, only lend on gold and silver, yet from her I accepted stones. That was my second thought about her then; that I remember. That time, that is when she came from Mozer's, she brought an amber cigar-holder. It was a connoisseur's article, not bad, but, again, of no value to us, because we only deal in gold. As it was the day after her 'mutiny', I received her sternly. Sternness with me takes the form of dryness. As I gave her two roubles, however, I could not resist saying, with a certain irritation, 'I only do it for *you*, of course; Mozer wouldn't take such a thing.'

The words 'for *you*' I emphasised particularly, and with a particular implication.

I was spiteful. She flushed up again when she heard that 'for you', but she did not say a word, she did not throw down the money, she took it – that is poverty! But how hotly she flushed! I saw I had stung her. And when she had gone out, I suddenly asked myself whether my triumph over her was worth two roubles. He! He!! He!!! I remember I put that question to myself twice over, 'Was it worth it? was it worth it?'

And, laughing, I inwardly answered it in the affirmative. And I felt very much elated. But that was not an evil feeling; I said it with design, with a motive; I wanted to test her, because certain ideas with regard to her had suddenly come into my mind. That was the third thing I thought particularly about her . . . Well, it was from that time it all began. Of course, I tried at once to find out all her circumstances indirectly, and awaited her coming with a special impatience. I had a presentiment that she would come soon. When she came, I entered into affable conversation with her, speaking with unusual politeness. I have not been badly brought up and have manners. H'm. It was then I guessed that she was soft-hearted and gentle.

The gentle and soft-hearted do not resist long, and though

they are by no means very ready to reveal themselves, they do not know how to escape from a conversation; they are niggardly in their answers, but they do answer, and the more readily the longer you go on. Only, on your side you must not flag, if you want them to talk. I need hardly say that she did not explain anything to me then. About the *Voice* and all that I found out afterwards. She was at that time spending her last farthing on advertising, haughtily at first, of course. 'A governess prepared to travel and will send terms on application', but, later on: 'willing to do anything, to teach, to be a companion, to be a housekeeper, to wait on an invalid, plain sewing, and so on, and so on', the usual thing! Of course, all this was added to the advertisement a bit at a time, and finally, when she was reduced to despair, it came to: 'without salary in return for board'. No, she could not find a situation. I made up my mind then to test her for the last time. I suddenly took up the *Voice* of the day and showed her an advertisement. 'A young person, without friends and relations, seeks a situation as a governess to young children, preferably in the family of middle-aged widower. Might be a comfort in the home.'

'Look here how this lady has advertised this morning, and by the evening she will certainly have found a situation. That's the way to advertise.'

Again she flushed crimson and her eyes blazed, she turned round and went straight out. I was very much pleased, though by that time I felt sure of everything and had no apprehensions;

nobody will take her cigar-holders, I thought. Besides, she has got rid of them all. And so it was, two days later, she came in again, such a pale little creature, all agitation – I saw that something had happened to her at home, and something really had. I will explain directly what had happened, but now I only want to recall how I did something *chic*, and rose in her opinion. I suddenly decided to do it. The fact is she was pawning the ikon (she had brought herself to pawn it!) . . . Ah, listen! listen! This is the beginning now, I've been in a muddle. You see I want to recall all this, every detail, every little point. I want to bring them all together and look at them as a whole and – I cannot . . . It's these little things, these little things . . . It was an ikon of the Madonna. A Madonna with the Babe, an old-fashioned, homely one, and the setting was silver gilt, worth – well, six roubles, perhaps. I could see the ikon was precious to her; she was pawning it whole, not taking it out of the setting. I said to her:

'You had better take it out of the setting, and take the ikon home; for it's not the thing to pawn.'

'Why, are you forbidden to take them?'

'No, it's not that we are forbidden, but you might, perhaps, yourself . . .'

'Well, take it out.'

'I tell you what. I will not take it out, but I'll set it here in the shrine with the other ikons,' I said, on reflection. 'Under the little lamp' (I always had the lamp burning as soon as the shop was opened), 'and you simply take ten roubles.'

'Don't give me ten roubles. I only want five; I shall certainly redeem it.'

'You don't want ten? The ikon's worth it,' I added, noticing that her eyes flashed again.

She was silent. I brought out five roubles.

'Don't despise anyone; I've been in such straits myself; and worse too, and that you see me here in this business . . . is owing to what I've been through in the past . . .'

'You're revenging yourself on the world? Yes?' she interrupted suddenly with rather sarcastic mockery, which, however, was to a great extent innocent (that is, it was general, because certainly at that time she did not distinguish me from others, so that she said it almost without malice).

'Aha,' thought I; 'so that's what you're like. You've got character; you belong to the new movement.'

'You see!' I remarked at once, half jestingly, half mysteriously, 'I am part of that part of the Whole that seeks to do ill, but does good . . .'

Quickly and with great curiosity, in which, however, there was something very childlike, she looked at me.

'Stay . . . what's that idea? Where does it come from? I've heard it somewhere . . .'

'Don't rack your brains. In those words Mephistopheles introduces himself to Faust. Have you read *Faust*?'

'Not . . . not attentively.'

'That is, you have not read it at all. You must read it. But I see an ironical look in your face again. Please don't imagine that I've so little taste as to try to use Mephistopheles to commend myself to you and grace the rôle of pawnbroker. A pawnbroker will still be a pawnbroker. We know.'

'You're so strange . . . I didn't mean to say anything of that sort.'

She meant to say: 'I didn't expect to find you were an educated man'; but she didn't say it; I knew, though, that she thought that. I had pleased her very much.

'You see,' I observed, 'one may do good in any calling – I'm not speaking of myself, of course. Let us grant that I'm doing nothing but harm, yet . . .'

'Of course, one can do good in every position,' she said, glancing at me with a rapid, profound look. 'Yes, in any position,' she added suddenly.

Oh, I remember, I remember all those moments! And I want to add, too, that when such young creatures, such sweet young creatures want to say something so clever and profound, they show at once so truthfully and naïvely in their faces, 'Here I am saying something clever and profound now –' and that is not from vanity, as it is with anyone like me, but one sees that she appreciates it awfully herself, and believes in it, and thinks a lot of it, and imagines that you think a lot of all that, just as she does. Oh, truthfulness! it's by that they conquer us. How exquisite it was in her!

I remember it, I have forgotten nothing! As soon as she had

gone, I made up my mind. That same day I made my last investigations and found out every detail of her position at the moment; every detail of her past I had learned already from Lukerya, at that time a servant in the family, whom I had bribed a few days before. This position was so awful that I can't understand how she could laugh as she had done that day and feel interest in the words of Mephistopheles, when she was in such horrible straits. But – that's youth! That is just what I thought about her at the time with pride and joy; for, you know, there's a greatness of soul in it – to be able to say, 'Though I am on the edge of the abyss, yet Goethe's grand words are radiant with light.' Youth always has some greatness of soul, if it's only a spark and that distorted. Though it's of her I am speaking, of her alone. And, above all, I looked upon her then as *mine* and did not doubt of my power. You know that's a voluptuous idea when you feel no doubt of it.

But what is the matter with me? If I go on like this, when shall I put it all together and look at it as a whole. I must make haste, make haste – that is not what matters, oh, my God!

II

THE OFFER OF MARRIAGE

THE 'details' I learned about her I will tell in one word: her father and mother were dead, they had died three years before, and she had been left with two disreputable aunts: though it is saying too little to call them disreputable. One aunt was a widow with a large family (six children, one smaller than another), the other a horrid old maid. Both were horrid. Her father was in the service, but only as a copying clerk, and was only a gentleman by courtesy; in fact, everything was in my favour. I came as though from a higher world; I was anyway a retired lieutenant of a brilliant regiment, a gentleman by birth, independent and all the rest of it, and as for my pawnbroker's shop, her aunts could only have looked on that with respect. She had been living in slavery at her aunts' for those three years: yet she had managed to pass an examination somewhere – she managed to pass it, she wrung the time for it, weighed down as she was by the pitiless burden of daily drudgery, and that proved something in the way of striving for what was higher and better on her part! Why, what made me want to marry her? Never mind me, though; of that later on . . . As though that mattered! – She taught her aunt's children; she made their clothes; and towards the end not only washed the clothes, but with her weak chest even scrubbed the floors. To put it plainly, they used to beat her, and taunt her with eating their bread. It ended by their scheming to sell her. Tfoo! I omit the filthy details. She told me all about it afterwards.

All this had been watched for a whole year by a neighbour, a fat shopkeeper, and not a humble one but the owner of two grocer's shops. He had ill-treated two wives and now he was looking for a third, and so he cast his eye on her. 'She's a quiet one,' he thought; 'she's grown up in poverty, and I am marrying for the sake of my motherless children.'

He really had children. He began trying to make the match and negotiating with the aunts. He was fifty years old, besides. She was aghast with horror. It was then she began coming so often to me to advertise in the *Voice*. At last she began begging the aunts to give her just a little time to think it over. They granted her that little time, but would not let her have more; they were always at her: 'We don't know where to turn to find food for ourselves, without an extra mouth to feed.'

I had found all this out already, and the same day, after what had happened in the morning, I made up my mind. That evening the shopkeeper came, bringing with him a pound of sweets from the shop; she was sitting with him, and I called Lukerya out of the kitchen and told her to go and whisper to her that I was at the gate and wanted to say something to her without delay. I felt pleased with myself. And altogether I felt awfully pleased all that day.

On the spot, at the gate, in the presence of Lukerya, before she had recovered from her amazement at my sending for her, I informed her that I should look upon it as an honour and happiness . . . telling her, in the next place, not to be surprised at the manner of my declaration and at my speaking at the gate, saying that I was a straightforward man and had learned the position of affairs. And I was not lying when I said I was straightforward. Well, hang it all. I did not only speak with propriety – that is, showing I was a man of decent breeding, but I spoke with originality and that was the chief thing. After all, is there any harm in admitting it? I want to judge myself and am judging myself. I must speak *pro* and *contra*, and I do. I remembered afterwards with enjoyment, though it was stupid, that I frankly declared, without the least embarrassment, that, in the first place, I was not particularly talented, not particularly intelligent, perhaps not particularly good-natured, rather a cheap egoist (I remember that expression, I thought of it on the way and was pleased with it) and that very probably there was a great deal that was disagreeable in me in other respects. All this was said with a special sort of pride – we all know how that sort of thing is said. Of course, I had good taste enough not to proceed to enlarge on my virtues after honourably enumerating my defects, not to say 'to make up for that I have this and that and the other'. I saw that she was still horribly frightened, but I softened nothing; on the contrary, seeing she was frightened I purposely exaggerated. I told her straight out that she would have enough to eat, but that fine clothes, theatres, balls – she would have none of, at any rate not till later on, when I had attained my object. This severe tone was a positive delight to me. I added as cursorily as possible, that in adopting such a calling – that is, in keeping a pawnbroker's shop, I had only one object, hinting there was a special circumstance . . . But I really had a right to say so: I really had such an aim and there really was such a circumstance. Wait a minute, gentlemen; I have always been the first to hate this pawnbroking business, but in reality, though it is absurd to talk about oneself in such mysterious phrases, yet, you know, I was 'revenging myself on society', I really was, I was, I was! So that her gibe that morning at the idea of my revenging myself was unjust. That is, do you see, if I had said to her straight out in words: 'Yes, I am revenging myself on society,' she would have laughed as she did that morning, and it would, in fact, have been absurd. But by indirect hints, by dropping mysterious phrases, it appeared that it was possible to work upon her imagination. Besides, I had no fears then: I knew that the fat shopkeeper was anyway more repulsive to her than I was, and that I, standing at the gate, had appeared as a deliverer. I understood that, of course. Oh, what is base a man understands particularly well! But was it base? How can a man judge? Didn't I love her even then?

Wait a bit: of course, I didn't breathe a word to her of doing her a benefit; the opposite, oh, quite the opposite; I made out that it was *I* that would be under an obligation to her, not *she* to me. Indeed, I said as much – I couldn't resist saying it – and it sounded stupid, perhaps, for I noticed a shade flit across her face. But altogether I won the day completely. Wait a bit, if I am to recall all that vileness, then I will tell of that worst beastliness. As I stood there, what was stirring in my mind was, 'You are tall, a good figure, educated and – speaking without conceit – good-looking.' That is what was at work in my mind. I need hardly say that, on the spot, out there at the gate she said '*yes*'.

But . . . but I ought to add: that out there by the gate she thought a long time before she said '*yes*'. She pondered for so long that I said to her, 'Well?' – and could not even refrain from asking it with a certain swagger.

'Wait a little. I'm thinking.'

And her little face was so serious, so serious that even then I might have read it! And I was mortified: 'Can she be choosing between me and the grocer!' I thought. Oh, I did not understand then! I did not understand anything, anything, then! I did not understand till today! I remember Lukerya ran after me as I was going away, stopped me on the road and said, breathlessly: 'God will reward you, sir, for taking our dear young lady; only don't speak of that to her – she's proud.'

Proud, is she! 'I like proud people,' I thought. Proud people are particularly nice when . . . well, when one has no doubt of one's power over them, eh? Oh, base, tactless man! Oh, how pleased I was! You know, when she was standing there at the gate, hesitating whether to say 'yes' to me, and I was wondering at it, you know, she may have had some such thought as this: 'If it is to be misery either way, isn't it best to choose the very worst?' – that is, let the fat grocer beat her to death when he was drunk! Eh! what do you think, could there have been a thought like that?

And, indeed, I don't understand it now, I don't understand it at all, even now. I have only just said that she may have had that thought: of two evils choose the worst – that is, the grocer.

But which was the worst for her then – the grocer or I? The grocer or the pawnbroker who quoted Goethe? That's another question! What a question! And even that you don't understand: the answer is lying on the table and you call it a question! Never mind me, though. It's not a question of me at all . . . and, by the way, what is there left for me now – whether it's a question of me or whether it is not? That's what I am utterly unable to answer. I had better go to bed. My head aches . . .

III

THE NOBLEST OF MEN, THOUGH I DON'T BELIEVE IT MYSELF

I COULD not sleep. And how should I? There is a pulse throbbing in my head. One longs to master it all, all that degradation. Oh, the degradation! Oh, what degradation I dragged her out of then! Of course, she must have realised that, she must have appreciated my action! I was pleased, too, by various thoughts – for instance, the reflection that I was forty-one and she was only sixteen. That fascinated me, that feeling of inequality was very sweet, was very sweet.

I wanted, for instance, to have a wedding *à l'anglaise*, that is only the two of us, with just the two necessary witnesses, one of them Lukerya, and from the wedding straight to the train to Moscow (I happened to have business there, by the way), and then a fortnight at the hotel. She opposed it, she would not have it, and I had to visit her aunts and treat them with respect as though they were relations from whom I was taking her. I gave way, and all befitting respect was paid the aunts. I even made the creatures a present of a hundred roubles each and promised them more – not telling her anything about it, of course, that I might not make her feel humiliated by the lowness of her surroundings. The aunts were as soft as silk at once. There was a wrangle about the trousseau too; she had nothing, almost literally, but she did not want to have anything. I succeeded in proving to her, though, that she must have something, and I made up the trousseau, for who would have given her anything? But there, enough of me. I did, however, succeed in communicating some of my ideas to her then, so that she knew them anyway. I was in too great a hurry, perhaps. The best of it was that, from the very beginning, she rushed to meet me with love, greeted me with rapture, when I went to see her in the evening, told me in her chatter (the enchanting chatter of innocence) all about her childhood and girlhood, her old home, her father and mother. But I poured cold water upon all that at once. That was my idea. I met her enthusiasm with silence, friendly silence, of course . . . but, all the same, she could quickly see that we were different and that I was – an enigma. And being an enigma was what I made a point of most of all! Why, it was just for the sake of being an enigma, perhaps – that I have been guilty of all stupidity. The first thing was sternness – it was with an air of sternness that

I took her into my house. In fact, as I went about then feeling satisfied, I framed a complete system. Oh, it came of itself without any effort. And it could not have been otherwise. I was bound to create that system owing to one inevitable fact – why should I libel myself, indeed! The system was a genuine one. Yes, listen; if you must judge a man, better judge him knowing all about it . . . listen.

How am I to begin this, for it is very difficult. When you begin to justify yourself – then it is difficult. You see, for instance, young people despise money – I made money of importance at once; I laid special stress on money. And laid such stress on it that she became more and more silent. She opened her eyes wide, listened, gazed and said nothing. You see, the young are heroic, that is, the good among them are heroic and impulsive, but they have little tolerance; if the least thing is not quite right they are full of contempt. And I wanted breadth, I wanted to instil breadth into her very heart, to make it part of her inmost feeling, did I not? I'll take a trivial example: how should I explain my pawnbroker's shop to a character like that? Of course, I did not speak of it directly, or it would have appeared that I was apologising, and I, so to speak, worked it through pride, I almost spoke without words, and I am masterly at speaking without words. All my life I have spoken without words, and I have passed through whole tragedies on my own account without words. Why, I, too, have been unhappy! I was abandoned by everyone, abandoned and forgotten, and no one, no one knew it!

And all at once this sixteen-year-old girl picked up details about me from vulgar people and thought she knew all about me, and, meanwhile, what was precious remained hidden in this heart! I went on being silent, with her especially I was silent, with her especially, right up to yesterday – why was I silent? Because I was proud. I wanted her to find out for herself, without my help, and not from the tales of low people; I wanted her to *divine of herself* what manner of man I was and to understand me! Taking her into my house I wanted all her respect, I wanted her to be standing before me in homage for the sake of my sufferings – and I deserved it. Oh, I have always been proud, I always wanted all or nothing! You see it was just because I am not one who will accept half a happiness, but always wanted all, that I was forced to act like that then: it was as much as to say, 'See into me for yourself and appreciate me!' For you must see that if I had begun explaining myself to her and prompting her, ingratiating myself and asking for her respect – it would have been as good as asking for charity . . . But . . . but why am I talking of that!

Stupid, stupid, stupid, stupid! I explained to her then, in two words, directly, ruthlessly (and I emphasise the fact that it was ruthlessly) that the heroism of youth was charming, but – not worth a farthing. Why not? Because it costs them so little, because it is not gained through life; it is, so to say, merely 'first impressions of existence', but just let us see you at work! Cheap heroism is always easy, and even to sacrifice life is easy too; because it is only a case of hot blood and an overflow of energy, and there is such a longing for what is beautiful! No, take the deed of heroism that is laborious, obscure, without noise or flourish, slandered, in which there is a great deal of sacrifice and not one grain of glory – in which you, a splendid man, are made to look like a scoundrel before everyone, though you might be the most honest man in the world – you try that sort of heroism and you'll soon give it up! While I – have been bearing the burden of that all my life. At first she argued – ough, how she argued – but afterwards she began to be silent, completely silent, in fact, only opened her eyes wide as she listened, such big, big eyes, so attentive. And . . . and what is more, I suddenly saw a smile, mistrustful, silent, an evil smile. Well, it was with that smile on her face I brought her into my house. It is true that she had nowhere else to go.

IV
PLANS AND PLANS

WHICH of us began it first?

Neither. It began of itself from the very first. I have said that with sternness I brought her into the house. From the first step, however, I softened it. Before she was married it was explained to her that she would have to take pledges and pay out money, and she said nothing at the time (note that). What is more, she set to work with positive zeal. Well, of course, my lodging, my furniture all remained as before. My lodging consisted of two rooms, a large room from which the shop was partitioned off, and a second one, also large, our living-room and bedroom. My furniture is scanty: even her aunts had better things. My shrine of ikons with the lamp was in the outer room where the shop is; in the inner room my bookcase with a few books in and a trunk of which I keep the key; of course, there is a bed, tables and chairs. Before she was married I told her that one rouble a day, and not more, was to be spent on our board – that is, on food for me, her and Lukerya whom I had enticed to come to us. 'I must have thirty thousand in three years,' said I, 'and we can't save the money if we spend more.' She fell in with this, but I raised the sum by thirty kopecks a day. It was the same with the theatre. I told her before marriage that she would not go to the theatre, and yet I decided once a month to go to the theatre, and in a decent way, to the stalls. We went together. We went three times and saw *The Hunt after Happiness*, and *Singing Birds*, I believe. (Oh, what does it matter!) We went in silence and in silence we returned. Why, why, from the very beginning, did we take to being silent? From the very first, you know, we had no quarrels, but always the same silence. She was always, I remember, watching me stealthily in those days; as soon as I noticed it I became more silent than before. It is true that it was I insisted on the silence, not she. On her part there were one or two outbursts, she rushed to embrace me; but as these outbursts were hysterical, painful, and I wanted secure happiness, with respect from her, I received them coldly. And indeed, I was right; each time the outburst was followed next day by a quarrel.

Though, again, there were no quarrels, but there was silence and – and on her side a more and more defiant air. 'Rebellion and independence', that's what it was, only she didn't know how to show it. Yes, that gentle creature was becoming more and more defiant. Would you believe it, I was becoming revolting to her? I learned that. And there could be no doubt that she was moved to frenzy at times. Think, for instance, of her beginning to sniff at our poverty, after her coming from such sordidness and destitution – from scrubbing the floors! You see, there was no poverty; there was frugality, but there was abundance of what was necessary, of linen, for instance, and the greatest cleanliness. I always used to dream that cleanliness in a husband attracts a wife. It was not our poverty she was scornful of, but my supposed miserliness in the housekeeping: 'He has his objects,' she seemed to say, 'he is showing his strength of will.' She suddenly refused to go to the theatre. And more and more often an ironical look . . . And I was more silent, more and more silent.

I could not begin justifying myself, could I? What was at the bottom of all this was the pawnbroking business. Allow me, I knew that a woman, above all at sixteen, must be in complete subordination to a man. Women have no originality. That – that is an axiom; even now, even now, for me it is an axiom! What does it prove that she is lying there in the outer room? Truth is truth, and even Mill is no use against it! And a woman who loves, oh, a woman who loves idealises even the vices, even the villainies of the man she loves. He would not himself even succeed in finding such justification for his villainies as she will find for him. That is generous but not original. It is the lack of originality alone that has been the ruin of women. And, I repeat, what is the use of your pointing to that table? Why, what is there original in her being on that table? O – O – Oh!

Listen. I was convinced of her love at that time. Why, she used to throw herself on my neck in those days. She loved me; that is, more accurately, she wanted to love. Yes, that's just what it was, she wanted to love; she was trying to love. And the point was that in this case there were no villainies for which she had to find justification. You will say, I'm a pawnbroker; and everyone says the same. But what if I am a pawnbroker? It follows that there must be reasons since the most generous of men had become a pawnbroker. You see, gentlemen, there are ideas . . . that is, if one expresses some ideas, utters them in words, the effect is very stupid. The effect is to make one ashamed. For what reason? For no reason. Because we are all wretched creatures and cannot hear the truth, or I do not know why. I said just now, 'the most generous of men' – that is absurd, and yet that is how it was. It's the truth, that is, the absolute, absolute truth! Yes, I *had the right* to want to make myself secure and open that pawnbroker's shop: 'You have rejected me, you – people, I mean – you have cast me out with contemptuous silence. My passionate yearning towards you you have met with insult all my life. Now I have the right to put up a wall against you, to save up that thirty thousand roubles and end my life somewhere in the Crimea, on the south coast, among the mountains and vineyards, on my own estate bought with that thirty thousand, and above everything, far away from you all, living without malice against you, with an ideal in my soul, with a beloved woman at my heart, and a family, if God sends one, and – helping the inhabitants all around.'

Of course, it is quite right that I say this to myself now, but what could have been more stupid than describing all that aloud to her? That was the cause of my proud silence, that's why we sat in silence. For what could she have understood? Sixteen years old, the earliest youth – yes, what could she have understood of my justification, of my sufferings? Undeviating straightness, ignorance of life, the cheap convictions of youth, the hen-like blindness of those 'noble hearts', and what stood for most was – the pawnbroker's shop and – enough! (And was I a villain in the pawnbroker's shop? Did not she see how I acted? Did I extort too much?)

Oh, how awful is truth on earth! That exquisite creature, that gentle spirit, that heaven – she was a tyrant, she was the insufferable tyrant and torture of my soul! I should be unfair to myself if I didn't say so! You imagine I didn't love her? Who can say that I did not love her! Do you see, it was a case of irony, the malignant irony of fate and nature! We were under a curse, the life of men in general is under a curse! (mine in particular).

Of course, I understand now that I made some mistake! Something went wrong. Everything was clear, my plan was clear as daylight: 'Austere and proud, asking for no moral comfort, but suffering in silence.' And that was how it was. I was not lying, I was not lying! 'She will see for herself, later on, that it was heroic, only that she had not known how to see it, and when, some day, she divines it she will prize me ten times more and will abase herself in the dust and fold her hands in homage' – that was my plan. But I forgot something or lost sight of it. There was something I failed to manage. But, enough, enough! And whose forgiveness am I to ask now? What is done is done. Be bolder, man, and have some pride! It is not your fault! . . .

Well, I will tell the truth, I am not afraid to face the truth; it was *her fault, her fault!* . . .

V

A GENTLE SPIRIT IN REVOLT

QUARRELS began from her suddenly beginning to pay out loans on her own account, to price things above their worth, and even, on two occasions, she deigned to enter into a dispute about it with me. I did not agree. But then the captain's widow turned up.

This old widow brought a medallion – a present from her dead husband, a souvenir, of course. I lent her thirty roubles on it. She fell to complaining, begged me to keep the thing for her – of course, we do keep things. Well, in short, she came again to exchange it for a bracelet that was not worth eight roubles; I, of course, refused. She must have guessed something from my wife's eyes, anyway she came again when I was not there and my wife changed it for the medallion.

Discovering it the same day, I spoke mildly but firmly and reasonably. She was sitting on the bed, looking at the ground and tapping with her right foot on the carpet (her characteristic movement); there was an ugly smile on her lips. Then, without raising my voice in the least, I explained calmly that the money was *mine*, that I had a right to look at life with *my own* eyes and – and that when I had offered to take her into my house, I had hidden nothing from her.

She suddenly leapt up, suddenly began shaking all over and – what do you think – she suddenly stamped her foot at me; it was a wild animal, it was a frenzy, it was the frenzy of a wild animal. I was petrified with astonishment; I had never expected such an outburst. But I did not lose my head. I made no movement even, and again, in the same calm voice, I announced plainly that from that time forth I should deprive her of the part she took in my work. She laughed in my face, and walked out of the house.

The fact is, she had not the right to walk out of the house. Nowhere without me, such was the agreement before she was married. In the evening she returned; I did not utter a word.

The next day, too, she went out in the morning, and the day after again. I shut the shop and went off to her aunts. I had cut off all relations with them from the time of the wedding – I would not have them to see me, and I would not go to see them. But it turned out that she had not been with them. They listened to me with curiosity and laughed in my face: 'It serves you right,' they said. But I expected their laughter. At that point, then, I bought over the younger aunt, the unmarried one, for a hundred roubles, giving her twenty-five in advance. Two days later she came to me: 'There's an officer called Efimovitch mixed up in this,' she said; 'a lieutenant who was a comrade of yours in the regiment.'

I was greatly amazed. That Efimovitch had done me more harm than anyone in the regiment, and about a month ago, being a shameless fellow, he once or twice came into the shop with a pretence of pawning something, and I remember, began laughing with my wife. I went up at the time and told him not to dare to come to me, recalling our relations; but there was no thought of anything in my head, I simply thought that he was insolent. Now the aunt suddenly informed me that she had already appointed to see him and that the whole business had been arranged by a former friend of the aunt's, the widow of a colonel, called Yulia Samsonovna. 'It's to her,' she said, 'your wife goes now.'

I will cut the story short. The business cost me three hundred roubles, but in a couple of days it had been arranged that

I should stand in an adjoining room, behind closed doors, and listen to the first *rendezvous* between my wife and Efimovitch, *tête-à-tête*. Meanwhile, the evening before, a scene, brief but very memorable for me, took place between us.

She returned towards evening, sat down on the bed, looked at me sarcastically, and tapped on the carpet with her foot. Looking at her, the idea suddenly came into my mind that for the whole of the last month, or rather, the last fortnight, her character had not been her own; one might even say that it had been the opposite of her own; she had suddenly shown herself a mutinous, aggressive creature; I cannot say shameless, but regardless of decorum and eager for trouble. She went out of her way to stir up trouble. Her gentleness hindered her, though. When a girl like that rebels, however outrageously she may behave, one can always see that she is forcing herself to do it, that she is driving herself to do it, and that it is impossible for her to master and overcome her own modesty and shamefacedness. That is why such people go such lengths at times, so that one can hardly believe one's eyes. One who is accustomed to depravity, on the contrary, always softens things, acts more disgustingly, but with a show of decorum and seemliness by which she claims to be superior to you.

'Is it true that you were turned out of the regiment because you were afraid to fight a duel?' she asked suddenly, apropos of nothing – and her eyes flashed.

'Is it true that by the sentence of the officers I was asked to give up my commission, though, as a fact, I had sent in my papers before that.'

'You were turned out as a coward?'

'Yes, they sentenced me as a coward. But I refused to fight a duel, not from cowardice, but because I would not submit to their tyrannical decision and send a challenge when I did not consider myself insulted. You know,' I could not refrain from adding, 'that to resist such tyranny and to accept the consequences meant showing far more manliness than fighting any kind of duel.'

I could not resist it. I dropped this phrase, as it were, in self-defence, and that was all she wanted, this fresh humiliation for me.

She laughed maliciously.

'And is it true that for three years afterwards you wandered about the streets of Petersburg like a tramp, begging for coppers and spending your nights in billiard-rooms?'

'I even spent the night in Vyazemsky's House in the Haymarket. Yes, it is true; there was much disgrace and degradation in my life after I left the regiment, but not moral degradation, because even at the time I hated what I did more than anyone. It was only the degradation of my will and my mind, and it was only caused by the desperateness of my position. But that is over . . .'

'Oh, now you are a personage – a financier!'

A hint at the pawnbroker's shop. But by then I had succeeded in recovering my mastery of myself. I saw that she was thirsting for explanations that would be humiliating to me and – I did not give them. A customer rang the bell very opportunely, and I went out into the shop. An hour later, when she was dressed to go out, she stood still, facing me, and said:

'You didn't tell me anything about that, though, before our marriage?'

I made no answer and she went away.

And so next day I was standing in that room, the other side of the door, listening to hear how my fate was being decided, and in my pocket I had a revolver. She was dressed better than usual and sitting at the table, and Efimovitch was showing off before her. And, after all, it turned out exactly (I say it to my credit) as I had foreseen and had assumed it would, though I was not conscious of having foreseen and assumed it. I do not know whether I express myself intelligibly.

This is what happened.

I listened for a whole hour. For a whole hour I was present at a duel between a noble, lofty woman and a wordly, corrupt, dense man with a crawling soul. And how, I wondered in amazement, how could that naïve, gentle, silent girl have come to know all that? The wittiest author of a society comedy could not have created such a scene of mockery, of naïve laughter, and of the holy contempt of virtue for vice. And how brilliant her sayings, her little phrases were: what wit there was in her rapid answers, what truths in her condemnation. And, at the same time, what almost girlish simplicity. She laughed in his face at his declarations of love, at his gestures, at his proposals. Coming coarsely to the point at once, and not expecting to meet with opposition, he was utterly nonplussed. At first I might have imagined that it was simply coquetry on her part – 'the coquetry of a witty, though depraved creature to enhance her own value'. But no, the truth shone out like the sun, and to doubt was impossible. It was only an exaggerated and impulsive hatred for me that had led her, in her inexperience, to arrange this interview, but, when it came off – her eyes were opened at once. She was simply in desperate haste to mortify me, come what might, but though she had brought herself to do something so low she could not endure unseemliness. And could she, so pure and sinless, with an ideal in her heart, have been seduced by Efimovitch or any worthless snob? On the contrary, she was only moved to laughter by him. All her goodness rose up from her soul and her indignation roused her to sarcasm. I repeat, the buffoon was completely nonplussed at last and sat frowning, scarcely answering, so much so that I began to be afraid that he might dare to insult her, from a mean desire for revenge. And I repeat again: to my credit, I listened to that scene almost without surprise. I met, as it were, nothing but what I knew well. I had gone, as it were, on purpose to meet it, believing not a word of it, not a word said against her, though I did take the revolver in my pocket – that is the truth. And could I have imagined her different? For what did I love her, for what did I prize her, for what had I married her? Oh, of course, I was quite convinced of her hate for me, but at the same time I was quite convinced of her sinlessness. I suddenly cut short the scene by opening the door. Efimovitch leapt up. I took her by the hand and suggested she should go home with me. Efimovitch recovered himself and suddenly burst into loud peals of laughter.

'Oh, to sacred conjugal rights I offer no opposition; take her away, take her away! And you know,' he shouted after me, 'though no decent man could fight you, yet from respect to your lady I am at your service . . . If you are ready to risk yourself.'

'Do you hear?' I said, stopping her for a second in the doorway.

After which not a word was said all the way home. I led her by the arm and she did not resist. On the contrary, she was greatly impressed, and this lasted after she got home. On reaching home she sat down in a chair and fixed her eyes upon me. She was extremely pale; though her lips were compressed ironically yet she looked at me with solemn and austere defiance and seemed convinced in earnest, for the first minute, that I should kill her with the revolver. But I took the revolver from my pocket without a word and laid it on the table! She looked at me and at the revolver. (Note that the revolver was already an object familiar to her. I had kept one loaded ever since I opened the shop. I made up my mind when I set up the shop that I would not keep a huge dog or a strong manservant, as Mozer does, for instance. My cook opens the doors to my visitors. But in our trade it is impossible to be without means of self-defence in case of emergency, and I kept a loaded revolver. In early days, when first she was living in my house, she took great interest in that revolver, and asked questions about it, and I even explained its construction and working; I even persuaded her once to fire at a target. Note all that.) Taking no notice of her frightened eyes, I lay down on the bed, half undressed. I felt very much exhausted; it was by then about eleven o'clock. She went on sitting in the same place, not stirring, for another hour. Then she put out the candle and she, too, without undressing, lay down on the sofa near the wall. For the first time she did not sleep with me – note that too . . .

VI

A TERRIBLE REMINISCENCE

NOW for a terrible reminiscence . . .

I woke up, I believe, before eight o'clock, and it was very nearly broad daylight. I woke up completely to full consciousness and opened my eyes. She was standing at the table holding the revolver in her hand. She did not see that I had woken up and was looking at her. And suddenly I saw that she had begun moving towards me with the revolver in her hand. I quickly closed my eyes and pretended to be still asleep.

She came up to the bed and stood over me. I heard everything;

though a dead silence had fallen I heard that silence. All at once there was a convulsive movement and, irresistibly, against my will, I suddenly opened my eyes. She was looking straight at me, straight into my eyes, and the revolver was at my temple. Our eyes met. But we looked at each other for no more than a moment. With an effort I shut my eyes again, and at the same instant I resolved that I would not stir and would not open my eyes, whatever might be awaiting me.

It does sometimes happen that people who are sound asleep suddenly open their eyes, even raise their heads for a second and look about the room, then, a moment later, they lay their heads again on the pillow unconscious, and fall asleep without understanding anything. When meeting her eyes and feeling the revolver on my forehead, I closed my eyes and remained motionless, as though in a deep sleep – she certainly might have supposed that I really was asleep, and that I had seen nothing, especially as it was utterly improbable that, after seeing what I had seen, I should shut my eyes again at *such* a moment.

Yes, it was improbable. But she might guess the truth all the same – that thought flashed upon my mind at once, all at the same instant. Oh, what a whirl of thoughts and sensations rushed into my mind in less than a minute. Hurrah for the electric speed of thought! In that case (so I felt), if she guessed the truth and knew that I was awake, I should crush her by my readiness to accept death, and her hand might tremble. Her determination might be shaken by a new, overwhelming impression. They say that people standing on a height have an impulse to throw themselves down. I imagine that many suicides and murders have been committed simply because the revolver has been taken in the hand. It is like a precipice, with an incline of an angle of forty-five degrees, down which you cannot help sliding, and something impels you irresistibly to pull the trigger. But the knowledge that I had seen, that I knew it all, and was waiting for death at her hands without a word – might hold her back on the incline.

The stillness was prolonged, and all at once I felt on my temple, on my hair, the cold contact of the iron. You will ask: did I confidently expect to escape? I will answer you as God is my judge: I had no hope of it, except one chance in a hundred. Why did I accept death? But I will ask, what use was life to me after that revolver had been raised against me by the being I adored? Besides, I knew with the whole strength of my being that there was a struggle going on between us, a fearful duel for life and death, the duel fought by the coward of yesterday, rejected by his comrades for cowardice. I knew that and she knew it, if only she guessed the truth that I was not asleep.

Perhaps that was not so, perhaps I did not think that then, but yet it must have been so, even without conscious thought, because I've done nothing but think of it every hour of my life since.

But you will ask me again: why did you not save her from such wickedness? Oh! I've asked myself that question a thousand times since – every time that, with a shiver down my back, I recall that second. But at that moment my soul was plunged in dark despair! I was lost, I myself was lost – how could I save anyone? And how do you know whether I wanted to save anyone then? How can one tell what I could be feeling then?

My mind was in a ferment, though; the seconds passed; she still stood over me – and suddenly I shuddered with hope! I quickly opened my eyes. She was no longer in the room: I got out of bed: I had conquered – and she was conquered for ever!

I went to the samovar. We always had the samovar brought into the outer room and she always poured out the tea. I sat down at the table without a word and took a glass of tea from her. Five minutes later I looked at her. She was fearfully pale, even paler than the day before, and she looked at me. And suddenly . . . and suddenly, seeing that I was looking at her, she gave a pale smile with her pale lips, with a timid question in her eyes. 'So she still doubts and is asking herself: does he know or doesn't he know; did he see, or didn't he?' I turned my eyes away indifferently. After tea I closed the shop, went to the market and bought an iron bedstead and a screen. Returning home, I directed that the bed should be put in the front room and shut off with a screen. It was a bed for her, but I did not say a word to her. She understood without words, through that bedstead, that I 'had seen and knew all', and that all doubt was over. At night I left the revolver on the table, as I always did. At night she got into her new bed without a word: our marriage bond was broken, 'she was conquered but not forgiven'. At night she began to be delirious, and in the morning she had brain-fever. She was in bed for six weeks.

Part 2
THE DREAM OF PRIDE

LUKERYA had just announced that she can't go on living here and that she is going away as soon as her lady is buried. I knelt down and prayed for five minutes. I wanted to pray for an hour, but I keep thinking and thinking, and always sick thoughts, and my head aches – what is the use of praying? – it's only a sin! It is strange, too, that I am not sleepy: in great, too great sorrow, after the first outbursts one is always sleepy. Men condemned to death, they say, sleep very soundly on the last night. And so it must be, it is the law of nature, otherwise their strength would not hold out . . . I lay down on the sofa but I did not sleep . . .

. . . For the six weeks of her illness we were looking after her day and night – Lukerya and I together with a trained nurse whom I had engaged from the hospital. I spared no expense – in fact, I was eager to spend money for her. I called in Dr Shreder and paid him ten roubles a visit. When she began to get better I did not show myself so much. But why am I describing it? When she got up again, she sat quietly and silently in my room at a special table, which I had bought for her, too, about that time . . . Yes, that's the truth, we were absolutely silent; that is, we began talking afterwards, but only of the daily routine. I purposely avoided expressing myself, but I noticed that she, too, was glad not to have to say a word more than was necessary. It seemed to me that this was perfectly natural on her part: 'She is too much shattered, too completely conquered,' I thought, 'and I must let her forget and grow used to it.' In this way we were silent, but every minute I was preparing myself for the future. I thought that she was too, and it was fearfully interesting to me to guess what she was thinking about to herself then.

I will say more: oh! of course, no one knows what I went through, moaning over her in her illness. But I stifled my moans in my own heart, even from Lukerya. I could not imagine, could not even conceive of her dying without knowing the whole truth. When she was out of danger and began to regain her health, I very quickly and completely, I remember, recovered my tranquillity. What is more, I made up my mind to *defer our future* as long as possible, and meanwhile to leave things just as they were. Yes, something strange and peculiar happened to me then, I cannot call it anything else: I had triumphed, and the mere consciousness of that was enough for me. So the whole winter passed. Oh! I was satisfied as I had never been before, and it lasted the whole winter.

You see, there had been a terrible external circumstance in my life which, up till then – that is, up to the catastrophe with my wife – had weighed upon me every day and every hour. I mean the loss of my reputation and my leaving the regiment. In two words, I was treated with tyrannical injustice. It is true my comrades did not love me because of my difficult character, and perhaps because of my absurd character, though it often happens that what is exalted, precious and of value to one, for some reason amuses the herd of one's companions. Oh, I was never liked, not even at school! I was always and everywhere disliked. Even Lukerya cannot like me. What happened in the regiment, though it was the result of their dislike of me, was in a sense accidental. I mention this because nothing is more mortifying and insufferable than to be ruined by an accident, which might have happened or not have happened, from an unfortunate accumulation of circumstances which might have passed over like a cloud. For an intelligent being it is humiliating. This was what happened.

In an interval, at a theatre, I went out to the refreshment bar. A hussar called A— came in and began, before all the officers present and the public, loudly talking to two other hussars, telling them that Captain Bezumtsev, of our regiment, was making a disgraceful scene in the passage and was, 'he believed, drunk.' The conversation did not go further and, indeed, it was a mistake, for Captain Bezumtsev was not drunk and the 'disgraceful scene' was not really disgraceful. The hussars began talking of something else, and the matter ended there, but next day the story reached our regiment, and then they began saying at once that I was the only officer of our regiment in the refreshment bar at the time, and that when A—, the hussar, had spoken insolently of Captain Bezumtsev, I had not gone up to A— and stopped him by remonstrating. But on what grounds could I have done so? If he had a grudge against Bezumtsev, it was their personal affair and why should I interfere? Meanwhile, the officers began to declare that it was not a personal affair, but that it concerned the regiment, and as I was the only officer of the regiment present I had thereby shown all the officers and other people in the refreshment bar that there could be officers in our regiment who were not over-sensitive on the score of their own honour and the honour of their regiment. I could not agree with this view. They let me know that I could set everything right if I were willing, even now, late as it was, to demand a formal explanation from A—. I was not willing to do this, and as I was irritated I refused with pride. And thereupon I forthwith resigned my commission – that is the whole story. I left the regiment, proud but crushed in spirit. I was depressed in will and mind. Just then it was that my sister's husband in Moscow squandered all our little property and my portion of it, which was tiny enough, but the loss of it left me homeless, without a farthing. I might have taken a job in a private business, but I did not. After wearing a distinguished uniform I could not take work in a railway office. And so – if it must be shame, let it be shame; if it must be disgrace, let it be disgrace; if it must be degradation, let it be degradation – (the worse it is, the better) that was my choice. Then followed three years of gloomy memories, and even Vyazemsky's House.

A year and a half ago my godmother, a wealthy old lady, died in Moscow, and to my surprise left me three thousand in her will. I thought a little and immediately decided on my course of action. I determined on setting up as a pawnbroker, without apologising to anyone: money, then a home, as far as possible from memories of the past, that was my plan. Nevertheless, the gloomy past and my ruined reputation fretted me every day, every hour. But then I married. Whether it was by chance or not I don't know. But when I brought her into my home I thought I was bringing a friend, and I needed a friend so much. But I saw clearly that the friend must be trained, schooled, even conquered. Could I have explained myself straight off to a girl of sixteen with her prejudices? How, for instance, could I, without the chance help of the horrible incident with the revolver, have made her believe I was not a coward, and that I had been unjustly accused of cowardice in the regiment? But that terrible incident came just in the nick of time. Standing the test of the revolver, I scored off all my gloomy past. And though no one knew about it, *she* knew, and for me that was everything, because she was everything for me, all the hope of the future that I cherished in my dreams! She was the one person I had prepared for myself, and I needed no one else – and here she knew everything; she knew, at any rate, that she had been in haste to join my enemies against me unjustly. That thought enchanted me. In her eyes I could not be a scoundrel now, but at most a strange person, and that thought after all that had happened was by no means displeasing to me; strangeness is not a vice – on the contrary, it sometimes attracts the feminine heart. In fact, I purposely deferred the climax: what had happened was, meanwhile, enough for my peace of mind and provided a great number of pictures and materials for my dreams. That is what is wrong, that I am a dreamer: I had enough material for my dreams, and about her, I thought she could *wait*.

So the whole winter passed in a sort of expectation. I liked looking at her on the sly, when she was sitting at her little table. She was busy at her needlework, and sometimes in the evening she read books taken from my bookcase. The choice of books in the bookcase must have had an influence in my favour too. She hardly ever went out. Just before dusk, after dinner, I used to take her out every day for a walk. We took a constitutional, but we were not absolutely silent, as we used to be. I tried, in fact, to make a show of our not being silent, but talking harmoniously, but as I have said already, we both avoided letting ourselves go. I did it purposely, I thought it was essential to 'give her time'. Of course, it was strange that almost till the end of the winter it did not once strike me that, though I loved to watch her stealthily, I had never once, all the winter, caught her glancing at me! I thought it was timidity in her. Besides, she had an air of such timid gentleness, such weakness after her illness. Yes, better to wait and – 'she will come to you all at once of herself . . .'

That thought fascinated me beyond all words. I will add one thing; sometimes, as it were purposely, I worked myself up and brought my mind and spirit to the point of believing she had injured me. And so it went on for some time. But my anger could never be very real or violent. And I felt myself as though it were only acting. And though I had broken off our marriage by buying that bedstead and screen, I could never, never look upon her as a criminal. And not that I took a frivolous view of her crime, but because I had the sense to forgive her completely, from the very first day, even before I bought the bedstead. In fact, it is strange on my part, for I am strict in moral questions. On the contrary, in my eyes, she was so conquered, so humiliated, so crushed, that sometimes I felt agonies of pity for her, though sometimes the thought of her humiliation was actually pleasing to me. The thought of our inequality pleased me . . .

I intentionally performed several acts of kindness that winter. I excused two debts, I gave one poor woman money without any pledge. And I said nothing to my wife about it, and I didn't do it in order that she should know; but the woman came herself to thank me, almost on her knees. And in that way it became public property; it seemed to me that she heard about the woman with pleasure.

But spring was coming, it was mid-April, we took out the double windows and the sun began lighting up our silent room with its bright beams. But there was, as it were, a veil before my eyes and a blindness over my mind. A fatal, terrible veil! How did it happen that the scales suddenly fell from my eyes, and I suddenly saw and understood? Was it a chance, or had the hour come, or did the ray of sunshine kindle a thought, a conjecture, in my dull mind? No, it was not a thought, not a conjecture. But a chord suddenly vibrated, a feeling that had long been dead was stirred and came to life, flooding all my darkened soul and devilish pride with light. It was as though I had suddenly leapt up from my place. And, indeed, it happened suddenly and abruptly. It happened towards evening, at five o'clock, after dinner . . .

II

THE VEIL SUDDENLY FALLS

TWO words first. A month ago I noticed a strange melancholy in her, not simply silence, but melancholy. That, too, I noticed suddenly. She was sitting at her work, her head bent over her sewing, and she did not see that I was looking at her. And it suddenly struck me that she had grown so delicate-looking, so thin, that her face was pale, her lips were white. All this, together with her melancholy, struck me all at once. I had already heard a little dry cough, especially at night. I got up at once and went off to ask Shreder to come, saying nothing to her.

Shreder came next day. She was very much surprised and looked first at Shreder and then at me.

'But I am well,' she said, with an uncertain smile.

Shreder did not examine her very carefully (these doctors are sometimes superciliously careless), he only said to me in the other room, that it was just the result of her illness, and that it wouldn't be amiss to go for a trip to the sea in the spring, or, if that were impossible, to take a cottage out of town for the summer. In fact, he said nothing except that there was weakness, or something of that sort. When Shreder had gone, she said again, looking at me very earnestly:

'I am quite well, quite well.'

But as she said this she suddenly flushed, apparently from shame. Apparently it was shame. Oh! now I understand: she was ashamed that I was still *her husband*, that I was looking after her still as though I were a real husband. But at the time I did not understand and put down her blush to humility (the veil!).

And so, a month later, in April, at five o'clock on a bright sunny day, I was sitting in the shop making up my accounts. Suddenly I heard her, sitting in our room, at work at her table, begin softly, softly . . . singing. This novelty made an overwhelming impression upon me, and to this day I don't understand it. Till then I had hardly ever heard her sing, unless, perhaps, in those first days, when we were still able to be playful and practise shooting at a target. Then her voice was rather strong, resonant; though not quite true it was very sweet and healthy. Now her little song was so faint – it was not that it was melancholy (it was some sort of ballad), but in her voice there was something jangled, broken, as though her voice were not equal to it, as though the song itself were sick. She sang in an undertone, and suddenly, as her voice rose, it broke – such a poor little voice, it broke so pitifully; she cleared her throat and again began softly, softly singing . . .

My emotions will be ridiculed, but no one will understand why I was so moved! No, I was still not sorry for her, it was still something quite different. At the beginning, for the first minute, at any rate, I was filled with sudden perplexity and terrible amazement – a terrible and strange, painful and almost vindictive amazement: 'She is singing, and before me; *has she forgotten about me?*'

Completely overwhelmed, I remained where I was, then I suddenly got up, took my hat and went out, as it were, without thinking. At least I don't know why or where I was going. Lukerya began giving me my overcoat.

'She is singing?' I said to Lukerya involuntarily. She did not understand, and looked at me still without understanding; and, indeed, I was really unintelligible.

'Is it the first time she is singing?'

'No, she sometimes does sing when you are out,' answered Lukerya.

I remember everything. I went downstairs, went out into the street and walked along at random. I walked to the corner and began looking into the distance. People were passing by, they pushed against me. I did not feel it. I called a cab and told the man, I don't know why, to drive to Politseysky Bridge. Then suddenly changed my mind and gave him twenty kopecks.

'That's for my having troubled you,' I said, with a meaningless laugh, but a sort of ecstasy was suddenly shining within me.

I returned home, quickening my steps. The poor little jangled, broken note was ringing in my heart again. My breath failed me. The veil was falling, was falling from my eyes! Since she sang before me, she had forgotten me – that is what was clear and terrible. My heart felt it. But rapture was glowing in my soul and it overcame my terror.

Oh! the irony of fate! Why, there had been nothing else, and could have been nothing else but that rapture in my soul all the winter, but where had I been myself all that winter? Had I been there together with my soul? I ran up the stairs in great haste, I don't know whether I went in timidly. I only remember that the whole floor seemed to be rocking and I felt as though I were floating on a river. I went into the room. She was sitting in the same place as before, with her head bent over her sewing, but she wasn't singing now. She looked cursorily and without interest at me; it was hardly a look but just an habitual and indifferent movement upon somebody's coming into the room.

I went straight up and sat down beside her in a chair abruptly, as though I were mad. She looked at me quickly, seeming frightened; I took her hand and I don't remember what I said to her – that is, tried to say, for I could not even speak properly. My voice broke and would not obey me and I did not know what to say. I could only gasp for breath.

'Let us talk . . . you know . . . tell me something!' I muttered something stupid. Oh! how could I help being stupid? She started again and drew back in great alarm, looking at my face, but suddenly there was an expression of *stern surprise* in her eyes. Yes, surprise and *stern*. She looked at me with wide-open eyes. That sternness, that stern surprise shattered me at once: 'So you still expect love? Love?' that surprise seemed to be asking, though she said nothing. But I read it all, I read it all. Everything within me seemed quivering, and I simply fell down at her feet. Yes, I grovelled at her feet. She jumped up quickly, but I held her forcibly by both hands.

And I fully understood my despair – I understood it! But, would you believe it? ecstasy was surging up in my head so violently that I thought I should die. I kissed her feet in delirium and rapture. Yes, in immense, infinite rapture, and that, in spite of understanding all the hopelessness of my despair. I wept, said something, but could not speak. Her alarm and amazement were followed by some uneasy misgiving, some grave question, and she looked at me strangely, wildly even; she wanted to understand something quickly and she smiled. She was horribly ashamed at my kissing her feet and she drew them back. But I kissed the place on the floor where her foot had rested. She saw it and suddenly began laughing with shame (you know how it is when people laugh with shame). She became hysterical, I saw that her hands trembled – I did not think about that but went on muttering that I loved her, that I would not get up. 'Let me kiss your dress . . . and worship you like this all my life . . .' I don't know, I don't remember – but suddenly she broke into sobs and trembled all over. A terrible fit of hysterics followed. I had frightened her.

I carried her to the bed. When the attack had passed off, sitting on the edge of the bed, with a terribly exhausted look, she took my two hands and begged me to calm myself: 'Come, come, don't distress yourself, be calm!' and she began crying again. All that evening I did not leave her side. I kept telling her I should take her to Boulogne to bathe in the sea now, at once, in a fortnight, that she had such a broken voice, I had heard it that afternoon, that I would shut up the shop, that I would sell it to Dobronravov, that everything should begin afresh and, above all, Boulogne, Boulogne! She listened and was still afraid. She grew more and more afraid. But that was not what mattered most for me: what mattered most to me was the more and more irresistible longing to fall at her feet again, and again to kiss and kiss the spot where her foot had rested, and to worship her; and – 'I ask nothing, nothing more of you,' I kept repeating, 'do not answer me, take no notice of me, only let me watch you from my corner, treat me as your dog, your thing . . .' She was crying.

'*I thought you would let me go on like that*,' suddenly broke from her unconsciously, so unconsciously that, perhaps, she did not notice what she had said, and yet – oh, that was the most significant, momentous phrase she uttered that evening, the easiest for me to understand, and it stabbed my heart as though with a knife! It explained everything to me, everything, but while she was beside me, before my eyes, I could not help hoping and was fearfully happy. Oh, I exhausted her fearfully that evening. I understood that, but I kept thinking that I should alter everything directly. At last, towards night, she was utterly exhausted. I persuaded her to go to sleep and she fell sound asleep at once. I expected her to be delirious, she was a little delirious, but very slightly. I kept getting up every minute in the night and going softly in my slippers to look at her. I wrung my hands over her, looking at that frail creature in that wretched little iron bedstead which I had bought her for three roubles. I knelt down, but did not dare to kiss her feet in her sleep (without her consent). I began praying but leapt up again. Lukerya kept watch over me and came in and out from the kitchen. I went in to her, and told her to go to bed, and that tomorrow 'things would be quite different'.

And I believed in this, blindly, madly.

Oh, I was brimming over with rapture, rapture! I was eager for the next day. Above all, I did not believe that anything could go wrong, in spite of the symptoms. Reason had not altogether come back to me, though the veil had fallen from my eyes, and for a long, long time it did not come back – not till today, not till this very day! Yes, and how could it have come back then: why she was still alive then; why, she was here before my eyes, and I was before her eyes: 'Tomorrow she will wake up and I will tell her all this, and she will see it all.' That was how I reasoned then, simply and clearly, because I was in an ecstasy! My great idea was the trip to Boulogne. I kept thinking for some reason that Boulogne would be everything, that there was something final and decisive about Boulogne. 'To Boulogne, to Boulogne!' . . . I waited frantically for the morning.

III

I UNDERSTAND TOO WELL

BUT you know that was only a few days ago, five days, only five days ago, last Tuesday! Yes, yes, if there had only been a little longer, if she had only waited a little – and I would have dissipated the darkness! – It was not as though she had not recovered her calmness. The very next day she listened to me with a smile, in spite of her confusion . . . All this time, all these five days, she was either confused or ashamed. She was afraid, too, very much afraid. I don't dispute it, I am not so mad as to deny it. It was terror, but how could she help being frightened? We had so long been strangers to one another, had grown so alienated from one another, and suddenly all this . . . But I did not look at her terror. I was dazzled by the new life beginning! . . . It is true, it is undoubtedly true that I made a mistake. There were even, perhaps, many mistakes. When I woke up next day, the first thing in the morning (that was on Wednesday), I made a mistake: I suddenly made her my friend. I was in too great a hurry, too great a hurry, but a confession was necessary, inevitable – more than a confession! I did not even hide what I had hidden from myself all my life. I told her straight out that the whole winter I had been doing nothing but brood over the certainty of her love. I made clear to her that my money-lending had been simply the degradation of my will and my mind, my personal idea of self-castigation and self-exaltation. I explained to her that I really had been cowardly that time in the refreshment bar, that it was owing to my temperament, to my self-consciousness. I was impressed by the surroundings, by the theatre: I was doubtful how I should succeed and whether it would be stupid. I was not afraid of a duel, but of its being stupid . . . and afterwards I would not own it and tormented everyone and had tormented her for it, and had married her so as to torment her for it. In fact, for the most part I talked as though in delirium. She herself took my hands and made me leave off. 'You are exaggerating . . . you are distressing yourself,' and again there were tears, again almost hysterics! She kept begging me not to say all this, not to recall it.

I took no notice of her entreaties, or hardly noticed them: 'Spring, Boulogne! There there would be sunshine, there our new sunshine,' I kept saying that! I shut up the shop and transferred it to Dobronravov. I suddenly suggested to her giving all our money to the poor except the three thousand left me by my god-mother, which we would spend on going to Boulogne, and then we would come back and begin a new life of real work. So we decided, for she said nothing . . . She only smiled. And I believe she smiled chiefly from delicacy, for fear of disappointing me. I saw, of course, that I was burdensome to her, don't imagine I was so stupid or egoistic as not to see it. I saw it all, all, to the smallest detail, I saw better than anyone; all the hopelessness of my position stood revealed.

I told her everything about myself and about her. And about Lukerya. I told her that I had wept . . . Oh, of course, I changed the conversation. I tried, too, not to say a word more about certain things. And, indeed, she did revive once or twice – I remember it, I remember it! Why do you say I looked at her and saw nothing? And if only *this* had not happened, everything would have come to life again. Why, only the day before yesterday, when we were talking of reading and what she had been reading that winter, she told me something herself, and laughed as she told me, recalling the scene of Gil Blas and the Archbishop of Granada. And with what sweet, childish laughter, just as in old days when we were engaged (one instant! one instant!); how glad I was! I was awfully struck, though, by the story of the Archbishop; so she had found peace of mind and happiness enough to laugh at that literary masterpiece while she was sitting there in the winter. So then she had begun to be fully at rest, had begun to believe confidently that I should leave her *like that*. 'I thought you would leave me like that,' those were the words she uttered then on Tuesday! Oh! the thought of a child of ten! And you know she believed it, she believed that really everything would remain *like that*: she at her table and I at mine, and we both should go on like that till we were sixty. And all at once – I come forward, her husband, and the husband wants love! Oh, the delusion! Oh, my blindness!

It was a mistake, too, that I looked at her with rapture; I ought to have controlled myself, as it was my rapture frightened her. But, indeed, I did not control myself, I did not kiss her feet again. I never made a sign of . . . well, that I was her husband – oh, there was no thought of that in my mind, I only worshipped her! But, you know, I couldn't be quite silent, I could not refrain from speaking altogether! I suddenly said to her frankly, that I enjoyed her conversation and that I thought her incomparably more cultured and developed than I. She flushed crimson and said in confusion that I exaggerated. Then, like a fool, I could not resist telling her how delighted I had been when I had stood behind the door listening to her duel, the duel of innocence with that low cad, and how I had enjoyed her cleverness, the brilliance of her wit, and, at the same time, her childlike simplicity. She seemed to shudder all over, was murmuring again that I exaggerated, but suddenly her whole face darkened, she hid it in her hands and broke into sobs . . . Then I could not restrain myself: again I fell at her feet, again I began kissing her feet, and again it ended in a fit of hysterics, just as on Tuesday. That was yesterday evening – and – in the morning . . .

In the morning! Madman! why, that morning was today, just now, only just now!

Listen and try to understand: why, when we met by the

samovar (it was after yesterday's hysterics), I was actually struck by her calmness, that is the actual fact! And all night I had been trembling with terror over what happened yesterday. But suddenly she came up to me and, clasping her hands (this morning, this morning!) began telling me that she was a criminal, that she knew it, that her crime had been torturing her all the winter, was torturing her now . . . That she appreciated my generosity . . . 'I will be your faithful wife, I will respect you . . .'

Then I leapt up and embraced her like a madman. I kissed her, kissed her face, kissed her lips like a husband for the first time after a long separation. And why did I go out this morning, only for two hours . . . our passports for abroad . . . Oh, God! if only I had come back five minutes, only five minutes earlier! . . . That crowd at our gates, those eyes all fixed upon me. Oh, God!

Lukerya says (oh! I will not let Lukerya go now for anything. She knows all about it, she has been here all the winter, she will tell me everything!), she says that when I had gone out of the house and only about twenty minutes before I came back – she suddenly went into our room to her mistress to ask her something, I don't remember what, and saw that her ikon (that same ikon of the Mother of God) had been taken down and was standing before her on the table, and her mistress seemed to have only just been praying before it. 'What are you doing, mistress?' 'Nothing, Lukerya, run along.' 'Wait a minute, Lukerya.' 'She came up and kissed me. "Are you happy, mistress?" I said. "Yes, Lukerya." "Master ought to have come to beg your pardon long ago, mistress . . . Thank God that you are reconciled."' 'Very good, Lukerya,' she said. 'Go away, Lukerya,' and she smiled, but so strangely. So strangely that Lukerya went back ten minutes later to have a look at her.

'She was standing by the wall, close to the window, she had laid her arm against the wall, and her head was pressed on her arm, she was standing like that thinking. And she was standing so deep in thought that she did not hear me come and look at her from the other room. She seemed to be smiling – standing, thinking and smiling. I looked at her, turned softly and went out wondering to myself, and suddenly I heard the window opened. I went in at once to say: "It's fresh, mistress; mind you don't catch cold," and suddenly I saw she had got on the window and was standing there, her full height, in the open window, with her back to me, holding the ikon in her hand. My heart sank on the spot. I cried, "Mistress, mistress." She heard, made a movement to turn back to me, but, instead of turning back, took a step forward, pressed the ikon to her bosom, and flung herself out of window.'

I only remember that when I went in at the gate she was still warm. The worst of it was they were all looking at me. At first they shouted and then suddenly they were silent, and then all of them moved away from me . . . and she was lying there with the ikon. I remember, as it were, in a darkness, that I went up to her in silence and looked at her a long while. But all came round me and said something to me. Lukerya was there too, but I did not see her. She says she said something to me. I only remember that workman. He kept shouting to me that, 'Only a handful of blood came from her mouth, a handful, a handful!' and he pointed to the blood on a stone. I believe I touched the blood with my finger, I smeared my finger, I looked at my finger (that I remember), and he kept repeating: 'a handful, a handful!'

'What do you mean by a handful?' I yelled with all my might, I am told, and I lifted up my hands and rushed at him.

Oh, wild! wild! Delusion! Monstrous! Impossible!

IV

I WAS ONLY FIVE MINUTES TOO LATE

IS IT not so? Is it likely? Can one really say it was possible? What for, why did this woman die?

Oh, believe me, I understand, but why she died is still a question. She was frightened of my love, asked herself seriously whether to accept it or not, could not bear the question and preferred to die. I know, I know, no need to rack my brains: she had made too many promises, she was afraid she could not keep them – it is clear. There are circumstances about it quite awful.

For why did she die? That is still a question, after all. The question hammers, hammers at my brain. I would have left her *like that* if she had wanted to remain *like that*. She did not believe it, that's what it was! No – no. I am talking nonsense, it was not that at all. It was simply because with me she had to be honest – if she loved me, she would have had to love me altogether, and not as she would have loved the grocer. And as she was too chaste, too pure, to consent to such love as the grocer wanted she did not want to deceive me. Did not want to deceive me with half love, counterfeiting love, or a quarter love. They are honest, too honest, that is what it is! I wanted to instil breadth of heart in her, in those days, do you remember? A strange idea.

It is awfully interesting to know: did she respect me or not? I don't know whether she despised me or not. I don't believe she did despise me. It is awfully strange: why did it never once enter my head all the winter that she despised me? I was absolutely convinced of the contrary up to that moment when she looked at me with *stern surprise*. *Stern* it was. I understood on the spot that she despised me. I understood once for all, for ever! Ah, let her, let her despise me all her life even, only let her be living. Only yesterday she was walking about, talking. I simply can't understand how she threw herself out of the window! And how could I have imagined it five minutes before? I have called Lukerya. I won't let Lukerya go now for anything!

Oh, we might still have understood each other! We had simply become terribly estranged from one another during the winter, but couldn't we have grown used to each other again? Why, why, couldn't we have come together again and begun a new life again? I am generous, she was too – that was a point in common! Only a few more words, another two days – no more, and she would have understood everything.

What is most mortifying of all is that it is chance – simply a barbarous, lagging chance. That is what is mortifying! Five minutes, only five minutes too late! Had I come five minutes earlier, the moment would have passed away like a cloud, and it would never have entered her head again. And it would have ended by her understanding it all. But now again empty rooms, and me alone. Here the pendulum is ticking; it does not care, it has no pity . . . There is no one – that's the misery of it!

I keep walking about, I keep walking about. I know, I know, you need not tell me; it amuses you, you think it absurd that I complain of chance and those five minutes. But it is evident. Consider one thing: she did not even leave a note, to say, 'Blame no one for my death,' as people always do. Might she not have thought that Lukerya might get into trouble. 'She was alone with her,' might have been said, 'and pushed her out.' In any case she would have been taken up by the police if it had not happened that four people, from the windows, from the lodge, and from the yard, had seen her stand with the ikon in her hands and jump out of herself. But that, too, was a chance, that the people were standing there and saw her. No, it was all a moment, only an irresponsible moment. A sudden impulse, a fantasy! What if she did pray before the ikon? It does not follow that she was facing death. The whole impulse lasted, perhaps, only some ten minutes; it was all decided, perhaps, while she stood against the wall with her head on her arm, smiling. The idea darted into her brain, she turned giddy and – and could not resist it.

Say what you will, it was clearly misunderstanding. It would have been possible to live with me. And what if it were anaemia? Was it simply from poorness of blood, from the flagging of vital energy? She had grown tired during the winter, that was what it was . . .

I was too late!!!

How thin she is in her coffin, how sharp her nose has grown! Her eyelashes lie straight as arrows. And, you know, when she fell, nothing was crushed, nothing was broken! Nothing but that 'handful of blood'. A dessertspoonful, that is. From internal injury. A strange thought: if only it were possible not to bury her? For if they take her away, then . . . oh, no, it is almost incredible that they should take her away! I am not mad and I am not raving – on the contrary, my mind was never so lucid – but what shall I do when again there is no one, only the two rooms, and me alone with the pledges? Madness, madness, madness! I worried her to death, that is what it is!

What are your laws to me now? What do I care for your customs, your morals, your life, your state, your faith! Let your judge judge me, let me be brought before your court, let me be tried by jury, and I shall say that I admit nothing. The judge will shout, 'Be silent, officer.' And I will shout to him, 'What power have you now that I will obey? Why did blind, inert force destroy that which was dearest of all? What are your laws to me now? They are nothing to me.' Oh, I don't care!

She was blind, blind! She is dead, she does not hear! You do not know with what a paradise I would have surrounded you. There was paradise in my soul, I would have made it blossom around you! Well, you wouldn't have loved me – so be it, what of it? Things should still have been *like that*, everything should have remained *like that*. You should only have talked to me as a friend – we should have rejoiced and laughed with joy looking at one another. And so we should have lived. And if you had loved another – well, so be it, so be it! You should have walked with him laughing, and I should have watched you from the other side of the street . . . Oh, anything, anything, if only she would open her eyes just once! For one instant, only one! If she would look at me as she did this morning, when she stood before me and made a vow to be a faithful wife! Oh, in one look she would have understood it all!

Oh, blind force! Oh, nature! Men are alone on earth – that is what is dreadful! 'Is there a living man in the country?' cried the Russian hero. I cry the same, though I am not a hero, and no one answers my cry. They say the sun gives life to the universe. The sun is rising and – look at it, is it not dead? Everything is dead and everywhere there are dead. Men are alone – around them is silence – that is the earth! 'Men, love one another' – who said that? Whose commandment is that? The pendulum ticks callously, heartlessly. Two o'clock at night. Her little shoes are standing by the little bed, as though waiting for her . . . No, seriously, when they take her away tomorrow, what will become of me?

The Dream of a Ridiculous Man

1877

I

I AM A RIDICULOUS person. Now they call me a madman. That would be a promotion if it were not that I remain as ridiculous in their eyes as before. But now I do not resent it, they are all dear to me now, even when they laugh at me – and, indeed, it is just then that they are particularly dear to me. I could join in their laughter – not exactly at myself, but through affection for them, if I did not feel so sad as I look at them. Sad because they do not know the truth and I do know it. Oh, how hard it is to be the only one who knows the truth! But they won't understand that. No, they won't understand it.

In old days I used to be miserable at seeming ridiculous. Not seeming, but being. I have always been ridiculous, and I have known it, perhaps, from the hour I was born. Perhaps from the time I was seven years old I knew I was ridiculous. Afterwards I went to school, studied at the university, and, do you know, the more I learned, the more thoroughly I understood that I was ridiculous. So that it seemed in the end as though all the sciences I studied at the university existed only to prove and make evident to me as I went more deeply into them that I was ridiculous. It was the same with life as it was with science. With every year the same consciousness of the ridiculous figure I cut in every relation grew and strengthened. Everyone always laughed at me. But not one of them knew or guessed that if there were one man on earth who knew better than anybody else that I was absurd, it was myself, and what I resented most of all was that they did not know that. But that was my own fault; I was so proud that nothing would have ever induced me to tell it to anyone. This pride grew in me with the years; and if it had happened that I allowed myself to confess to any one that I was ridiculous, I believe that I should have blown out my brains the same evening. Oh, how I suffered in my early youth from the fear that I might give way and confess it to my schoolfellows. But since I grew to manhood, I have for some unknown reason become calmer, though I realised my awful characteristic more fully every year. I say 'unknown', for to this day I cannot tell why it was. Perhaps it was owing to the terrible misery that was growing in my soul through something which was of more consequence than anything else about me: that something was the conviction that had come upon me that *nothing in the world mattered.* I had long had an inkling of it, but the full realisation came last year almost suddenly. I suddenly felt that it was all the same to me whether the world existed or whether there had never been anything at all: I began to feel with all my being that there was *nothing existing*. At first I fancied that many things had existed in the past, but afterwards I guessed that there never had been anything in the past either, but that it had only seemed so for some reason. Little by little I guessed that there would be nothing in the future either. Then I left off being angry with people and almost ceased to notice them. Indeed this showed itself even in the pettiest trifles: I used, for instance, to knock against people in the street. And not so much from being lost in thought: what had I to think about? I had almost given up thinking by that time; nothing mattered to me. If at least I had solved my problems! Oh, I had not settled one of them, and how many they were! But I gave up caring about anything, and all the problems disappeared.

And it was after that that I found out the truth. I learned the truth last November – on the third of November, to be precise – and I remember every instant since. It was a gloomy evening, one of the gloomiest possible evenings. I was going home at about eleven o'clock, and I remember that I thought that the evening could not be gloomier. Even physically. Rain had been falling all day, and it had been a cold, gloomy, almost menacing rain, with, I remember, an unmistakable spite against mankind. Suddenly between ten and eleven it had stopped, and was followed by a horrible dampness, colder and damper than the rain, and a sort of steam was rising from everything, from every stone in the street, and from every by-lane if one looked down it as far as one could. A thought suddenly occurred to me, that if all the street lamps had been put out it would have been less cheerless, that the gas made one's heart sadder because it lighted it all up. I had had scarcely any dinner that day, and had been spending the evening with an engineer, and two other friends had been there also. I sat silent – I fancy I bored them. They talked of something rousing and suddenly they got excited over it. But they did not really care, I could see that, and only made a show of being excited. I suddenly said as much to them. 'My friends,' I said, 'you really do not care one way or the other.' They were not offended, but they all laughed at me. That was because I spoke without any note of reproach, simply because it did not matter to me. They saw it did not, and it amused them.

As I was thinking about the gas lamps in the street I looked up at the sky. The sky was horribly dark, but one could distinctly see tattered clouds, and between them fathomless black patches. Suddenly I noticed in one of these patches a star, and began watching it intently. That was because that star gave me an idea: I decided to kill myself that night. I had firmly determined to do so two months before, and poor as I was, I bought a splendid revolver that very day, and loaded it. But two months had passed and it was still lying in my drawer; I was so utterly indifferent that I wanted to seize a moment when I would not be so indifferent – why, I don't know. And so for two months every night that I came home I thought I would shoot myself. I kept waiting for the right moment. And so now this star gave me a thought. I made up my mind that it should certainly be that night. And why the star gave me the thought I don't know.

And just as I was looking at the sky, this little girl took me by the elbow. The street was empty, and there was scarcely anyone to be seen. A cabman was sleeping in the distance in his cab. It was a child of eight with a kerchief on her head, wearing nothing but a wretched little dress all soaked with rain, but I noticed particularly her wet broken shoes and I recall them now. They caught my eye particularly. She suddenly pulled me by the elbow and called me. She was not weeping, but was spasmodically crying out some words which she could not utter properly, because she was shivering and shuddering all over. She was in terror about something, and kept crying, 'Mammy, mammy!' I turned facing her, I did not say a word and went on; but she ran, pulling at me, and there was that note in her voice which in frightened children means despair. I know that sound. Though she did not articulate the words, I understood that her mother was dying, or that something of the sort was happening to them, and that she had run out to call someone, to find something to help her mother. I did not go with her; on the contrary, I had an impulse to drive her away. I told her first to go to a policeman. But clasping her hands, she ran beside me sobbing and gasping, and would not leave me. Then I stamped my foot, and shouted at her. She called out 'Sir! sir! . . .' but suddenly abandoned me and rushed headlong across the road. Some other passer-by appeared there, and she evidently flew from me to him.

I mounted up to my fifth storey. I have a room in a flat where there are other lodgers. My room is small and poor, with a garret window in the shape of a semicircle. I have a sofa covered with American leather, a table with books on it, two chairs and a comfortable arm-chair, as old as old can be, but of the good old-fashioned shape. I sat down, lighted the candle, and began thinking. In the room next to mine through the partition wall, a perfect Bedlam was going on. It had been going on for the last three days. A retired captain lived there, and he had half a dozen visitors, gentlemen of doubtful reputation, drinking vodka and playing *stoss* with old cards. The night before there had been a fight, and I know that two of them had been for a long time engaged in dragging each other about by the hair. The landlady wanted to complain, but she was in abject terror of the captain. There was only one other lodger in the flat, a thin little regimental lady, on a visit to Petersburg, with three little children who had been taken ill since they came into the lodgings. Both she and her children were in mortal fear of the captain, and lay trembling and crossing themselves all night, and the youngest child had a sort of fit from fright. That captain, I know for a fact, sometimes stops people in the Nevsky Prospect and begs. They won't take him into the service, but strange to say (that's why I am telling this), all this month that the captain has been here his behaviour has caused me no annoyance. I have, of course, tried to avoid his acquaintance from the very beginning, and he, too, was bored with me from the first; but I never care how much they shout the other side of the partition nor how many of them there are in there: I sit up all night and forget them so completely that I do not even hear them. I stay awake till daybreak, and have been going on like that for the last year. I sit up all night in my arm-chair at the table, doing nothing. I only read by day. I sit – don't even think; ideas of a sort wander through my mind and I let them come and go as they will. A whole candle is burned every night. I sat down quietly at the table, took out the revolver and put it down before me. When I had put it down I asked myself, I remember, 'Is that so?' and answered with complete conviction, 'It is.' That is, I shall shoot myself. I knew that I should shoot myself that night for certain, but how much longer I should go on sitting at the table I did not know. And no doubt I should have shot myself if it had not been for that little girl.

II

YOU see, though nothing mattered to me, I could feel pain, for instance. If anyone had struck me it would have hurt me. It was the same morally: if anything very pathetic happened, I should have felt pity just as I used to do in old days when there were things in life that did matter to me. I had felt pity that evening. I should have certainly helped a child. Why, then, had I not helped the little girl? Because of an idea that occurred to me at the time: when she was calling and pulling at me, a question suddenly arose before me and I could not settle it. The question was an idle one, but I was vexed. I was vexed at the reflection that if I were going to make an end of myself that night, nothing in life ought to have mattered to me. Why was it that all at once I did not feel that nothing mattered and was sorry for the little girl? I remember that I was very sorry for her, so much so that I felt a strange pang, quite incongruous in my position. Really I do not know better how to convey my fleeting sensation at the moment, but the sensation persisted at home when I was sitting at the table, and I was very much irritated as I had not been for a long time past. One reflection followed another. I saw clearly that so long as I was still a human being and not nothingness, I was alive and so could suffer, be angry and feel shame at my actions. So be it. But if I am going to kill myself, in two hours, say, what is the little girl to me and what have I to do with shame or with anything else in the world? I shall turn into nothing, absolutely nothing. And can it really be true that the consciousness that I shall *completely* cease to exist immediately and so everything else will cease to exist, does not in the least affect my feeling of pity for the child nor the feeling of shame after a contemptible action? I stamped and shouted at the unhappy child as though to say – not only I feel no pity, but even if I behave inhumanly and contemptibly, I am free to, for in another two hours everything will be extinguished. Do you believe that that was why I shouted that? I am almost convinced of it now. It seemed clear to me that life and the world somehow depended upon me now. I may almost say that the world now seemed created for me alone: if I shot myself the world would cease to be at least for me. I say nothing of its being likely that nothing will exist for anyone when I am gone, and that as soon as my consciousness is extinguished the whole world will vanish too and become void like a phantom, as a mere appurtenance of my consciousness, for possibly all this world and all these people are only me myself. I remember that as I sat and reflected, I turned all these new questions that swarmed one after another quite the other way, and thought of something quite new. For instance, a strange reflection suddenly occurred to me, that if I had lived before on the moon or on Mars and there had committed the most disgraceful and dishonourable action and had there been put to such shame and ignominy as one can only conceive and realise in dreams, in nightmares, and if, finding myself afterwards on earth, I were able to retain the memory of what I had done on the other planet and at the same time knew that I should never, under any circumstances, return there, then looking from the earth to the moon – *should I care or not?* Should I feel shame for that action or not? These were idle and superfluous questions for the revolver was already lying before me, and I knew in every fibre of my being that *it* would happen for certain, but they excited me and I raged. I could not die now without having first settled something. In short, the child had saved me, for I put off my pistol shot for the sake of these questions. Meanwhile the clamour had begun to subside in the captain's room: they had finished their game, were settling down to sleep, and meanwhile were grumbling and languidly winding up their quarrels. At that point I suddenly fell asleep in my chair at the table – a thing which had never happened to me before. I dropped asleep quite unawares.

Dreams, as we all know, are very queer things: some parts are presented with appalling vividness, with details worked up with the elaborate finish of jewellery, while others one gallops through, as it were, without noticing them at all, as, for instance, through space and time. Dreams seem to be spurred on not by reason but by desire, not by the head but by the heart, and yet what complicated tricks my reason has played sometimes in dreams, what utterly incomprehensible things happen to it! My brother died five years ago, for instance. I sometimes dream of him; he takes part in my affairs, we are very much interested, and yet all through my dream I quite know and remember that my brother is dead and buried. How is it that I am not surprised that, though he is dead, he is here beside me and working with me? Why is it that my reason fully accepts it? But enough. I will begin about my dream. Yes, I dreamed a dream, my dream of the third of November. They tease me now, telling me it was only a dream. But does it matter whether it was a dream or reality, if the dream made known to me the truth? If once one has recognised the truth and seen it, you know that it is the truth and that there is no other and there cannot be, whether you are asleep or awake. Let it be a dream, so be it, but that real life of which you make so much I had meant to extinguish by suicide, and my dream, my dream – oh, it revealed to me a different life, renewed, grand and full of power!

Listen.

III

I HAVE mentioned that I dropped asleep unawares and even seemed to be still reflecting on the same subjects. I suddenly dreamed that I picked up the revolver and aimed it straight at my heart – my heart, and not my head; and I had determined beforehand to fire at my head, at my right temple. After aiming at my chest I waited a second or two, and suddenly my candle, my table, and the wall in front of me began moving and heaving. I made haste to pull the trigger.

In dreams you sometimes fall from a height, or are stabbed, or beaten, but you never feel pain unless, perhaps, you really bruise yourself against the bedstead, then you feel pain and almost always wake up from it. It was the same in my dream.

I did not feel any pain, but it seemed as though with my shot everything within me was shaken and everything was suddenly dimmed, and it grew horribly black around me. I seemed to be blinded and benumbed, and I was lying on something hard, stretched on my back; I saw nothing, and could not make the slightest movement. People were walking and shouting around me, the captain bawled, the landlady shrieked – and suddenly another break and I was being carried in a closed coffin. And I felt how the coffin was shaking and reflected upon it, and for the first time the idea struck me that I was dead, utterly dead, I knew it and had no doubt of it, I could neither see nor move and yet I was feeling and reflecting. But I was soon reconciled to the position, and as one usually does in a dream, accepted the facts without disputing them.

And now I was buried in the earth. They all went away, I was left alone, utterly alone. I did not move. Whenever before I had imagined being buried the one sensation I associated with the grave was that of damp and cold. So now I felt that I was very cold, especially the tips of my toes, but I felt nothing else.

I lay still, strange to say I expected nothing, accepting without dispute that a dead man had nothing to expect. But it was damp. I don't know how long a time passed – whether an hour, or several days, or many days. But all at once a drop of water fell on my closed left eye, making its way through a coffin lid; it was followed a minute later by a second, then a minute later by a third – and so on, regularly every minute. There was a sudden glow of profound indignation in my heart, and I suddenly felt in it a pang of physical pain. 'That's my wound,' I thought; 'that's the bullet . . .' And drop after drop every minute kept falling on my closed eyelid. And all at once, not with my voice, but with my whole being, I called upon the power that was responsible for all that was happening to me:

'Whoever you may be, if you exist, and if anything more rational than what is happening here is possible, suffer it to be here now. But if you are revenging yourself upon me for my senseless suicide by the hideousness and absurdity of this subsequent existence, then let me tell you that no torture could ever equal the contempt which I shall go on dumbly feeling, though my martyrdom may last a million years!'

I made this appeal and held my peace. There was a full minute of unbroken silence and again another drop fell, but I knew with infinite unshakable certainty that everything would change immediately. And behold my grave suddenly was rent asunder, that is, I don't know whether it was opened or dug up, but I was caught up by some dark and unknown being and we found ourselves in space. I suddenly regained my sight. It was the dead of night, and never, never had there been such darkness. We were flying through space far away from the earth. I did not question the being who was taking me; I was proud and waited. I assured myself that I was not afraid, and was thrilled with ecstasy at the thought that I was not afraid. I do not know how long we were flying, I cannot imagine; it happened as it always does in dreams when you skip over space and time, and the laws of thought and existence, and only pause upon the points for which the heart yearns. I remember that I suddenly saw in the darkness a star. 'Is that Sirius?' I asked impulsively, though I had not meant to ask any questions.

'No, that is the star you saw between the clouds when you were coming home,' the being who was carrying me replied.

I knew that it had something like a human face. Strange to say, I did not like that being, in fact I felt an intense aversion for it. I had expected complete non-existence, and that was why I had put a bullet through my heart. And here I was in the hands of a creature not human, of course, but yet living, existing. 'And so there is life beyond the grave,' I thought with the strange frivolity one has in dreams. But in its inmost depth my heart remained unchanged. 'And if I have got to exist again,' I thought, 'and live once more under the control of some irresistible power, I won't be vanquished and humiliated.'

'You know that I am afraid of you and despise me for that,' I said suddenly to my companion, unable to refrain from the humiliating question which implied a confession, and feeling my humiliation stab my heart as with a pin. He did not answer my question, but all at once I felt that he was not even despising me, but was laughing at me and had no compassion for me, and that our journey had an unknown and mysterious object that concerned me only. Fear was growing in my heart. Something was mutely and painfully communicated to me from my silent companion, and permeated my whole being. We were flying through dark, unknown space. I had for some time lost sight of the constellations familiar to my eyes. I knew that there were stars in the heavenly spaces the light of which took thousands or millions of years to reach the earth. Perhaps we were already flying through those spaces. I expected something with a terrible anguish that tortured my heart. And suddenly I was thrilled by a familiar feeling that stirred me to the depths: I suddenly caught sight of our sun! I knew that it could not be *our* sun, that gave life to *our* earth, and that we were an infinite distance from our sun, but for some reason I knew in my whole being that it was a sun exactly like ours, a duplicate of it. A sweet, thrilling feeling resounded with ecstasy in my heart: the kindred power of the same light which had given me light stirred an echo in my heart and awakened it, and I had a sensation of life, the old life of the past for the first time since I had been in the grave.

'But if that is the sun, if that is exactly the same as our sun,' I cried, 'where is the earth?'

And my companion pointed to a star twinkling in the distance with an emerald light. We were flying straight towards it.

'And are such repetitions possible in the universe? Can that be the law of Nature? . . . And if that is an earth there, can it be just the same earth as ours . . . just the same, as poor, as unhappy, but precious and beloved for ever, arousing in the most ungrateful of her children the same poignant love for her that we feel for our earth?' I cried out, shaken by irresistible, ecstatic love for the old familiar earth which I had left. The image of the poor child whom I had repulsed flashed through my mind.

'You shall see it all,' answered my companion, and there was a note of sorrow in his voice.

But we were rapidly approaching the planet. It was growing before my eyes; I could already distinguish the ocean, the outline of Europe; and suddenly a feeling of a great and holy jealousy glowed in my heart.

'How can it be repeated and what for? I love and can love only that earth which I have left, stained with my blood, when, in my ingratitude, I quenched my life with a bullet in my heart. But I have never, never ceased to love that earth, and perhaps on the very night I parted from it I loved it more than ever. Is there suffering upon this new earth? On our earth we can only love with suffering and through suffering. We cannot love otherwise, and we know of no other sort of love. I want suffering in order to love. I long, I thirst, this very instant, to kiss with tears the earth that I have left, and I don't want, I won't accept life on any other!'

But my companion had already left me. I suddenly, quite without noticing how, found myself on this other earth, in the bright light of a sunny day, fair as paradise. I believe I was standing on one of the islands that make up on our globe the Greek archipelago, or on the coast of the mainland facing that archipelago. Oh, everything was exactly as it is with us, only everything seemed to have a festive radiance, the splendour of some great, holy triumph attained at last. The caressing sea, green as emerald, splashed softly upon the shore and kissed it with manifest, almost conscious love. The tall, lovely trees stood in all the glory of their blossom, and their innumerable leaves greeted me, I am certain, with their soft, caressing rustle and seemed to articulate words of love. The grass glowed with bright and fragrant flowers. Birds were flying in flocks in the air, and perched fearlessly on my shoulders and arms and joyfully struck me with their darling, fluttering wings. And at last I saw and knew the people of this happy land. They came to me of themselves, they surrounded me, kissed me. The children of the sun, the children of their sun – oh, how beautiful they were! Never had I seen on our own earth such beauty in mankind. Only perhaps in our children, in their earliest years, one might find some remote, faint reflection of this beauty. The eyes of these happy people shone with a clear brightness. Their faces were radiant with the light of reason and fulness of a serenity that comes of perfect understanding, but those faces were gay; in their words and voices there was a note of childlike joy. Oh, from the first moment, from the first glance at them, I understood it all! It was the earth untarnished by the Fall; on it lived people who had not sinned. They lived just in such a paradise as that in which, according to all the legends of mankind, our first parents lived before they sinned; the only difference was that all this earth was the same paradise. These people, laughing joyfully, thronged round me and caressed me; they took me home with them, and each of them tried to reassure me. Oh, they asked me no questions, but they seemed, I fancied, to know everything without asking, and they wanted to make haste and smooth away the signs of suffering from my face.

IV

AND do you know what? Well, granted that it was only a dream, yet the sensation of the love of those innocent and beautiful people has remained with me for ever, and I feel as though their love is still flowing out to me from over there. I have seen them myself, have known them and been convinced; I loved them, I suffered for them afterwards. Oh, I understood at once even at the time that in many things I could not understand them at all; as an up-to-date Russian progressive and contemptible Petersburger, it struck me as inexplicable that, knowing so much, they had, for instance, no science like ours. But I soon realised that their knowledge was gained and fostered by intuitions different from those of us on earth, and that their aspirations, too, were quite different. They desired nothing and were at peace; they did not aspire to knowledge of life as we aspire to understand it, because their lives were full. But their knowledge was higher and deeper than ours; for our science seeks to explain what life is, aspires to understand it in order to teach others how to live, while they without science knew how to live; and that I understood, but I could not understand their knowledge. They showed me their trees, and I could not understand the intense love with which they looked at them; it was as though they were talking with creatures like themselves. And perhaps I shall not be mistaken if I say that they conversed with them. Yes, they had found their language, and I am convinced that the trees understood them. They looked at all Nature like that – at the animals who lived in peace with them and did not attack them, but loved them, conquered by their love. They pointed to the stars and told me something about them which I could not understand, but I am convinced that they were somehow in touch with the stars, not only in thought, but by some living channel. Oh, these people did not persist in trying to make me understand them, they loved me without that, but I knew that they would never understand me, and so I hardly spoke to them about our earth. I only kissed in their presence the earth on which they lived and mutely worshipped them themselves. And they saw that and let me worship them without being abashed at my adoration, for they themselves loved much. They were not unhappy on my account when at times I kissed their feet with tears, joyfully conscious of the love with which they would respond to mine. At times I asked myself with wonder how it was they were able never to offend a creature like me, and never once to arouse a feeling of jealousy or envy in me? Often I wondered how it could be that, boastful and untruthful as I was, I never talked to them of what I knew – of which, of course, they had no notion – that I was never tempted to do so by a desire to astonish or even to benefit them.

They were as gay and sportive as children. They wandered about their lovely woods and copses, they sang their lovely songs; their fare was light – the fruits of their trees, the honey from their woods, and the milk of the animals who loved them. The work they did for food and raiment was brief and not laborious. They loved and begot children, but I never noticed in them the impulse of that *cruel* sensuality which overcomes almost every man on this earth, all and each, and is the source of almost every sin of mankind on earth. They rejoiced at the arrival of children as new beings to share their happiness. There was no quarrelling, no jealousy among them, and they did not even know what the words meant. Their children were the children of all, for they all made up one family. There was scarcely any illness among them, though there was death; but their old people died peacefully, as though falling asleep, giving blessings and smiles to those who surrounded them to take their last farewell with bright and loving smiles. I never saw grief or tears on those occasions, but only love, which reached the point of ecstasy, but a calm ecstasy, made perfect and contemplative. One might think that they were still in contact with the departed after death, and that their earthly union was not cut short by death. They scarcely understood me when I questioned them about immortality, but evidently they were so convinced of it without reasoning that it was not for them a question at all. They had no temples, but they had a real living and uninterrupted sense of oneness with the whole of the universe; they had no creed, but they had a certain knowledge that when their earthly joy had reached the limits of earthly nature, then there would come for them, for the living and for the dead, a still greater fullness of contact with the whole of the universe. They looked forward to that moment with joy, but without haste, not pining for it, but seeming to have a foretaste of it in their hearts, of which they talked to one another.

In the evening before going to sleep they liked singing in musical and harmonious chorus. In those songs they expressed all the sensations that the parting day had given them, sang its glories and took leave of it. They sang the praises of Nature, of the sea, of the woods. They liked making songs about one another, and praised each other like children; they were the simplest songs, but they sprang from their hearts and went to one's heart. And not only in their songs but in all their lives they seemed to do nothing but admire one another. It was like being in love with each other, but an all-embracing, universal feeling.

Some of their songs, solemn and rapturous, I scarcely understood at all. Though I understood the words I could never fathom their full significance. It remained, as it were, beyond the grasp of my mind, yet my heart unconsciously absorbed it more and more. I often told them that I had had a presentiment of it long before, that this joy and glory had come to me on our earth in the form of a yearning melancholy that at times approached insufferable sorrow; that I had had a foreknowledge of them all and of their glory in the dreams of my heart and the visions of my mind; that often on our earth I could not look at the setting sun without tears . . . that in my hatred for the men of our earth there was always a yearning anguish: why could I not hate them without loving them? why could I not help forgiving them? and in my love for them there was a yearning grief: why could I not love them without hating them? They listened to me, and I saw they could not conceive what I was saying, but I did not regret that I had spoken to them of it: I knew that they understood the intensity of my yearning anguish over those whom I had left. But when they looked at me with their sweet eyes full of love, when I felt that in their presence my heart, too, became as innocent and just as theirs, the feeling of the fullness of life took my breath away, and I worshipped them in silence.

Oh, everyone laughs in my face now, and assures me that one cannot dream of such details as I am telling now, that I only dreamed or felt one sensation that arose in my heart in delirium and made up the details myself when I woke up. And when I told them that perhaps it really was so, my God, how they shouted with laughter in my face, and what mirth I caused! Oh, yes, of course I was overcome by the mere sensation of my dream, and that was all that was preserved in my cruelly wounded heart; but the actual forms and images of my dreams, that is, the very ones I really saw at the very time of my dream, were filled with such harmony, were so lovely and enchanting and were so actual, that on awakening I was, of course, incapable of clothing them in our poor language, so that they were bound to become blurred in my mind; and so perhaps I really was forced afterwards to make up the details, and so of course to distort them in my passionate desire to convey some at least of them as quickly as I could. But on the other hand, how can I help believing that it was all true? It was perhaps a thousand times brighter, happier and more joyful than I describe it. Granted that I dreamed it, yet it must have been real. You know, I will tell you a secret: perhaps it was not a dream at all! For then something happened so awful, something so horribly true, that it could not have been imagined in a dream. My heart may have originated the dream, but would my heart alone have been capable of originating the awful event which happened to me afterwards? How could I alone have invented it or imagined it in my dream? Could my petty heart and my fickle, trivial mind have risen to such a revelation of truth? Oh, judge for yourselves: hitherto I have concealed it, but now I will tell the truth. The fact is that I . . . corrupted them all!

V

YES, yes it ended in my corrupting them all! How it could come to pass I do not know, but I remember it clearly. The dream embraced thousands of years and left in me only a sense of the whole. I only know that I was the cause of their sin and downfall. Like a vile trichina, like a germ of the plague infecting whole kingdoms, so I contaminated all this earth, so happy and sinless before my coming. They learned to lie, grew fond of lying, and discovered the charm of falsehood. Oh, at first perhaps it began innocently, with a jest, coquetry, with amorous play, perhaps indeed with a germ, but that germ of falsity made its way into their hearts and pleased them. Then sensuality was soon begotten, sensuality begot jealousy, jealousy – cruelty . . . Oh, I don't know, I don't remember; but soon, very soon the first blood was shed. They marvelled and were horrified, and began to be split up and divided. They formed into unions, but it was against one another. Reproaches, upbraidings followed. They came to know shame, and shame brought them to virtue. The conception of honour sprang up, and every union began waving its flags. They began torturing animals, and the animals withdrew from them into the forests and became hostile to them. They began to struggle for separation, for isolation, for individuality, for mine and thine. They began to talk in different languages. They became acquainted with sorrow and loved sorrow; they thirsted for suffering, and said that truth could only be attained through suffering. Then science appeared. As they became wicked they began talking of brotherhood and humanitarianism, and understood those ideas. As they became criminal, they invented justice and drew up whole legal codes in order to observe it, and to ensure their being kept, set up a guillotine. They hardly remembered what they had lost, in fact refused to believe that they had ever been happy and innocent. They even laughed at the possibility of this happiness in the past, and called it a dream. They could not even imagine it in definite form and shape, but, strange and wonderful to relate, though they lost all faith in their past happiness and called it a legend, they so longed to be happy and innocent once more that they succumbed to this desire like children, made an idol of it, set up temples and worshipped their own idea, their own desire; though at the same time they fully believed that it was unattainable and could not be realised, yet they bowed down to it and adored it with tears! Nevertheless, if it could have happened that they had returned to the innocent and happy condition which they had lost, and if someone had shown it to them again and had asked them whether they wanted to go back to it, they would certainly have refused. They answered me:

'We may be deceitful, wicked and unjust, we *know* it and weep over it, we grieve over it; we torment and punish ourselves more perhaps than that merciful Judge Who will judge us and whose Name we know not. But we have science, and by means of it we shall find the truth and we shall arrive at it consciously. Knowledge is higher than feeling, the consciousness of life is higher than life. Science will give us wisdom, wisdom will reveal the laws, and the knowledge of the laws of happiness is higher than happiness.'

That is what they said, and after saying such things everyone began to love himself better than anyone else, and indeed they could not do otherwise. All became so jealous of the rights of their own personality that they did their very utmost to curtail and destroy them in others, and made that the chief thing in their lives. Slavery followed, even voluntary slavery; the weak eagerly submitted to the strong, on condition that the latter aided them to subdue the still weaker. Then there were saints who came to these people, weeping, and talked to them of their pride, of their loss of harmony and due proportion, of their loss of shame. They were laughed at or pelted with stones. Holy blood was shed on the threshold of the temples. Then there arose men who began to think how to bring all people together again, so that everybody, while still loving himself best of all, might not interfere with others, and all might live together in something like a harmonious society. Regular wars sprang up over this idea. All the combatants at the same time firmly believed that science, wisdom and the instinct of self-preservation would force men at last to unite into a harmonious and rational society; and so, meanwhile, to hasten matters, 'the wise' endeavoured to exterminate as rapidly as possible all who were 'not wise' and did not understand their idea, that the latter might not hinder its triumph. But the instinct of self-preservation grew rapidly weaker; there arose men, haughty and sensual, who demanded all or nothing. In order to obtain everything they resorted to crime, and if they did not succeed – to suicide. There arose religions with a cult of non-existence and self-destruction for the sake of the everlasting peace of annihilation. At last these people grew weary of their meaningless toil, and signs of suffering came into their faces, and then they proclaimed that suffering was a beauty, for in suffering alone was there meaning. They glorified suffering in their songs. I moved about among them, wringing my hands and weeping over them, but I loved them perhaps more than in old days when there was no suffering in their faces and when they were innocent and so lovely. I loved the earth they had polluted even more than when it had been a paradise, if only because sorrow had come to it. Alas! I always loved sorrow and tribulation, but only for myself, for myself; but I wept over them, pitying them. I stretched out my hands to them in despair, blaming, cursing and despising myself. I told them that all this was my doing, mine alone; that it was I had brought them corruption, contamination and falsity. I besought them to crucify me, I taught them how to make a cross. I could not kill myself, I had not the strength, but I wanted to suffer at their hands. I yearned for suffering, I longed that my blood should be drained to the last drop in these agonies. But they only laughed at me, and began at last to look upon me as crazy. They justified me, they declared that they had only got what they wanted themselves, and that all that now was could not have been otherwise. At last they declared to me that I was becoming dangerous and that they should lock me up in a madhouse if I did not hold my tongue. Then such grief took possession of my soul that my heart was wrung, and I felt as though I were dying; and then . . . then I awoke.

It was morning, that is, it was not yet daylight, but about six o'clock. I woke up in the same arm-chair; my candle had burned out; everyone was asleep in the captain's room, and there was a stillness all round, rare in our flat. First of all I leapt up in great amazement: nothing like this had ever happened to me before, not even in the most trivial detail; I had never, for instance, fallen asleep like this in my arm-chair. While I was standing and coming to myself I suddenly caught sight of my revolver lying loaded, ready – but instantly I thrust it away! Oh, now, life, life! I lifted up my hands and called upon eternal truth, not with words but with tears; ecstasy, immeasurable ecstasy flooded my soul. Yes, life and spreading the good tidings! Oh, I at that moment resolved to spread the tidings, and resolved it, of course, for my whole life. I go to spread the tidings, I want to spread the tidings – of what? Of the truth, for I have seen it, have seen it with my own eyes, have seen it in all its glory.

And since then I have been preaching! Moreover I love all those who laugh at me more than any of the rest. Why that is so I do not know and cannot explain, but so be it. I am told that I am vague and confused, and if I am vague and confused now, what shall I be later on? It is true indeed: I am vague and confused, and perhaps as time goes on I shall be more so. And of course I shall make many blunders before I find out how to preach, that is, find out what words to say, what things to do, for it is a very difficult task. I see all that as clear as daylight, but, listen, who does not make mistakes? And yet, you know, all are making for the same goal, all are striving in the same direction anyway, from the sage to the lowest robber, only by different roads. It is an old truth, but this is what is new: I cannot go far wrong. For I have seen the truth; I have seen and I know that people can be beautiful and happy without losing the power of living on earth. I will not and cannot believe that evil is the normal condition of mankind. And it is just this faith of mine that they laugh at. But how can I help believing it? I have seen the truth – it is not as though I had invented it with my mind, I have seen it, seen it, and *the living image* of it has filled my soul for ever. I have seen it in such full perfection that I cannot believe that it is impossible for people to have it. And so how can I go wrong? I shall make some slips no doubt, and shall perhaps talk in second-hand language, but not for long: the living image of what I saw will always be with me and will always correct and guide me. Oh, I am full of courage and freshness, and I will go on and on if it were for a thousand years! Do you know, at first I meant to conceal the fact that I corrupted them, but that was a mistake – that was my first mistake! But truth whispered to me that I was *lying*, and preserved me and corrected me. But how establish paradise – I don't know, because I do not know how to put it into words. After my dream I lost command of words. All the chief words, anyway, the most necessary ones. But never mind, I shall go and I shall keep talking, I won't leave off, for anyway I have seen it with my own eyes, though I cannot describe what I saw. But the scoffers do not understand that. It was a dream, they say, delirium, hallucination. Oh! As though that meant so much! And they are so proud! A dream! What is a dream? And is not our life a dream? I will say more. Suppose that this paradise will never come to pass (that I understand), yet I shall go on preaching it. And yet how simple it is: in one day, *in one hour* everything could be arranged at once! The chief thing is to love others like yourself, that's the great thing, and that's everything; nothing else is wanted – you will find out at once how to arrange it all. And yet it's an old truth which has been told and retold a billion times – but it has not formed part of our lives! The consciousness of life is higher than life, the knowledge of the laws of happiness is higher than happiness – that is what one must contend against. And I shall. If only everyone wants it, it can all be arranged at once.

And I tracked out that little girl . . . and I shall go on and on!